A CHOICE OF LOVE

HOME TO OSCEOLA

BOOK ONE

ALENA MENTINK

Paperback ISBN: 979-8-9890967-0-1

E-book ISBN: 979-8-9890967-1-8

Editing by Mountain Peak Edits & Design, Tessa Emily Hall, and Kristina Hall

Cover design by Hannah Linder

FICTION / Christian / Romance / Historical

FICTION / Romance / Historical / America

Printed in the United States of America

ALSO BY ALENA MENTINK

Settle My Heart

HOME TO OSCEOLA SERIES

A Bargain to Keep

A Choice of Love

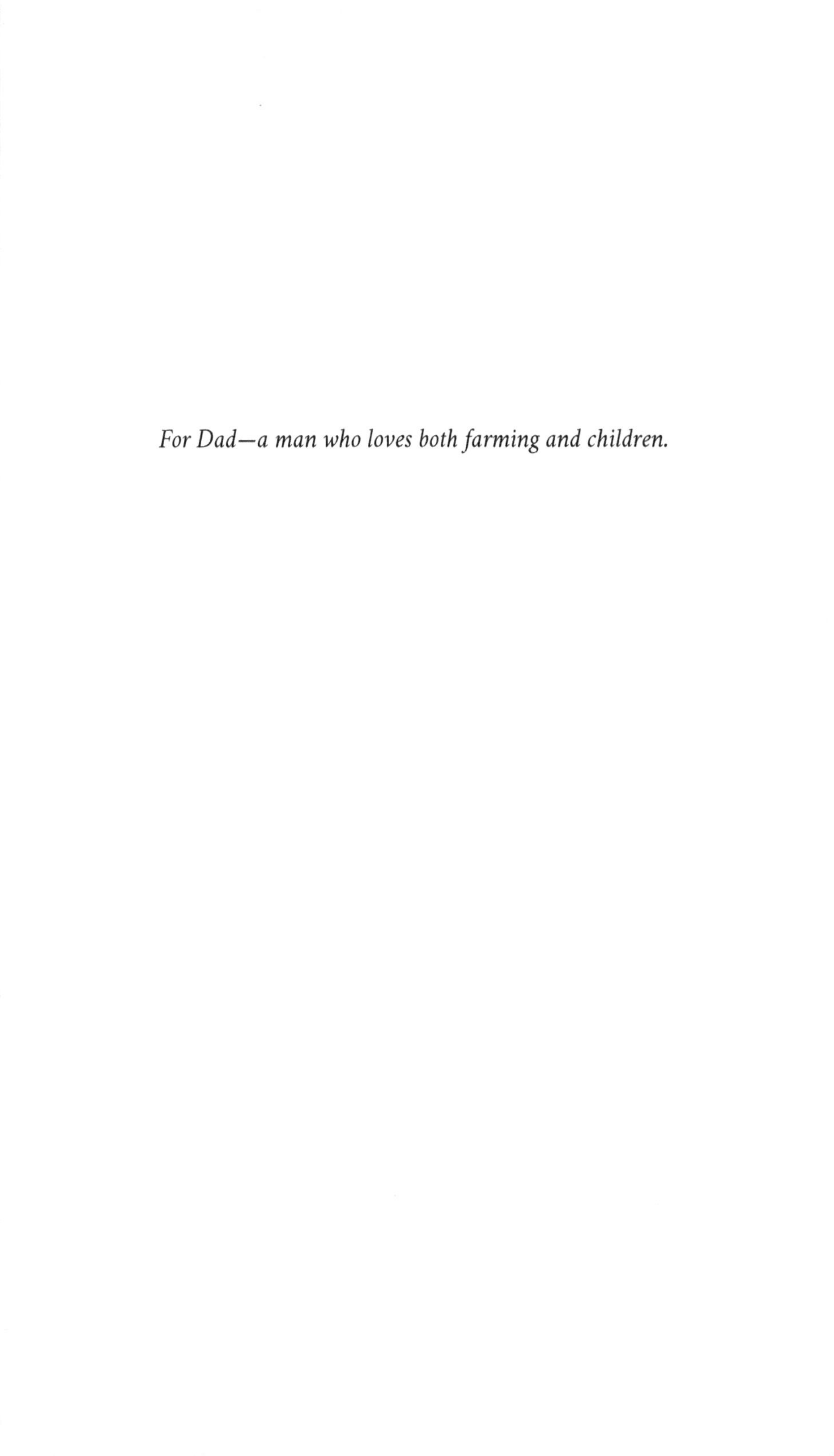

For Dad—a man who loves both farming and children.

"Love bears all things, believes all things, hopes all things,
endures all things. Love never ends."

1 Corinthians 13:7-8

PROLOGUE

Osceola, Nebraska
April 1879

"What will you do now?"

The question that had been looming in the atmosphere for days, taunting her, mocking her, finally escaped from her brother's mouth. His regret-filled eyes did nothing to keep the question from piercing deep into her heart.

Emily Keath averted her gaze and instead stared at the horizon where yellowish blades of grass contrasted with the deep blue sky. She shouldn't have to address this question. *No woman should ever be faced with it.*

But life didn't always happen the way it should.

She leaned against the sod house that she had called home for the last six years, the wall's uneven surface digging against her back. All the unknowns in her life felt like salt being poured on her lacerated heart. As soon as she caught her breath after one dose, another round of salt trickled in to aggravate the pain. Was it ever going to stop?

"Emily, I'm sorry it has to be this way, but you need to make some plans." Her sister-in-law, Sadie, slid one arm around her waist, squeezing her tightly.

Emily swallowed. Ephraim and Sadie were trying to help, but . . .

"It's just too soon." Her words emerged as little more than a whisper—and they sounded hollow to her own ears. She knew as well as they did that she needed to make some decisions and she needed to do so quickly. After all, the planting season was almost upon her.

Ephraim cleared his throat. "This isn't what you'll want to hear, but I had a man come into the store yesterday asking about land for sale around Osceola. If you're going to sell, now would be the time."

"I'm not selling." Emily gripped a fistful of fabric from her black dress, her chest heaving. How could he suggest that she sell the land that Colton had loved more than anything else in the world—other than herself and their children? He had devoted his life to it, and she would sooner starve than give it up.

Ephraim's eyebrows drew together, but he made no effort to change her mind. He simply nodded and gestured toward the fields still filled with stubble from last year's harvest. "And how will you make a living from the farm?"

Emily stared at the fields as well, the hopelessness of the situation washing over her afresh. Maybe *she* would rather starve than sell the farm, but she had the children to look after as well. She was all they had, and it was up to her to provide for them this year—and every year after that.

She bit her lip. Maybe she could learn how to work the fields. Maybe she could figure out a way to bring the children with her—

"Emily." Ephraim took her by the shoulders and looked into her eyes. "You aren't alone in this. I'll help you, and so will Pa and the other neighbors. But we need a plan that will work long-term."

The tears that seemed to always hover just beneath the surface sprang into her eyes. "I can't lose the farm, Ephraim. The children and this land are all that I have left of Colton, and I just can't let it go."

Ephraim's throat jogged. "But what about you? How would Colton feel if he knew that you've been running yourself ragged to hang on to this land? He loved you far more than the farm. He wouldn't want to see you do this to yourself."

Emily inched away, and Ephraim's hands fell from her shoulders. "Just let me try to keep the farm. I don't deny that I'll need help from all of you men, but I'll try to do most of the work myself."

Sadie heaved a deep sigh beside her. "And that's the problem, honey. You can't keep on like this."

Emily kept her gaze fixed on Ephraim. "Please?"

Ephraim shifted, rubbing his hand along his jawline. His shoulders rose and fell. "I can't stop you from trying, but it isn't going to be easy, Emily. You'll need to let me and Pa help you as much as we can."

A wave of relief washed over Emily. *Good.* If she could just hold on to the land until the boys grew older, she would have nothing to worry about.

But that was still years away.

Emily lifted her chin. One day's problems at a time.

She pushed away from the sod house that served as a home for her and the children, letting her gaze sweep over the squat structure. It was a solid building. Rustic, but built with care by Colton's own hands. He had intended to build them a frame house in a couple of years, but that was just one more dream that had died with him. It seemed that she and the children would be living in the soddy as long as the dirt walls held.

She took a deep breath. "If you'll both excuse me, I have one more matter to deal with before we can move on with life. I need to write to Colton's brother, but I've been delaying."

Sadie grasped Emily's hand, stopping her retreat. "Do you suppose Colton's brother might help?"

Emily shook her head. "He's busy with his own life."

And she would *never* ask a favor of Matthew Keath. Not even if she had nothing more than bread crusts in her pantry.

She'd heard enough stories about Matthew to warn her that he ran a little on the wild side. Definitely not a man she wanted to expose her children to, even if he was their uncle.

No, she and the children would wrestle through this on their own. Somehow. At least, she prayed they could.

CHAPTER 1

Bar K Ranch, Scottsbluff, Nebraska
May 1879

W as there ever a season that compared to spring?

Matt Keath surveyed the land from atop his horse. Gradually, the earth was being freed from its icy winter prison, snowdrifts turning to slush beneath the weight of the sun's warmth and new blades of green shooting through last year's withered growth. Calves bucked alongside their mothers in the pasture, and birds sang their sweet serenades from the sky.

Even the atmosphere was changing; it no longer pierced Matt's lungs with cold when he breathed in deeply.

A smile tugged at his lips. A man couldn't find a day better than this.

Matt urged his horse, Bowie, toward the corral.

Riding for the Bar K had been the best decision of his life. He loved spending his days outdoors, even if the weather could be brutal at times. He didn't mind the loneliness either. Working as a deputy for a couple of years had given him his fill of others and their violence.

Matt tilted his head back, allowing the setting sun's rays to slip past the brim of his Stetson and caress his face. Nope, being a ranch hand wasn't a bad job. Not at all. He'd dreamed of this job from the time he was a kid, even though the idea was met by disbelief and scoffs from Pa and his brother, Colton. Neither of them understood Matt's thirst for adventure or his drive to become anything but a farmer. At one point or another, they had both tried talking him out of his dreams, but Matt wouldn't hear a word of it. He couldn't stand the thought of following a plow and milking cows for the rest of his days.

Matt drew Bowie to a stop in front of the corral and dismounted, shrugging as he did so. Pa and Colton had found their life's work in farming, and he wasn't about to start fault-finding with his family. Pa had gone on to his reward years ago, and Colton seemed to find joy in plowing and milking, if his last letter was any indication.

Matt stripped Bowie of his saddle and bridle, his fingers deft. Before long, Juan would be calling them all to supper, none too soon for Matt. Working out in the fresh spring air had a way of awakening an appetite within a man.

Besides that, Juan's supper was sure to be a treat. He had a reputation for being one of the best cooks on this side of the Mississippi, making the hands at the Bar K the envy of all the neighboring ranches.

"Hey, Matt!"

The call prompted Matt to turn. Another Bar K employee sauntered toward him, waving a rolled-up newspaper above his head. It could only be Flick, walking with the swagger that no one else could duplicate.

"Mail came in today." Flick opened the newspaper as he drew closer, producing a cream-colored envelope and holding it for Matt to see. "This one's yours."

"Thanks." Matt reached out and took the letter, sticking it in his vest pocket without looking at the return address. Colton was the only person who ever wrote to him. He would read it later when he had some privacy.

Flick leaned against the corral, resting his elbows against one of the rails as if settling in for a long stay. "Say, I got something I think you'll be interested in."

"Oh yeah?" Matt rubbed a hand along Bowie's neck. On second thought, maybe he *wouldn't* get to eat his supper soon. Flick always did like to drag fresh news out for as long as possible.

"How many years has it been since you were a deputy in town?"

Matt blinked. That was not the question he anticipated. "Uh, two—no, three years ago. Why?"

"You remember Frank Harvey?"

"Sure I do." A crawling sensation crept along the base of Matt's neck. Frank Harvey wasn't a good fellow. He'd started several brawls at the saloon, and one night, he'd shot the place up, resulting in two deaths. Matt had helped Sheriff Telmond arrest him for the murder.

Flick jabbed the newspaper at Matt's chest. "Well, you might want to read this."

Casting a sideways glance at Flick, Matt took the newspaper and unrolled it, his gaze falling on an advertisement for the mercantile. He started to read through what they were selling, but Flick snatched the paper back and turned it to the front page.

"Not that. Look at the headlines, fool."

Matt rewarded Flick with a glare, then turned his attention back to the paper. The headlines turned his blood cold.

MAN WANTED FOR KILLING SCOTTSBLUFF SHERIFF.

Matt jerked his head up. "Somebody killed Sheriff Telmond?"

Flick smiled, obviously enjoying Matt's shock. "Guess who?"

"Frank Harvey?"

"Way to rope the steer around the neck."

Matt stared down at the paper, feeling as if he'd just been punched in the stomach. His breath came in shallow jerks that failed to fill his lungs. "But why?"

Flick rolled his eyes. "Use your head. You know Frank Harvey has reasons to resent Telmond for locking him up after that shooting. He would've been hung if he hadn't made a break from jail and escaped."

"But why now? If he was so upset with Telmond, why now and not three years ago when he first escaped?"

"For a former deputy, you really aren't that good at putting the pieces of the puzzle together." Flick scowled at him, shifting so that he stood taller against the corral. "Three years ago, he was running for his life and didn't have time to plan revenge. Besides, he probably couldn't have caught Telmond off guard then like he did now."

"He must be mighty bitter to hold a grudge against Telmond for this long." Matt lingered on Frank Harvey's picture that was spread across the paper's front page. The black and white image didn't give a very accurate view of the man. It sharpened the lines of his face too much, giving him a sinister look.

In truth, Frank Harvey was a deceptively normal-looking man. It was only the glint in his eyes that hinted at his evil. Matt hadn't forgotten them in the three years since he'd last seen Frank Harvey.

"Yeah, and just think, you were the one who helped Telmond lock him up. You wonder if he's got a grudge against you too?"

A chill ran down Matt's spine. That was the question he'd been wondering as well. "I was only the deputy. He probably didn't notice me as much."

"Well, just be careful. He could be lurking around here even now, waiting for you to end up in some lonely corner where he could jump you." Flick leaned closer, his stale breath hitting

Matt's face. "I sure would hate to see a good man like you killed, and at such a young age too."

Suddenly the ranch didn't feel so safe. Matt's gaze strayed to the horizon in spite of himself, but all was still. He darted a glance toward the shadows of the cook shack and bunkhouse, but nothing moved there either. He shifted uncomfortably.

Flick burst out a cackle of laughter. "You look so serious, Matt. Ain't scared, are you?"

Matt glared at him. "I'm not scared."

"Then why so jumpy? You afraid Frank's a better shot than you?"

That was the problem with Flick. He never took other people's problems seriously.

Matt pressed his lips together to keep from snapping at Flick. Then he took a breath and the words spewed out anyway. "I'd like to see how calmly *you'd* react if you heard that a man you helped arrest a few years back was in the area and on the warpath."

"You hold your life pretty highly, don't you?" Flick smirked. "Maybe Frank doesn't think you're worth a bullet."

Matt gritted his teeth. "Who knows what Frank thinks? But either way, I think it would be wise for me to be extra careful. Being off guard is what wound up getting Telmond killed."

"Whatever. Just don't get trigger-happy. If you don't know for sure that your target is Frank Harvey, then don't shoot, 'cause I sure don't want to end up with a bullet in my skin if I happen to pass your bed on my way to the privy tonight."

"Ha. Very funny, Flick." Matt folded his arms across his chest. He cast a glance at the horizon, then forced his gaze away, giving his shoulders a shake. "Can we talk about something else now?"

"I was having a heap of fun talking about good ol' Frank, but if you're too spooked, I suppose we can move on." Flick shifted from one foot to the other, making his spurs clink. "You know that the boss is looking for a new foreman, huh?"

Matt merely stared back at him. Of course he knew. The open foreman position had been the only talk on the Bar K Ranch for a week.

"Well, I was talking with some of the boys, and a number of them think the boss is considering you for the job."

Matt's next breath tangled in his throat. "Are you pulling my leg?"

"Why would I? Everyone knows you're one of the Bar K's top riders. You've had years of experience with cattle, and you know how to handle men too, or else you never would've been a deputy. You seem like a good choice for the job."

Matt worked to keep his face expressionless. Truth was, he'd had his fingers crossed that Keller would consider him for the position. Riding as foreman for the Bar K would be one of his biggest dreams come true, but he wasn't about to let that on to Flick. He'd learned long ago that every word he told Flick was sure to travel through the bunkhouse faster than a prairie fire.

"Can't believe everything those boys tell you," Matt said instead. "Guess we'll just see what happens."

"I think there might be some truth to what they're saying this time. You better start thinking on your words of acceptance for when Keller asks if you want the position." Flick studied Matt, fingers drumming the top board of the corral. "That is, if you think it would be the best idea."

"What do you mean?"

"Well, if Frank's after you . . ." Flick shrugged. "Maybe Scottsbluff isn't the best place for you. There are other places looking to hire hands. Like Texas. Maybe you wouldn't be offered a foreman's position right away, but better safe than dead, right?"

Matt frowned. Texas? The thought put a strange feeling in his middle. Maybe he just disliked change—or maybe his senses really did detect something dangerous about Texas. Either way, he wasn't about to downplay intuition. "I'm not looking to run, Flick."

"Who said anything about running? I was talking about safety and opportunities. Why, if you do want to go to Texas, I might just go with you. I'd like to see Texas. What do you have to say to that?"

Matt wanted to say that there was *no way, no how* that he was going to saddle up and leave behind the life he had built for himself here in Scottsbluff. But instead, he heard himself muttering, "Texas? Seriously?"

"Think it over, partner." Flick clapped him on the shoulder and swiveled away. "I see Billy by the cook shack, and I've got a letter for him. See you at supper."

"Sure." Matt watched Flick leave, then realized he was still holding the newspaper. "Hey, you want your newspaper back?"

Flick waved his hand. "Keep it. You might want to give the Telmond story a closer going over. Maybe it'll help you change your mind about Texas."

Matt shook his head, but he set the newspaper on top of his gear. Maybe he would read it more thoroughly later.

In the meantime, he had a letter to read from Colton. Leaning back against Bowie, Matt reached into his vest pocket and retrieved his brother's letter, a twinge of guilt pricking him as he opened it. He ought to write more often to Colton, but time got away from him. He'd never liked writing. Colton, however, *did* like writing, and that made it easy for Matt to let him shoulder the bulk of their correspondence.

But a correspondence shouldn't be one-sided.

Matt pulled the letter out of its envelope, sensing something different about it. He squinted his eyes at the paper and discovered that there was only one page of text, with nothing on the other side.

That was it. Colton never left any of his paper blank. He

always said that since he wasn't lacking for things to write about, he might as well not waste any money in sending blank paper. Every inch of space was always crammed with his handwriting.

Frowning, Matt unfolded the page. *Odd.* The handwriting wasn't even Colton's. This handwriting was more delicate, feminine, and even more perfect than Colton's penmanship. Matt skimmed down the page until he found the signature. *Emily Keath.*

Emily? She was Colton's wife, but Matt had never met her. She'd never written to him, either, and Matt's stomach did a funny little twist, leaving it hard and knotted.

Matt forced himself to start reading:

Dear Matthew,

It is with a heavy heart that I write to you now, for the news I have to share is one of great tragedy. Three weeks ago, Colton's life was taken from us in an unexpected manner—

"What?" The single word escaped from Matt's lips as little more than a whisper. *Colton's life was taken?* Matt's pulse raced. That couldn't be true. Emily must have confused her words, surely.

Colton passed from this life and into the arms of his Savior. He had left home early in the morning to cut wood, perfectly healthy and strong. When he hadn't returned on time, my father went searching for him and found that Colton had been injured. His ax had slipped, leaving his leg severely cut. He brought Colton home and sent for the doctor, but it was too late. Colton had already lost too much blood to be saved.

"No." Matt tore his gaze away from the letter, unable to comprehend what he'd just absorbed. His eyes burned and each breath felt as if it was tearing through him. This had to be someone's mad idea of a joke. Colton was too young to die, only twenty-eight, two years older than Matt. He had always been a strong man, a man with good health and a clean lifestyle. He ought to have lived well into his old age.

A shudder ran through Matt's frame. His hold on the letter tightened, and he crumpled the paper in his hand as if destroying it could somehow erase the painful words that it contained.

But glancing down at the paper, he realized that it was foolish to let his emotions out on the paper. He had to read it through to completion. Even from miles away, he needed to know what had happened to Colton.

Matt smoothed the letter out again, but one glance at the handwriting sent a tremor through his body. He couldn't do this. Not now, at least.

Matt thrust the letter back into his vest pocket, hands shaking. Maybe later, when he was calmer, he'd be able to make it through the entire thing without feeling like a knife had been plunged into his chest.

CHAPTER 2

Matt used his fork to prod at the last bites of meat and gravy on his plate, attempting to summon an appetite. After a day of outdoor labor, he should have been famished, yet all thoughts of hunger had been stolen by Emily's letter. He hadn't been able to think straight ever since he'd read the horrible news just one hour ago.

He didn't want to think. He didn't want to even consider that his big brother was gone. But every time Matt closed his eyes, the image of the letter flashed through his mind, the words inscribed across it: *Colton passed from this life.*

Setting aside his fork, Matt gave his supper up as a lost cause. He reached into his pocket and pulled out the terrible letter again. Much as he dreaded reading it, he had to get it over with before he lost the nerve.

He moved close to the lamp on the table, blocking out the sounds of clattering as Juan stacked dishes into the wash basin in the corner of the shack and Flick piled more food onto his plate across the table. He angled the paper so he could see the words more clearly.

Emily informed Matt that Colton's family had been doing

well, as well as they could under the circumstances at least. They had received much support from the community during their time of grieving. Emily found the church to be a source of great comfort, and the pastor had been most generous in devoting extra time to spend with her.

Things will continue much the same for us, I suspect, despite Colton's death. We will continue to run the farm, since my father and several others have offered their assistance in the upcoming planting, she finished. *And of course, we shall trust that our Heavenly Father knows our needs and will provide for us during this difficult time.*

Matt clenched his jaw. There was far more that went into running a farm than merely planting crops. Surely she didn't think she could handle all the fieldwork after the planting. She wouldn't have the strength to swing a scythe to put up enough hay for her livestock to last through the winter. She couldn't handle harvesting all of her fields in the fall. She couldn't cut enough wood to keep the stove stoked. And how did she expect to take care of her children, maintain the garden, handle all the cooking and cleaning, and do all the other chores a woman had to do on top of tending the farm?

Either the woman wasn't thinking clearly or she was placing way too much trust in her neighbors' assistance. Maybe she had some remarkable neighbors who were willing to help her all year, but each of them would have their own fields and families to care for, and Emily's farm would by necessity come second.

Matt leaned back in his seat, studying the flame in the lantern as if it could unveil all the mysteries of life to him.

You should go help her, a voice nagged in his mind. Matt almost laughed aloud. Him, play farmer when he'd always had a particular hatred for plows and scythes? The idea was ludicrous.

He let his eyes skim over the letter again. Emily was simply stating facts. At no point did she even hint that she wished for his assistance.

He had never even met the woman, so there was no need for

him to throw his own life out the window and run to her aid. If she thought she needed to hold on to her farm, then fine. Let her deal with her own problems.

Maybe she doesn't have a choice except to try to make the farm profitable, another inner voice whispered to Matt. *She is your sister-in-law, after all. Family helps family.*

He knew exactly what his father would say if he were in the room with him: "Son, quit your dawdling and go out there and give your sister-in-law a hand."

He'd also have plenty to say about Matt even *thinking* of letting Emily try to run the farm all by herself—a young woman who had children in tow.

But this is her problem. Not mine.

You think she wanted Colton to die and leave her like this?

Of course not. But she's not my family by blood. She's Colton's wife, and I don't even know her well enough to think of her as my sister-in-law.

And whose fault is that?

Matt cringed. Now *that* was an uncomfortable turn of thought. It wasn't for lack of invitation that he'd never met Colton's family. Colton had invited him many times, asking him to come for his wedding, the birth of his first child, and then because he simply wanted to see Matt again. Something had come up each time, keeping Matt from going. Truthfully, he hadn't wanted to make the long journey to visit his brother's farm. There was always next year, he'd told himself, and maybe by then he'd feel more like making the week-long journey to visit Colton.

And look at where that left him now. Time had run out for Colton, and Matt had never made the effort to see him again.

Matt set the letter on the table and buried his face in his palms. He should have burned that letter when he first received it. Then maybe he could continue to fool himself into thinking Colton was still alive.

Juan crossed the room and collected Matt's plate from the table, his dark eyes studying Matt. "You have been given bad news, Matt?" he asked, his faint Spanish accent lilting his words.

"Yeah, pretty bad." Matt didn't want to believe the news that he had just received, let alone vocalize it, but he forced the words out. "My brother's dead."

"Aw, that's tough." Bread crumbles escaped from Flick's mouth as he spoke while chewing.

"I am sorry to hear that." Juan dropped the plates into his dish tub with a clatter. "You were close with your brother, yes?"

Matt clenched his hands under the table. Just how much did he dare speak to Juan and Flick? He liked the two men—as coworkers. But he had a reputation to uphold. He couldn't let them think he actually had emotions—even if those emotions were tearing at his insides like a beast right now.

He kept his response an understatement. "We were always pretty close."

Matt's throat closed as memories flooded his mind. Images of Colton laughing when they were just boys. Memories of the hours they spent whispering to each other on their beds in the dark after Pa blew out the lamp. The comforting feel of Colton's arm wrapped around Matt's shoulders as they stood together in front of their parents' graves, sharing a grief that they had never before experienced.

Matt swallowed, trying to banish the ache in his heart. "Haven't seen him in close to ten years. Not since back when I was sixteen on the farm in Ohio."

Juan nodded and looked in the distance as though searching through his own memories. "I've not been home in eighteen years. Sometimes I dream about it, but . . ." His words trailed off. He gave a nonchalant shrug and set to work wiping down the table.

Flick used a fork to scrape the last of the gravy from his

plate. "Boy, but this room's turned gloomy all a sudden. Hanky, anyone?"

Juan frowned at him. "Shame, Flick. Matt's brother has passed, and you are still cracking your not-so-funny jokes? Maybe you have no sense of family, but I understand how Matt is feeling."

Flick had the grace to inch a little lower in his seat.

Juan looked back at Matt. "Where does your brother live?"

"Osceola."

At Juan and Flick's blank looks, Matt added, "Small town over a week's ride east of here. Colton's got a homestead outside of town."

"Homestead?" Flick wrinkled his nose. "He's a sodbuster?"

Matt nodded, and Juan and Flick grimaced. Matt wasn't the only one around there who looked down on farming.

Farmers were a threat in cattle country. The more land they plowed for crops, the less grass there was for the herd. And when farmers complained about the cattle trampling their crops underfoot, they often used a shotgun to emphasize their point.

Colton wasn't one of those farmers. His land was far removed from the open range and cattle wars—but no Westerner liked the idea of a man who followed the plow.

"Does your brother have a family?" Juan asked.

"A wife and two kids. Or was it three?" Matt glanced down to skim through the letter, but Emily's flowing script didn't offer him the answer. "Guess I can't remember. Time gets away from a man."

"I didn't know you were an uncle." Flick nudged him with his boot underneath the table. "*Uncle Matt.* Bet you'd scare the living daylights out of those kids if you showed up there."

Juan shot Flick a pointed look and added, "No offense, but you don't seem like a very kid-friendly type of man."

"Hardly." Matt wasn't bothered by Flick's observation. It was only the truth. Kids were one thing he'd never been overly fond of, and he was content to let Colton handle the duty of carrying on the Keath name. For him, he figured that his life was a far sight easier without a woman or children roping him down.

"How will your brother's family continue?" Juan asked. "Who will provide for them?"

Of course Juan had to go straight for the hard questions. Matt dropped his gaze to the table and gave what he hoped would pass as a careless shrug. "Emily said neighbors would help. Neighbors and—well, God."

Flick snorted. "Neighbors ain't worth the bother they cause. And God? What's He going to do? Drop manna from the sky for her?" His laugh made Matt cringe. "Sounds like she's aiming to starve this winter."

Who did Flick think he was to offer his opinion on this matter? Sure, Matt had been thinking along the same lines. That didn't mean he appreciated Flick's callousness. "Oh, they won't starve. I'll see to that personally."

Both Flick and Juan stared at him, their jaws dropping.

"What're you talking about?" Flick asked.

"Just don't seem right to have a woman out in the fields working like a man. I've been thinking I might head out that way and lend her a hand this summer." Matt felt a sweet sense of triumph at the look of shock on Flick's face.

Then Flick tipped his head back and howled. "Of all the dumb ideas you've ever had! You really think you can pull off being a farmer for any length of time? You'll come crawling back here whipped before a single day is over!"

Something hot flared inside Matt, sweeping into his face and making him clench his hands. "I was a farm boy before I even dreamed of being a ranch hand. Maybe *you* don't have the grit to stick with something you don't like, but I could last through the whole summer if I had to." Matt straightened his posture. "I reckon I'd manage just fine."

"*If?* Didn't you make up your mind that you're going?"

Matt bit his lip. He hadn't intended to sound *that* decided. Traveling to Osceola was still an option. Nothing more than that. The only reason he couldn't push the crazy idea aside was because he was still trying to figure out how to clear his conscience.

Flick's brow lifted. "Two minutes and you've already chickened out?"

The grin hovering on Flick's lips and the mockery that dripped from his tone scalded Matt. More heat pumped into his face. "I haven't chickened out. I meant to say *when* I go, not *if.*"

Great. He was good and stuck now.

Flick smirked. "I wager you'll give up, and I'll lay down twenty dollars on it. How much you willing to bet?"

Matt drew himself up straighter. "You know I don't bet."

"Only because you're too scared."

"You probably don't even have twenty dollars."

Flick half rose from his seat, making the table rock. "You looking for a fight, Keath?"

"Settle down, boys, or I will throw you outside to cool your heads," Juan warned them, and then he spouted off something in Spanish that undoubtedly was not complimentary.

Matt cast Flick a glare. What a heap of trouble he'd caused tonight! If it weren't for Flick, he wouldn't have declared that he was going to help Emily. He would have waited a while to think it over and then probably decided against going. That would've been far more sensible than running headlong into a mess he hadn't made.

Flick shoved back from the table and stalked the five feet to the door. "Do what you want, Matt, but I'm warning you that you're gonna wreck your own life if you're always trying to help other people. I wouldn't stoop to sodbusting for nobody." Flick darted his gaze back at Matt. "There's never an end to farming. Watch out, 'cause if you aren't careful, you'll never escape it, and you'll never come back to real life."

Matt stared after Flick as the door shut behind him. Something inside Matt warned him that there might be a measure of truth to Flick's words.

"I shouldn't have let him rile me," he muttered, glaring one more time toward the door.

"Don't listen to Flick. He never thinks of anyone but himself." Juan wiped a towel around his freshly washed plate and grinned at Matt. "I think you are making a good choice."

Juan sounded more sure of his decision than he did. "You do?"

"Oh yes. It caught me off guard for a moment, but now that I think it over, you are right. Cattle can do without you for one summer, but your family cannot."

His words sounded logical, and Matt let himself relax. "One summer," he said aloud. "I'm only doing this for one summer, and then I'll be back here as fast as Bowie can travel. I can survive one summer of farming, don't you think?"

"Of course," Juan agreed.

Matt leaned back in his seat. He had to believe this was the right thing to do. Just a few months, and then he'd be back here to show Flick that he did, in fact, have the grit to stick with farming through harvest—and that he was cowboy enough to escape the farm as soon as his job was accomplished.

Then another thought struck him. If Frank Harvey did want to finish him off, it might not be such a bad idea to lay low for a spell. And what better place to hide out than a little town of sober, church-going farmers?

Matt smiled. Maybe this wasn't such a bad idea after all.

He pushed away from the table and stood. "Guess I better go have a little talk with Keller. My mind's made up, so there's no use sticking around here. I'll leave before sunup tomorrow so I can get a good day's ride in."

"Solid plan." Juan's towel stopped its circuit around the pan he was drying, his expression hardening as he looked at Matt.

"The boys will laugh—but you just let them. You are right in what you are doing, so don't let anyone stop you."

Matt waved a hand at him and turned the door handle. "No worries. They can laugh all they like, but it won't change a thing in my mind."

CHAPTER 3

"Matt Keath, you're just the man I wanted to talk with tonight."

Matt eased himself into the chair across from Jack Keller, owner of the Bar K Ranch. Juan's encouragement still rang in his ears, and he felt ready to take on anything. Even Keller, the man he had worked so hard for so long to impress, couldn't intimidate him tonight. He was a man on a mission to rescue his destitute family.

He squirmed forward in his chair, but the leather upholstery failed to fit his frame right. Nothing in Keller's office sat comfortably with him. The furnishings were too plush. The paintings on the wall showed people from a higher status than him. Even the ceiling was too high, leaving him feeling exposed.

Keller lifted a pile of papers off the desk in front of him and shuffled them. "Let's start with you. What can I do for you, Matt?"

Matt inhaled. Here it came, the blow that would change his whole life—at least for a summer. "I've come to tell you I won't be riding for you anymore. I intend to leave tomorrow before sunrise."

"Leave?" Keller stopped shuffling the papers. "You mean to say that you aren't happy working for me?"

"No, sir, it's not that. I've been most happy working for you."

Keller's eyes narrowed. "Someone offered you a bigger pay?"

"No, it's not that either."

"Then why?"

"I received a letter today telling me that my brother has passed on. He's got a homestead, and a wife and kids who need help, so I figured I'd head that way and lend a hand." Matt pushed a smile onto his face, but his muscles protested. *Farming.* He still cringed at the thought.

Keller nodded slowly and began to shuffle the papers again. "I see. So, your sister-in-law asked you for help?"

"Well, no," Matt admitted. He had no desire to disclose that he and Emily were complete strangers—and she was smart enough not to beg for help from a stranger.

"Then what makes you think that someone's not helping them already? Or that they even need help in the first place?"

"There's something that tells me that's not the way it is. If that is the case, then I guess I'll just turn around and come back here."

Keller frowned. "So you *want* to help them?"

Matt shifted in his seat, the leather feeling even more uncomfortable than when he first sat down. "It's not a matter of whether I want to or not. It's a matter of being needed."

Keller leaned forward, looking Matt straight in the eyes. "Do you want to help them or not?" he asked, emphasizing each word.

The question was point blank, giving Matt no way to dodge it. "No."

"Then why go?"

The subtle implications Keller gave, indicating that he thought Matt was deranged, were beginning to step on his nerves. "Because I'm needed, that's why."

"And what if I needed you here?"

Matt studied the man's face. Usually, he was quick at reading others' intentions, but Keller was proving hard to understand. Maybe his mind wasn't working its best after a long day's work —or maybe Keller had a deeper purpose for his questions. "I'm not sure what you mean, sir."

"No, probably not." Keller rose from his chair and paced to the other side of the room, his boots clicking against the polished wood floor.

Matt rubbed his jaw, watching as Keller stopped in front of an image of a man in a top hat and stared at him, almost as if he were asking for advice. What was going on here? He'd quit at ranches before and never had trouble. He had simply informed the boss of his upcoming departure, they figured up his pay, he collected it, and then rode on. Simple.

"Matt, I have an offer for you." Keller spun to face him. "I want you to ride for me as foreman. You'll have more responsibilities, but you'll also make more money. What do you say?"

Matt stared at him, his heart rate kicking into full gear. He was being offered the position of foreman at the Bar K Ranch? He'd dreamt of being offered this position for months.

But then an uneasy sensation curled in the pit of his stomach. He was leaving. He'd made his decision and vowed that he wouldn't be dissuaded from it. He could almost picture his pa's eyes, drilling into him as he said, "If you violate what you know is right, all the money in the world will never make you a successful man."

He swallowed, wishing he could forestall the disappointment. "I'm sorry, but I'm afraid I can't."

"I'll pay you top dollar. Fifty-five a month."

Matt would have staggered if he hadn't been sitting down. This man really wanted Matt to ride for him. "Why do you want me to be your foreman so bad? There are plenty of other men in the bunkhouse who would gladly take the job for a lot less than what you just offered me."

Keller scowled, his black mustache quivering. "I said I wanted *you* to ride for me, not any of those other yahoos out there. How long have you been working for me?"

"Three years."

"Three years, and I ain't had a single problem with you yet. You've done a thorough job on every task you're given, and you've had some good ideas on making things more efficient around here. I've never seen you get drunk. You're one of my top riders, and I don't see why you should be so surprised that I want you as my foreman."

Matt gripped both sides of his chair just to make sure he was still grounded. He hadn't dared to hope that Keller noticed him. "I guess I am surprised. You never hinted of this to me."

"Didn't know I was required to."

Now Keller was getting testy, and Matt figured he had better back off a little. "Riding for you would be a pleasure, Keller, but—"

"Good, then what are we waiting for?"

Matt held up a hand. "I wasn't finished. I can't take the position because—"

"Young man, I am starting to lose some of my respect for you," Keller said between gritted teeth. "This is an opportunity you won't get at any other ranch, and you must realize that the money I'm offering you is nothing to scoff at. I'm offering to pay you the very top dollar of what a foreman can expect to make. Period. If you are as enterprising as you first appeared, you'll be wise to leap on this offer before it passes you by."

"Under any other circumstances, I'd be honored to ride for you as your foreman. I'm not refusing because I don't consider it a good offer. Indeed, you've been more than fair in your terms."

Keller started to interrupt, but Matt stopped him. "My

brother's family needs me right now, so I'm not free to accept your offer."

Keller stared at him, his gaze hardening. "This is the dumbest thing I've ever heard. Ever!"

Matt stiffened. He was growing tired of hearing people call him a fool. "When I was young, my pa made it very clear to me that a family sticks together and comes to each other's aid, no matter the personal cost. Right now, my family comes first for me, no matter what my personal feelings are. Do you have family, Keller?"

Keller glared at him. "That's enough, young man. You can leave. Right now."

Matt rose and moved toward the door, barely restraining himself from stomping. So Keller was going to blow up at him because he happened to hold an opinion different than his. Fine. Matt was quitting anyway.

As Matt opened the door to leave, Keller called out, "Hold on, Matt. Come back here one moment."

Matt hesitated, then shut the door and returned to Keller's table. "Yes?"

Keller returned to shuffling around the papers in his hands. "If I considered raising your pay even more than my first offer —say, to sixty a month—would you be willing to take the job?"

Matt could hardly keep from smirking. So, Keller hadn't dismissed him after all. He'd expected Matt to fall down begging for the job rather than walking away.

"Your money means nothing to me. It would only be under one condition that I will accept the position," Matt said, locking eyes with Keller.

Keller's hands stilled, and he studied Matt warily. "Yes?"

"I'll accept the job if you will hold it for me until I return in the fall."

Keller's nostrils flared, red sweeping into his face. "I'll figure up your pay and you can collect it before you ride out tomorrow, Keath. Now, get out of here this instant. I'm glad you refused my offer because I changed my mind. I don't want you as my foreman anyway!"

Matt gave a tight nod and turned to leave, determined that he was not going to lose his temper in front of Keller.

"Oh, and Keath? If you do return in the fall, don't bother to come looking here for a job. Any man who puts his family ahead of my cattle isn't worth his salt to me," Keller called after him.

Matt sent him a final backwards glance. "Well, Keller, I wasn't planning on hiring on with you again anyway. I don't like working for bullheaded men who get what they want by pushing others around."

He slammed the door shut before Keller could respond. He wasn't sure if he had quit or if he had been fired, but he knew one thing for sure. He was done with Bar K Ranch.

Osceola was his next destination.

CHAPTER 4

"Well, Bowie, guess this must be it."

Matt stared at the town looming ahead of him, already feeling out of place. With the benefit of a hill and Bowie's added height, he had a good overview of the town's layout. Every street lay perfectly straight in a grid pattern that spoke of someone's careful plotting. Two church spires rose from the heart of the community.

This was no Wild West town. These people were building something they intended to last. Something that would no doubt still be standing generations later.

He inhaled, telling himself he wasn't nervous. He'd been a deputy, facing men of unsavory character, and he'd been a cowboy, a job that was not for the weak. He shouldn't have any cause to feel uneasy about the upcoming meeting with Colton's family or facing a town of upstanding citizens. So why did he wish that he could push everything off for just a little longer, have one more day to think things over?

More time would do nothing to banish his uncertainties.

Matt rode through the outskirts of town and down Main Street, unable to keep his gaze on the path straight ahead.

Osceola was a young town, with just enough brick business fronts to make it look established, yet plenty of new construction to give it a fresh, up-and-coming feel. Several new buildings were being built right on Main Street, and the echo of pounding hammers rang in the air.

Matt's gaze slipped to the hitching rail around the square, and he noticed that while there were a few saddled horses waiting for their owners to return, teams and wagons lined the streets for the most part. Welcome to farming country.

Not many pedestrians were out and about, but as he continued down the street, Matt noticed that the people he did meet stared at him a little longer than necessary. Their eyes widened as they studied his hat, his chaps, and his boots. Evidently cowboys were not a common sight around these parts. Matt tipped his hat to the next passerby. Nothing like making a grand appearance.

He had to find someone who knew where Colton's family lived. He had already passed a lumberyard, a farm machinery dealer, a livery, and a bank. Now, his gaze fell on the store in front of him, Mayfield Mercantile. He guided Bowie to the hitching rail. A mercantile should be as good a place as any to try his luck.

After tethering Bowie securely, he sauntered toward the building with his most confident step. The door creaked as he opened it, and the bell above his head jangled.

"Be with you in a minute," a woman's voice called from somewhere near the back of the store.

"That's fine." Matt stepped a little farther inside, surveying his surroundings. He took in the sight of the fabrics stacked on the shelves, the line of boots, the collection of shovels and hoes, the jars filled with lemon candy and peppermints, and all other home goods that lined the store's cramped aisles.

Yep, he was definitely in a mercantile.

Matt took it all in, memories from his childhood flashing

through his mind of Pa letting him tag along on his trip to the general store in their hometown of Ohio. As a kid, he'd been amazed by all the different products for sale crammed together in one room. That awe hadn't worn off as an adult.

"All right, sir, how can I help you today?" A woman emerged from one of the aisles, her face flushed and blonde hair seeking to escape from the bun that was supposed to contain it.

Matt pulled his attention away from the shelves. Before he could respond, the woman rushed on.

"Forgive all the noise outside. I can't get used to all that hammering. Ever since the Omaha and Republican Valley Railroad promised to bring a line through here this summer, people have been flocking here to build. Can't believe how many new people are pouring in here; too many for me to even keep track of. Times are changing, and the town's surely growing. A good thing for business, of course."

Matt's heart dipped. She didn't know *everyone* around, but would she know where Emily lived?

The woman blew a strand of hair out of her face and smiled at him. "Now, sir, how can I help you today?"

There was only one way to find out if she could truly help him. He gave his hat brim a tug. "Hello, ma'am. I'm Matt Keath, and I was trying to find someone who might know where my brother—" He faltered. "That is, where my sister-in-law's farm is located."

The woman's eyes went round. Then she let out a shriek and ran toward him. "Well, I'll be! You surely are a Keath, and more than that, I'm sure you must be an angel!"

Before Matt could make sense of what was happening, she threw her arms around him and hugged him. What did this woman think she was doing? Matt stumbled back a step, his arms dangling at his sides like limp rags.

The woman had already turned and run toward the back of the store. "Ephraim, come quick! Colton's brother is here."

"Who?" A man emerged from the back room, broom in hand.

"Colton's brother!"

Ephraim looked toward Matt and studied him. A smile curved his mouth upwards, and he stroked his chin. "Well, I'll be. You sure do look like Colton."

"Doesn't he though?" The woman looped her arm through Ephraim's, and they both stood beaming at Matt in a most unnerving way.

Matt reached up to adjust his hat, belatedly realizing that the action betrayed his nervousness. "You own this store?"

"Oh, pardon me! We clean forgot to introduce ourselves. I'm Sadie Mayfield." The woman motioned to herself and then to the man beside her. "This is my husband, Ephraim."

"Emily is my sister," Ephraim added.

Matt looked from one to the other, understanding dawning on him. "*Mayfield.* I remember that name now. Emily was a Mayfield before she married Colton."

"It's just a pity about Colton." Sadie shook her head. "He was a fine man and took such good care of his family."

"He was one of my best friends." Ephraim's gaze dropped to the floor. "He's greatly missed around here."

"And leaving behind those poor fatherless children of his. It just breaks my heart." Sadie's eyes filled with tears. "We're sorry for your loss, Matt."

Matt jerked his head in a nod, tension mounting. He didn't want to hear of their sympathy. He didn't want to hear people refer to Colton in past tense.

The bell above the door clinked, mercifully turning Ephraim and Sadie's attention from him.

"Mrs. Durmond, how good to see you," Sadie said as a woman with an angular face and hawkish nose entered the store. Matt noted that her tone had turned more reserved, lacking the warmth she'd spoken with to him. "How are you?"

"I could be better." The woman looked at Matt, and her eyebrows rose, mouth pursing into a thin line. "My, but those are some outlandish clothes. How can you have the nerve to wear those out in town?"

Something about the woman reminded Matt of a neighbor he'd known back in Ohio, a woman who was always checking behind his ears for dirt that he might have missed, always making him tell her what verse the sermon had been on and scolding him for the scrapes he'd gotten into. She claimed that her undue interest in him was only because he didn't have a mother. And since Grant Keath showed no signs of remarrying, she took it upon herself to make sure that his boys grew up properly. Without fail, Matt was the one who fell under her disapproving eye. Colton had always been far more mature than other boys his age, and he was a model in politeness and manners. But Matt had been . . . *lacking* at times, and she took it upon herself to correct him.

But now he wasn't a little boy who had no choice but to writhe under the woman's observations. Meeting Mrs. Durmond's eye, he gave her his most charming smile. "Actually, I tend to like my clothes quite well, thank you."

"Well." Mrs. Durmond frowned. "Are you just passing through town, or are you staying?"

"Oh, I'm staying. For a few months at least. Perhaps you know Emily Keath? She's my sister-in-law, and I thought I'd come and give her a hand now that her husband—well, you know."

Mrs. Durmond blinked. "You're Colton Keath's brother?" She studied him as if she thought he might be lying. "Guess you do look a heap like him, although he was sane enough that he wouldn't have worn such getup for anything. You say you're staying for a few months?"

"Yes, ma'am."

Her eyes narrowed. "Why aren't you busy with your own farm?"

"I don't have a farm. I'm a cowboy."

Matt watched with satisfaction as first shock, then horror, crossed her face. "A *cowboy*? I've heard things about them—nothing good. Ephraim, are you really going to allow this man to be around Emily's children? Think of how this will harm them!"

Ephraim's face remained impassive. "It's Emily's decision."

"But she needs help so badly that you know she's not going to turn him away. Do something, Ephraim!"

"It's Emily's decision," Ephraim said again.

"It's a pleasure to meet you, Mrs. Durmond, and I'm sure we'll become well acquainted in the next few months." Matt smiled, secretly enjoying seeing her get ruffled.

"So that's the way it's going to be." Mrs. Durmond glared at him, then she spun on her heel and marched toward the door. "I expect to see you in church on Sunday!"

The door shuddered as she slammed it shut behind her. Matt risked a glance at Ephraim and Sadie. Neither of them were looking at him and instead had their eyes fixed on the stock on their shelves.

"So." Ephraim turned back to Matt, a hint of a smile on his face. "Did you mean what you told her? You're going to stay and help Emily?"

"Of course." Matt tried his best to sound enthusiastic. "I'm planning to stay until the harvest is in."

"Bless you, Matt. Sadie and I have been worried about her getting through the summer. Of course, plenty of people have said they'd help her. Pa, Zane, and me were planning to give her a hand as much as we could, but it's hard to make time, you know?" Ephraim rubbed at his temples. "Emily is a dear woman, but I'm afraid she's also got some pride. She's bad about asking for help. If she feels something needs to be done, she's going to take it upon herself to try and do it all on her own."

"She's already wearing herself out with trying to take care of everything," Sadie added. "She's been handling all of Colton's chores on top of her normal work. Keeping up with her three kids is enough to wear anyone out in the first place. I should know since I've got four of my own."

"You're an answer to prayer, Matt. A real answer to prayer." Ephraim clapped Matt on the shoulder.

Matt blinked. *An answer to prayer?* He'd been called many things in his life, but never that. He really didn't think he was the kind of man the Good Lord would want to use as an answer to prayer. And he wasn't about to admit that he'd been seriously hoping someone else had already stepped in to oversee Colton's farm.

"Can I have directions to Emily's place?" he asked. Sometimes it was best just to change the subject.

"Why, of course," Ephraim replied. Both he and Sadie kept their wide smiles locked in place.

Matt shifted from one foot to the other. He felt as if a noose was slowly settling around his neck and strangling him. This was not his territory. He wasn't a farmer. He wasn't fond of kids. He certainly couldn't be an answer to prayer.

And yet, it seemed he was stuck.

CHAPTER 5

Matt let Bowie choose his own pace as he rode out of town toward Colton and Emily's farm. He tried his best to block out the cheerful bird calls and the lush green vegetation surrounding him, wishing for winter's chill to come and dim the sunlight so at least his environment would match his dismal mood.

Ephraim's words still rang in his mind—*"You're an answer to prayer."*

Flick would roar if he heard that. As for Matt, he felt more unsettled than anything. He didn't pretend to understand how God worked. He'd given up on that years ago, deciding that if there really was a God, He sure didn't know what He was doing. It seemed the "Most High" was always taking, taking, taking. And He was always taking the best people who had no cause to die. After all, wasn't it God who had caused both Colton and their parents to die?

Matt closed his eyes. He'd felt searing pain as a boy when his mother passed. Matt had only been five when their family contracted diphtheria. Pa, Colton, and Matt had only gotten light cases and were soon as well as ever, but Ma always had frail health, and the sickness claimed her life, leaving only shadowy memories of her in Matt's mind. In the days before her passing, Matt spent more time on his knees than ever, pleading that God would spare her life, but to no avail.

She'd died. And praying hadn't stopped the terrible deed from happening.

It had been just him and Pa and Colton after that. The three of them had clung to each other, sharing both the housekeeping duties and the farm work. The only time they separated was when the boys went off to school, and then they loitered at home as long as possible, barely making it to school on time and leaving as soon as school was dismissed, racing to be with their pa again.

And then Pa passed away. Matt was only sixteen the day it happened. "His heart," the doctor had said. His passing had shaken Matt's life to the core.

He and Colton had stayed on the farm a couple of months longer, neither of them wanting to rush into making any decisions. Colton was all for selling the Ohio farm with its too-painful memories and buying a farm together farther west. Matt wanted to go West as well, but not to farm. He wanted excitement, enough excitement that he could forget the hollow place that his parents' deaths had created inside of him.

At last, they sold the farm, split the money between them, and then parted ways. Colton landed a town job while deciding where he was going to homestead, and Matt headed out West and on to the adventure he craved. They'd promised to stay in touch, and they'd both been faithful—until now, separated by death.

Matt sucked in a deep breath, barely able to swallow the memories that still pained him, even after all this time. No wonder he rarely spent time in retrospect, preferring instead to run headlong into each adventure and challenge that came his way. The only dilemma he faced with this one was that there was nothing tangible he could do; no outward battles to fight. He was caught up in something he couldn't change.

Ripping his thoughts away from the backward path they had followed into the past, Matt lifted himself slightly in the stirrups. He ought to be getting close to the farm. He shaded his eyes against the sun and replayed Ephraim's instructions in his mind. He should have been paying closer attention to where he was going rather than letting his mind wander off.

A farm jutted out from the landscape, and Matt's pulse quickened. Was this Colton's place? He steered Bowie onto the lane that led to the farmhouse and crept closer, taking in the view before him. He squinted at what he could make out to be the wooden barn, then a small sod house. As he leaned forward, Matt noticed that the sod house was still in use; Colton had been living there since day one and apparently never left. Why did Colton build the barn out of wood before the house? One would think he'd want to get his growing family out of the sod house as soon as possible.

Bowie neared the sod building. Matt reined him in, dismounted, then tied Bowie to a handy post.

Walking toward the house, Matt hooked his thumbs in his pockets, trying not to look as nervous as he felt. This felt all wrong. He ought to be seeing Colton appear at any moment, a welcoming grin on his face. But instead, Matt was about to meet strangers—people who were the closest thing he had to family now.

Why had he waited so long to visit? The question crossed his mind for what must have been the hundredth time since receiving Emily's letter.

Before he reached the door, a little girl came around the corner of the house, singing to a doll in her arms. She stopped short and stared at him, her eyes wide.

Matt studied her face, scrutinizing her deep blue eyes, her brown braids, and the smattering of freckles on her nose. This wasn't one of Colton's kids. He could remember like yesterday when he received a letter from Colton telling him that he was an uncle. None of Colton's kids could be as old as this girl, though the ages of his children slipped Matt's mind.

"Hello." A grin broke across the girl's face. "You coming to visit us?"

"No—actually, I'm looking for another family." Matt looked away and searched the yard for someone older than this girl. Someone capable of giving him directions to Emily's.

"Oh." The girl's voice held disappointment. Then she brightened. "Well, you could stay with us a while, and *then* go find your family. We have some kitties in the barn I could show you." She seemed convinced that kitties would be enough to keep Matt with her. As if Matt cared anything about cats.

"How old are you?"

"Five." She grinned at him and held up her doll. "This is Susan. My mama made her 'specially as a gift on my birthday a couple years ago. One time my little brother chewed off one of her eyes, and Mama and Pa were scared he'd swallowed it, but then they found the button on the floor, so it was okay, and Mama sewed a new eye back on her. She's my very own baby."

She apparently had no hesitation about talking to a stranger. For some reason, he felt unnerved by that. The way she fixed those bright eyes on him and grinned made him want to squirm. What had he done to get her attention? He didn't even like kids.

He cleared his throat. "Where are your parents?"

"Mama's workin' around." She raised a hand toward the farm. "And my pa's deaded."

Matt jerked. Her pa was dead? Was she talking about Colton? But then, who else? There couldn't be too many fatherless families on this road.

"What's your name?"

"Joyanna. My mama says–"

"Is your mama's name Emily Keath?" Matt interrupted her before she could gather steam.

The little girl stared up at him, her blue eyes wide. "No."

"Oh." Relief swept through Matt. If he'd had to put up with this little chatterbox for a few months, he would have been sure to lose his mind.

"Guess I'll be leaving, then." He started to turn back toward Bowie, but Joyanna blocked his way.

"You don't have to leave right away, do you? You just got here. You could stay and eat supper with us. My mama's a really good cook." Her eyes pleaded with him. "You could leave another time."

"No, I need to leave now." Matt tried to sidestep around her, but she blocked his way again.

"You got a real pretty horse. We used to have a horse that looked kind of like that, only not quite so pretty, but Mama sold it after Pa got deaded."

Matt flinched. How could she speak so casually of someone getting "deaded"? Chances were that she was too young to fully grasp what being "deaded" even meant.

This kid must be starved for someone to talk to. That was the only explanation for why she was so desperate to keep talking to *him*.

"Look, I need to leave right now, so why don't you go find your mama?" Matt cast a desperate glance over his shoulder, hoping to find help. A girl up ahead caught his attention. She strode toward him, a baby on one hip and a little boy clinging to her skirts. Probably her older sister. Matt had never felt so relieved to see someone in all his life.

The girl drew nearer, her eyes narrowing as she looked him over. "Hello, sir. Can I help you?"

Matt glanced at Joyanna. If she could just get this kid out of his way, that would be the biggest help.

"I'm a little mixed up and need some directions. Is your mother around here?"

The girl stiffened. "If you're looking for my mother, you'll have to go north a couple miles. But for your information, I am fully capable of giving you directions to any farm within a few miles of here."

Matt shot her a glance and all at once realized she wasn't quite as young as he'd first thought. Did that mean she was the mother of all these children? Heat climbed up his neck toward his face. Swallowing his pride, he said, "In that case, I'd be grateful if you could give me directions. Do you know where Emily Keath lives?"

The woman arched one eyebrow. "You're talking to her."

A jolt of shock ran through Matt, rooting him to the ground. *This was Emily Keath?* But nothing quite matched up to his expectations, least of all his introduction to her.

"But—but . . ." His gaze fell on Joyanna, and he pointed at her accusingly. "You told me your mama wasn't named Emily Keath."

Joyanna looked back at him with innocent eyes. "She's not. She's Mama."

Matt swiveled his gaze back to Emily, scrambling to think of how Colton had described her in his letters. Black hair—she had that. A delicate chin—she had that too. Blue eyes—yes, she had those.

And since she matched Colton's description and claimed herself that she was Emily Keath, Matt had no choice but to accept that as the truth.

Matt smiled weakly, removing his hat. "Pleased to meet you, ma'am."

Emily gave a quick intake of breath. The stoic mask she wore crumbled, and her hand flew over her mouth. "Oh my. Pardon me, but you—you look almost like my husband, Colton."

Matt grimaced. "Funny, but you're not the first to say that. I'm Matt, Colton's brother."

"Colton's brother," she repeated, still staring at him in awe.

"You wrote to me not too long ago."

His words seemed to snap Emily out of her daze, and her tone turned cool again. "Yes, I remember. Please, Mr. Keath, won't you come in?"

Mr. Keath? So, she was going to treat him with freezing politeness. Well, two could play that game.

"I'd be most happy to, Mrs. Keath," he said, meeting her gaze. He tried to decipher the emotion that lingered behind her eyes. Resentment? Frustration? Pain? Maybe fear.

She averted her gaze, motioning for him to follow her toward the sod house. "I see you already met Joyanna," she said as they fell into step. "This is Grant." She pointed to the round-eyed boy still clinging to her skirts. "He's three. And Austin here just turned one." She pointed to the baby on her hip who was staring at Matt with the same wide eyes as his brother.

Matt studied both boys. How could Colton have been the father of boys who were this old? He still pictured them as babies. "Hi," he said to them with another weak smile.

Instantly, both of their faces crumpled and they started crying, crowding closer to Emily.

Emily shushed them, murmuring words of comfort. Matt stared in bewilderment. "What'd I do?"

Emily shrugged. "I guess they're just a little sensitive."

This was a disaster. All he said was hi, and they started screaming. Matt shook his head, wishing he could return back to cattle country where no one stared at him as if they suspected that he was a monster bent on devouring them.

Emily herded them into the house, the boys still sniffling and looking anywhere except at Matt. Joyanna hovered at Matt's side, and he almost tripped on her as he walked through the door. That girl was *still* clinging to him.

Ducking into the sod house, Matt blinked, his vision struggling to adjust to the darkness after hours out in the sun. The home was merely one small room, with a stove, a rocker, and a table squeezing in between two narrow beds—one against each wall. He barely had any room to move around.

"I'll cut some bread, and we can all sit and have a snack," Emily said.

Matt watched as Emily tried unsuccessfully to set Austin down on the bed, but he howled and clung to her. With a sigh, she hoisted him back onto her hip, then with her free arm, she pulled out a knife and a cutting board. "Wash up and have a seat, Mr. Keath."

Matt almost missed the dip of her head, indicating that the basin was on a little shelf behind him. He retreated and scrubbed his hands with the bar of soap, then he dried them off with the towel that hung from a hook.

He stepped toward the table and slid into a chair. Joyanna took the seat next to his and scooted it just a little closer to him. Matt ignored her, instead turning his face to the window. If only they could return outside. The two windows in the house were not letting in much light, thanks to the thick slabs of sods that made up the walls. As a result, the room was dim.

"So, Mr. Keath, what brings you here to Osceola?" Emily placed a loaf of bread on the cutting board with such finesse that Matt figured she must have plenty of experience doing so while having one arm occupied by her child.

"Well, after I got your letter, I thought it might be best for everyone if I came and helped you out for the summer."

Her hands stilled and her jaw tightened. "I wasn't trying to make you think I wanted your help."

"I know." Why was she so prickly? Was everything he said really that offensive?

Emily appeared to struggle for control. "It is very kind of you to offer your assistance, Mr. Keath, but we don't need your help. We are doing just fine here without you." She gave him a pointed look. "You can go back West."

Matt stared at her. She was serious, he could tell. The look on her face told him that she didn't want him there.

Something akin to anger ignited in his chest. He had just left his job as a cowboy, abandoning the range he loved, turning down a position as foreman—a position he'd dreamt of for a long time—and he traveled over a week to arrive, only to have Emily tell him that she wanted him to leave?

Well, she wasn't going to get rid of him that easily.

Matt drew a breath to calm himself. "Oh, it's no problem for me. I don't have anything pressing going on this summer, and I'm sure you must have something for me to do around here. There's never an end to farm work, Mrs. Keath."

Emily tensed. "I can't pay you."

"That's all right. I wouldn't accept it even if you did have the money."

"In case you haven't noticed, we don't have extra room in here. Joyanna and Grant share one bed, and me and Austin share the other."

"No trouble. I brought my bedroll, so I'll just bunk down in the hayloft at night."

"You can't do that!"

"Sure I can. I've slept in worse places before."

He could tell her frustration was mounting. She had to be running out of excuses to make him leave.

"Do you know anything about farming?" she asked, her eyes challenging him.

"Oh, sure. I grew up on a farm, remember?"

"Colton said you don't like farming."

Matt straightened. "Look, ma'am, you're not getting rid of me. I intend to stay until harvest, and I promise I'll leave right after that. The only reason I'm agreeing to do this is for Colton's sake and to free it from my conscience. Don't want my help?

Fine. But do you think Colton would want you to accept my help?"

He had struck a nerve. Emily's eyes welled up with tears as she busied herself with slicing the bread, pretending to be focused solely on that task. Matt felt a twinge in his middle. He probably shouldn't have said that. She was obviously still in a lot of pain after her husband's death.

Without a word, Emily handed out everyone's slice of bread, and they began to eat. Even Joyanna—the unstoppable chatterbox—seemed to sense the room's tension and remained silent.

Matt took one bite of the bread and was instantly transported back to his childhood before his ma died. Pa had never mastered the art of making good bread, and none of the neighbor ladies' bread tasted quite like Ma's. But this—this was delicious. The crust had just the right firmness to it while the middle had a soft texture and rested on his tongue lightly.

"Good bread," he said as he took another bite and nearly finished off his slice.

Emily eyed him as if making sure he was serious. Then, without a word, she rose and retrieved another piece for him. Matt ate that one almost as quickly. He didn't miss that hint of a smile that sneaked onto Emily's lips as she watched him.

On second thought, with an endless supply of the best bread he'd tasted in years, this might not be such a bad deal after all. Remarkable how a man's opinion could change once his appetite became involved.

He leaned back in his chair. "I suppose you have chores that need to be done?"

She nodded. "Milking, feeding, and watering the animals."

"I guess I'll get to work then. Where's your milk bucket?"

Emily stiffened again, her eyebrows arching. "Do you know how to milk?"

She seemed to doubt that Matt could do *anything* useful.

Drawing himself up to his full height, Matt said, "Sure I do. Why, I've been milking cows since before you were born."

Emily smirked. "Really? You must have been a remarkable one-year-old."

Was there really only one year between them? If Emily said so, then it was probably true. In Matt's experience, women had an uncanny way of keeping track of people's ages and birthdays.

Matt's face heated. "The bucket. Please."

Emily rose to fetch it. Joyanna bounded out of her seat too. "Can I join you? Pa always said I was a good help when it came to milking, and I want to be with you."

Matt shook his head. "No. Not this time."

"Oh." Joyanna's smile faded, but then she shrugged. "I'll wait here for you to come back, okay?"

Matt made a noncommittal response, determined not to give her further cause to seek his attention. He couldn't for the life of him understand why she didn't cower like her brothers. At least they acted naturally.

Emily handed the milk bucket to him, her face betraying her doubt. Matt turned to leave.

"Mr. Keath," she called out.

Matt turned. "Yes?"

She hesitated only a little before she said, "I agree. I think Colton would want me to accept your help."

Matt hid his smile. He'd thought she would come to that conclusion sooner or later.

"I'll accept your help. As long as you don't mind having no pay and having to sleep in the barn. You'll eat with us, and I'll do your laundry. Are you fine with that?"

She sounded as if she was trying to make a business deal out of it. But wasn't that what it was? A profitless business deal?

Matt nodded. "Sounds fine."

Emily met his gaze, her features tense. "The only reason I'm doing this is for Colton, all right?"

"Of course. The only reason *I'm* doing this is for Colton."

Their gazes locked and held for one moment, neither of them willing to be the first to look away. Matt's irritation grew. What a stubborn woman. What an *incredibly* stubborn woman!

"Mama!" Grant tugged at Emily's dress. "Gotta go!"

Emily glared one more time at Matt, then she turned to her son. "Just hold on until we make it to the outhouse." She took his hand and hurried out the door, Austin still on her hip.

Matt released a sigh as he watched her go. Where had his brother found such a woman? And whatever had possessed him to marry her?

"If she keeps this up all summer, I'm going to be a saint by the time harvest arrives," he muttered. Taking a deep breath of the late afternoon air, he stepped out of the house and trudged toward the barn and the tasks that awaited him there.

CHAPTER 6

This was not supposed to happen. Emily hadn't even *thought* to foresee it coming, and now she'd been caught off guard and hardly knew how to string a coherent sentence together.

She pushed the outhouse door open, causing the hinges to squeak. She allowed Grant to hop out, adjusted her hold on Austin, and followed him outside.

She closed the door and straightened, her gaze snagging on the one figure who had no business standing on her farmland. *Matthew Keath.* What had she written to make him think that she needed him? She'd tried hard to strip her letter of any emotion that might evoke his pity.

She trailed him with her gaze as he sauntered across the barnyard and opened the gate that led to the milk cow's pasture. He walked so easily, his arms swinging free at his sides—and no children hanging on to him. She couldn't do anything lately without three pairs of hands latched onto her skirts.

That man shouldn't be doing her work for her. He shouldn't be here at all, and she definitely should *not* be feeling indebted to him. Why did he think he could just show up and take over her farm anyway? His words and the confidence in his voice still irked her: *I thought it might be best for everyone if I came and helped you out for the summer.*

She doubted it would be for the best. Colton's occasional comments about his brother had never left a good impression with her. To sum Matthew up, Colton described Matthew as wild, rugged, and a loner. The way he forced himself onto her family was only going to create friction.

Emily blew out her breath. He should have stayed out West where he belonged.

She glanced down at Grant. He stood on the path and stared after Matthew, his forehead creased. He looked up at her and jabbed a finger in Matthew's direction. "I don't like him."

Emily smoothed down his hair, another sigh lifting her shoulders. "Neither do I, Grant."

Grant leaned against her skirt, grabbing a fistful of the material. "Is he leaving?"

"Maybe."

Colton had always said that Matt hated farming. If she kept letting him know that she didn't need him to stay, then he would tire quickly of the farm. And if she kept the atmosphere between them from getting too pleasant—well, that could only hurry him on his way, right?

She'd agreed to let him help for Colton's sake. But if he changed his mind about staying all summer, she wouldn't say a word to hold him in place.

Matt had already broken a sweat by the time the milk cow walked into the stanchion. Herding her up from the pasture had been easy enough—until she reached the barn door. She stopped short there and wouldn't move for the longest time, despite Matt's pushing and coaxing that turned to cursing. Then she turned around, shoving through him as if he wasn't even there, and trotted off to a nearby patch of grass where she began to graze.

Finally, Matt managed to turn her back to the barn *and* through the door—a simple job that had turned into a big hassle. And now, as she thrust her head into the stanchion as calmly as if she hadn't wasted a good twenty minutes of his time, Matt felt mad enough to want to hit her.

"Dumb old cow," he muttered, slamming the bar into place to lock her in. He looked around, trying to remember where he'd dropped the milk bucket in his struggle with her. He spotted it by the door.

Fetching it, he pulled a stool close to the cow's side and grimaced. He'd once thought that the day he left the farm in Ohio was the last time he'd ever milk a cow. But there he was, back at a job he'd always despised.

"Let's get this over with, girl. And as long as you're gentle with me, I'll be gentle with you," he said, grasping the cow's udders.

Over ten years had passed since the last time he'd milked. At first, the motion felt clumsy, but within a few minutes, his hands remembered the motion and milk began to ping into the bucket at a steady pace, the milk foaming as it struck the bottom. *A person can forget a lot of things, but never how to milk,* Pa had always said. Matt swallowed hard, feeling closer to his father than he had in a long time. Closer to Colton too.

A smile tugged at Matt's lips. Colton would have a good laugh if he saw Matt now, stooping to the dreaded job of milking.

The cow shifted, and Matt snatched up the bucket just before she had a chance to knock it over. *Close one.* This cow surely didn't like him—but then, he didn't like her either. He just knew she was waiting for him to let his guard down.

Falling back into the rhythmic motion of milking, Matt

allowed his thoughts to shift to the summer ahead. He'd accomplished his first goal of convincing Emily to let him stay. That was one victory at least.

Or was it? He never would have dreamed that she would need to be *convinced* to let him stay. He thought she would've hailed him a hero. But that hurdle had been dealt with, so now he could move on to more important matters.

Like crops. What had Colton been intending to plant this year? Matt remembered Colton mentioning both corn and wheat in his letters. One year, he'd planted a patch of sorghum, and when it was harvested, they'd had a party to turn it into sweetener.

Maybe Emily knew Colton's plans. He'd have to ask her.

Matt hated to admit it, but she probably knew much more about the farm work than he did. Matt knew little about the timing of planting, harvesting, and haying. Pa had always been the one who kept track of that kind of stuff, and Matt did whatever he told him to.

Asking Emily all these questions would sting and prove how pitifully ignorant he was. Surely there was someone else around here he could talk to so that he wouldn't look quite so dumb. Not that he cared what she thought—but he did have a sense of pride. He was a man, after all. Besides, Emily apparently already thought he was incapable.

What a mess. Colton was the farmer, the one who knew all these things. Why couldn't he have stayed alive?

The cow shifted. Before Matt could grab the bucket, her hoof slammed into it, sending it flying. The bucket crashed into the wall behind her, and milk flew in every direction.

Matt swore and stalked over, picking it up from the hay-covered ground. She'd hit it so hard that it had left a dent in the bucket.

Marching back to the cow, Matt glared at her. "You are the nastiest critter I've ever seen this side of the state," he said, emphasizing each word. "If I had my way, you know what I'd do? I'd have you turned into roasts and steaks. That's what I'd do."

She stared at him balefully.

"But you know I can't do that, don't you? Pity, because I would just love to wring your neck right now."

Swearing again, Matt returned to his stool and repositioned the bucket. "Let's give it another go, girl."

"Mr. Keath?" Emily walked up next to him. Her sudden presence and voice caused him to startle, and he almost tipped the bucket again.

"Do you gotta scare a person like that?" he snapped. *Oh, boy.* He hoped she hadn't heard him swearing. Riding herd had given him a full vocabulary of choice expletives that he wasn't against using around other men, but never would he dare to use words like those around women and children.

"I was just checking to see how the milking is coming along." Her lips formed a tight line. He suspected that she *had,* in fact, overheard him.

"It's going splendidly, Mrs. Keath. Just splendidly," Matt said through gritted teeth. As if to prove that he was lying, the cow slapped him in the face with her tail, and Matt had to bite his tongue hard to hold back a word he knew he'd regret saying later.

"I see." Emily's eyebrows rose in a way that said she wasn't convinced, but she turned and walked away, leaving Matt alone in the quiet of the barn once again.

Matt glowered at the cow. "I said that if you would treat me gently, then I'd be gentle with you. And you've not been gentle with me tonight. Shape up or you're going to regret it."

The cow sighed, slapping him in the face again. Matt hunched lower on his stool, wishing with all his heart that he could actually carry through with his threat.

CHAPTER 7

Exhausted, Matt made it back to the sod house with only a quart of milk in his bucket. Emily watched him pour it out, her lips pressed in a thin line. "Did you milk her out well? We usually get at least a couple gallons, and I don't want Candy to get mastitis, Mr. Keath."

Candy? The name was entirely out of keeping with that cow's disposition, and Matt silently christened the cow with a name that suited her far better—*Snooty.*

"There's more out in the barn," he said, moving to run the milk through the strainer.

"In the barn? Why didn't you bring it all in at once?" Emily asked, disapproval lacing her voice.

"Because I couldn't." Matt kept his back toward her. "Because it was all over the floor and along the wall."

A beat passed, and Emily didn't speak. Finally, she said, "I think you need to be more gentle with her. She's never caused trouble for me or Colton before."

"I was being gentle. I was being *extremely* gentle. The problem is that cow just plain ole doesn't like me." *Along with everyone and everything else around here.*

Emily started to speak, presumably to scold him some more, but Joyanna interrupted her. "Can I go with you now? Please, sir?" Joyanna asked, popping up at Matt's side. "I'll be a good help."

Angry about Snooty and how Emily blamed him, Matt didn't trust his voice and simply shook his head *no*. But Joyanna was too busy jumping from one foot to another as she asked her mother, "Can I go with him, Mama? Please?"

"Why, I think Mr. Keath would like that just fine," Emily said, her voice dripping with honeyed sweetness.

Oh, he was just sure she thought he would like that. What was that woman trying to do, drive him out of his mind?

More likely, she was making up for being forced to accept his help—or maybe she was still trying to scare him away. Well, he'd just have to prove her wrong. He'd take whatever she delivered like a man and surprise her by how long-suffering he could be when he tried.

But he still didn't like Joyanna tagging along. She seemed to be the only one around here who liked him, and she was nothing but a pain.

Without a word, Matt marched out the door. Joyanna skipped along beside him, singing some little ditty to herself.

He glanced back over his shoulder and was sure he caught a slight smirk sneaking onto Emily's lips.

Matt took in the view of the farm while tending to the chores. Colton had a fine little spread for a farmer. There were hens strutting around near a coop and a pig being fattened up for butchering in the upcoming fall. Horses resided in a nearby paddock, and cows grazed from a haystack in their pen, three of them steers fattening up for meat and the other two heifers.

He checked the hay supply and found that it was almost

depleted. But spring was here and before long, the grass would be grown out enough to turn the whole herd out to pasture. Snooty had already been turned out to graze, maybe a little too soon, but Matt couldn't blame Emily. Milk always tasted best when the cow had been out on pasture.

Matt was pleased with what he saw. With the eggs from the chickens and milk from the cow, Emily should be able to get along just fine until harvest, no matter how much money she had on hand. Colton had done a good job of building up the farm. Looking at it now, it was hard to tell that this land had been virgin prairie that no white man had ever set foot on not long ago. It must have taken tremendous effort for Colton to construct the sod house, fences, and outbuildings, along with preparing the land for cultivation. Matt had to admire his brother. Homesteading was no job for the faint of heart.

Everywhere he looked, Matt could tell that there was still a lot of work to be done. One section of the fencing near the barn was lopsided, one post on the chicken coop was rotting, and the woodpile needed restocking. Matt caught a whiff of an odor coming from the outhouse when the wind blew in his direction —it needed some lime thrown down its hole. There was going to be no time for idle hands around here, but Matt didn't mind. Working hard would help him forget why he was here and the pain that came with that reason.

Joyanna trailed at his heels as he did the chores, her tongue never stopping. Matt tuned out her prattle for the most part, but she was useful for answering his questions. In the barn, he interrupted her and pointed to the corner where a pen had been built out of wooden rails. "What is that?" he asked.

"Mama made it to hold Austin while she did the milking and chores. One time, Grant got too close to the stock tank while she was milking and almost drowned himself, so she tied him up to it after that too."

Matt stared at her, horrified.

"Mama said that tonight she's gonna make a plum pie. She hasn't made that since Pa got deaded." Joyanna bent to pet a cat winding around her ankles, obviously not too bothered by her brother's near-death experience. "Ever since Pa got deaded, she hasn't made a lot of stuff. Too busy. Usually we eat real late 'cause it takes so long for Mama to get the chores done and make supper." She stole a glance at Matt and grinned. "Maybe she'll make more extra stuff, like pie, now that you're here."

Matt shrugged and measured out feed for the pig, still processing everything Joyanna had said. So Emily didn't need him, did she? If she was struggling to keep up with everything now, how had she planned to manage when planting began?

What a stubborn woman.

After finishing the last of the chores, Matt and Joyanna returned to the soddy. As Matt pushed the door open, a delicious smell wafted out to meet him. His stomach let out an audible growl. He had skipped lunch, and with only two pieces of bread to tide him over since breakfast, he was starving.

Grant and Austin played on the floor together as Grant showed Austin how to bang one of his mama's spoons against a pan. But as soon as Matt stepped into the room, they froze. In a flash, Grant ran for the protection of his mother's skirts, and Austin crawled after him faster than Matt had known a baby could move. They screamed as they reached her. Emily turned from the stove to look at them first, and then she looked up at Matt, her forehead creasing into a frown.

"What did you do? They were playing just fine until you came."

Matt raised both hands. "I did absolutely nothing. Promise."

Emily didn't look too convinced. She picked Austin up and walked over to a chair at the table, Grant still clinging to her legs and wiping his tears on her skirt. "We're ready to eat, so let's pray. Maybe by then these two will have calmed down enough for me to set the food on the table."

She looked pointedly at Matt. He looked back at her, not understanding what she was trying to tell him.

"Mr. Keath," she said at last, "Will you bless the meal for us?"

Oh, so *that* was what she wanted out of him? Matt's heart began to pound faster than if he'd run a mile. Of course, it was the man's place to lead in religious duties, but he didn't have a clue of what to say. He never prayed. Not even in private. That was a practice he'd dropped with his childhood.

Emily kept staring at him, and Matt realized he had no choice.

With a dry mouth, Matt removed his hat and ducked his head.

"Dear God, thank You for this food." He paused a moment, and then he quickly added, "Amen."

When he opened his eyes, Emily's frown indicated that he'd done something wrong again. Yet, without saying a word, she stood, each of the boys still clinging to her.

"You shouldn't talk so fast when you're talking to God," Joyanna told Matt, shaking her head reproachfully. "Pa always says that we gotta think through what we say and make sure we aren't just sayin' empty phrases. And we gotta be respectable."

"*Respectful,*" Emily corrected her. She didn't turn from the stove, but Matt could sense she was amused by her daughter's scolding.

Matt's face burned. It didn't seem right to be lectured about prayer by his five-year-old niece, but he suspected that she probably knew far more about it than he did.

Emily handed Austin to Joyanna so that she could set the table, and Grant sat on the floor within reach of his mother's skirts. Matt looked his way and found the boy staring at him, his blue eyes round. Matt averted his gaze, remembering what happened the last time he'd tried to greet him.

He took another peek at Grant. The boy still had his eyes on him, but he had crawled just a little closer. So, he'd changed his mind, had he? The big man at the table wasn't that scary after all.

Matt waited, counting the seconds as the boy inched even closer. At last, he looked down and found the boy at his feet, staring at his boots. Then one of Grant's hands reached out, fingers grabbing for the shiny spurs on the back of Matt's boots—

"No, Grant." Matt jerked his foot back, out of reach.

Grant stared up at him in shock, tears flooding his eyes. He tipped his head back and wailed, the sound bouncing off the sod walls and making Matt's ears ring.

"For pity's sake, what now?" Emily marched toward her son and scooped him up, her expression demanding an explanation from Matt.

"I'm telling you it wasn't my fault. He tried to grab my spurs."

"It's been one thing after another since you came, Mr. Keath." Emily glared at him and then spun around, setting Grant in the rocker and going to the cupboard for bowls. Matt thought she set them on the table with more force than necessary.

Matt dished up some stew, his face still hot from her reprimand. Maybe it *had* been foolish to come here. Her neighbors would surely be more help to her than him. They were farmers. He was just a cowboy. It had become apparent that the thing he excelled at since his arrival was riling Emily up.

Tension radiated through the air, suffocating Matt. Desperate to turn Emily's attention to something other than his list of shortcomings, which seemed to be piling higher than ever, Matt blurted out, "Why is the barn built out of wood while you're still living in the soddy?"

Emily shot him a glance, probably wondering why he asked that, but she replied, "Simple. Colton built the house when he first came here and was short on money. A couple years later, after we were married, we decided we needed a barn to keep the stock better protected, and I told him to make the barn the way he wanted right from the first. Out of wood. Of course, Colton argued that our house should come before the animals, but I told him not to worry about that. We were getting along fine in the soddy, and it didn't make sense to waste time building a sod barn when we both knew he wanted a wooden one."

Her gaze traveled around the room. "It's cramped, and I can't say I particularly like having dirt for my walls and floor, but we manage. Besides, a soddy has one advantage. It keeps the inside more insulated than a frame house. It's always cool in here in the summer and warm in the winter."

"Interesting." Matt smeared a thick spreading of butter on his bread and took a bite. *Ah. Pure bliss.* "When will the fields need planting?"

Emily bit her lip. "Well, I don't really know, Mr. Keath. You'll have to ask my father. He would know."

Matt felt a little smug that she was forced to admit her own lack of knowledge.

"I'll need the garden turned soon. The ground is warming up, and it's almost time for planting. My father already helped me get the potatoes in." Emily took a bite of her stew, then said, "Pass the salt please, Mr. Keath."

Mr. Keath. Matt was growing sick of the name. "Sure, I'll pass you the salt, but not until you stop this nonsense of calling me Mr. Keath. It's unnerving."

Emily's expression held pure innocence, but her eyes sparked with a challenge. "You've been calling me Mrs. Keath. Isn't it only proper that I call you Mr. Keath?"

Oh, Emily understood that she was bothering him, and she seemed downright pleased about it too.

"We're the next thing to family, so I consider it to be entirely proper for you to use my given name. And from now on, I'm calling you Emily, not *Mrs. Keath.*"

Emily looked at him hard, but at last her shoulders lowered. "Fine, Matthew. If that's the way you want it."

Matthew? Matt looked at her sharply, but she had turned away from him and fixed her attention solely on Austin. Matt clenched his jaw. If she was trying another approach at plaguing him, she was doing well. The only person he'd ever allowed to call him Matthew was his mother. Why, being referred to as *Matthew* was even more unnerving than Mr. Keath!

"What can *I* call you?" Joyanna asked, tugging on his sleeve. "I don't want to call you Mr. Keath either."

Matt bit his lip, then said, "You can call me Uncle Matt." Better that he be the one to tell her what to call him, or else Emily would have her calling him Matthew too.

"Uncle Matt." Joyanna grinned. "That means that now I've got three uncles. Uncle Ephraim, Uncle Zane, and now *Uncle Matt.*" She counted them off on her fingers.

Matt almost explained to her that he'd always been her uncle, even before coming here—but then he thought better of it. It would take too much effort to get the idea through the little girl's head.

Without warning, pain shot through the instep of Matt's foot, and he jerked back from the table with a half-smothered yell. *What in the world?* He reached for his foot and looked down at it. Sticking out of the shaft of his boot was the handle of a fork. And there, underneath the table, Grant stared at him with those round blue eyes of his.

"What on earth are you trying to do? *Kill* me?" Matt asked him, his voice rising until it was about as loud as a windstorm on an open prairie. "Maybe you don't like me, but that's no excuse for stabbing me!"

Grant burst into tears and fled for the shelter of his mother's arms. His screams set Austin off, and both boys began to try and outdo each other's howls, crowding close to Emily.

"Oh, now you've done it again." Emily scowled at Matt,

looking close to tears herself. "I declare, there's going to be no peace as long as you're here."

Matt gripped the edge of the table with both hands, trying to rein in his temper. So everything that went wrong around here was his fault, was it? Here he was trying to do a good deed, and he was scolded and screamed at and stabbed at every turn. It was enough to make him want to clap his hands over his ears and ride west as fast as Bowie could run.

CHAPTER 8

The next morning, the barn roof echoed with a steady rhythm of raindrops as Snooty kicked the milk pail across the expanse of the barn. Matt had to chase down the bucket, all the while feeling sorry for himself for disregarding Flick's advice about going to Texas. Everything had been going from bad to worse ever since he arrived in Osceola, despite his best intentions.

"I swear I'll turn you into ground beef one of these days, Snooty," Matt muttered, setting the milk bucket in place harder than necessary. Emily was going to have another fit with him when he returned to the house unless a good night's sleep had improved her temperament at all, which Matt highly doubted.

Matt heaved a sigh. With a wife like her, how had Colton lived as long as he had? Of course, he seemed to have been on Emily's good side, and Matt doubted that his sons had screamed every time he looked at them. Snooty had probably treated him better than she treated Matt.

After the trauma of this experience, Matt would never wish for a wife and kids. Not that he had wanted a wife or kids before, but if he'd had even a hint of interest, it was gone. All he felt now was hard desperation to get out of this mess with all his body parts intact and at least most of his sanity.

Standing, he grimaced as he noticed how little milk covered the bottom of the pail. He unlocked Snooty from the stanchion then drove her out of the barn and to the pasture, grateful that she was a little more cooperative this morning as far as moving was concerned.

He studied the pasture fence in the gray morning light. He needed to check the entire fence for holes soon. There was much that he needed to do, but if it continued to rain, it would be difficult to accomplish anything.

After returning to the barn, he grabbed the milk pail and brought it to the soddy. A light shone from the window and smoke curled from the chimney, signaling to him that Emily was awake. Matt paused outside the door, trying to scrape some of the mud from his boots, then laughed at himself. The soddy's floor was made of dirt, so why worry about tracking in more?

Emily turned from the stove as he opened the door and gave him a nod that he considered almost friendly. Matt nodded in return, then moved to strain the milk. He could see three mounds still underneath the covers of the beds, so he kept his movements as quiet as he could, not wanting to wake them up and arouse Emily's wrath—or have the boys screaming and Joyanna begging to follow him outside.

Emily's gaze fell on Matt as he emptied the last of the milk from the pail, and Matt braced himself for a scolding.

"What did she do today?" Emily asked, eyebrows raised.

"Sent me on a little game of chase, that's all." Matt set down the bucket, still annoyed that Snooty had waited until he was almost finished before she pulled her nasty trick. She'd wasted nearly a whole bucket of milk.

"Maybe she doesn't like you," Emily said.

Matt looked at her. "Emily, there's no *maybe* about it in my mind. I *know* she doesn't like me."

"Hmm," was all Emily said. "If you go out to the well, you'll find a basket where you can put the milk to keep it cool. Breakfast will be ready when you finish the rest of the chores."

She turned her back to him as if she'd said everything necessary and couldn't stand the strain of talking politely to him any longer. Matt shrugged and headed outside, determined that he, too, was going to keep a civil tongue this morning.

By the time he returned to the soddy, the aroma of bacon, eggs, and pancakes hung in the air. He inhaled deeply and made his way to the basin to wash his hands. At least Emily was a good cook. She'd be downright unbearable if it weren't for that.

As Matt turned around, he noticed Joyanna sitting in the rocker, her eyes fixed on him. She broke into a grin when he looked at her, and Matt averted his gaze.

"Breakfast is almost ready," Emily said, setting the table with plates and forks. "Joyanna, can you wake up your brothers?"

Grant stirred in the bed, the quilt shifting above him. He propped himself up on one arm and rubbed a hand across his face, then squinted at Matt. He froze, his eyes flaring wide.

Matt couldn't help but feel sorry for the boy. Here he was only a few seconds into his day, and already he was faced with his worst nightmare come to life.

Joyanna bounced Austin on her hip as she brought him to the table, and the children giggled. Grant looked at them, rolled to the edge of the bed, and slid to the floor before running to the safety of his big sister.

"Grant, you don't got to be scared of Uncle Matt," Joyanna said, hugging him against her. "Uncle Matt's a good man. He likes you. Go over there and give him a big hug and tell him good morning."

Matt was sure his eyes must have gone as wide as Grant's. What made Joyanna think he liked any of them?

Grant cast a dubious look at his big sister, as if making sure she *really* wanted him to endanger his life, then he turned and walked toward Matt. Throwing his arms around Matt's legs, he said, "Mornin'."

Matt felt as if he'd been rooted to the spot. He'd never been hugged by a child before. Not that being squeezed around the legs was much of a hug.

Grant backed away and ran back to Joyanna, but he didn't appear quite so frightened as he looked at Matt.

As for Matt, he felt more frightened of those three children than ever.

"To the table, everyone," Emily called, setting a dish of butter next to a stack of pancakes.

They slid into their chairs, and Joyanna scooted close to Matt. His stomach rumbled. He reached out to dish up his plate, but Emily coughed slightly. *Oh yeah.* They had to pray.

Matt glanced at Emily to see if she was again going to make him do the praying. From the look on her face, that was exactly her intention. Sighing, Matt bowed his head, trying to think of something better to say than what he'd said the night before. "Dear God, thank You for this food—and for this day. Amen."

Matt felt pleased with himself. He'd spoken slowly, and he'd even added another phrase this time. But when he looked up, Emily had that pinched look on her face again. Bother, could he do nothing right?

Matt dished up his plate and ate in silence, but Joyanna kept a steady stream of conversation. He suspected most of her words were aimed at him, but he ignored her. What she said, he had no clue, except that several times she paused to ask, "Isn't that right, Mama?" And Emily agreed with her.

What was a person supposed to do on a rainy day? Matt thought of his father, who had never been idle for a minute and always had some kind of work in his hands. Harness to repair, leather to bore holes into, and projects to whittle. Matt remembered seeing a little workplace Colton had formed in the barn, and he decided to check that out after breakfast. There was sure to be something for him to do there, and he was *not* going to spend the day sitting on his hands in the already overcrowded soddy.

Finishing his plate, Matt started to push back from the table, but Emily stopped him. "We always do Bible reading after breakfast. Perhaps you'd like to start reading in the book of Psalms, Matthew?"

First prayer, and now Bible reading? She couldn't be speaking the truth about always doing Bible reading. Did they *really* waste time every day on reading, or was she simply trying to make an effort to see a heathen cowboy get saved?

And yet she looked sincere.

Matt sighed and accepted the Bible that Joyanna brought to him. He thumbed through the pages, Emily's gaze resting on him like a heavy weight. Was she expecting him to ask where the Psalms were located? Or maybe *what* a psalm even was?

He might not have touched the Good Book in years, but he *had* grown up in church. He knew where the Psalms were, even if he was less certain about his ability to find all those little prophets like Nahum or Jonah.

"Uncle Matt?" Joyanna appeared at his elbow. "Could I sit on your lap? Pa always let me before he got deaded."

Matt fumbled and lost his place in the Bible. *Good for him, but I'm not your pa,* he wanted to snap, but she was already scrambling into his arms.

Matt had never felt so uncomfortable or so incredibly clumsy. He looked helplessly at Emily, hoping she would take pity on him and tell her daughter to leave him alone. She was absorbed in cutting Austin's pancake into tiny bites and didn't seem to notice his discomfort.

This wasn't right at all. Here he was, sitting in Colton's chair, holding Colton's daughter, with Colton's wife sitting across from him, under the roof of Colton's house, on Colton's farm—

Matt had never felt so defenseless in his life. Emily raised her head, her eyes questioning why he wasn't reading, and he ducked his head. It seemed like a good idea to read before he started screaming over how wrong everything was in his life.

Matt read through the psalm, trying not to flinch when he read about walking through the valley of the shadow of death. It didn't make sense to him. The psalmist said that God walked through that valley with him. But if there really *was* a God who was all powerful, couldn't He have prevented the psalmist from walking through the valley in the first place? If God was really loving, why would He ever allow His followers to suffer?

Matt finished the psalm and shut the Bible, aware that Joyanna was staring at him again.

"Now you gotta give us an explanation, like Pa always did," she told him.

Matt pinched the bridge of his nose. He had endured all he could. Pushing back from the table, he set Joyanna off his lap and turned for the door. "I'm not your pa, and I have work to do."

Before anyone could interfere, Matt slammed the door shut, a spray of rain striking his face. Sprinting toward the barn, he wished that all of life's problems were as easy to flee from as that soddy.

CHAPTER 9

About midmorning, Matt heard a scuffling against the barn door, and he swore softly to himself. Joyanna was no doubt looking for him. Was it too much to hope that she would go away if he ignored her?

Matt studied the harness that he mended. At least Pa had thought it necessary to teach him to recognize places of wear in the harness and how to fix them. *No point in getting out to the field only to turn around again because of a broken harness,* he'd said. Now, that wisdom was paying off.

The door creaked and Matt looked up. Sure enough, there was Joyanna, boots spattered with mud and coat dripping with rainwater.

"Hi, Uncle Matt!" she said, rushing into the barn. "Mama said I could come and visit. Whatcha doing?"

"Fixing something." Matt fixed his attention on his work. Hopefully she'd grow bored and leave. But instead, Joyanna took a low stool and pulled it next to him.

"Pa used to do stuff like that, too, before he got deaded." Joyanna watched his hands, her expression shadowing. "I miss

Pa. I wish he'd come home. Mama says he's happy in heaven, but I'd like him here."

Oh, please don't start that. I'm not good at giving comfort to anyone, not even myself.

Joyanna brightened. "But then God sent you to us, and that's about as good as Pa."

Matt almost dropped the harness. What was the girl talking about? He was no kind of a replacement for Colton.

"Oh, I almost forgot. Mama said I could bring this to you." Joyanna fumbled around in her pocket and retrieved a pair of slightly crumbling cookies. She studied them, then she gave the bigger of the two over to Matt.

"Thanks," Matt mumbled, unable to meet her eyes. Here he'd tried to ignore her so she'd leave, and she had brought him a cookie. Well, if she thought she could win her way into his heart by being nice, it wasn't going to work. It only made him feel guilty.

"I usually like my cookies with milk, but they're good like this too. Mama made 'em fresh this morning," Joyanna said after taking a bite, not even attempting to close her mouth while she chewed.

Matt could tell the cookies were freshly baked. His treat still held a slight warmth that felt comforting against his chilly palms.

They ate their cookies, and Matt was all too aware of Joyanna's observant gaze that was locked on him.

"Did you like sleeping in the hayloft last night?" Joyanna asked.

"I guess. It was comfortable enough." Matt finished his last bite and brushed away a few stray crumbs.

"I could sleep with you tonight to keep you company, you know." Joyanna spoke casually, but her eyes pleaded with him.

"No!" Realizing how harsh the word sounded, Matt added, "Your mama wouldn't like having you away from her."

"Oh." Joyanna frowned, then she gave a nonchalant shrug. "Well, at least you live here. Uncle Ephraim and Uncle Zane both have their own houses, and they never stay as long as you."

He was there for only one day and already she was speaking of him as if he'd been here for years. If she had accepted him so quickly, what was she going to do when he left? Matt pushed the thought aside. By the time he needed to leave, she'd probably be over her infatuation with him, especially if he didn't pay much attention to her.

A wagon jingled outside. Matt stood and headed for the barn door. He stopped in the doorway, Joyanna beside him. Sure enough, a team plodded down the lane toward them, an elderly couple huddled together against the rain.

"Who's that?" Matt asked, but Joyanna didn't hear as she sprinted toward the couple.

The team drew to a stop in front of the soddy and the man and woman dismounted from the wagon. Joyanna ran straight toward the man, and he swept her up in his arms, both of them laughing.

Joyanna ran her mouth, appearing to talk a mile a minute. Then she motioned toward Matt. Both the man and woman looked toward him, then back at Joyanna. *Oh boy.* What was she saying now?

Well, he better make sure the couple didn't get any wrong impressions about him. He walked toward them, away from the protection of the barn.

"And so now I call him Uncle Matt, and Mama calls him Matthew. Grant and Austin are still kinda scared of him, but Uncle Matt hasn't yelled as much this morning, so they aren't quite as scared of him today," Joyanna told the couple.

Matt's face heated. She made it sound as if he'd been yelling at them for no reason, when in truth he had *not* been yelling. Well, not much, anyway.

The soddy door opened and Emily stepped outside, her face

wreathed in the first true smile that Matt had seen from her yet. The smile gave her face a completely different look, and Matt caught a glimpse of why Colton might have married her. She was beautiful when she smiled.

"Morning, Ma and Pa," she called as she approached them.

"Good morning, Emily, honey." The woman reached out to give her a hug.

Ah. Emily's parents.

"Have you met Matthew?" Emily motioned toward him. "He arrived yesterday. He's Colton's brother."

"Colton's brother?" The man tipped his hat brim back and looked at Matt more closely. "Well, I'll be. You are just about the spitting image of him."

Matt flinched. Why did every new acquaintance have to compare him to Colton?

"I'm terribly sorry about your brother. He was a good man, about like a son to me. He's certainly missed around here. But, anyhow, that's in the past." The man held his hand out toward Matt. "My name's Josiah Mayfield. Emily's pa."

Matt grasped the man's hand and shook it. "Matt Keath."

"Pleasure to meet you, Matt. How long you planning on sticking around these parts?"

"Through harvest."

"Through *harvest?*" Josiah's eyebrows rose, and then his weathered face broke into a grin. "Well, glory be. It's an answer to prayers, ain't it, Margaret?"

His wife beamed at Matt. "Indeed, a very evident answer to prayer."

Matt squirmed at being called an answer to prayer yet again. But even in his discomfort, he noticed Emily. She looked from one parent to another, her mouth open and eyes reflecting her disbelief. Then she promptly closed her mouth into that familiar tight line and said nothing, her shoulders rigid. Maybe she disliked hearing him called an answer to prayer about as much as he did.

"Please, come inside and escape the rainfall, everyone." Emily beckoned everyone to enter the soddy. Matt noticed Grant and Austin standing in the entrance, their eyes gleaming with enthusiasm.

"Grandpa!" Grant hollered, waving with all his might.

Josiah waved back, and Grant beamed. Matt felt a stab of irritation. Why couldn't the boy have a little of that enthusiasm when he saw Matt? Not that he wanted Grant to be all over him like Joyanna, but it would be nice if Matt could *at least* enter the soddy without setting off ear-shattering screams.

"I'll take care of your team." Matt reached for the team's harness, guessing that Josiah would want to go inside and warm up after his cold drive.

Josiah waved him aside. "It's no trouble for me to take care of them, but I would be pleased if you came with me."

Matt nodded, relieved to have an excuse to avoid the soddy a little longer. Two chattering women and three giggling children was enough to make his head spin.

The two fell in step as they headed toward the barn with the horses.

"I remember Colton mentioning you now that I think of it. You lived out West, right?" Josiah asked, rain dripping off the brim of his hat.

"Yeah. I was a cowboy." *Was.* What a sad word.

"A cowboy, huh? Bet you enjoyed that."

Matt nodded. "It's my life."

"I thought about going to Texas and helping run beef up to Kansas at one time. But I had a family, and doing the calculations, the pay wasn't enough to make it worth it."

Matt shot the man a sideways glance. Josiah Mayfield didn't strike him as that adventurous of a man.

Josiah must have guessed his thoughts because he chuckled.

"I went all over the country in my younger days, so it wasn't as far-fetched of an idea as it seems. Worked for the railroad until all that traveling away from Margaret and the kids just got to be too much."

"I wouldn't have guessed," Matt admitted.

"Well, that was a long time ago. Now I'm mighty happy with where God has placed me, farming right here in Osceola."

As soon as they reached the barn, Josiah unhitched his team. He placed them in a spare stall while Matt pitched them some hay.

"Nothing like a rainy day for visiting," Josiah said, brushing his hands on his pants. "Hard to get stuff done when it's wet like this. Me and Margaret have been checking in on Emily pretty frequently since Colton died, so we figured this was as good a time as any. We've been worried about her."

First Ephraim, and now Josiah expressed concern about her? Matt shook his head. "Seems to me she's still got plenty of fire to her."

The corners of Josiah's eyes crinkled. "She didn't want you here, did she? Tried to give you a piece of her mind?"

"Many pieces."

Josiah laughed. "Well, you're still here, and I'm glad." He sobered. "I'm afraid that Emily's a lot like me in some ways. Too proud to ask for help. Me? I've learned a lot through the years. Had enough hard bumps and humbling times that I'm willing to take help when it comes, but Emily—she struggles."

"Guess we all struggle at one time or another," Matt said, surprising himself with the comment. It felt a little too vulnerable for his liking.

"Sure, but some of us more than others." A beat passed between them. Then Josiah asked, "Are you looking forward to being a farmer this summer?"

Matt hesitated. Just how open should he be? "To be honest, I don't know much about what I'm doing. I grew up on a farm, but Pa and Colton were always the true farmers. I don't even know when the crops should be planted."

Josiah gave a slow nod. "I see. Don't worry, Matt. You'll find that you learn fast. And truly, it's not all that complicated."

Unless you have a woman who wishes you far away, three kids who vary between loving and hating you to death, a cow that would just as soon take your head off as kick the bucket, and clumsy hands with everything farm-related. Matt bit back his complaint.

"And I'm happy to help you," Josiah added. "I'll help you know the timing on things and the art of doing them. I understand how you feel. I haven't always been a farmer either, and I know it can feel overwhelming."

Overwhelming. That was the perfect word to describe Matt's circumstances.

He smiled at Josiah. "I'd appreciate any help you can offer."

"Well, then, I guess I'll give you my first bit of advice, and then you can see if you still appreciate what I have to say." Josiah stroked his chin. "If you plan on lasting throughout the summer here, I'd advise you to change your clothing."

Matt looked down at himself. "My clothing?"

"Yes. I'm afraid chaps and spurs aren't common around here. They're not practical. Those are what a *cowboy* wears, not a farmer."

Matt bit his lip. Josiah was right. What use did a farmer have for spurs? A farmer didn't ride a horse. He followed it.

But the knowledge didn't make giving up his gear any easier. Matt had been wearing spurs and high-topped boots for years, even back when he was a deputy. Something within him rebelled at the idea of dressing like a farmer, as if the clothing would somehow make him less of a cowboy. And yet, if he was going to do his best at farming, then he ought to make things as easy as possible for himself. The odds were stacked up against him high enough as it was.

Practicality won out in the end. "Fine." Matt gave a short nod. "I guess you're right."

Josiah's mouth curved into a smile. "Good. You'll get on just fine, Matt."

They hurried back to the soddy to avoid getting drenched. As they opened the door, laughter spilled out, a sound that had been lacking since he had arrived. Margaret Mayfield sat in the rocker with Grant on her lap, and Joyanna perched at her side. Emily had one of the chairs at the table. They were trying to coax Austin into making the step from Emily to Margaret, but he seemed content to stay where he was by Emily, bouncing up and down on his chubby legs and grinning for everyone.

"Would you look at that boy, standing up on his own?" Josiah walked over and scooped Austin into his arms. "Since when did you get so big?"

Austin squealed. Matt felt that nagging sense of annoyance flare up once again. He was unsuccessful in drawing any laughter from the boys. Not that he'd ever sought to make them giggle.

"We stopped by Zane and Sarah's to see Audrey. Two weeks old, and she's already got everyone wrapped around her little finger." Josiah settled into a chair and looked back at Matt. "Sarah's our daughter. She and Zane have two of the cutest kids that have ever set foot on this earth, in my opinion. But since they are my grandkids, I might be a little biased."

"I need to get over there sometime to see Audrey—and Byron, of course. I haven't seen Audrey since she was first born." Emily sighed. "I just love babies."

Margaret and Josiah agreed, but Matt kept silent. He wasn't going to fib and claim to love babies when he didn't. Not in the least.

As the talk turned to other neighbors and family, Matt drew back, feeling as if he were drowning in a deluge of meaningless names. His time would have been far better spent out in the barn. He toyed with the idea of excusing himself, but something kept him where he was.

His gaze strayed toward Josiah who sat with Austin perched on his knee. It was probably the similarities to his own pa that drew him to Josiah. Both men were farmers, both of them obviously loved children, and both of them had that gleam in their eye that said they were at peace with their world.

Mostly, though, Matt was grateful that Josiah didn't stare at him as if he were an unwanted vermin. He glanced at Emily. Unlike *some* people.

Suddenly, something icy-cold splashed against Matt's nose and he recoiled, catching the attention of the others.

"Something just dripped from the ceiling," Matt said, rubbing his nose. When he pulled back his hand, his fingers were muddy.

"Oh, that." Emily shrugged. "The roof leaks when it rains. It usually takes a couple days for the rain to leak through, but I did notice that the corner is a little thin and it leaks sooner than the rest of the roof. Welcome to life in a soddy."

Welcome to life in a soddy, indeed.

CHAPTER 10

"C'mon, now. Get up there."

Matt flicked the lines across the team's back, a trickle of sweat tracing down his face. He tilted his head back and glared at the sun. How could the weather go from cold and rainy just days ago to scorching hot today?

Five days had passed since he'd arrived in Osceola. Five of the worst days in his life. Nothing had changed in the soddy. Grant and Austin still cowered from him. Joyanna plagued him. Emily snapped at him and he at her. Snooty delighted in making him chase down the milk bucket.

His sanity was slipping.

Matt had expected things to improve by now. They should have, by all means. Emily should have realized that she needed him badly. She should have considered him her rescuer, the one who had ridden to her aid in a time of dire need. But no. Instead, she still glared ice at him and hinted about him going back West. If only he could! As it was, both his word and his conscience pinned him right there, refusing to allow him to escape.

Matt wiped a hand across his forehead. At least his Stetson

shielded his eyes from the worst of the sun's glare. His Stetson was one of the few things that felt familiar to him. Following Josiah's advice, he'd laid aside his chaps and spurs just days before. He still felt strange without the jangle of his spurs when he walked. He knew some men who liked the sound so much that they purposefully added more metal to their spurs just to heighten the sound. But Matt had to admit that spurs and farm work didn't meld well and laying them aside had been best.

He'd even given up his high-topped boots. The heels, while perfect when sitting in a saddle and wrangling cattle, were not good when following a plow. Now he wore a pair of Colton's old boots which were a little on the large side for his feet.

Matt cast a glance over his shoulder at the row he'd finished plowing, and he grimaced. The row was crooked, obviously so. Josiah had instructed him on all that he would need to do, telling him "plowing is an easy job, but it's one that takes some technique."

Boy was he right about the technique.

"Uncle Matt!"

Matt turned toward the call. Joyanna rushed toward him, bucket swinging at her side as she gave him a big wave. The sight of the bucket made Matt realize that he was parched. Reining in the team, he waited for Joyanna to reach him.

"Hi, Uncle Matt!" She turned her face up toward him and grinned. "Brought you some water. Mama said I could bring it out to you all by myself. Want some?"

"Yeah, reckon I do." Matt rested his arm on the handle of the plow while she grabbed the dipper in the pail and scooped out some water, spilling some over the edge of the bucket as she handed him the dipper.

Matt raised it to his lips but paused as the team shifted. "Hold on, you two," he told them, then he took a swallow of water that was more refreshing than anything on the planet.

"More?" Joyanna asked as he handed the dipper back to her.

He nodded.

Joyanna started to hand the filled dipper to him again when the team moved forward.

"Whoa!" Matt yelled, grabbing the reins just in time.

The team stopped. Muttering uncomplimentary words aimed at the team, Matt held their reins with one hand and took his drink with the other.

When he lowered the dipper, he found Joyanna staring at him with her wide blue eyes. "You shouldn't say that, Uncle Matt."

"Hmm? Say what?"

She shook her head slowly. "I can't say it, 'cause it was a bad word."

Matt's face heated. That girl must have sharp ears.

"Pa always said we've gotta be real careful of what comes into our ears and out of our mouths." Joyanna tilted her head to one side. "If it's somethin' that God doesn't like, then we shouldn't listen to it and we 'specially shouldn't say it. We gotta do everything in a way that pleases God. So you won't say that anymore, will you?"

Matt wanted to snap at her for lecturing him, but he couldn't. After all, he was the one who had provoked her sermon. If he didn't want her to look at him with those reproachful eyes, then he ought to pay closer attention to what he said.

If you never used those words, then you wouldn't slip up and say them around Emily and the kids, an accusing voice whispered.

On second thought, maybe it *was* a good idea to clean up his language while he was helping Emily. Holding his tongue couldn't be that hard, could it? He only used that kind of language when he was really frustrated. It wasn't in his daily vocabulary.

Joyanna still waited for his response.

Matt found himself nodding. "Fine. I won't say those words anymore."

Her face relaxed. "And if you do, you will wash your mouth out with soap, right?"

"What?" That wasn't part of what Matt had bargained for.

"Pa and Mama always said that if they heard one of us use a bad word, they would wash our mouths out with soap. My cousin Walter said a bad word once, so Aunt Sadie washed his mouth out. He said it was so awful that he won't never say that again, so I guess it works, all right. You will do that if you say a bad word, won't you?"

Oh boy. Now he was in a fix. If he said no, then Joyanna would think he was criticizing her parents' and Aunt Sadie's discipline—but if he said yes, then what if he *did* slip up and needed to use the soap bar?

But he wasn't going to slip up. The tongue was one of the easiest things to control. If he made up his mind to never again use certain words, then all he had to do was keep his mouth shut.

"Fine," Matt agreed, handing her the empty dipper. "I'll use soap if I say another word like that, but I'm not going to use words like that."

Joyanna beamed. "Good. I knew you would like the idea, Uncle Matt."

Bucket in hand, she skipped back toward the soddy. Matt shook his head. It took the smallest things to hurt her or to make her happy. Colton and Emily sure had given that girl a fine sense of right and wrong, and she wasn't afraid to tell people when they were doing something they shouldn't.

Had Colton ever had his own lessons thrown back in his face by his daughter?

Probably not. Unlike Matt, Colton had always seemed to find it easy to do the right thing.

The team shifted again, and Matt swung his attention back

to them, pinning them down with the full weight of his glare. "Blast it! Can't you hold still for just one minute? By the time I'm through with you—" Matt clamped his mouth shut just before one of those "bad words" could fly off his lips.

He glanced around. No one was within hearing distance, but it might be a good idea to start practicing now.

Maybe this was going to be harder than he'd originally thought.

By the time Matt had unhitched the team, milked Snooty, and finished the chores, he felt so tired that he didn't dare stop moving lest he fall asleep. He'd never realized just how physically demanding farming was.

He stretched, wincing as muscles complained in places where he'd never even known that he had muscles. Then he picked up the milk pail and headed for the soddy. Being a cowboy was physically hard too, but its demands were different than walking behind a plow all day.

Matt paused at the door to switch the bucket to his other hand, flinching at the pain as the handle ground into his fingers. He needed to ask Emily if Colton had any gloves he could use. Handling the team's reins for so long had formed blisters, the last thing he needed if he planned to put in a full day's work tomorrow, and the day after that and the day after that . . .

Matt sighed. Not only was he doing Colton's work, but now here he was wearing his gear too.

Entering the soddy, Matt cast a glance around the room to gauge the atmosphere. Grant sat on the floor in the middle of the room, holding a rag against his finger, tears rolling down his cheeks. Joyanna occupied the rocker, her doll tucked beneath her arm and tears rolling down her cheeks. Something had obviously happened to them, but the worst of the storm seemed over.

Emily bent over Austin on the bed as she changed his diaper. She spared Matt a single glance and then returned to her task, the lines on her forehead etched deeper than usual.

Not too happy a crowd tonight.

By the time Matt strained the milk and returned from taking it to the well, the room was no longer silent.

"I didn't mean to slam his finger in the door," Joyanna wailed at Emily.

Grant started crying again, his finger clutched in his other hand. Then, as though Austin didn't want to be left out, he too began to howl.

Matt flinched. Maybe he should skip supper just so he could escape the noise of the soddy. Tired as he was, the noise was louder than a bunch of cowboys whooping up a town.

Emily caught sight of him and gestured for him to sit at the table. "We're ready to eat," she said above the racket of her children.

The sight of the chicken pie and a plate piled with Emily's fresh-baked cookies made Matt's stomach rumble. *Never mind.* There was no way he could skip supper, no matter how tired he was or how loud the kids might be screaming.

After washing up at the basin, he slid into his usual chair. Matt waited until Emily was seated across from him with Austin on her lap. Joyanna and Grant took their places on either side of him, Grant's chair pushed as far from him as possible and Joyanna's chair scooted as close to his as she could manage.

Matt bowed his head, then slowly said, "Dear God, thank you for this food and for this day—and for the work we've gotten done. Amen."

Lifting his head, Matt met Emily's gaze from across the table. Her eyebrows had that quirk to them, telling him he'd messed up. Again.

Matt frowned.

"Would you mind telling me why you never like the way I pray?" Words spilled from his mouth before he could stop them.

Emily grabbed the spoon to dish up Austin's plate, her forehead furrowed. "It's not the words that bother me. I just don't think you mean them."

Matt's muscles coiled tight. "Fine. How about you pray from now on?"

Emily flushed. "I wasn't trying to hint that I wanted you to stop praying. I want you to pray, but I want you to know the God you're praying to."

Know the God he was praying to? Matt could feel his temper flaring. He might have his doubts about God, but he wasn't heathen. He *did* know about God.

Deciding it would be best to keep quiet for now, Matt dished up his plate and dug into it. "Good supper," he said, both because the food was good and because it seemed like a way to make peace.

That seemed to do the trick, because sure enough, Emily's shoulders relaxed. "Thank you."

Pleased that he had pulled the conversation back to more peaceful grounds, Matt said, "By the way, does Colton have any gloves I could use tomorrow? Those reins are hard on the hands."

Emily's lips tightened. *Oh, no.* He must have said something wrong again.

"Tomorrow's Sunday," she said, cutting Austin's food into bite-sized pieces.

"Sunday? Oh. I lost track of time." Matt took another bite, sneaking a glance across the table at Emily. Surely she wasn't trying to hint at what he thought she was, right? "So, is there a pair of gloves I could use?"

"Yes, but not tomorrow. Tomorrow is Sunday."

"So? As I see it, the field needs to get finished no matter what day it is, and I intend to work on it tomorrow."

Emily shot a fiery glare at him. "No one around here works on Sunday, and neither will you. I will not allow it."

Matt met her gaze squarely. "Oh really? I don't see how you can stop me. I came to help you with the farm, not idle away the Sabbath, and I *will* be working on that field tomorrow."

"No, you will *not*." Emily pushed back from the table and rose, her eyes snapping. "I may have agreed to let you help, but let me tell you one thing, Matthew. *No one* in this family is going to work in the fields on a Sunday, and if you don't like it, then you can just leave."

"You don't realize how hard it would be for you if I left. Do you realize how much work those fields take, along with all the farm chores and your own usual work? It's a heap more work than you'd think, Emily Keath." Matt spoke through a clenched jaw.

Emily folded her arms across her chest. "That trick's not going to work. We don't need you, Matthew. I appreciate your help, but we *do* have neighbors and family members who would be happy to help us if you weren't here. We are a community, and community helps one another." Her eyes narrowed. "And let me tell you this. I do not want you to be a bad influence on the children. If it comes down to it, I would rather see you leave than to see my children grow up to be like you."

Her words struck Matt like a slap across the face. How could she say that? He'd known that she didn't like him, but *that* was a low opinion indeed. Did she really think he was a wicked man?

Of course, it didn't matter. He didn't like her anyway—but her words hurt more than they should have.

Emily sighed and dropped back into her seat. "I expect you to come to church with us tomorrow."

"No." *Go to church?* Why, he hadn't set foot in a church since Pa's funeral. Churches were one thing he had no tolerance for, with everyone all dressed up and acting sickeningly sweet to one another. He would never set foot in a church again.

Emily seemed to lose all patience with him. "Yes, you will, Matthew Keath, and I will not take no for an answer. I will drag you there if I have to."

As she leaned toward him, both arms braced against the table, Matt had a vivid image of his ma standing in Emily's place. His mother's eyes held that exact same spark and the same stubborn tilt of her chin. Even the way she said his name was the same way Ma had said it. Matt sucked in his breath, and the vision faded. He sat across from Emily again, but it took him a moment to collect himself after the startling revelation.

He rarely thought of his mother, but the woman sitting across the table from him forced him to remember. If Ma could hear him now, she would be hurt that a son of hers would turn his back on church. He knew that. Guilt stirred within his gut and he could not bring himself to meet anyone's gaze. He looked at the tabletop instead.

Fear was a powerful motivator—and he was scared out of his wits lest she give him another look like Ma. He swallowed hard. "Fine."

Emily eyed him, obviously unable to believe he would give in without putting up more of a fight. "Really? You'll go to church tomorrow?"

"Yes. I'm not a heathen." Matt blew out his breath, irritated that he'd been roped into yet another thing he didn't want to do. That seemed to happen regularly to him lately.

Emily pushed the cookie plate toward him. "Have a cookie, and then go to bed, Matthew. You're getting crabby."

Matt snorted. As if he were the only crabby person in the room. Still, the cookies looked good, so he took one anyway.

He nibbled at the crisp edge, the flavor of oatmeal and cinnamon flooding his taste buds. Emily's baking was a treat, but he was going to need more than a sweet cookie to forgive her this time.

Church. He wasn't even certain he could sit still for an entire service. Tomorrow was bound to set the record for the worst day of his life.

Matt could still scarcely believe what he was doing as he guided the team into Osceola, Emily jostling on the seat beside him. Austin sat on his mother's lap, grinning at everything and everyone except for Matt. Joyanna and Grant giggled with each other in the back. If a stranger were to witness this sight, they might have assumed that the Keaths were like any other happy family on their way to church together.

But by now, Matt knew Emily well enough to tell that she was still upset with him over their "discussion" at the kitchen table the night before. She hadn't said much to him that morning, and now she stared straight ahead without giving him a single glance.

Fine. Matt didn't want to talk to her anyway.

A half a mile passed with both Matt and Emily intently studying each farm they passed. Then Matt remembered that maybe there *was* something he wanted to talk to Emily about.

He cleared his throat. "Emily, where's Colton buried?"

"At the cemetery in town." Emily's grip on Austin tightened.

"I hadn't thought of it, but I suppose you'd want to see it sometime?"

"I guess." Matt tried to sound careless, but the lump gathering in his throat made it difficult.

"Maybe today after church?"

Matt nodded.

"That could be arranged." Emily straightened. "Oh, I forgot to tell you. We're planning to eat lunch at my parents' house today. Ephraim and Sadie's family will be there, as well as Zane and Sarah."

Matt tensed. "I thought we were going home. Isn't going to church enough for one day?"

Emily flushed. "Look, if you don't want to come, that's fine. You can go home and we'll just ride over with Pa and Ma. It's enough that you're coming to church."

Matt hadn't expected her to sound apologetic. His annoyance was mostly because she hadn't given him further warning, not because they were going to the Mayfields'.

"I guess it's all right," he said in a more subdued voice.

Neither of them spoke until they reached town. As they headed into downtown, Emily leaned forward and said, "Our church is on the east side of the square,"

"Which denomination is that?"

"Oh, it's not a mainline denomination. Osceola does have a Methodist and a Congregational church, but we go to the one that people call The Mission Church. Pastor Drew started it when the town was first laid out."

Matt followed her directions, trying to still his nerves as they drew closer to the church. He nodded briefly to other families they passed, some driving and some walking. It seemed as if the whole town was on their way to church.

Emily pointed ahead to a white-painted wooden building—obviously The Mission Church. Matt drew the team up in front of it to let Emily and the children out. He reached for Emily to help her down, but she was faster than he. With a swish of her black skirts, she hoisted herself over the wheel and landed safely on the ground.

Matt tamped down his hurt that she had purposefully avoided his assistance.

She shifted Austin on her hip and said, "Joyanna, Grant, come with me."

Grant ran to her side, but Joyanna glanced back at Matt. "Mama, can't I stay with Uncle Matt?"

"No," Matt and Emily said in unison.

Without a word, Joyanna trudged toward her mother.

Matt clicked the team forward and drove until he found an empty spot on the hitching rail. Swinging down from the wagon, he tied the team then headed for church building. His palms grew damp. What had possessed him to agree to this? He would rather try to rope and brand a bear than face this churchyard that was filled with Emily's neighbors who were visiting as they waited for the service to begin.

Matt felt several people looking at him, and he tried to shake off his self-consciousness. He shouldn't be self-conscious. He thrived on attention—except when it came from decent men who looked like they belonged in the churchyard. Unlike him.

A couple of men nodded to him. Matt gave them a brief nod in return and hurried past. If he could just avoid interacting with them, maybe then no one would realize that he had no business entering their bell-topped chapel.

"Hi, Uncle Matt."

Glancing down, Matt found Joyanna grinning up at him.

Matt frowned. "I thought you were supposed to be with your mama."

"Mama's fine with me going wherever, just long as I don't leave the churchyard. I thought I'd wait for you." Joyanna tried to take his hand, but Matt pulled back and stuck his hands in his pockets where she couldn't reach them.

Her face shadowed, but then she shrugged and smiled, skipping along beside him as they climbed the church steps.

A gray-haired man in a black suit greeted them at the door. "Good morning," he said, holding out his hand. "I don't believe we've met yet. I'm Drew Willard, the pastor."

Matt accepted his hand. "Matt Keath."

"Why, bless you, son." The man's eyes widened. "You look like—"

"Colton. I know," Matt said grimly. "He's my brother. Or, rather, *was* my brother."

"Ah, yes. I'd heard that you were here to help Emily. News travels fast in a small town." Pastor Drew smiled. "Allow me to welcome you to Osceola and our church this morning. We're glad to have you here and to see dear Emily being well taken care of."

Matt jerked his head in a nod and moved on. He had sounded sincere, but Matt suspected it was just a ploy to prime him to put plenty of money in the offering plate. He didn't trust preachers any farther than he could throw them. They might talk smoothly and say they cared nothing for the things of this world, but Matt could think of a couple he'd known in his lifetime who had been more than happy to accept money that they used to line their own vests.

He spotted Emily in a pew a few rows from the back. Easing out his breath, he made his way over, weaving through the crowd until he reached her side. Too late, he realized that she was busy talking with Sadie Mayfield, but he couldn't turn back now.

Sadie looked his way, her face brightening. "Why, Matt Keath, how good to see you this morning! How's the farm life going?"

Matt forced a smile. "Very well, thank you." He didn't dare look at Emily, but he guessed her eyes were accusing him of being a liar.

"Great! Emily said you're all still planning on lunch, so I'll look forward to seeing you then." She looked at the blonde-haired little girl wiggling in her arms. "In the meantime, I think this here girl needs a diaper change. We'll visit more later, all right, Emily?"

"Yes, of course," Emily said.

Watching the two women exchange meaningful looks, Matt had to resist the urge to squirm. He wouldn't be surprised if they had been discussing him before he interrupted.

A man stepped to the front of the church, and Matt lowered himself to the wooden bench beside Grant. The boy sent him a wary look, but he relaxed when Joyanna scooted in between him and Matt.

"Turn to hymn number sixty-three, 'Rock of Ages,'" the man said.

As the pianist began, Joyanna pushed a hymnal into Matt's hands. Matt had no choice but to accept it. Opening it up, he fumbled through the pages until he found the right hymn. Emily leaned closer to share the book with him, and Matt held it out so she could see better.

At that moment, he happened to look across the aisle. Two women had their gazes fixed on him. The first was none other than Mrs. Durmond from the mercantile. Her lips were pursed into one thin line of disapproval, her eyes narrowed above her hawkish nose.

The other woman was younger. She wore a purple dress that was lavish with lace and a hat with a ridiculous feather on top drooping down and curling against her cheek. Her brilliant green eyes met his and she smiled, batting her long lashes.

Matt quickly looked back at the hymnal, heat creeping up his face. What kind of a woman would flirt like that with a complete stranger, and in church, of all places? He glanced at Emily. To his relief, she didn't seem to have noticed anything.

They sang a couple more hymns and then took their seats

again. Pastor Drew stepped to the front, and Matt eased back in his seat. Now for the boring part. Preachers always gave insufferably long sermons, probably to make people think their money was going to good use. Too bad preachers didn't have to sit on one of these hard wooden benches and hear their own sermon thrown back at them. The world would be a far better place if there were fewer preachers and more people who acted on their own advice.

Pastor Drew's voice rang through the church with conviction. "This world is filled with those who think they know best and fail to consider the thoughts of others—isn't that right?" Matt stared at him, sure that he was speaking directly to him. He couldn't read minds, could he?

"There are those who would gladly run your life for you if they could. People who would be happy to tell you what they think you should be doing. There are people who try to shame others into doing things that the Word of God never tells us we must do. There are those who do their best to control the world." The pastor rested both palms on the pulpit. "But I'm here to tell you that what those people have to say doesn't matter. Not if their advice doesn't line up with what the Bible tells us. What people think we should do means nothing. The biggest question we must ask ourselves each day is this: What does *God* want us to do? How does He want us, His creation, to live?"

Matt shifted in his seat as the pastor continued.

"If we want our lives to gain true meaning, then we must seek the One who gives meaning to all things. If we have formed our lives around mere things, then when those things go away, we are left empty and worthless. We have no purpose, and we are miserable."

Pastor Drew peered over his glasses at those in the room. "Friends, there is only One who is worth living for. He wants to be involved in each of our lives, and He has spoken to us very plainly through the pages of His Word. But we can't hear Him if we've blocked our ears to His voice. Sometimes, we get so focused on the creation that we fail to notice the Creator. And sometimes, perhaps often, the creation we are focused on is *ourselves*."

Pastor Drew opened his Bible. "Psalm twenty-four says, 'The earth is the Lord's and the fullness thereof, the world and those who dwell therein . . . Who will ascend the hill of the Lord? And who will stand in his holy place? He who has clean hands and a pure heart . . . He will receive blessing from the Lord and right-eousness from the God of his salvation.'

"We read there that not only is the earth the Lord's, but the people in it are His as well. And He has spoken of how He wants the people who have experienced His salvation to live. We must focus our attention on Him alone, not those around us, and especially not ourselves."

Matt remained rooted in his seat. That was a psalm he'd read aloud just a few days ago, and he hadn't pulled any of that out of the verses. He forgot all about his plans to doze off during the sermon. This preacher was unlike any he'd ever met.

Matt continued to listen closely, right up until Pastor Drew gave his final prayer. Then Pastor Drew stepped aside for the first man who had led the singing. *That's it?*

The sunlight filtering through the windows had shifted since he first sat down. It had to be close to noon. That meant the sermon had been almost an hour long, even if it felt like only minutes for Matt.

When the last notes of the final hymn faded away, the room began to hum with activity again. Matt still couldn't shake free of the sermon's hold on him. He hadn't expected to enjoy—or, at least, tolerate—it as much as he did. And he sure hadn't thought he would feel convicted by Pastor Drew's words.

"I need to talk with Ma," Emily said, brushing past him. "Come with me, Grant, Joyanna."

Her words brought Matt back to the moment, and he watched them walk away. What was he supposed to do while she visited? Follow her? Or should he just stand there looking out of place and foolish?

"Yoo-hoo!" a voice sang out at his elbow, and Matt jumped. It was *that* woman again. The woman with the ridiculous hat and fluttering eyelashes.

The woman tittered. "Good morning! How are you doing on this fine day? It's a pleasure having you in church with us today."

Before Matt could say a word, she rushed on. "I'm Maude Reynolds. My father is the owner of the harness shop here in town. Maybe you've met him? It's a pleasure to meet you. What did you say your name was?"

He *hadn't* said. Matt resisted the urge to squirm. "Matt Keath."

"Matt." She dragged his name out. "Such a nice name. Matt. I heard there was a man helping poor Emily with her farm work, but I didn't realize you would be so young. How old are you?"

Matt edged away from her. "Twenty-six, miss."

"Ah, twenty-six. Twenty-six, and already with a fine sense of selflessness. You can't truly enjoy working for your sister-in-law for nothing, can you?"

The pity in her expression made the back of Matt's neck itch. "I like it," he said recklessly. "It's been good to meet my brother's family, and I can't say I'm entirely selfless in the whole thing, because Emily's cooking sure is a treat."

The look in her eyes changed. Why, it almost seemed that she was jealous of Emily.

Then she fluttered her lashes again, setting the feather on her hat bobbing. "I suppose you get tired of farming all the time, though. Don't you ever wish for a little fun?"

"Miss, I've been here for less than a week. I'm more concerned about getting the fields planted than about having fun."

Maude sighed. "Ah, a hardworking man too."

Matt took another step back. Surely this was how an animal felt while it was being hunted.

A shadow fell across the floor between Matt and Maude Reynolds. Matt lifted his head and found himself looking into Mrs. Durmond's stern face. At that moment, he welcomed the distraction that even she provided.

"Young man, I'm glad to see you decided to come to church today." Her tone implied that she doubted he'd come willingly. "Most of all, I am glad to see that you discarded the outlandish garb you were wearing the last time we met. It would have been a sin had you come to church flaunting such ridiculous clothing, if you can even call it that. Especially those spiky metal contraptions on your boots."

Instantly, Matt vowed that next Sunday he would wear his spurs and high-topped boots.

Mrs. Durmond's gaze shifted from Matt to Maude, whose lip had protruded at Mrs. Durmond's interruption. Her eyes narrowed.

"The Lord doesn't approve of His house being used as a place of flirtation," she said, the weight of her glare settling on Matt. "You shouldn't be leading young women into temptation and sin. And on the Lord's Day, no less! You should be ashamed of yourself."

Matt's face burned. Had he really been glad when she first appeared? She was even worse than Maude, and obviously, Pastor Drew's sermon had gone right over her head.

"I don't think you understand," he began, but she cut him off.

"Oh, I understand your type. You are the kind of man who has no sense of shame to restrain yourself from doing evil. I watched you during church, and I don't approve of what you were doing."

Matt raked his mind but couldn't remember making any significant blunders. "And what was that?"

"Don't play innocent. I saw how you and Emily stood entirely too close to one another during the singing. Knowing Emily like I do, I'm sure she was unaware of what you were doing, or perhaps you have been leading her astray since the day you arrived."

They had stood too close to each other, even when they had two kids between them? The idea was incredulous.

Maude giggled, and Mrs. Durmond turned on her. "And you! I've spoken with you about your unruly conduct, and I know you aren't innocent either. The way you flirt with every young man you meet makes you a disgrace to your parents."

Maude let out another giggle, and Mrs. Durmond's eyes flashed fire. Matt realized he was cornered between the two women blocking his exit from the pew. He scanned the room for a way to escape but found none.

His gaze fell on Emily, visiting with Pastor Drew. She glanced his way at that moment, and something flashed in her eyes—maybe sympathy? He felt pitiful, all right.

He didn't expect any help out of her, but with a final word to Pastor Drew, Emily headed his way.

"Good morning, Mrs. Durmond. Maude. Would you mind moving over a bit so I can grab my things from the pew?" Emily asked with the sweetest smile.

The two women moved away, and Emily looked at Matt as if she were noticing him for the first time. "Oh, Matthew. I talked with Pa, and he said he'd bring you to the cemetery. Ma and I will drive our wagon to the farm, and you and Pa can take their wagon."

Matt was sure she must be an angel. At that moment, he felt he could forgive her for any cold shoulders and sarcastic comments she might make. That was far better than flirting like Maude did.

Mrs. Durmond *tsked*. "Emily, do you really think it's proper to call the young man by his first name?"

Emily's expression didn't change. "I see absolutely nothing wrong with it. Calling him Mr. Keath every day would get to be quite a mouthful."

"Well, as I like to say, 'let not a trace of unseemliness mar your conduct, and you'll never have reason to be reproached.'" Mrs. Durmond pursed her lips. "Sometimes it's easier to do wrong than right, but that shouldn't stop us from doing the right thing."

"I agree," Emily said in an even tone. "But in this case, I don't believe there is any unseemliness at all. Matthew is family, and it's entirely proper for families to use each other's given names."

Matt was tempted to applaud just to see Mrs. Durmond's reaction. Instead, he decided to make an escape while the way was still open. He slipped from the pew and searched the room for Josiah.

"Goodbye, Matt. So nice to meet you. And if you ever get bored with farming, remember that there are plenty of fun things to do here in town, especially if you have a good companion." Maude batted her eyelashes.

Mrs. Durmond glowered at her, then leaned closer to Matt, one eyebrow raised. "I've heard things about cowboys. After your scandalous conduct this morning, I am forced to believe them."

"Oh really?" Matt lowered his voice as well. "Well, I've heard things about farmers . . ." He let his voice trail off meaningfully.

Mrs. Durmond's lips curved into an almost smile. "You aren't going to get me with that one, young man. My husband isn't a farmer. He's a well digger."

The woman was impossible. Rather than lingering to think of a good retort, Matt turned and left.

Sometimes the better part of wisdom was knowing when to stay and fight and when to make a run for it instead.

CHAPTER 12

Matt had trouble escaping from the church. People wouldn't let him pass without saying hello and introducing themselves, remarking all the while about how much he reminded them of Colton. The constant comparison between him and Colton was making him uneasy, though he couldn't tell why. He brushed the feeling aside for later dissection and moved through the throng until Josiah stood before him.

Josiah and Pastor Drew were oblivious to the time as they talked, leaving Matt to stand idly by. He began to wonder if he might be stuck waiting there all day, and his attention went back to Mrs. Durmond and Maude. Mrs. Durmond was still going on with Emily, and though he was relieved to have been spared her scolding, Matt felt a pang for Emily. Meanwhile, Maude had chosen to leave rather than face further reprimands from Mrs. Durmond.

At last, Josiah turned and caught sight of him. "Why, Matt, didn't see you there. Have you been there long?"

"Not too long." Matt gave a weak smile.

"Don't hesitate to interrupt next time. Me and Drew could talk all day if we were given a chance. Have you met Pastor yet?"

Matt nodded.

"A good man, Drew is." Josiah clapped Pastor Drew on the shoulder. "Not only is he a good preacher, but he also makes some of the best furniture you'll ever see."

"Don't get his expectations up. I'm afraid my furniture is hardly *that* fine." Pastor Drew smiled good naturedly. "Again, it was a pleasure to have you join us, Matt. Will you be here next week?"

Matt lifted his shoulders. "I expect so."

"Good." Pastor Drew beamed. "I'll look forward to seeing you then. Take care, Matt and Josiah."

Mumbling his goodbye, Matt turned and followed Josiah toward the door. He was quite sure that Pastor Drew would look forward to seeing him next Sunday. Didn't all pastors look forward to the prospect of a new member?

The man could preach a decent sermon—still, Matt couldn't trust him.

Josiah seemed in no hurry to be on his way. As they walked back to the wagon, he introduced Matt to even more people. As the whirl of people paraded past him, Matt met the sheriff, Ethan Becker, who couldn't have been much older than he, and his wife Jeanne. And then he was introduced to Doctor Nelson Stoning, as well as Josiah's son-in-law, Zane Hoffman, and his twin brothers, Adam and Benjamin. The Hoffman brothers were friendly, but he wasn't sure if their father, Elkanah, liked him or not. He didn't smile once during their introduction.

Ephraim, with one of his children riding on his shoulders, waved to Matt from across the yard, and Matt waved back. While he looked around, Matt did not see a single family packing up and leaving. All the neighbors seemed happy to stay and chat as if they genuinely enjoyed each other's company.

Community. That's what Emily had called it. Matt had never seen anything like it. At his church back home in Ohio, everyone acted polite but insincere. And they were always in a hurry to leave each other's presence. Out West, it had been every man for himself. Not like here where everyone acted like one big family.

Gradually, Matt was beginning to understand why Colton had liked Osceola and even enjoyed going to church. But it wasn't his kind of place. This was a town for people like Colton, not a solitary cowboy who threw steers and rode broncs. Attending church every Sunday might not be as bad as he had originally thought, but he would attend only as long as he was in Osceola. Once he returned West, his church days were over. And Pastor Drew had better not get the wrong idea that Matt would be making donations to the offering plate. He liked the man all right, but he didn't want to encourage him too much.

Josiah indicated for Matt to drive, so Matt picked up the reins and backed the team away from the hitching rail. His stomach twisted at the thought of their destination, and he was grateful to have something to keep his hands busy.

He and Josiah rode in silence as they drove through town to the cemetery, with Josiah giving him only directions. As they drew closer, Matt's apprehension grew, particularly when they crossed Davis Creek Bridge and he saw the graveyard ahead of him. He was tempted to tell Josiah that he had changed his mind, but he knew in his heart that he had to do this. Until Matt visited Colton's grave, it would be hard to comprehend that he was gone for good.

"Stop here," Josiah said as they entered the cemetery's driveway. "That marker over there is Colton's."

Matt swallowed hard, his gaze following Josiah's pointing finger. Sure enough, he could see a round-topped marker protruding from the ground, its presence a grim proof that death had struck.

Josiah patted his knee. "Go on, son. I'll wait here."

Matt nodded, just as he was expected to do. Then he climbed

down from the wagon, inhaling deeply before he walked toward Colton's grave.

This was going to be harder than he'd thought.

Step by step, he inched closer, feeling as if time stood still as he drew near. He didn't want to look. He didn't want to admit that Colton was dead. Even though he was living on Colton's property with his family, it was easy to keep pretending that Colton would someday return.

But now, Matt forced himself to look down at the grave in front of him. *Colton John Keath, 1851-1879,* the marker read. The bare dirt in front of it announced that death had recently won, but already a few new blades of grass had dared to make an appearance, striving to reclaim the spot for the prairie around it.

Matt reached out one hand and touched the marker. Why? Why Colton, of all people?

It wasn't right. His family needed him. His children needed their father. Emily needed her husband. The farm needed its owner.

"I'm trying to do my best for your sake, Colton, but it isn't enough," Matt whispered aloud. It was far from enough, and there in that moment, Matt was unable to acknowledge any differently. He'd kept himself running like crazy this last week until all time to think had been drowned out, but now he was left empty. Why did he even come to Osceola? He wasn't Colton. Colton's family needed a strong man to lead them, protect them from pain, and to provide for them.

Matt had never considered himself a weak man. But compared to his brother, he felt incredibly small. Just thinking of how badly he'd muddled the last week made him flinch. He doubted that Colton had ever raised his voice with Emily and the kids. He doubted he had sworn at the milk cow or said an insincere prayer. He would have known how to care for his family the *right* way, unlike Matt.

Perhaps that was why it bothered him so much when people compared him to Colton. Because if they really knew him, they would realize that while he and Colton might have been brothers with many physical similarities, there was a world of difference between the two of them on the inside.

And yet there was nothing Matt could do to bring Colton back.

Anger spurted through him, creating a roar in his ears. Did God not understand that Colton would be better off on this earth than in heaven? Did He not recognize that Matt couldn't replace Colton? Why had He allowed all of this to happen?

The Lord's ways are higher than ours, his father had been fond of saying. Matt shoved the thought aside, unwilling to consider that God had not just *allowed* these things to happen but had actually *planned* them. He would have to be one cruel God to do that.

Matt took in the sight of Colton's grave one more time, his anger draining away and leaving only a pain that seemed to scrape at his soul. His brother, along with his parents, was dead. He was completely alone.

Tears stung against his eyes, but he blinked hard to chase them away. He refused to cry—not now or ever.

He clenched his jaw and wheeled around, marching back to the wagon. Emily and the kids were depending on him, and he would not let them down. So he swallowed his emotions and trudged onward. There was no other option.

Josiah and Matt kept the conversation light as they traveled to the Mayfields'. Much as he liked Josiah, he couldn't think of making him his confidant. No one had ever played that role for him apart from his pa and Colton, and he wasn't ready to let anyone else be privy to his innermost thoughts. He didn't even want to ponder them himself.

As they pulled into the Mayfields' farm lane, a group of children ran by yelling and laughing. Matt spotted Joyanna and Grant, and Joyanna grinned at him and hollered, "Hi, Uncle Matt!"

Josiah chuckled, watching the children run off. "Margie, Walter, and Isaac are Ephraim and Sadie's kids. The more that the years go by, the more kids get added to this family. The youngest children are probably at the house with the women."

He sounded pleased with all his grandchildren. Matt felt overwhelmed by the thought of so many kids.

Josiah pulled the team up in front of the barn. "I'll unhitch the team. You just go on and find Ephraim and Zane. I'll join you in a few minutes."

Matt nodded, even though he wished to protest. He would have much preferred sticking close to Josiah's side, but that seemed cowardly.

Mustering all his self-confidence, he walked toward the house. Josiah and Margaret had a frame house, not a soddy. It wasn't very big but it didn't need to be; Josiah and Margaret were only two people living there. Matt observed Ephraim and Zane in a couple of rocking chairs on the porch, chuckling at something they shared.

Matt's steps slowed as he drew closer, and he hesitated to barge in on their conversation. He hadn't felt this shy since his first day of school back when he was a kid.

Ephraim spotted him and waved him over. "Hey, Matt! How's it going?"

"Fine," Matt said as he approached.

"Come over and have a seat." Zane used one foot to keep the rocker in motion so that the baby in his arms would remain asleep. As Matt lowered himself to one of the porch steps, Zane added, "It's good that you could join us today."

Ephraim nudged him. "Yeah, you would think so. You're just looking to show off that new baby to as many people as possible."

"Hey, that's not fair." Zane nudged him back. "Whenever you have a new baby, you do your own share of showing off."

"Point taken. But that's because they're so cute that it would be doing the world a pity to keep that little one in a corner and out of sight."

Matt glanced between the two, resisting the urge to flee to the barn and Josiah. He felt like an intruder. Worse than that, he couldn't think of a word to say. He wasn't a father like they were. He didn't even *like* kids.

He must have made a slight movement, because Zane looked at him and gave an apologetic smile. "Sorry. Ephraim and I like to argue. The only excuse I have is that I grew up with three brothers, and he grew up with two sisters."

"Now, I like that," Ephraim spoke up. "I never thought I'd hear the day you said it was Sarah's fault for anything, not even if I'm an arguer."

Zane blew out his breath. "Didn't say it was Sarah's fault, so don't blame your actions on her. The reason Sarah's such an angel is probably because she had to put up with the likes of you for a brother."

Ephraim let out a low whistle. "That was a good one, Zane."

"Anyway." Zane waved a hand at Ephraim. "Be quiet, Ephraim. Let's give Matt a chance to talk. Why don't you tell us a little about yourself? I take it you don't have a family of your own."

Matt shook his head. "No."

"Any young lady you're going to make Mrs. Keath soon?" Ephraim asked.

Matt's face heated. "No." *And hallelujah,* he was tempted to add.

"Oh." Both Ephraim and Zane looked so serious that Matt couldn't help but chuckle.

"Really, it's not a tragedy. I like being by myself."

Zane lifted an eyebrow. "You *think*. Isn't there some saying that 'ignorance is bliss?' You won't be able to stand the thought of being alone after you meet the right lady."

Matt said nothing. *He* knew better. All of the women he'd met lately only made him more desperate to return to his comfortable life by himself.

"So what do you do for a living?" Ephraim asked, thankfully changing the topic.

"I'm a cowboy. Worked for a big spread out in Scottsbluff for several years. Before that, I did some work as a deputy."

Both men stared at him. "You were a deputy?" Ephraim asked, leaning forward in his seat. "Did you ever run into any real desperadoes?"

Matt chuckled, easing some of the tight bands around his chest. "Not really. Mostly just men in the saloon who'd had a few too many drinks."

Zane stroked his jaw. "Did you ever have your life threatened?"

Matt shook his head. "No, but I have been punched and kicked a few times. One man even bit me. Eventually I grew tired of dealing with other men's violence, so I went back to being a cowboy, a much simpler job."

"I've always heard that Western towns are pretty wild places," Zane commented.

Matt shrugged. "It depends. The wild towns are usually at the end of the trail where the cowboys coming in have been driving cattle for months and they're ready to party it up a bit. Scottsbluff was pretty tame." He hesitated and then added, "When I left, there was some big news going around. A wanted man returned to the area and shot the sheriff I used to work with."

Zane's and Ephraim's eyes widened.

"Did you know the man who did it?" Zane asked.

"Not in a friendly way. I was the one who helped Telmond lock him up."

Ephraim let out a low whistle. "Do you think he's mad at *you?*"

"Nah. I was just the deputy, and deputies aren't as great of targets as sheriffs." Matt tried to sound convincing, but he couldn't shake his sense of unease. He hadn't thought of Frank Harvey since his time spent at Bar K, yet here he was again. If Frank wanted to take something out on him, surely he wouldn't be able to find Matt all the way in Osceola, right?

The door opened, and Emily stepped onto the porch. "Dinner's ready," she said, shading her eyes against the sun.

Both Zane and Ephraim stood, but Matt could sense they still had plenty of questions for him. He kept his face impassive, but he couldn't help but smile on the inside. Maybe this was the beginning of a real friendship. He hoped so. It was going to be a lonely summer if he was always hanging on the outskirts of things.

Emily's forehead furrowed. "Where did the kids go?"

"Over by the barn. I'll get them." Ephraim crossed the porch, marched past Matt, and descended the steps.

Emily stood beside Zane and looked down at the baby, her face softening. "What a dear. Could I hold her?"

Zane nodded and passed the baby to her. "She's light as a feather compared to Byron. I hadn't realized just how much he's grown until he came into the room to see his new sister. He looked huge."

"I know that feeling." Emily's eyes grew distant, and her smile faded a bit. Matt's gaze intercepted hers momentarily, and he thought he saw a tear welling in the corner of her eye, though it vanished as fast as it had come. In its place was a look of disapproval directed at him.*What did I do now to deserve that?* Matt couldn't voice his question, though, because Emily whirled away and marched into the house.

"Hurry in," she called over her shoulder. Matt rose to follow as she sent him another scowl. Out of all the women in the world, she was the most complicated to understand.

Matt felt as if he had been snatched away into a tornado of activity the moment he stepped inside. Ephraim and the kids exploded into the place, making a ruckus loud enough that Matt couldn't think. He was directed to the table and directed to sit next to Emily in the only unoccupied seat in the room. Josiah prayed briefly and quieted the room for a second before saying amen. Then, it burst back to life with full force once more.

Matt dished up his plate and passed along the platters of food, feeling as if he were in a daze. This was the loudest house he'd ever been in, and he feared the sound might just overpower him. Emily, seated beside him, offered no solace and kept her gaze lowered away from him.

Halfway through his meal, the truth kicked him in the midsection. He had unknowingly taken the spot that Colton usually occupied.

His throat tightened and the food in his mouth turned metallic. Placing his fork down, he took in a deep breath. It all made sense; he was sitting in the one remaining chair—right next to Emily. That was why she didn't even glance at him and acted so distant.

Around him, the talk and laughter swirled, but a wave of nausea washed over Matt. He was *not* Colton. He should have just gone home after the church service. He shouldn't have come to this family gathering where there was no place for him except in Colton's vacant spot. His job was to provide for Colton's family—farming, labor, cutting wood. Not to fill in his shoes and take over his family role.

Matt wished for nothing more than to return to the farm and the soil that he was meant to tend, back to work that actually made sense in the craziness that had taken over his life. But he was trapped at the table now, unable to move for fear of offending the women. He even felt obligated to finish his plate.

Matt lifted a forkful of food into his mouth and forced himself to chew and swallow.

He had only one choice now—to endure. He would carry through with that resolve even if it killed him.

After dinner, Matt followed the other men out to the porch, as was expected of him. He would have preferred to stay near Emily so he could urge her toward the door, but knew he'd only be in the way. The women needed to clean the kitchen, and they didn't need him hanging around and in their way.

Matt lowered himself to sit on the steps. As he relaxed against the railing, Joyanna appeared beside him, tugging on one of her braids. "Uncle Matt, can I sit with you?"

Matt gripped the edge of the steps. "Don't you want to go play?"

"No."

Matt bit his lip. After all his revelations that morning, he had less interest than ever in cuddling up with Colton's daughter. And yet, if he said no, he would look like a hardhearted brute.

He sighed. "Sure. You can sit next to me."

Joyanna looked like she would protest, but then Matt repeated, "Next to me."

She shrugged, gave him her usual grin, and plopped next to him. She snuggled as close to his side as she could. Matt leaned against the railing and heaved another sigh. Why was she so obsessed with him? He had been there for nearly a week and it wasn't like he was encouraging her.

Josiah, Ephraim, and Zane fell into a conversation, and though Matt knew he ought to pay attention, it was easier to let his mind drift.

His thoughts flew in the direction they always traveled when he allowed himself a moment of thought, back to how his life *could* have been at this moment. Had he not received Emily's letter, he would still be at the Bar K Ranch, probably adjusting to his new promotion to foreman.

You didn't want to keep working for the likes of Keller, he told himself.

Still, his heart dipped low at the thought of how his dreams had gone awry.

He wondered about Flick and how he was doing. The answer to that was obvious. He was probably doing just fine, doing the same things he always had. Matt assumed he was working cattle with his usual flair, getting into hot arguments with Hal, and blowing his paychecks at the saloon in town. Matt had often tried to intervene and keep Flick out of one scrape or another, usually without much success. That was one thing he *didn't* miss—although, at that moment, even a glimpse of Flick might make all the hassle worth it.

Joyanna slumped against him, and twisting to look at her, Matt saw that she was sound asleep. Her head started to slide forward, and to keep her from falling off the step, Matt wrapped his arm around her.

"Wow, she was out fast." Ephraim rose from his seat. "Come sit here, Matt."

Matt shot him a quick glance, a sense of helplessness overpowering him. He didn't know the first thing about children, let alone how to hold one properly. He didn't trust himself to hold Joyanna sitting down, let alone when he was carrying her across the porch to Ephraim's chair. But he had no choice but to try.

Matt held Joyanna delicately in his arms, stepped across the porch, and eased himself into Ephraim's chair, relieved that he didn't drop her.

I guess you win, Joyanna. He wiped away the sweat that had formed on his forehead.

Even with all the shifting around, Joyanna hardly stirred. Now she snuggled with him, her cheek pressed against his chest and braids falling down her back. She *was* rather cute, Matt had to admit, and the way she seemed so trusting of him was appealing. But he shook those thoughts aside. Maybe, if he were merely her visiting uncle, he could let his guard down. But as it was, he didn't dare allow her to wrap her fingers around his heartstrings. He had a job to do, and once that was over, he would leave. Both of those things—doing his job and leaving— would only be more difficult to accomplish if he clung to this little girl.

The front door opened, and Sadie stepped onto the porch. Turning to her husband, she said, "We're going on a little walk, but we'll be back soon."

We? Matt looked beyond her and noticed Emily standing in the doorway.

"All right, just don't wear out Emily's ear with all your talk." Ephraim smiled at his wife. "What'd you do with the kids?"

"Christina's asleep, and your mother is reading the others a story." Sadie patted his shoulder, then she skipped down the steps. "Come on, Emily, before these men find something else for us to do."

Emily started after her and then looked at Matt. He felt a distinct sense of smugness as her eyes went wide and she looked from him to her daughter. Now she had to admit that he wasn't all torture to her children.

Emily stared at him for one long moment. Then, without a word, she turned and hurried down the steps. Unexpected disappointment stabbed Matt in the gut. He'd thought she was on the verge of praising him, perhaps for the first time.

He pushed the feeling aside. It didn't matter. The truth was that Joyanna fell asleep in spite of—not *because of*—him. And he didn't care anything about her praise.

CHAPTER 13

"Slow down, Emily. If you keep up that pace, you'll be in Osceola before I reach the end of the lane." Sadie made a show of gripping her side and swiping the back of her hand across her forehead.

Emily sighed and slowed her pace to match Sadie's, even though she'd rather break into a sprint and never stop. That was how she'd felt lately. If she could run fast enough, perhaps she could outrun all the chaos that had overtaken her life.

Sadie slowed still more and came to a stop. "All right, I think it's time to talk. Something's bothering you. I could tell from the moment I saw you in church this morning."

Emily looked back at her parent's house, but they were far enough away that she couldn't easily make out the men seated on the porch. Her lower lip began to tremble, and she bit down on it. She didn't want to cry in front of Sadie *again*. She'd cried enough lately. Sadie was going to think that crying was the only thing she could do nowadays.

Ever since Colton's death, the tears rose at the slightest provocation. Usually, she restrained them until nighttime when the children were asleep and she didn't have to worry about upsetting them. But sometimes, they caught her by surprise, like now, and it was all she could do to fight them back.

Emily looked back at Sadie and forced a shaky laugh. "I'm sorry. It's been a long week."

Sadie nodded, her eyes not leaving Emily's face. "Is it Matt?"

"Matthew?" Emily clasped her hands together. "Of course it's Matthew. He's practically ruined this week!"

"*Ruined* it?" Sadie's eyes went wide. "How? I had the impression that he was a good man. After all, he shares the same blood as Colton."

Colton. The tears stung. "Matthew is nothing like Colton. Colton was a good man, but Matthew—" Emily's voice broke.

"He hasn't been pulling his fair weight?"

Emily shook her head. "No, no, that's not it. I wouldn't put up with him if he wasn't. He has a good work ethic."

"Then what's wrong with him?"

"Everything else, that's what. The house hasn't had a moment of peace since he arrived. Grant and Austin are terrified of him and scream every time he even looks at them. Joyanna is obsessed with him for some strange reason, and she won't stop talking about him and begging that I give her a little errand to run so she can see Uncle Matt. And Matthew and I just can't get along. I've tried my best, but he is the most irritating man I've ever met. We clash on every little thing."

"Are you sure *he's* the problem?" Sadie asked, her voice soft.

"Of course. Our house was just fine until he came."

"He does look a lot like Colton. Does that bother you?"

Bother her? Yes, sitting down to eat dinner across from a man who bore a distinct resemblance to her late husband bothered her. Driving to church next to that man bothered her. And watching him snuggle with her sleeping daughter hurt the worst of all. He'd never looked so much like Colton as he did in that moment.

Emily closed her eyes, thinking back to the day when

Matthew Keath first rode into their yard. She could still recall the shock she'd felt as she stared into a pair of blue eyes that were a perfect copy of Colton's. That moment had unraveled all the progress her broken heart had made toward healing. It brought back to her every ounce of the agony she experienced when her father and Doc Stoning told her Colton had died.

Of course, Matt wasn't identical to Colton. A closer inspection of him revealed that his looks were distinctly different, and he certainly had a personality that set him apart from her easygoing, loving husband. It was those differences that jarred her, causing her to long for her late husband. When he was contrasted against Colton, Matt's faults glared worse than ever and Emily's dislike for him grew more intense.

Emily's gaze fell to the ground. "Sometimes, especially if I catch a glimpse of him out of the corner of my eyes, I forget that he isn't Colton. When he's out working in the field, it's easy to mistake Matt for him. They have the same height, the same broad shoulders—" Her voice trailed off, and she raised her eyes to meet Sadie's, the motion sending a tear rolling down her cheek. "I miss Colton so badly. Do you think it will ever get better?"

"Of course it will." Sadie wrapped an arm around her shoulders. "Think of it this way: when you get injured, the pain is awful at first, but as time goes by, you start to heal. The hurt fades away bit by bit, and before you know it, there's only a scab left. You'll mend in your own time too, Emily."

"I don't know. It doesn't seem possible just now." Emily's jaw tightened. "And Matthew doesn't help. I think he likes annoying me."

"I hardly believe that can be true. I think you're being over-sensitive."

If anyone other than Sadie told her that, Emily would have flared and tried to argue. But this was coming from Sadie, who was not only her sister-in-law but also her best friend. She was forced to consider what she said.

"I guess I haven't been easy to get along with this week," she admitted. "Not quite everything has been Matthew's fault, but I think I'd feel better if he would just leave. Instead, he insists on staying through harvest, and he refuses to talk about it anymore. We were getting on just fine without him."

"Were you?" Sadie quirked one brow. "You were looking pretty tired, so tired that Ephraim and I were worried about you. I can't imagine how run down you'd be if you were trying to get through spring planting without Matt. I know the neighbors said they would help, but they all have farms of their own to maintain. Your fields probably would have been planted late, and you would have tried to do it all yourself. You *do* need a man's help, Emily."

Emily clamped down her trembling bottom lip. "I know. I can't deny that I need a man—but I don't need Matthew."

"But you just said he's been doing a good job."

"Forget about the fields. I'm concerned about my children. A swearing heathen cowboy is not a good influence for them. Children pick up on things quickly, and spending as much time as they do with Matthew can't be healthy for them. He's not a good example for them to follow. Just look at Joyanna. She's obsessed with the man, and I have no idea why."

"I think I know why." Sadie rested a hand on Emily's shoulder. "She misses her father, and she's trying to fill in the gap his death has created in her life. You know how close she and Colton were. Her uncle seems like the perfect solution to her."

Her words stabbed at Emily. Clenching her hands together, Emily shook her head. "No. Matthew Keath is no replacement for Colton, and if he thinks he can just waltz in here and fix everything—"

"I'm sure Matt doesn't think that."

Emily swiveled her gaze toward Sadie. "What makes you so sure?"

"Because. That man seems utterly out of place. As far as appearance goes, he fits in fine, especially now that he's dressed like a farmer rather than a cowboy. But he's got this look in his eyes that plainly says he's miserable."

Emily frowned. "Well, if he's miserable then he should just go West. I'm not holding him here."

"No, but something is. I'm thinking he must miss Colton quite a bit."

Emily paused a moment to think. He'd hardly said a word about Colton, apart from this morning when he'd asked where Colton was buried. If it weren't for his looks, Emily might have forgotten that he was Colton's brother.

"I don't know," she said, shrugging. "He doesn't act sad. He's never even said he was sorry that Colton was dead."

"That doesn't mean much. Men often try to act tougher than they really are. Why, when I lost my baby after Christina, I thought Ephraim didn't even care. He wouldn't talk about it, and he didn't cry. It made me angry for a time." Sadie blinked quickly. "But then one night I found him standing in front of the empty cradle. He was just standing there—and I knew he hurt too. We talked and cried after that, and I realized I could never again think that Ephraim didn't feel. The more he feels, the more he tries to hide it. I wonder why we do that."

"Maybe because we can't let other people consider us to be weak." Emily had hurt enough these past couple of months that she should know. Many times, she acted like Ephraim and hid her pain out of sight of those around her, trying to act like everything was just as fine as it had been before Colton died. In truth, though, her whole world had collapsed.

Sadie fingered the collar of her dress, her brow furrowed. "Did Colton ever talk about Matt?"

"Yes." Emily sighed. "He and Matthew were always close.

Almost every childhood memory he talked about involved Matthew, and he often said that he wished Matthew lived closer."

"So, Colton would approve of Matt helping out?" Sadie turned the question into more of a statement.

Emily ignored her. "He read me parts of Matthew's letters as well. I always had the impression that Matthew was a little wild—and I was glad he never took up Colton's offer to visit. Of course, I understand why Colton was fond of him, being his brother and all. But I think living out West ruined his character more than Colton was willing to admit."

"Hmm." Sadie looked off to the horizon. "I still think Matt's arrival was an answer to prayer. You needed him."

Emily could feel her frustration mounting. After all she'd said about Matt, Sadie still thought he was a good man, the man Emily needed to keep her farm going?

"You don't understand. No one understands." Anger drove Emily's tears away more effectively than her previous efforts. "I don't believe he's an answer to prayer. I can't believe that God would send a cowboy who swears, yells, and upsets the kids."

Sadie frowned. "That sounds like something Mrs. Durmond would say."

Emily's jaw dropped. Had she sounded like Mrs. Durmond? That was the last thing she wanted. Nearly everyone around had endured Mrs. Durmond's tongue lashings at one time or another. Most recently, Emily seemed to be her main target. Mrs. Durmond was upset because she thought Emily ought to wear black all the time, not just on outings. *"It isn't proper,"* she'd insisted.

But Emily had no intention of caving to the woman's demands. She didn't have the money to change her entire wardrobe to black, even if it would be proper. At least, that was her excuse. In truth, the idea of working in the hot sun in a black dress did not appeal to her.

Mrs. Durmond never filtered her words when she spoke. How Albert Durmond put up with such a wife, Emily would never know.

Silence stretched between them, and Sadie spoke again. "God uses imperfect people, Emily."

"But Matthew isn't even a Christian." Emily folded her arms across her chest. "He didn't want to come to church today."

"Going to church doesn't make you a Christian."

"No, but there are other signs. He doesn't like to pray or read the Bible. And he swears. He has never even claimed to be a believer."

Sadie took Emily's hands in hers. "If that's true, then it sounds to me like he needs you. He needs you even more than you need him. Your problems are only physical, but his are spiritual. And we both know that a soul is more important than anything on this earth."

Emily stared at her. She'd never thought of Matt as needing her and the children. He was a strong, self-sufficient man. The idea seemed preposterous.

And yet, maybe he *did* have needs that he kept out of sight.

Emily lowered her head. "I'm afraid I haven't been doing a good job of being a Christian this week. If anything, he's probably decided that Christians have short tempers, snap at everything, and shove Bibles down people's throats."

Sadie smiled and squeezed Emily's hands. "Good thing it's never too late to make a fresh start."

"I still don't like having him here."

Sadie's lips curved. "Too bad. It doesn't seem like you'll get rid of him any time soon."

Matt stepped away from the pig pen, set down the empty bucket, and wiped the back of his sleeve across his forehead. It was evening, yet still hot enough to make him sweat. Now that they were nearing the end of June, the days had grown warm—a good thing for growing crops but hard to bear while working. Come July, it would become even more unbearable with humidity making everything miserable.

Matt began to walk back toward the barn, but as he turned, something caught his peripheral vision. He frowned as he bent to inspect the area around the corner post of the pig pen. The post was rotting out, and the dirt behind it had been scraped away, creating a hole that would eventually become an escape route for the pigs. He sighed. He'd have to fix it before they all ran off.

"Why do animals have to be so destructive?" Matt muttered an oath, and then remembered that he wasn't going to swear anymore. He grimaced. The words had become a bigger part of his vocabulary than he'd first realized. He'd never been so aware of how often he used them until he made his vow to Joyanna.

He'd been slipping up more often lately—but since Joyanna wasn't around, it didn't matter that much.

A whinny came from Bowie's nearby pen. Matt walked over to his horse and rubbed his neck, weaving his fingers through his mane. "Hey there, old boy. I've been neglecting you lately, huh? It's hard to get everything done."

That was an understatement. It seemed to Matt that no matter how early he rose in the morning or how late he went to bed, there were never enough hours in a day to get everything done.

Bowie thrust his head over the fence and nuzzled Matt's hand, making him chuckle. He ached to saddle his horse up and go for a ride, even just a short one, but there wasn't time. Supper would be ready soon, and he needed to split wood before then.

Still rubbing Bowie's neck, Matt leaned against the fence and surveyed the land. He had wondered for a time if he could survive another week, let alone over a month. And yet here he was in June, still hanging on. He'd made it through the planting, putting in long days until the fields were planted and he was exhausted. But there wasn't much time to rest between planting and the first round of haying. That was yet another new lesson Matt had needed to learn. Josiah had taught him how to use a scythe and then how to rake the hay after it was down.

Finally, Matt, Josiah, and Zane had started on the task of putting up the dry hay—a chore that Matt found he actually enjoyed. While Sarah drove the team of horses, Emily and her mother prepared lunch for everyone. It was funny how working with other people could turn a big job almost into a party. And seeing all the hay neatly tucked away in the hayloft felt fulfilling, giving him a sense of pride as he reflected on a job well done.

Matt's gaze fell on the soddy, and he let it linger. Things had been going surprisingly well between him and Emily. She hadn't scolded him as often, and he'd been doing his best to stay on her good side. Grant and Austin had accepted him as unavoidable. They still refused to get too close to him, but they had offered him a couple of shy smiles when they were near the protection of their mother.

They might not be friends, but all of them were learning to get along.

The door opened and Joyanna came bounding outside. "Hi, Uncle Matt! You got more chores to do?"

As she neared him, her foot caught on something, and she stumbled. Matt moved quickly and caught her before she could hit the ground.

"Be careful," he said, helping her stand back up.

Joyanna grinned back at him. "Sorry. Can I help you with your chores?"

"I'm done. I was going to cut some wood until your mama has supper ready."

"Can I come with you?"

Matt sighed. "I guess." He leveled a stern expression at her. "But if you get too close, I'll send you inside, all right?"

Joyanna bobbed her head in agreement. "All right. Thanks, Uncle Matt."

Giving Bowie a final pat, Matt picked up the grain bucket, and they both walked toward the barn to put it away. Joyanna tried to grab his hand, but Matt pulled it out of reach. She acted just as taken with him as ever. He found himself constantly having to steel himself against her, reminding himself not to let her too close. But she *did* have a way of growing on a person. Matt feared that if he wasn't more careful, his heart might soften too much.

Matt left the bucket in the barn and grabbed the ax, resting it on his shoulder. Then he set off for the woodlot next to the soddy. Joyanna skipped alongside him, humming to herself.

"Uncle Matt, do you have three names?"

"What?"

"Three names," she repeated. "I do. My whole name is Joyanna Margaret Keath. The Margaret is after my Grandma Mayfield, and the Anna is after my Grandma Keath that I never met 'cause she got deaded."

His mother. Matt flinched, wishing the girl wouldn't talk so bluntly about death. Looking down at Joyanna, he realized that she *did* look a lot like his mother. His memories of Ma had blurred with time, but her picture had always hung over the fireplace when he was a boy. He knew every detail of that image —he had studied it every day in an attempt to recapture those fading memories.

"What about you?" Joyanna asked. "Do you have three names?"

"Sure. My full name is Matthew Grant Keath."

Joyanna's face brightened. "Keath, just like me, huh? And you've even got the same name as Grant."

Of course, Matt was tempted to respond. Instead, he chose to remain polite. "My pa's name was Grant. He would've been your grandpa."

They arrived at the woodlot, where Matt placed the ax in preparation to cut some logs. There were only a few trees in this part of the state, usually planted and cared for by settlers, with wild trees growing near riverbanks. Most of these trees were small but could be used as fuel, something highly valued in this area.

Matt raised the ax above his head and slammed it down onto the log. The blade sank into the wood, but Matt could tell that the edge wasn't as sharp as it should have been. *Bother.* He'd noticed it was getting dull the last time he used it, but he'd forgotten to sharpen it. Now he would need to trudge back out to the barn and re-sharpen the ax, and that would delay how much wood he could chop before dinner.

Matt muttered an expletive under his breath, threw the wood he'd just split onto the pile against the side of the soddy, and grabbed his ax. He started to stomp back toward the barn when Joyanna said, "Uncle Matt."

Matt turned, surprised she was still there. But then, he shouldn't have been surprised. She was always trying to get as close to him as possible.

Joyanna shook her head slowly, her eyes full of reproach. "You've done it again. You said you weren't gonna use those words anymore, remember? The bad ones."

"Oh." Matt could have smacked himself. *This* was what he got for failing to take more care with his tongue—yet another lecture from his niece. "I'm sorry. I'll try harder not to say those things."

Joyanna didn't look appeased. "You shouldn't say them *ever*. But since you just did, you're gonna have to wash your mouth."

Matt blinked. "What? But—"

"You made a promise," Joyanna reminded him. "And when you promise something, you've always got to do your best to keep it."

She really meant to hold him to his word. Matt wanted to argue, but he *was* the one who had agreed to her terms. If he wanted to avoid the mouth washing then he shouldn't have cursed.

"Look. I've got wood that I need to chop..." He gestured toward the stack, hoping she'd let him off the hook.

"You can do that *after* you wash your mouth out." Joyanna shot him a stern glance that reminded him of Emily.

There was no getting out of this. Matt was stuck, and now he'd have to take it like a man.

Matt set his ax against the wall. "All right. I'll get some soap and wash my mouth out."

Her shoulders relaxed. "Good. Do you want Mama to help?"

"No!" Matt swung around to give her his full attention. "I don't think your mama needs to know anything about this, all right?"

Joyanna seemed to think about it for a moment, and at last she nodded. "I guess."

Matt breathed a sigh of relief and turned to fetch the soap. He might as well get this over with as fast as possible.

≈

It was no wonder a mouth washing was the punishment for using profanity. The bitter taste and stinging sensation lingered, and Matt figured he'd be talking funny for a week.

After rinsing his mouth out with water at least a couple dozen times, Matt lifted his head from the pump and ran his hand down the damp stubble on his jaw. His gaze fell on Joyanna, who had hovered at his side the whole time just to make sure he used the soap long enough. "Are you satisfied?" he asked, trying not to sound too sarcastic.

"You did good." She gave him a nod of approval. "And now you won't ever say that again, right?"

"Right." Matt was sure that if he had to put up with that punishment again, his tongue would become permanently damaged. "And you won't tell your mama, remember?"

"Nope." Joyanna rocked back on her heels to look up at him. "Have you ever washed your mouth out with soap? Before now, I mean."

"No. It's not something I'd do for fun."

"Did your mama ever make you do it?"

"My mama? No, she died when I was only five." Funny how the pain had never completely left. The thought of Mama still made Matt's heart ache.

Joyanna was quiet for a moment, her eyebrows drawn together. "My pa's deaded, and I'm five, too. I guess we aren't too much different, huh?"

Matt stared at her, surprised she'd formed such a connection. He never had.

She'd lost her father, and he'd lost his mother. And of course she was hurting, just like he'd hurt when his mama was taken away. He was too familiar with the feelings of insecurity, the hurt, and the grief that came when an important person was taken from this life. No one could take their place. Their role was too big for just anyone to come along and fill.

As Matt gazed at his niece, something within him cracked. It was wrong that a small child should have to suffer so much sadness, and he desired to protect her from any more hurt. It was too late to think about keeping her at arm's length. She had already stolen a place in his heart.

Swallowing hard, Matt reached out and rested a hand on her shoulder. "You're right. I guess we aren't all that different."

CHAPTER 15

Emily glanced across the table at Matt for what must have been the tenth time during supper. He was strangely subdued tonight, and she couldn't figure out why. It had been odd enough when Matt and Joyanna came inside hand in hand, Joyanna chattering away with her usual abandon. Normally he wanted her as far away from him as possible. And now he'd hardly said a word since praying for the meal.

"How was your day?" Emily asked, buttering her slice of bread.

Matt stared at his plate and said nothing.

Emily waited for an answer, then said, "Matthew?"

His gaze snapped to her face. "What? Oh. It was fine." Silence stretched between them, then he asked, "How was your day?"

"Fine."

The clank of forks and knives against their plates filled the silence that followed.

Matt seemed content with the quiet. Emily, however, couldn't settle down and scoured her mind for something else to discuss.

"I saw you with the ax," she said. "Were you able to split much wood?"

Matt couldn't seem to keep eye contact. "No."

Emily took a bite of her bread, frustration welling up inside her. None of her efforts were bearing fruit. She might as well have kept her mouth shut for all the good her words were doing.

But she couldn't completely fault Matt. The two of them never attempted small talk with one another, so why should tonight have been any different?

Because she was tired of talking to herself and to children. Because she missed Colton and being able to have a conversation with another adult. Mealtimes used to be her favorite part of the day, the time when they took a break from their responsibilities and came together around the table for food, talk, and laughter. Nowadays, mealtimes were her least favorite part of the day. No one said much more than "pass the salt, please," or, "good meal."

And no one ever laughed.

"What are you doing this evening?" she asked Matt, making a final attempt at conversation.

Matt shrugged. "Guess I'll chop wood. That stove seems to eat it like a starving critter."

"That would be good. I used up quite a bit of wood with wash day yesterday and ironing today."

Matt nodded. And just like that, the conversation was over.

Before Emily had time to feel irked, Joyanna leaned toward Matt and whispered, "Uncle Matt, you forgot the soap outside."

Matt sank lower in his seat, his face reddening. "I thought we weren't going to talk about that," he whispered back to Joyanna.

"I didn't break my promise. I didn't tell Mama about the mouth washing. All I said was you gotta remember to bring the soap inside."

Mouth washing? Emily fixed her attention on Matt, waiting for an explanation.

Matt's flush deepened. "Now you've done it," he muttered, glaring at Joyanna.

Joyanna's wide blue eyes revealed her innocence. "Done what?"

Matt seemed to struggle to find the right words. At last he hissed, "*It.*"

"Oh!" Joyanna clapped a hand over her mouth. "Sorry, Uncle Matt!"

"Would one of you please explain?" Emily darted her gaze from one to the other.

Matt released a sigh that sounded more like a growl. "It wasn't important."

Joyanna shook her head slowly at him. "My pa always says that every sin is important, and that we should never try to make it seem insig–insignif–something."

"*Insignificant,*" Emily corrected.

Matt pushed back from the table and stood, hands fisted at his sides. "That's not what I meant, and both of you know it. Everyone around here's always trying to twist my words." He stomped toward the door and yanked it open. "I'm going to go chop some wood."

Joyanna's expression crumpled. "I said I was sorry, Uncle Matt. I didn't mean to break my promise."

Her words jerked Matt to a stop. He swallowed, then released the door handle and returned to the table. Stopping in front of Joyanna, he knelt until he was at eye level with her. "I'm sorry. It's all right, Joyanna. I didn't mean to get upset." He stopped, then mumbled again, "I'm sorry."

Then Matt stood and walked back to the door, shutting it behind him as he left.

Matt's apology echoed in Emily's ears. He was sorry? That was new.

She rubbed her forehead, baffled at how a regular conversation could descend into such chaos. She had tried her best to be cordial this evening, yet things still went wrong the same way they always did when Emily and Matt were together.

Austin fussed from the chair where Emily had secured him with a towel, and Emily guessed he was probably ready to nurse. The cleaning of the supper dishes would need to wait.

As she untied Austin and scooped him into her arms, Emily released a deep sigh. The loneliness of the cabin crept in even closer with Matt's departure, threatening to smother her. If only Ma, Sadie, or Sarah were there to keep her company.

Or, most of all, Colton.

You really must be one of the worst men on earth. How could you go and make Joyanna cry like that? Especially after you realized that you care about her too?

Matt's thoughts seemed to beat at his mind in rhythm to the thud of the ax. He split wood until his shirt was drenched with sweat and his arms burned, but he still couldn't seem to escape the accusing voices in his mind.

The problem with you is that when you lose your temper, you just let it all out, even when you try to hold it in. It leaks out anyway, and then somebody gets hurt. It's no wonder Emily doesn't like you.

Matt swung the ax harder, his breathing ragged. He wanted to be a better man, he truly did, but it just didn't seem to work. He'd been attending church, reading a passage from the Bible each day, and praying. He even tried to clean up his language, but none of the changes seemed to go any deeper than the skin.

He had to try harder. Surely if he really set his mind to it, he could improve,

He did possess a lot of willpower. If he put that behind his desire to be better, it would work, right?

Yeah, just like how it "worked" with the profanity. He'd tried hard on that, yet he still messed up.

But Matt wasn't willing to give up just yet. There had to be some way for him to become more like Colton and not so much a man who let everything spill out. He could never take Colton's place, but he was here and Colton wasn't. Without their father, those children at least deserved a good uncle. Matt only wished he could talk to Colton. His brother would have known how to help him.

But now that he thought of it—he did have all the letters Colton had written to him over the years. He hadn't thrown away a single one.

Matt drove his ax into the log before him, splitting it in half. He picked up the two pieces and tossed them onto the wood-pile, then brushed the dirt and chips of wood from his hands. It was time to get some answers. Maybe the key to becoming a better man had been before him all along.

Shouldering his ax, he set off for the barn, unable to keep from whistling. He should have thought to read Colton's letters a long time ago.

Matt slipped into the barn and stashed the ax away, then rushed up the ladder that led to the loft where he kept his bedroll, saddle bags, and other belongings. Pitch darkness swallowed the hayloft, but Matt had become used to finding his way around without the light. He rummaged around until he found his saddle bag, then he picked it up and started back toward the ladder.

Matt climbed down, the saddle bag tucked under one arm. Bringing it over to the workbench, he set it down to light the lantern. He wouldn't have dared bring the lantern up to the hayloft—that was just asking for a fire—but there wasn't too much danger here with the lantern on a level surface. Besides, he was right there and would keep an eye on it.

Matt opened his saddle bag and drew out the packet of

Colton's letters, picking up the top envelope, the first letter Matt had received from his brother out West. Matt read through each letter, beginning with Colton's time working in Ohio and ending with his settling near what would become Osceola. Matt was especially interested when Emily's name first appeared after a Christmas program the year of his arrival. Colton seemed to have been impressed with her from that day onward, writing that he'd never met a woman who affected him like Emily Mayfield.

Neither had Matt. He had never met a woman who stepped on his nerves so much.

Matt continued, reading about Colton and Emily's courtship, their wedding, and Colton's plea for Matt to visit.

Matt flinched. If only he had.

Then came Joyanna's birth.

She has a way of grabbing your heart right from the first. I never realized until now just how special a little girl can be.

Then came the summer following Joyanna's birth, the year a swarm of grasshoppers blotted out the sky and devoured every living thing, dashing the farmers' hopes of a good harvest. Matt was hit with a wave of sadness he hadn't felt when he first read Colton's letter. He might not be a farmer, but he felt protective of the growing crops in his fields. The thought of something happening to them sickened him.

By the time he read about Grant's and Austin's births in the letters, Matt could hardly keep his eyes open. Putting the letters back into his saddlebag, Matt blew out the lamp and climbed up the ladder to his bedroll.

Rather than the surge of hope he'd expected to feel after Colton's letters, emptiness gnawed at Matt. Colton made it appear so easy to be a good person. Compared to Matt's flaws, Colton had been perfection itself. Was Matt just a hopeless case?

No, that couldn't be. He had to try harder.

Lying there in the dark, Matt pieced together a plan for the next day and every day after that. He would try to become more like Colton. More patient. A better man.

Your efforts aren't going to be good enough.

Matt groaned and pushed the thought aside. He couldn't allow himself to consider the idea.

As he was just about to drift off, it hit him that tomorrow was the first of July. He growled and rolled onto his side, burying his head in his arms. Of all the days to make this decision, why did he have to pick Colton's birthday to make these changes? He dreaded thinking about the next day. The day Colton would have turned twenty-nine.

Would have.

Matt was beginning to hate those words with a passion.

CHAPTER 16

A new day meant a fresh start for Matt—even if it was Colton's birthday.

He grabbed the milk pail and closed the barn door behind him. Things could be worse. Snooty hadn't attempted to spill the milk this morning, but she had stepped on his foot. It hadn't felt good, but Matt refused to do anything other than grit his teeth.

Now if he could just endure the rest of this day . . .

Matt had just secured the door when a bright bolt of lightning illuminated the sky, followed by a deluge of rain. He held the milk bucket close and ran for the house, keeping his head tucked so that his hat took the brunt of the downpour. It seemed that the rain was settling in to give the ground a good soaking and would block him from the fields today. Of all the days to be stuck around the place, why did it have to be on Colton's birthday?

Matt reached the soddy and pushed the door open, stumbling into the room as another bolt of lightning lit the sky and thunder rumbled.

"It sure is coming down out there," he said, closing the door.

The only response he received was a muffled sob from Grant who was curled in the rocker. He'd obviously been crying for a while.

"What happened to you?" Matt asked, moving to strain the milk.

"He fell out of bed." Emily knelt on the floor, rummaging around in a box for something. Her hair still tumbled down her back, uncombed, and the lines on her forehead were etched deeper than usual. "I don't know where I could have put it," she muttered, moving aside something else in the box.

Joyanna walked past Matt, bouncing Austin on her hip to keep him from fussing. Even she seemed to have lost her customary smile.

Maybe it would have been best if everyone just went back to bed and forgot about trying to get through this difficult day.

The sound of the stovetop sizzling alerted Matt to the coffee pot boiling over.

"No!" Emily leaped from the floor and ran for the stove. Using a towel as a potholder, she pushed the coffee pot back off the heat, then grabbed a spoon to stir the eggs. Matt had never claimed to be a cook, but it didn't take a chef to smell that the eggs were beginning to burn.

"Why couldn't something go right today?" Emily muttered at the stove.

Once Matt was done straining the milk, he slipped outside to deliver it to the well. He pulled out the empty basket from below and placed the jars of milk inside, then sent it back down into the depths of the well. The job didn't take as long as he would have liked, and he was tempted to loiter on his errand just to get away from the soddy a little longer. But the wind picked up and the rain came down harder than before. He dashed the rest of the way back to the soddy.

He burst through the door, his wet clothes clinging to his frame. Water trickled down his face from his hair and puddled beneath him. He pulled off his Stetson and gave his head a shake, sending more water droplets flying.

Emily turned to look at him. "Oh my. You're soaked clear through."

Yes. He was well aware. Matt clenched his jaw to keep his teeth from chattering.

"Here, let me get you a towel." Emily grabbed a dry towel and brought it to him. "You ought to change out of those clothes or you're going to catch a chill."

"I'll be fine. After breakfast, I'm going to head to the barn to get something done, so I'll be getting wet again anyway." His heart warmed at the thought that she cared about him and his health—at least a little.

"That would be the last thing we need, you getting sick. There's enough work around here without you taking ill because you got wet in a rainstorm." Emily's words doused that warm feeling.

"I've got a better constitution than that." A bite crept into his words, but then Matt remembered that he was trying to guard his temper. Pasting on a smile, he added, "This towel will do me just fine, thank you."

Emily still seemed worried, and she urged him to take her spot nearer the fire. Matt chaffed at being told what to do, but he knew it would be unwise to contest her. So he obediently went where she asked and sat.

Emily returned to the stove. As Matt listened to her worry over the eggs, he decided that today she was going out of her way to find things to fret over. Maybe it was just a way of coping and trying to keep her mind off Colton.

"*Ma-a-a,*" Grant called from the rocker.

"What is it?" Emily asked, sounding distracted.

"Wanna be held."

"Not now. Mama's busy."

The boy's pout grew deeper, a clear sign that if something

wasn't done soon, he would throw a tantrum.

Matt gripped the edge of his seat, debating with himself. He could grab the boy and quiet him—or wait for Emily to deal with his fussing. After all, he never held the boy.

But today is a new day, and you're going to be different from now on.

That was true. Inhaling deeply, Matt rose from his spot and moved to the rocking chair. "C'mon, Grant," he said, scooping the boy into his arms.

Grant looked up at Matt, and his eyes widened. He released a piercing shriek, flailing in Matt's arms.

Caught off guard, Matt staggered to regain his balance. A small fist struck him in the nose, and boots drummed against his midsection. He flinched.

Before he could tighten his grip on the boy, Grant slipped out of his arms and fell to the floor.

Emily shrieked, pressing her hand against her heart. "What do you think you're doing?"

Joyanna stopped jiggling Austin and stared, her eyes reflecting genuine horror that Uncle Matt would dare abuse her precious brother.

Grant ran for safety behind Emily's skirts, piercing Matt's ear drums with his screams. The boy was obviously doing just fine if his screams were loud enough to almost break the roof.

Emily marched the few steps over to Matt, her eyes flashing. "Matthew Keath, you tell me right now, what were you trying to do to Grant?"

Matt raised his hands. "I was just trying to help."

"*Help?* By throwing Grant on the floor?" She planted her hands on her hips. "Is that your version of *help*?"

She was nothing short of furious when her children were wronged, as if she were a mother bear ready to pounce. Matt half feared he was about to get a slap across the face. He nervously stumbled back, but she kept right on coming for him.

Matt kept his palms faced outward. "I didn't expect him to react like that." Grant didn't react that way to his uncle Ephraim or to his uncle Zane.

"You never even hold him. Why did you think you should now?"

"He wanted to be held."

Emily eased back, her forehead furrowed. "I don't understand."

"Well I don't understand *him*." Matt pointed at Grant who remained standing next to the stove.

"Next time, think before you act." Emily rubbed her temples and blew out her breath. "Breakfast is ready, so sit down."

Matt would think twice before he dared to come within arm's length of Grant again.

Matt sat at the table close to the fire. Joyanna pulled her chair up to his, her presence assuring Matt that at least *she* forgave him for dropping her brother.

Emily took her seat and folded her hands, signaling for Matt to say the blessing. Matt bit his lip. If only he could skip saying the blessing today. His thoughts couldn't stop churning around Colton and his absence. Matt knew that Emily wanted him to be honest in his prayers, but if he were truly honest in speaking to the Lord, he might start screaming against the injustice of it all.

Suddenly, an idea hit him. "Joyanna, do you want to pray for us today?"

Joyanna blinked. After a moment of considering, she smiled and nodded "Dear God," she began, lowering her head, "thank you for this food that Mama's cooked, and thank you for it rainin', but please help it not to leak through the roof too bad today, 'cause that's pretty hard to deal with. Thanks for Mama and Grant and Austin and Uncle Matt and Pa, and thanks for it bein' Pa's birthday today. We wish Pa was here, but since he's not, please take good care of him in heaven. Thanks for all You do for us. In Jesus' name, amen."

Matt responded with a nod and even managed to produce a small grin, though his vision blurred from tears.

Each of them dished their plates in silence, aside from the sound of the rain drumming against the roof. Matt glanced toward the leaky corner. Sure enough, a drop of muddy rainwater plopped to the floor.

Something ought to be done about that roof. If the rain came down for longer than a day, this place would turn into a pond.

Matt risked a glance across the table at Emily. Although she looked down at her plate, she seemed to be pushing her food around more than she was eating.

Matt cleared his throat. "Do you have plans for the day?"

She continued to prod at her egg with her fork. "Yes. Survive."

"Oh."

Silence stretched into awkwardness.

"Good breakfast."

Finally, Emily glanced up at him. "Don't you dare say that, Matthew. Just say the plain truth that the eggs and ham are burned, and the porridge is lumpy. It's terrible!"

"Better than most meals I've cooked."

"Then I pity anyone who ever ate your meals. It must have nearly been suicide."

Well. All Matt had tried to do was cheer her up a little, and instead she lashed back at him.

He chose to change the subject to neutral ground. "The other day I saw an article in the paper that said farmers were expecting—"

Emily jerked back in her chair. "Who cares what the paper says? I certainly don't."

Matt's irritation kindled. "I was only trying to make conversation."

"Conversation! You of all people care about conversation?" Emily gave a short laugh that was anything but mirthful. "First, you try to grab Grant, and then you try to make conversation. What's wrong with you today?"

"What's *wrong* with me?" Matt repeated, his voice growing louder. "What's wrong with *you?*"

"Stop yelling, Matthew. You'll scare the children."

Matt took in a long breath and released it slowly, trying to keep his temper in check. "Like I said. It's nice to have someone else to talk to instead of being stuck talking to just myself or the animals."

"Then why wouldn't you talk to me last night? I tried to start a conversation and you hardly said anything!"

"What? I don't remember that." Matt thought back to the night before. Everything had been peaceful before Joyanna brought up the mouth washing incident. Emily hadn't said anything.

Or had she? Now that he thought about it, it did seem like she'd said something to him—but he couldn't remember what it was. He'd been too busy trying to sort out his thoughts.

"What did you say last night?" he finally asked.

"It doesn't matter now. You don't care anyway." Emily stood and stomped across the room to the dish tub, thrusting her plate into the water with enough force that her frame quivered.

"What do you mean I don't care?" Matt watched as she grabbed a rag and scrubbed at one of the dirty pans, her skirts swaying with her effort.

"You don't care about any of us. Not really."

Matt's breathing hitched, his heart thumping painfully against his ribs. "You have no right to say that. I wouldn't be here if I didn't care."

"I still doubt it." Emily rinsed the pan and set it down with a *thud*.

"I care about you for Colton's sake."

Emily turned from the dish tub, tears streaming down her cheeks. "I'm not sure I trust that."

Her tears unnerved Matt. He couldn't stand watching a woman cry. He may have run straight from the room if her gaze hadn't pinned him to his seat.

"You don't trust me," he said slowly, her words still sinking in. "But Colton—"

"Colton! Did you really care about Colton?" Emily's question spilled out about as fast as her tears. "You never act like you miss him. You go on living like he's not even gone. You don't talk about him. Do you ever even think about him?"

Matt recoiled, feeling as if he'd been struck. No, worse. How could she dare think he didn't care about Colton? Didn't she realize that his whole world had crumbled around him since Colton's death?

His heart bled out just as much as hers did.

Matt tried to speak, but words escaped him.

Joyanna broke down in tears beside him. "I don't like fights."

Grant and Austin joined in, and the sound of their combined sobs drowned out the noise of the rain outside.

Emily covered her face with her hands, shoulders shaking. "I'm sorry." Her words came as a gasp. "I didn't mean that."

"I think you did." His voice rasped through the air—cold, a reflection of how he felt on the inside.

Matt pushed back from the table and stood. "Go on and let it out. Tell me you hate me. I know you want to." It was the bitter truth, and Matt couldn't deny it any longer.

Emily shook her head, hands still clamped over her face. "It's not that I hate you. I only wish—" She stopped, but Matt knew what was left unsaid.

His voice shook as he choked out, "Bringing him back is beyond my abilities."

With one last look at Emily, Matt stepped outside and closed the door firmly behind him.

CHAPTER 17

Matt secluded himself in the barn for the remainder of the day, too heartsick to return inside. He'd tried so hard to please Emily and the kids, but he would never meet their expectations. He wasn't Colton. He couldn't change who he was.

He would have felt better if Emily had kicked him in the chest rather than slung those words at him, accusing him of being callous.

At noon, Emily called that it was time for dinner, but he ignored her. He wasn't hungry, and he had no inclination to go inside and sit. He would only add tension to the already uncomfortable atmosphere of the soddy.

Footsteps approached from outside. Matt tensed and ducked out the barn's north door. The footsteps drew closer, and then a knock tapped on the south door.

"Matthew?" Emily called. "It's dinner time."

Matt leaned against the wall and closed his eyes, wishing she'd go away and leave him alone. He didn't want to be fussed over.

"Matthew?"

The barn door creaked open. Emily's footsteps rustled the straw as she entered.

"I know you're here." Silence stretched. "Matthew, I'm sorry. I shouldn't have said what I did. It was wrong, and—and I'm terribly sorry."

Matt refused to respond. He wasn't ready to talk to her yet. The ache was too deep.

Emily sighed and finally turned back toward the barn's entrance. "Come in when you're ready. I'll save a plate for you."

The door swung shut, leaving Matt in the stillness. He waited a few minutes then slipped inside again, clothes damp from the rain. Returning to the worktable, he slumped onto the bench and rested his forehead against both palms. Each throb of his heart thudded through his temples.

Tools lay scattered across the worktable's surface, but he couldn't summon the focus to work on repairs. He jerked to his feet again and paced the barn floor from one side to the other.

He couldn't stand this any longer. He was tired of dealing with one problem after another. This trip had devolved into a mess that he *had* to escape from.

There isn't anyone holding you here. You could go back West, a voice whispered. *It was Emily's suggestion from the start that you go back West. She didn't want you here and she clearly despises you.*

Matt flinched and walked faster. He hated the idea of giving up. He'd vowed that he would stay on the farm until harvest, and the corn was nowhere near ready to be brought in for the winter.

Matt could see the mocking gleam in Flick's eyes as clearly as if he were standing before him, could hear the words he would spew at him. "Well, Matt, you lasted longer than I thought you could, but it was too much to expect for you to make it until harvest. You never should have left cattle country, but I suppose you know that now, huh? Playing farmer might be fun for a little bit, but you've eventually gotta get back to real life."

And Keller was sure to laugh at Matt when he found out that he'd given up and returned to Scottsbluff. "So much for taking care of the family," he would say. "You should have taken that job I offered when you had the chance. Now you lose all around."

Matt clenched his hand into a fist. He never liked admitting that he was licked, but he'd handled about as much as any man could. He should have left long ago, before he tangled his heart into his work and had it torn to pieces.

Now was the time to leave. The longer he stayed, the deeper the knife would cut into his heart. He hurt every time he saw disappointment in Joyanna's eyes. He hurt when the boys shied away from him despite his attempts to befriend them. And he ached when Emily shot him that glare that made him feel like he was nothing compared to Colton, like she couldn't stand the mere sight of him.

Matt paced the room, debating with himself until the unrelenting sound of rain pelting the rooftop threatened to drive him crazy. His departure was in everyone's best interest. Emily had family and neighbors to assist her with farm work before Matt showed up; why couldn't she rely on them when he left?

Matt collapsed onto the workbench and buried his face in his hands. He never should have come. He'd caused far more trouble than he was worth.

The door creaked open. Matt jerked upright and swung around, wishing he could just disappear. He didn't want to talk to anyone. Especially Emily.

But it wasn't Emily who stepped into the barn.

Josiah entered the room wearing his perpetual smile. "Why, Matt, how good to see you! Mind if I visit with you for a while? I left Margaret at the house, and she and Emily will be chattering about their womanly things. Gets downright boring at times."

Josiah didn't wait for Matt to respond before he grabbed a nearby pail and flipped it upside down, then sat across from Matt. "How are you doing?"

Matt dropped his gaze to the floor, unable to meet his eyes. "Fine."

"Are you sure?" Josiah's voice was gentle, but it held something subtle that called Matt out on his lie. "I know today is probably tough, with it being Colton's birthday and all. That first birthday is always hard, realizing all anew that your loved one is gone."

The back of Matt's eyes began to burn. "It can be hard." Inhaling to steady his emotions, Matt pushed his brother from his mind. "I'm going to head back to Scottsbluff. It's high time that I got back to doing something I'm good at. It's clear to everyone that farming is not a strength of mine."

"You're leaving?" Josiah sounded mildly surprised. "I thought you were staying until harvest."

"I was, but..." Matt shrugged. How could he explain that Emily was the reason he was leaving? She was Josiah's daughter, so he had to be careful about his choice of words. "There are others who can be a better help to Emily than what I can offer. Men who are real farmers, not fakes."

Josiah reached out and patted Matt's knee. "You've been doing just fine. You're learning fast, and things look good around here."

Matt wanted to say that he hated farming, but the words froze on his tongue. Hatred wasn't the right word. Farming had its own rewards, and if it weren't for all the conflict, then maybe he would have *wanted* to stay.

The idea was so foreign that Matt couldn't catch his next breath. He would miss seeing his crops harvested in the fall. He'd looked forward to seeing how they turned out.

"The kids will miss you," Josiah said.

Matt snorted. "No. They already have two good uncles, so they don't need me. They'll count my absence a blessing. The boys are scared stiff of me."

"Joyanna loves you to pieces."

The simple words penetrated deep into Matt's heart, unleashing more pain. He swallowed. "I guess so. But I don't know why. I've never done anything to deserve her love." He hesitated. "I've tried to be more worthy of it lately, but it doesn't work. Despite all my good intentions, I've made her cry twice in the last two days. She's a sweet girl and so easy to please that I don't have any excuse. There's just something wrong with me." He laughed, trying to rid the comment of some of its weight, but the sound was hollow.

Josiah looked beyond Matt. "I've heard of worse cases. I know one man who worked for the railroad, and every time he came home from one of his stints, his children ran and hid from him. His very own flesh and blood. And his wife was always upset with him because of the language he used around his family, because he refused to go to church, and because he never thought of anyone other than himself. He thought he was doing all he needed by making a paycheck that provided for his family's physical needs."

Josiah looked at Matt intently. An idea popped into Matt's head that he found too absurd to voice.

"You're right." Josiah nodded, confirming Matt's suspicion. "I was that man. Sometimes I have a hard time believing it myself. Did you know that at one time I had six children? The last three were younger than Sarah."

Matt shook his head. He had no idea.

"They died. Whooping cough. It took all three of them within mere days of each other. I wasn't there when they died—didn't even know they were sick until I stepped through the door and Margaret laid into me for always being gone when she needed me." Josiah's eyes glistened. "Of course, there was nothing I could do then. Nothing but help bury them."

Matt's chest squeezed tight, making it hard to force out the words, "I'm sorry."

"So am I." Josiah leaned forward, pinching the bridge of his nose. "But terrible as that time was, the Lord can use even the bad things to accomplish His purposes. As ironic as it may sound, their deaths paved the way for a spiritual awakening within me. I realized that I'd been living life my own way, doing my own thing, and as a result, I never really knew those three precious children of mine. I was always gone."

He looked up, regret carving lines upon his face. "And when I was home, they wouldn't get near me. They'd only cling to Margaret. I'll admit—that upset me. But it was only natural. I was a stranger to them. It was my own fault that I'd never attempted to win their affection." A deep sigh shuddered his shoulders. "After they were gone, I recognized that I had been a terrible man, but Margaret showed me I could surrender my will to the Lord, accept His forgiveness and live as a new man by His grace. I had no power to make myself better—it was all Him working within me who cleaned away my sins and made me anew."

Matt shifted, fidgeting with a splinter on the work table. "I take it that you're pretty sure there's a God?"

"Sure I do." Josiah's voice rang with a certainty Matt envied. "I can see God's fingerprints everywhere I look, in nature, in history—even in my own life. I've seen Him work in such a powerful way that nothing can match it. I can see in His Word who He is, and most convincing of all, I can feel what He has done in me, changing my desires so that I wish to live for Him and not myself."

"But here's what I don't understand." Matt spoke slowly, his insides churning. He hated making himself vulnerable—but he was too desperate *not* to. "If God really is in control of everything, then why does He allow bad things to happen? Like Colton and my parents dying. What did they ever do to deserve to die?" Tears blurred Matt's vision. "It feels like He's taken away everyone I care about."

Josiah laid his hand on Matt's shoulder. "Son, I can't say why Colton and your parents died, but I can tell you this. I trust God even when I can't clearly see what He's doing, and I know that His plan is far greater than what I can comprehend." Josiah gave Matt's shoulder a squeeze. "And you know what? It's hard when someone we love dies, but our loved ones—those who knew Christ—have only gone on ahead of us. Colton and your folks are in heaven in the glory of God, where there's no more pain or sorrow. If there's anyone to feel sorry for, it's not them, but rather us who are still here on earth."

The tears refused to be restrained any longer. Matt covered his face with his hands, struggling to control his sobs.

"It's all right, son. Just let it out. There's nothing wrong with a man crying, and don't let anyone ever make you think so." Josiah patted Matt's back gently in a soothing, fatherly way.

"I just want Colton back! Why would God send me here when Emily and the kids need Colton and not me? I'm just not good enough. I want Colton back." Matt's sobs filled the room as he was overwhelmed with emotion—something he hadn't experienced since his mother had passed away when he was five. Josiah stayed silent, giving him support by simply rubbing his back.

At last, the sobs subsided and Matt sat a little straighter.

"Better?" Josiah asked, offering him a clean handkerchief.

Matt accepted it and blew his nose. "Maybe. There's still a lot I don't understand."

Josiah smiled. "Join the rest of us. It's hard when we don't know what to make of what's going on around, but knowing the One who controls it all is a big source of comfort."

Matt let the idea linger. Perhaps Josiah was right. He'd

already found that ignoring God was *not* a comfortable way to live. "You never finished your story."

"I didn't? What did I leave out?"

"How did you make things right with your wife and kids?"

"Ah." Josiah leaned back on his bucket, hooking one ankle over his knee. "After I made the ultimate decision to give my life to the Lord, that part was simple. You see, before I'd experienced the Lord's love for me, I had no idea of what true love was. I always thought it was a feeling that certain people pulled out of you in various strengths.

"But then I learned that true love is a choice, even when it doesn't come easily. It's not selfish. It's about giving to the one I love, even when I don't feel like it. After I learned that, it became easier to love Margaret, Ephraim, Emily, and Sarah. And they were willing to forgive me for neglecting them. It's still a wonder." Josiah shook his head slowly. "I quit my job with the railroad so I could have more time with family, even though that left us with little money to live on. When the opportunity came, we decided to come here to Osceola to homestead. And you know all that happened after that."

Matt nodded, his mind spinning.

Josiah remained silent for a moment, then leaned forward. "If I were you, I'd wait on making any final decisions about leaving."

Matt sighed. He may as well come clean before the older man. After all, Josiah had been honest with *him*. "I'd be willing to stay, but Emily doesn't want me to."

"She doesn't?" Josiah's eyebrows lifted. "Then why did she ask me to come out here and make sure you were all right? She's been worried about you all day, and she sounded relieved that your horse was still here. Seems to me that she wants you to stay."

Matt narrowed his gaze at Josiah. Should he believe him, or

would that just be wishful thinking? "Emily and I haven't been getting along too well. We haven't since the day I arrived."

Josiah gave a slow nod. Maybe the man knew all along how things were going in the Keath home. He'd only been waiting to offer his advice until it was requested.

"Perhaps you should pray about it," Josiah said. "You'd be surprised at how powerful prayer is, not just for the person you're praying for, but for you too. Sometimes it changes the person who's praying even more profoundly than the person who is being prayed for."

"I've never thought much about God. Not until coming here," Matt admitted.

"But now?"

"Now..." Matt drew a deep breath. "I'd like to know more about Him. And I want to know more about how to love. Will you pray with me?"

Josiah's face creased into a smile. "Son, I'd be happy to."

CHAPTER 18

Emily huddled across the table from her mother, teacup clenched between her hands. The room should have felt cozy with the fire crackling in the stove behind her and raindrops bouncing off the windowpane, but the emotions tearing through her annihilated any comfort she might have otherwise felt.

Thinking back to how she'd treated Matt earlier that morning made Emily want to sink into the floor with embarrassment. The poor man had done nothing to deserve her tongue lashing. It wasn't his fault that Colton had died, leaving her alone with a young family and a farm to run.

Matt had been most helpful, but rather than thanking him like she should have, Emily had allowed her distrust to flow out for him to see. And more than that, she'd accused him of not even caring about Colton. She'd been wrong. The pain in his eyes had revealed just how deeply he did, in fact, miss his brother.

Why hadn't she noticed before now? Even Sadie had been perceptive enough to guess that he was hurting. But Emily, who saw him every day, had been blind to it. She'd been wrong about many things, and now she had no clue of how to fix it.

"Ah, Emily." Ma held on to Austin with one arm and reached across the table to take Emily's hands. "You're much like me, you know. We both speak too quickly at times. If I could just keep my mouth closed at times, I would save myself a good deal of trouble."

"I always seem to forget in the heat of the moment." Emily looked at her mother helplessly. "What should I do now?"

"A good place to start is to pray."

"I have been. All day."

"The next step would be to apologize to the young man."

"I tried. I'm sure he heard me, but he didn't seem to want to accept my apology." Emily heaved a sigh, tears stinging her eyes.

"Then wait." Ma gave her hands a squeeze. "Take a lesson from this day and remember that being hasty leads to all kinds of trouble. He'll come around eventually."

Emily made a face. She wasn't so sure about that. It would be a wonder if he stayed after today's events.

Emily rose from her seat, crossed to the stove, and picked up the kettle. "Can I pour you more tea?"

Ma shook her head. "This would be my fourth cup. I don't think I can drink any more."

Emily set the kettle back on the stove and returned to her chair, rubbing her temples. How could she feel so tired when she'd accomplished so little? All she wanted to do was crawl into bed and curl beneath the covers, allowing the tears to fall freely.

Some days were harder than others to keep a brave front for the children.

"Things will get better eventually, Emily," Ma said, her voice gentle.

"I miss him so badly, Mama. Some days I don't even want to

keep on living." Emily's chin quivered. "I've never felt so alone before."

Emily closed her eyes, thinking back to the year before. It had been a beautiful day, with clear skies and just the right amount of heat. All day she'd restrained herself from making any mention of Colton's birthday, waiting until evening when Pa and Ma, Ephraim and Sadie, and Zane and Sarah arrived with each of their families. Colton had received the shock of his life when he stepped through the door of the soddy and found them crammed inside, hollering out, "Happy birthday!"

"Happy birthday, dear," Emily told him, throwing herself into his arms.

Colton's arms tightened around her as he looked around, still shaking his head. "I thought you forgot it was my birthday. How long have you been planning this?"

"Long enough." Emily grinned at him. "I love you, Colton."

"You do?" Colton's azure eyes sparkled. "I happen to love you too, Emily. You're an amazing woman, did you know that?"

And then, ignoring the noisy crowd of family that surrounded them, he bent down and kissed her.

That was just one short year ago. Emily blinked quickly, trying to keep the tears from spilling over. She never would have guessed that, come this year, Colton would be in the grave. He'd been so young and strong.

"It will get easier," Ma said again. "Even though that isn't comforting to hear right now. God is still in heaven, and you have not been forsaken by Him. Keep trusting, Emily, and it will get easier."

"Maybe." Emily took a sip from her cup. The tea was luke-warm, and she rose to pour some fresh tea from the kettle. At least *that* was one problem she could fix.

The door handle rattled. Emily swung around, her heart leaping into her throat as her father entered the room. How she hoped he had found Matt.

Pa's gaze met hers and he nodded, stepping farther into the room. Behind him, another figure entered the soddy.

Matt.

Joyanna leapt from the floor where she'd been playing with Grant and flung herself at him. "Uncle Matt! I haven't seen you almost all day. I missed you."

Matt swung her into his arms. "I've missed you too."

His gaze slid to Emily, and he offered her a tentative smile. Emily relaxed and smiled back. He didn't seem upset with her.

"You ready, Margaret?" Pa asked.

Ma set Austin on the floor next to Grant and rose. "Yes, I figure we better get home. Goodbye, Emily. You take care. Good to see you, Matt."

She and Pa both waved, and then they left, the door closing behind them with a soft thud.

Emily exhaled. Now she just needed to be careful with how she proceeded.

"Have a seat, Matthew. I'll get you a plate," Emily said. Even though Matt wasn't a very big man, he still seemed to fill the room. Just like Joyanna, she'd missed his presence today.

"Actually, could we talk first?" he asked. "There's something I want to tell you."

Emily tensed. Maybe he *was* still upset with her. Maybe he intended to leave.

From the day he'd arrived, she'd wanted him gone. But now that his leaving was actually a possibility, she had to fight back her panic. She'd never been so aware of how much he did around the farm and how safe she felt knowing there was a man nearby. If he left, she'd be on her own again, only this time it would be worse. When Colton died, she'd been in a fog and the full reality of her own helplessness hadn't fully set in. Now she was aware of how desperate her situation would be if Matt had left.

Emily sat at the table and motioned him toward the chair

across from her. He settled down, still holding onto Joyanna as if he were never going to let her go.

Emily twisted her hands together in her lap. "Before you say anything, I want you to know just how sorry I am. I was so wrong—"

Matt held up a hand, stopping her. "It's all right, Emily. I don't blame you."

"It still wasn't right—"

"I forgive you." Matt's gaze held hers. "And now, I want to ask, can you forgive me?"

"Forgive you?" Emily tilted her head to one side. "For what?"

"For not being caring. For thinking of myself. For just being me." Matt smiled. "You know I haven't been easy to get along with."

"I haven't been easy to get along with either," Emily admitted.

"I guess we both could use some work. But will you forgive me, Emily?"

"Of course I will."

"Good." Matt's shoulders lowered a little. "Earlier I thought I'd tell you that I was leaving."

Emily didn't dare look at him lest he see just how much she wanted him to stay. "Earlier?"

"Yes, earlier."

Matt was silent for so long that Emily was forced to look at him.

"I know I pushed myself on you in the beginning," he said. "If you don't want me here then I'm willing to leave. I don't want you to feel put out. The decision is entirely yours."

Emily lowered her gaze again. "If you wish to go, that's fine." She swallowed against the lump in her throat. The words were hard to speak, but she didn't want him to feel that he needed to stay, especially if he'd rather go back West.

"And if I wished to stay?"

"That would be fine as well." It was all Emily could do to keep her voice steady.

"What do you say, Joyanna? Would it be okay if I stayed?" Matt gave the little girl on his lap a bounce.

Joyanna didn't blink an eye. "Of course. Where else would you go, Uncle Matt?"

Matt looked toward Grant and Austin. "Is all right with you if I stayed?"

Grant stuck his thumb in his mouth. Both boys leaned toward Emily, but they each rewarded Matt with a shy smile.

Matt laughed. "I'll take that as a yes. Just as long as I keep my distance."

Emily smiled too. "So you'll stay?"

"Seems like I will." He leaned back in his seat. "I'm glad, because I've actually been curious to see how my first crop turns out."

"You wouldn't want to miss out on that." Relief made Emily want to jump out of her seat and dance. "I'm glad you aren't leaving, Matthew."

"So am I. Your father is a wise man, you know?"

"He talked with you?"

"Yes." Matt looked down at the soddy's dirt floor. "Do you remember that line in the song 'Amazing Grace' that talks about being blind, but now seeing?"

Emily nodded, although she didn't see how the hymn pertained to anything in their discussion.

"That's how I feel right now. Like I've been walking in darkness my entire life without even realizing it. But now the scales have fallen off and I can suddenly see." He toyed with the end of Joyanna's braid, wrapping the ribbon around his finger. "It's been a long time since I've been sure that there really is a God. I've been trying with all my might to be a better man, but it didn't seem to accomplish anything. That's because it's impossible. I can't do that in my own strength. I need the Lord to change my heart and His forgiveness for when I fall short." His throat jogged "I've made a lot of mistakes since I've been here. How did you put up with me?"

"I'm not a perfect person either." Emily reached across the table for his hand. He turned his hand palm up, his fingers engulfing her smaller ones. "I'm so glad you've realized that, Matthew. I'm only sorry I didn't help you see it before now."

"I was too knot-headed." A twinkle appeared in his eyes. "Maybe your own stubbornness helped me more than anything. It helped to bring out the worst in me, helping me to see that I really wasn't as good of a person as I thought I was."

"What? I've heard of people telling others that they bring out the best in them, but what kind of a compliment is it to say that 'you bring out the worst in me'?"

Matt tipped his head back and laughed. "You know, I'm pretty hungry. I'd love some of whatever it is that you're cooking for supper."

Emily shook her head. "I don't know what to do with you. First, you tell me that I bring out the worst in you, and then you ask me to provide you with supper."

"Please? I'll try to be on my best behavior."

"As much as you can manage around me, hmm?" Emily almost laughed, something she hadn't done since Colton's passing. Her heart warm, she stood and moved to the stove to check on supper.

"The last thing I want to say is that I love you, Joyanna. You too, boys."

Joyanna threw her arms around Matt's neck. "I love you too, Uncle Matt."

Matt held one arm toward the boys. Grant and Austin stood in the middle of the floor, Grant's thumb still tucked in his mouth. Emily was sure they would run back to her. Instead, both of them inched forward. Matt pulled them and Joyanna close to him in a big embrace.

Tears sprang to Emily's eyes. But unlike her earlier tears, she didn't mind these. These were tears of happiness as she watched her family begin to heal after being so deeply hurt by Colton's death.

If Colton could see his younger brother just now, he'd be mighty pleased with him. Emily was sure of it.

CHAPTER 19

Cicadas hummed outside the open window as Matt set his plate in the basin. Another day was almost through—a good day, even if the fields were still too wet to work in after yesterday's rain. Instead, he had spent his time fixing the boundary fence so that Snooty wouldn't have an opportunity to escape.

At a tug on his arm, he turned to find Joyanna at his side

"Uncle Matt, can you read to me?" Joyanna held a book out toward Matt.

Matt took it from her hands. *"Pilgrim's Progress?* That looks like a mighty big book for a little girl."

Joyanna straightened her posture, as though trying to appear more mature. "Pa was reading it to me. See, it's got a bookmark right here."

Matt inspected the book closer. A white, crocheted cross marked the page where Colton had left off. Sorrow tugged at Matt, but the pain wasn't as sharp as it had been before he spoke with Josiah yesterday. The torment of Colton's death had begun the process of retreat.

There were plenty of projects that Matt could work on

outside while he still had some daylight, but Joyanna was too hard to resist. Especially since she rarely asked him for anything.

"All right. As long as your mama's fine with putting off your bedtime a little longer."

Joyanna seemed confident that her mama would agree. "Uncle Matt's gonna read me a story," she called to Emily, who was clearing supper dishes from the table.

"Sounds good." Emily offered Matt a brief smile and then returned to her work. Matt's heart warmed.

"Over here, Uncle Matt." Joyanna grabbed his hand and drew him to the wooden rocker. "When we read a story, we always gotta sit here so you can fit all of us on your lap."

"Oh." For a brief second, the recluse inside Matt shrank back from the idea of squeezing into that small of a chair with three children, but he pushed the feeling aside.

"Grant, Austin, you want to read a book?" he asked, easing into the rocker. Without hesitation, the boys dropped their toys and came to his side—Grant running and Austin crawling. He leaned down to pick up Austin, and Grant scrambled up onto the chair all by himself.

"They like books," Joyanna said. "Pa used to read to us a lot." Joyanna claimed the last of the space on his lap, wiggling until she was comfortable.

Matt struggled to free his arms from the tangle of children on top of him, then he took the book from Joyanna and opened it where the crocheted bookmark indicated. Starting at the top of the page, he began to read. Not everything about the story made sense to him, but the children seemed to enjoy it. Maybe someday he'd find the time to read it from the beginning.

When he reached the end of the chapter, Matt inserted the bookmark back into place. "That's all for tonight."

"And that means it's time for bed." Emily hung up the dish

towel and faced her children. "Thank Uncle Matt for reading to you, and then go change into your night clothes."

"Thank you, Uncle Matt," Joyanna and Grant said together as they slid off his lap.

"Keep rocking, Matthew," Emily whispered, looking at Austin. "He's almost asleep."

Matt nodded and kept the rocker in motion. Emily turned away to help Grant out of his shirt, and Matt pulled his gaze away from her. Funny how a single look or word of approval from Emily made him feel such pleasure. Really, it was almost embarrassing. He was worse than one of the children.

Shifting Austin to a more comfortable position, Matt reached down and picked up the copy of the *Osceola Record* that Josiah had left yesterday. The entire front page held news of the upcoming Fourth of July celebration to be held in town. Osceola was going to be celebrating in style, complete with speeches, a picnic, games, and dancing. Returning to the top of the page, Matt read more details.

About halfway through he realized that Emily was at his side.

"Want me to take Austin?" she whispered.

Matt shook his head. "Give him a few more minutes. I don't mind holding him."

Emily nodded. Picking up her sewing basket, she took a seat at the table. Matt set the paper aside and watched Emily as she pulled out a needle, threaded it, and set to work mending a pair of Grant's pants. How could she be so deft at making such tiny stitches?

She caught him watching her and asked, "What are you thinking?"

"Not much." Matt glanced back at the paper. "I saw there's a party planned for the Fourth. Do they always plan such big events?"

"Usually. The Fourth is a big holiday around here. Nearly everyone around heads into town for it."

"Maybe we should go."

Emily nearly dropped Grant's trousers. "What?"

"It sounds fun, and things have been quiet around here lately. We could use a little excitement." Looking back at Emily, Matt could tell that she didn't like his idea. She had *that* pinch to her forehead. "Have you ever gone to the celebration?"

"I've gone every year, as far as I can remember. Almost everyone does."

And yet, something was bothering her. Something big enough to make her avoid eye contact with him. "So you don't want to go this year?"

Emily bit her lip and shrugged. The squeak of Matt's rocker was the only sound that filled the room until she softly said, "Things are different this year. It's our first holiday without Colton, and I guess I don't feel like going to a party."

"Oh." Her words quenched Matt's enthusiasm.

He understood how Emily felt. But now that he'd gotten the idea of a party into his head, he felt restless at the idea of putting in a normal day's work and missing out on the celebration.

"You could go if you wanted to, of course," Emily added. "I just don't think the children and I will this year."

"No, that's all right." Attending the celebration without Emily and the children would take the fun out of it. He still felt like an outsider in Osceola and would be out of place by himself.

Emily returned to her stitching, but Matt kept working the problem over in his mind. There had to be a way to convince Emily to change her mind. They could all benefit from some fun, especially the children.

"Emily," he began, drawing a deep breath. "Maybe you should think about going to the celebration."

"What? Why?"

"The way I see it, you have two options." Matt kept his voice as gentle as possible. "One, you could stay home. It's the easier of the two, because then you could ignore that the day is different than others and you wouldn't have to think about moving on beyond Colton." He paused. "The other choice would be to go and face the truth that he is no longer with us, but that life goes on. It's hard, but you just may find that it's another step toward healing."

Emily shook her head even before he finished. "I can't. It's too soon."

"I see." Matt caught a glint of tears in her eyes and decided it was time to back off. "I understand how you feel, Emily. Just think about it and let me know if you change your mind. But if you don't, then that's fine, too."

Emily jerked her head in a nod, keeping her gaze lowered on her work.

Silence settled between them. Matt adjusted Austin again, trying to think of something to take away the strain between them.

His gaze snagged on his father's old clock, a family heirloom that had always held a place of honor when he was a boy. Now the clock occupied the wall above Emily's bed. He studied its familiar lines, then let his gaze linger on the shelf where it rested.

"Who made that shelf?" he asked.

Emily glanced in the direction he pointed. "Colton did shortly before our wedding."

"I didn't know he was a carpenter."

"Colton was always learning something new. He also made this." She patted the kitchen table beside her.

"Really?" Matt's admiration for his brother grew. He rubbed his fingers along the butter-smooth arm of his chair "Did he make this rocker too?"

"No, that would have been a little too complicated. One of my old students made that for me."

"Colton never mentioned that you were a teacher."

Emily shrugged. "I only taught for one year. Colton and I met that Christmas. We had a whirlwind courtship and were married the week after school let out. I liked teaching, but . . . I *loved* Colton."

Even though Colton was gone, it was evident that Emily was still just as in love with him as ever. The emotions on her face plainly expressed that.

"Someone must have had a great deal of admiration for you to make such a special gift," Matt muttered as he again caressed the chair's arm. "It sounds like the boy was quite smitten with you." He glanced at her, trying to gauge her reaction to his teasing.

"Jase?" Emily smiled. Based on the way the light danced in her eyes, Matt thought she might actually laugh. But she didn't.

"No. He was only twelve. And besides, he made it as a wedding present and was quite happy for me and Colton. He had a bright mind and was a natural woodworker." Her eyes lingered fondly on the rocker. "Jase was Elkanah Hoffman's youngest son."

"Jase?" Matt frowned, trying to place a face to the name. "I've met Zane, Adam, and Benjamin, but I don't remember a Jase."

"You haven't met him." Emily's smile dimmed. "He left the area. Jase and his father were always butting heads. He had a passion for building, but Elkanah thought the only acceptable occupation for his sons was farming. And then Jase was accused of a crime I know he didn't commit, and when Elkanah refused to back him up, Jase ran off. That was over three years ago, and we haven't heard from him since."

Matt shook his head. "That's too bad."

"Yes." Emily looked at the ground for a long moment, then

blurted out, "Sometimes I've felt guilty over Jase's sudden departure. The day before he left, he stopped by, gave me a slip of paper, and asked me not to open it but to give it to his parents in two days and no sooner. I promised, but I didn't expect Jase to disappear overnight." Emily sighed. "Since I didn't want to break my promise, I waited until the next day to give the note to his parents. Turns out the note told them not to worry about him and that he was going to make his own way in the world. I've often wondered what would have happened if I gave the note to Elkanah and Florence right away. Maybe Jase would still be with us."

Matt rubbed Austin's back, thinking through what he should say. "It seems like the boy was determined to leave no matter what and that he wouldn't have appreciated it if you broke your word."

Emily's forehead lined. "He was only sixteen. Too young to be away from home."

Matt smiled. "Guess it depends on how you look at it. I was sixteen when I left home—or what was left of home, at least."

Emily's eyebrows lifted. "You were?"

Matt nodded. "I figured I could take on the whole world. 'Course, that feeling changed about halfway across Nebraska. It had been pouring rain for the past few days, there wasn't a soul for miles, and I'd been living off what cooking I could manage without a fire. That was a low time, to say the least. I started to wonder what had possessed me to wander away from Colton."

Emily studied him. "Matthew, I don't know you very well. I know little more than what Colton's told me."

"I could say the same about you." Matt leaned back in his chair and folded his hands. "Maybe we should fix that. Tell me about yourself, Emily."

Setting aside her sewing, she did. She told him about her childhood and moving to Osceola, about how she became one of the first white settlers in the county. And then she spoke about the time she met Colton and fell in love with him.

"Both of us immediately knew that we were meant for each other. After we met, I had no doubts that Colton Keath was the man for me." Emily glanced at Matt. "Do you have a girl waiting for you out West?"

"Me?" Matt could feel his face redden. "No. I've never been interested in marriage."

"Maybe you should. You might find that you like it."

Matt shrugged. Although some things had altered since he'd arrived, that was one decision he determined to stick with.

And yet . . .

Matt glanced down at Austin and hugged him tighter. After meeting his niece and nephews, he wouldn't mind having a couple of kids of his own. The thought of coming home after a long day's work to a pretty lady with supper on the table and a smile just for him wasn't bad either.

"Now, tell me. What was it like living out west?" Emily asked.

Instantly, Matt remembered with clarity all the aspects he'd appreciated from the area. The rugged beauty of the great outdoors. The open vistas. The sense of adventure and freedom. All things he struggled to relay in words yet wanted to share with Emily.

He recounted his journey to Scottsbluff, where he had initially sought work as a cowboy before landing the role of deputy. He told her about some of the less savage confrontations during his time as deputy that eventually caused him to return to being a ranch hand. And about how he wished he'd come sooner to see Colton again and meet his niece and nephews.

"I wish you had too," Emily said. "Maybe with Colton to intercede between us, we would have had a less rocky start." A brief smile flitted across her face and then disappeared. "But the past has been written and it can't be changed. All we can do now is move forward."

Matt nodded. Emily turned to gaze out the window at the darkening sky, a distant expression on her face. Did she realize that she had said the very words he'd been trying to get through to her? Maybe she *would* think his words over after all.

Matt rose from his chair with Austin. "I should get to bed. Sunup comes mighty quickly."

Emily stood as well. "Here, let me take him."

Matt handed Austin over to her and noted how she avoided his gaze. "Goodnight, Emily."

She barely even looked at him as she said, "Goodnight."

Matt started to leave, but then Emily called, "Matthew."

Matt turned. Standing in the middle of the soddy, the lamplight casting a soft glow around her, she looked small and alone. She was a brave woman and had strength to fight obstacles that would have defeated someone of less determination.

Yet despite that, she was still vulnerable.

Something protective welled up inside Matt, similar to what he felt for Joyanna and the boys. With everything inside him, he wanted to shield her from all hurt.

Emily tilted her head. "I've been thinking about what you told me."

Matt fought to focus on her words rather than his emotions. "Yeah?"

"You're right. I think we should go."

"To the Fourth of July celebration?"

Emily nodded. "It's tempting to stay home, but you're right. This is a time to heal. I need to keep moving forward, no matter how hard it is." A spark glinted in her eyes. "But if Mrs. Durmond complains, just know that I'll be sending her to you."

A smile tugged at the corners of Matt's mouth. "I'm willing to handle the bear if it means you'll come."

Matt would have gladly taken on *any* challenge for her sake.

Osceola was alive with more people than Emily could remember ever seeing in town before.

The American flag fluttered above the courthouse as families milled about the lawn, some of the mothers still packing away the remains of picnic dinners. Games had been set up at one end of the square

After delivering her picnic basket to the wagon with Sadie, Emily walked alongside her sister-in-law, hands swinging free at her side. A group of children raced by, their giggles pulling a smile to her own mouth. Everyone was in high spirits today.

Sadie grabbed her hand and gave it a quick squeeze. "I'm so glad you came today. I wasn't sure you would, given how things are this year, but celebrating the Fourth wouldn't have been as much fun without you."

"You can thank Matthew. I didn't want to come at first, but he convinced me it would be best. I'm glad he did."

Sadie grinned. "Since when did you start listening to Matt Keath's advice? I thought you didn't like him."

Emily's cheeks warmed. "I do now. We've had one of the roughest weeks yet but also one of the best."

A yell came from up ahead, and Sadie strained to see over the shoulder of the man in front of them. "I'd love to hear more of this story, but we better keep moving if we hope to find our children."

Emily nodded. They hurried their steps, careful to keep the hems of their skirts out of the dust.

A train whistled nearby, the sound grating against Emily's ears. The Omaha and Republican Valley Railroad Company had extended its line to run through Osceola, and mere weeks ago, the first train had come through. Emily still wasn't used to the idea of having a train weave through their little town.

But it would have its advantages, especially come harvest time. The one thing about farming that Colton had hated was the long, tiring trip he had to take to Columbus to sell the grain, especially since he had to ford the Platte River. This railroad would be a blessing, even if Emily didn't entirely trust those noisy, smoke-spewing locomotives that went far faster than what she considered to be safe.

When Emily and Sadie reached the white clapboard building that served as the courthouse, they paused and scanned the area for their families.

"We ought to have more parties like this," Sadie said. "The town never comes alive as much as it does on the Fourth."

Emily smiled. Her sister-in-law clearly thrived on excitement. "I like Osceola the way it is. A celebration is fine once a year, but it would become tiring if this was the town's daily atmosphere."

Before Sadie could respond, a woman called, "*Yoo-hoo!* Over here!"

A sense of dread filled Emily. She knew exactly who was walking toward her even before she saw the brilliant green eyes and the broad-brimmed hat, complete with a bobbing feather.

"Emily, how delightful to see you today," Maude Reynolds

gushed, but she looked past Emily, searching the area around her. "You did bring Matt with you, didn't you?"

"Of course." Emily pressed her lips together, miffed that Maude thought she would attend a party while leaving Matt working at home.

Maude's smile turned dazzling. "Wonderful! Where is that charming man?"

"I don't know," Emily said between clenched teeth. Maude had a tendency to pick out helpless men to flirt with, a habit she'd refined back when Emily was her schoolteacher. Maude was tenacious, so when she chose a man to give her attention to, the only way out for them was either fleeing or tying the knot with someone else. Lately, Archer Baker had been in the spotlight of her affections, but now he was betrothed so it seemed that Matt was her next pick.

Maude looked beyond Emily and broke into an even wider smile. "There he is! *Matt!* Over here!"

Emily followed Maude's gaze. Sure enough, Matt stood on the sidelines, holding Austin while he visited with Ephraim. He glanced their way, and Emily watched his expression change from friendly to caged. Maude broke away from Emily and dashed toward him, her feather dancing crazily, arms waving. Matt seemed to measure the distance between him and the oncoming Maude.

If only there were some way that Emily could help him. There was no chance that she could distract Maude by conversation. She and Maude had never gotten along—probably because Maude carried too many sore memories of Emily punishing her for paying more attention to the boys across the aisle than her lessons.

Matt leaned down and whispered something to Joyanna, then stood and placed Austin into Ephraim's arms. Grabbing Joyanna's hand, the two of them hurried off in the opposite direction of Maude.

"Matt!" Maude called after him, running still faster. "Where are you going?"

Matt quickened his pace. Joyanna had to sprint to keep up with him.

"Going to do the three-legged race with Joyanna," Matt said. "Sorry. I'll see you later."

Maude slowed, seeming to realize that she'd been outwitted. Her smile gave way to a pout. Sadie winked at Emily, and Emily fought the urge to giggle. It wasn't very often that Maude was outwitted.

"Come on." Sadie grabbed Emily's hand. "It looks like Ephraim could use some help with all those little ones. And I don't know about you, but I'm not going to miss out on watching Matt and Joyanna race."

Emily squeezed Sadie's hand. "Neither am I."

"On your mark, get set, go!"

Emily thought she possibly yelled louder than Sadie for a change as they stood with their kids and watched the race. Ephraim had taken his daughter Margie so they could challenge Matt and Joyanna. They now hopped along together in a clump.

"Go, Ephraim! Go, Margie!" Sadie called, jumping about as much as her three-year-old son, Isaac. "Sorry, Emily, but for once I'm hoping my niece doesn't win."

"Sorry, Sadie, but I'm rather hoping my brother doesn't win." Emily rose up on her tiptoes to get a better view of Matt's and Joyanna's movements. She shouted as they skipped past two little girls. It looked like they'd gotten the hang of it and were doing far better than Emily would have expected.

Sadie let out a groan that ended in a laugh. Emily glanced toward the start of the line where Ephraim and Margie were sprawled across the ground. Their grins made Emily assume that neither of them were hurt.

She looked back at Matt and Joyanna and squealed at how close to the end of the line they were. Only a couple more contestants were ahead, and Matt and Joyanna were gaining on them.

Sadie turned her attention from her husband and daughter, yelling, "Go Matt and Joyanna! Keep going!"

"I think they're going to win!" Emily clapped her hands, making Austin squeal as Matt and Joyanna passed another set of contestants.

But then the two boys ahead of Matt and Joyanna tripped and fell. To avoid them, Matt and Joyanna swerved to the side. Emily held her breath as she watched them stumble. They spread out their arms, trying to regain their balance, but it was no use. They both sprawled next to the two boys. Pastor Drew and another young girl hopped past them and over the finish line.

"So close!" Emily groaned.

Sadie chuckled. "I didn't know Drew could move so fast. He's outdone himself today."

Emily smiled as well, watching as Matt and Joyanna untied their legs and climbed to their feet. Matt called something to Drew that made those around them laugh, and Drew wagged a finger at him.

"Emily Keath, what are you thinking, allowing your little girl to go around with that uncouth man?" a familiar voice hissed behind Emily.

Emily's stomach clenched into a hard knot as she slowly faced her accuser.

"Mrs. Durmond, how good that you came today." Emily struggled to keep her smile in place. Austin buried his face in her shoulder, and Grant leaned in closer to her skirts, his grip on her hand tightening. "We have beautiful weather this after-noon, wouldn't you agree?"

Mrs. Durmond's lips tightened. "Don't try to get me off track, young lady. Do you realize the rotten influence that man is going to have on sweet little Joyanna?"

Emily stared back at her evenly. "By 'that man,' I presume you're speaking of Matthew?"

"Who else? Cowboys are nothing but trouble, and I'm convinced that your brother-in-law is the lowest of the low. Never in my life have I ever met such a shameless young man."

Emily's temper flared. It was one thing for Mrs. Durmond to attack her but quite another for her to go after Matt, something Emily could not put up with. "Matthew is an honorable man, Mrs. Durmond, and I have no worries about my children asso-ciating with him. No one apart from you has ever accused him of lacking in character."

"Is that so?" Mrs. Durmond stood up straight, her posture conveying her disapproval. "Perhaps no one saw what happened on his first Sunday in town. He was being overtly flirtatious with Maude Reynolds and ever since then, I couldn't help but notice how he looks at her, even when talking to the other men. He can't seem to keep his eyes off her."

Yes, Emily *had* noticed that Matt kept an eye on Maude when she was in sight, but his expression was anything but love struck; it was more like a horse preparing to bolt.

Emily drew herself up straighter. "I saw what happened that Sunday as well, and Matthew did nothing to encourage Maude's behavior. You and I are both familiar with Maude Reynolds's ways, and you have no right to cast aspersions on Matthew because of her actions."

Mrs. Durmond narrowed her gaze. "Well, well, look who's made herself Matt Keath's keeper. And what has you so defen-sive about him?"

Emily inhaled deeply. "Matthew has done nothing but good to us since he's arrived. I would appreciate it if you would refrain from tearing apart his character. Try to see the real Matthew, not the man you've made him out to be."

"Look here, Emily, *you're* the one who isn't seeing the real man. I know you've had a hard time lately and you're desperate for help, but your children will suffer for your foolishness. You aren't thinking clearly. And if you have any sense, you ought to take advice from others."

Emily set her jaw. "I am thinking quite clearly, thank you. I am grateful for Matthew's help, and I have no intention of turning down his assistance."

Mrs. Durmond leaned closer, a challenge in her eyes. "Is it the man's *help* or the man *himself* that you desire more?"

The implication of her words struck Emily like a blow. She pressed her hand against her chest, her heartbeat erratic beneath her fingers. "How could you even ask that? Colton has only been gone for a few months. I don't want another man. *Ever!*"

Mrs. Durmond eased back. "If you were to chase after another man so soon after your husband's death, it would be most improper, a desecration to your husband's memory. No woman should remarry within a year of her husband's death, no matter the circumstances. I do hope that you are being truthful, both with me and yourself."

Emily clenched her free hand into a fist, aware that she was trembling. "Mrs. Durmond, don't you *ever* accuse me of desecrating Colton's memory. Colton was a wonderful man, and we shared a deep love, the kind that only comes once in a lifetime. I don't want to hear another word about me desiring another man."

Mrs. Durmond pinned her with a cold glare. "You sure don't seem to be mourning much for Colton. If you were, seems to me you'd be at home, not gallivanting around a party in the company of another man."

A wave of nausea burned against the back of Emily's throat. Mrs. Durmond had no clue of how close Emily had come to not attending. She could never guess how deeply Emily missed Colton and wished for him to return. She had no idea of all the nights Emily had cried herself to sleep, longing for her husband.

Emily could sense a strong presence behind her. Even before she turned, she somehow knew who it was.

"Mrs. Durmond, I trust you're enjoying yourself this afternoon." Matt tipped his hat.

"Matt Keath," Mrs. Durmond said with a frown. "I'm not surprised to see you here. You're always getting in the middle of the excitement, aren't you?"

Matt's smile remained pleasant. "Why, yes, ma'am, I reckon that's true. Seems you and I are alike in that way."

"Well!" Mrs. Durmond's eyes measured Matt. "Where did you leave your niece? I hope you didn't lose her on your way over here. The responsibility of looking after a child in these crowds is no joke, young man."

"I left her with Ephraim and Margie, and I know they'll keep a good eye on her. But thank you for your concern."

Mrs. Durmond paused, her lips pursed and eyes narrowed. "I see you're wearing those outlandish boots again. Don't know how you can feel respectable going out among people wearing those."

"I rather like them. If you want a pair for your husband, I can tell you where to find them." Matt's smile turned a little smug, and Emily felt a sneaking suspicion that he may have worn those boots just to rile Mrs. Durmond.

Mrs. Durmond sniffed. "The idea! My Albert wouldn't be caught dead wearing those."

"You might be surprised. A man will do a lot of things he never thought he would when it comes down to a matter of life or death." Matt tilted his head back to look at the sun. "You know, Mrs. Durmond, I'd love to stay and visit, but I think Emily and I better get a move on. Pleasure seeing you."

Matt picked up Grant and set him on his shoulders. Then, tipping his hat one last time to Mrs. Durmond, he took Emily's arm and led her away. Emily could feel Mrs. Durmond's gaze drilling into her, and her face warmed with more than just the heat. She may have escaped this time, but knowing Mrs. Durmond, she was not about to let this go. The woman was sure to try and corner her another time.

Matt leaned closer. "Sorry I didn't come sooner. I saw her come up to you, but the crowds were so thick I couldn't get there right away. It *was* my intention to take her on if necessary, not to leave you to face her alone."

Thinking of what Mrs. Durmond had told her, Emily felt relief that Matt *hadn't* come sooner. Mrs. Durmond had been determined to tell her all that she did, and Emily wouldn't have put it past her to say it in front of Matt.

Emily shrugged. "It's fine."

Emily felt the weight of Matt's hand on her arm and discreetly removed herself from his grasp. His touch would have meant nothing before, but now Mrs. Durmond's words left Emily wanting to keep a comfortable distance between them.

"I'd like to go home now," she said, unable to make eye contact. As shaken as her emotions were, she desperately needed to escape the crowd and be alone to sort through all that had happened.

"Already?" Matt's voice was incredulous. "It's hardly after lunch."

Emily's chin trembled. "I'd rather be home."

Matt took her arm and drew her to a stop. "Emily, look at me."

He waited until Emily slowly raised her gaze to his, then spoke. "Don't let Mrs. Durmond make you think there's a thing wrong with you being here. You can't be expected to remain holed up on the farm just because you've been widowed, and if anyone tries to make you think you should, send them to deal with me. With all you've been through this year, you need fellowship with other people more than ever."

He thought Mrs. Durmond had been lecturing her merely about attending a party so soon after Colton's death. If only that were all!

Grateful that he hadn't guessed any of Mrs. Durmond's dirty accusations about the two of them, Emily kept her attention on the ground. "I'd still like to go home."

"Going home is only going to give Mrs. Durmond the satisfaction that she managed to cow you into doing her bidding. I think we should stay a little longer. I'll remain close to you and make sure that Mrs. Durmond doesn't bother you again."

Matt was offering to stay close to her? Far from protecting her, his presence would only fuel Mrs. Durmond's indignation further.

But now she was letting Mrs. Durmond cow her into her bidding, as Matt had phrased it. His presence hadn't bothered her earlier, so why should she shun him now? He was only trying to help.

Matt applied more pressure. "Sadie's going to miss you if you leave now. And Joyanna's having the time of her life with her cousins."

"Fine." Emily released a sigh that made her shoulders sag. "I'll trust that you're making the right decision."

"You won't regret it. I'll make sure of that." Matt smiled, and then Grant tipped Matt's hat down over his face, covering Matt's eyes.

"Hey!" Matt exclaimed, and Emily couldn't resist giggling. Reaching out, she took Matt's hat from his head and plopped it onto Grant's.

"There, that should help."

"That's one way to take care of the problem." Matt grinned and patted Grant's leg. "C'mon, cowboy, we better keep moving."

He offered his arm to Emily. Without allowing herself to think about Mrs. Durmond, Emily accepted it.

Matt stood along the sidelines as couples whirled past to the music of a rather rusty fiddle. He made no effort to join in, but he couldn't keep his foot from tapping in time to the music.

A heavy hand settled on his shoulder. Matt jumped, then realized it was only Ephraim.

Ephraim flicked a finger toward the dancers. "What are you doing here when you should be out there dancing?"

Matt shrugged. Sure, he liked to dance with the right partner, but he didn't feel like asking any of the young ladies who were still unclaimed. Or any of the ones on the dancefloor, either.

Ephraim settled in beside him. "Where'd you lose Emily?"

"Austin needed a diaper change and a feeding, so she took him out to the wagon."

A gleam in Ephraim's eyes warned Matt that teasing was coming. "You've been sticking awfully close to her this afternoon, hardly even letting her out of your sight. I wondered how she'd managed to escape."

Matt stared ahead, coughing to clear his throat. "She had a

little run-in with Mrs. Durmond earlier and it shook her up. I talked her out of going home, but I'm determined not to allow that woman to get another chance to harass Emily."

Ephraim patted Matt's shoulder. "You've been taking good care of my sister and her kids, Matt. You've lifted a heavy weight of worry off my shoulders. Thank you. Let me know if you ever need anything, all right? We're practically family."

Matt looked at Ephraim, warmth spreading through his chest. Ephraim's teasing could sometimes step on a person's nerves, but underneath the laughter, Ephraim was a good, solid man, one Matt would be proud to think of as family. "Thanks," he murmured.

Ephraim smiled, then turned at a tap on his shoulder.

"Ephraim, you haven't asked me to dance yet." Sadie planted her hands on her hips and made a show of frowning at him.

Ephraim raised his eyebrows. "Seems to me you just extended the invitation."

"Well, you weren't getting around to it." Sadie rolled her eyes then smiled at Matt. "Sorry, but I'm going to steal my husband for this dance."

"Whether he's willing or not?" Ephraim asked, allowing Sadie to lead him away.

"You better be willing, or you're in deep water," Sadie replied.

Matt smiled as he watched them disappear into the crowd, then he glanced around to make sure Joyanna and Grant were still nearby. His gaze fell on a woman pressing through the crowd toward him. Dread gathered in Matt's middle. Only one woman he knew wore a dress with *that* much lace on it, and only one woman would ever dare to wear a hat sporting *that* curling feather.

Matt edged backward, hoping to blend in with those around him, but it was too late.

"*Yoo-hoo!*" Maude sang out, dashing the final steps to his side.

"I've been looking everywhere for you, Matt! You're a sneaky one, aren't you?"

Matt gave a weak smile. He thought he'd been flashing plenty of signals, trying to tell her that he wasn't interested, but she didn't seem to receive any of them. No, Maude probably thought that he was head over heels in love with her and that any reticence he showed was merely due to shyness.

Guilt nibbled at him. He hadn't done a thing to encourage her; in fact, he'd tried to keep a safe distance. But he still disliked having a young woman deceived over his feelings toward her, even if she'd drawn her own conclusions.

"Miss Reynolds," he began, but Maude gushed on.

"Hasn't it been just a marvelous party today? So many things to do and such lovely weather! Wonderful company as well." Maude fluttered her eyelashes at him.

Panic gripped Matt. Emily wasn't there to save him this time. It was his job alone to get himself out of this awkward situation.

Matt cleared his throat. "Miss Reynolds, I can't help but notice that you seem rather—um . . .attracted to me. But I think you've misunderstood—"

Maude laughed, the silvery sound drowning out everything else he'd intended to say. "I always like a man who can speak what's on his mind. And since you're so open, why don't you tell me what you think of my dress?"

She turned a circle for him, showing off the ruffles of her lacy pink dress. Matt's sense of desperation increased.

"Miss Reynolds, I'm not exactly interested in dresses—"

She spun to face him again, smiling broadly. "Neither am I. But I do agree with you that we should go dance."

"What?" Matt stared at her. How had she pulled that out of his words? Before he could say another word, she grabbed his hand and pulled him onto the dancefloor.

Matt tried to move away. "Now, wait, I never said—"

"I'm so glad you asked me to dance with you; no one's invited me yet. I *so* love to dance, practically thrive on it, and I was beginning to fear that if someone didn't ask me soon, I would miss out on my only chance," Maude gushed, beaming up at him.

Helplessness overpowered Matt. Looking around, he realized that almost all the onlookers were focused on them. If he ran from Maude now, news would surely spread throughout town tomorrow that Emily Keath's brother-in-law was scared of Maude Reynolds.

Maude had him cornered, and he didn't like it. She knew just as well as Matt that he hadn't asked her to dance with him, nor had he intended to.

Matt made one last escape attempt. "I need to keep an eye on my niece and nephew. I can't dance until Emily—"

"No worries." Maude's expression turned smug. "They're not too far away, and Emily's with them."

Matt darted a glance in the direction Maude looked. Sure enough, Emily stood there with Austin in her arms, bending down to say something to Joyanna. Matt's heart sank. There was no way out now.

Squaring his jaw, Matt determined not to create a spectacle and fell into step with Maude. But though he outwardly remained pleasant, on the inside, he stormed. The one thing he could not stand was deceit. If Maude had hoped to win him over by making him dance with her, she was dead wrong. She couldn't have chosen a worse thing to do. Matt vowed that, from that moment on, he would not fall for Maude Reynolds. *Ever.*

Maude kept up a steady stream of chatter during the dance, jarring Matt's nerves. The music dragged on until he wanted to lunge at the fiddler and snap his bow in half. He couldn't endure the woman any longer—and yet there was no escape. Keeping his smile on his face, Matt tried not to look too sick.

Finally, the fiddler stretched out the last notes, and the dance ended.

Matt attempted to back away from Maude, but she caught him by the sleeve.

"Come, let's get something to drink at the refreshments table. Dancing always gives me a powerful thirst." Maude sent him an overly sweet smile.

Matt's patience with her was at the end of its rope. He'd sent enough hints about his feelings toward her that only a person who was both blind and deaf could miss them. But it seemed she was determined to hear him put his sentiments into plain words.

"Maude," he said, his voice steely. "You will need to find someone else. I know you think I like you in a special way, but that's not true. Now, I need to go find Emily, so you run along, you hear?"

Maude's expression plainly said that she had heard—and she was mad. "You're sweet on Emily Keath, aren't you?" she spat out.

"Emily?" Matt felt the corner of his mouth twitch. "Of course not. I'm not sweet on anyone."

Maude eyed him. "And you never have been?"

"No."

Maude's smile turned shrewd. "Then how do you know what it feels like to be in love? Maybe you don't understand your own feelings."

"I understand myself, thank you." Matt pulled his sleeve from her fingers and backed away. "Goodbye, Miss Reynolds."

Maude's face darkened. "You don't understand yourself, Matt Keath. Get back here so we can talk this over!"

"We've already talked as much as necessary." Matt tipped his hat to her, then spun away on his heel.

"Don't trick yourself into thinking Emily Keath would ever

marry you! She's just a sour widow who doesn't like anyone— and she's real mean with a ruler, too!" Maude hollered.

Matt didn't waste his breath responding. Pressing his way through the crowd, Matt nearly ran back to the area where he'd last seen Emily. He heaved a breath of relief when he saw her with Sadie. They stood together talking, and he hurried toward them.

Emily glanced his way and lifted an eyebrow. "What's wrong?"

"Nothing." Matt glanced at Sadie, then motioned for Emily to come closer. He did *not* want Sadie to overhear what he was about to say. "Maude Reynolds has just taken a year off my life, and I don't know how to get her to understand plain English. She's made up her mind that I'm going to like her *or else*. And if she bats her eyelashes at me one more time, I'm going to go insane."

Emily smiled in amusement. "I'm sorry."

"Sorry? That's all you have to say?"

"What can I do?" Emily looked beyond Matt and grimaced. "And not to be the bearer of bad news, but it looks like we're about to have company."

Matt cast a glance over his shoulder and groaned aloud at the sight of Maude Reynolds elbowing her way through the crowd. All traces of anger were gone, and her smile had returned in all its brilliance.

Matt turned back to Emily. "Quick! I need your help."

"How?" Emily asked, still frowning at Maude.

"Dance with me."

"What?" Emily's gaze snapped to his face. "Are you crazy? It's one thing for me to attend a party, but quite another to *dance*. Colton hasn't been gone for more than a few months!"

"So? I don't know any law against widows dancing."

"Mrs. Durmond's law decrees it a crime."

"Now, hey. I thought we had agreed that we weren't going to listen to Mrs. Durmond."

"She might be right on this one." Emily folded her arms across her chest. "I'm sorry, Matthew, but I just can't do it."

Matt had to think fast. He didn't want Emily to dance if it would hurt her more, but he didn't think she was as against dancing as she sounded. He'd noticed the interest in her eyes as she watched the other dancers, and he figured it was only people like Mrs. Durmond who kept her from joining them.

"Is it a crime to do good?"

"What?" Emily raised both eyebrows.

"Is it a crime to do good?" Matt repeated.

"Well, no, but how…"

"Then come dance with me. There's no way I can survive another dance with Maude Reynolds, so if anyone questions you, just tell them that your intentions were good. You were trying to save life."

Emily burst into laughter—the first real laugh that Matt had managed to coax out of her. He wasn't prepared for how the laughter changed her face.

Land sakes, no wonder Maude warned him against falling for her! Had Matt been interested in taking a wife, he might well have gone tumbling head over heels for Emily—not that there was any danger of that with their current circumstances.

Maude drew dangerously closer, and without waiting for Emily to continue, Matt grabbed her hand and pulled her toward the other couples.

Emily tried to free her hand. "Matthew, I can't. I need to watch the children."

Matt turned and called, "Sadie, can you keep an eye on the kids?"

"No trouble. You two go along and enjoy yourselves." Sadie didn't even attempt to hide her grin.

"See? You have no excuses."

Emily stopped trying to pull away, and a smile curved her lips upward. "I guess not."

Matt half bowed. "May I have this dance, Mrs. Keath?"

"Very well, Mr. Keath." Emily glanced back at Maude. "I see that you really do need my help."

"Oh, I do," Matt said grimly. "I need all the help I can get when it comes to that woman."

Dancing with Emily didn't even compare to dancing with Maude Reynolds. Emily was a good dancer, and even though she said little, peace emanated from her, and it soothed Matt's soul.

Now it seemed to Matt that the fiddler purposefully played fast. Was it really so hard for the man to find a balance?

But Matt guessed that the real reason his dance with Emily seemed shorter was not because of the music, but rather because of his partner. He could dance all afternoon with Emily.

When the tune ended, Matt started to ask Emily for another dance, but someone tapped his shoulder. Turning, Matt found himself face to face with a man he'd never met. He had to be years older than Matt, in his mid-thirties at least. He was a fine-looking man, tall and broad shouldered with thick brown hair that was slicked smooth.

"Hello." The man's gaze rested on Matt for a second, then slid past him to Emily. His mouth curved. "Mrs. Keath, what a pleasure to see you today. You appear to be doing well."

Emily smiled in return. "Mr. Grady, it's good to see you too. You haven't visited lately."

"I'm most sorry about that, but I heard you had help to care for your needs, and I became busy with farm work..." The man waved his hand. "Pitiful excuses, I know."

"Don't worry. I understand how it is with a farm. Time goes

faster than you realize." Emily glanced at Matt. "Matthew, I don't believe you've met Obadiah Grady yet. Obadiah, my brother-in-law, Matthew."

The man turned toward Matt. "A pleasure to meet you, Mr. Keath," he said, but the lines around his eyes tightened as his gaze measured Matt up.

"Same, Mr. Grady." Matt studied the man, aware of an odd churning in the middle of his stomach. Something about the man didn't set well with him, but he couldn't tell why. Obadiah Grady looked decent, and his manners were flawless. Emily seemed to know him and like him too. Maybe too well.

Obadiah Grady turned back to Emily. "I'm glad you came to the celebration today. It's a bold step so soon after your husband's passing, and I admire you for it."

Emily's cheeks turned pink, and she glanced at Matt. "Thank you, but I probably wouldn't have come if Matthew hadn't encouraged me."

"Indeed." Again, Obadiah Grady looked at Matt.

He returned the stare, a familiar tingling sensation running through his veins. It was a feeling he always had in the moments leading up to a fight, and now he found his deputy's instincts kicking in, calculating each of the man's movements, every tensing of his muscles—

Matt caught himself and stepped backwards. What was he thinking? He didn't like Obadiah, and somehow, he could sense that Obadiah didn't like him either. But that was no cause to jump into a fight.

Matt wasn't one to look for trouble.

Obadiah sent him a sharp look, then he turned to Emily as the fiddler began playing again. "Would you allow me to have this dance, Mrs. Keath?" He held his hand out toward her.

Emily's eyes reflected her uncertainty. "No, I don't think so. I hadn't intended to dance today, and I only danced with Matthew because..." Her words trailed off.

"Yes, we should probably get back to Sadie and the kids." Matt took Emily's arm. The sooner he could get the two of them away from this man, the better he would feel.

"Not so fast. One dance won't hurt, Emily. And really, I'd be most honored if you would allow me the privilege." Obadiah's gaze didn't leave Emily's face.

"Well…" Emily hesitated. "Matthew, do you mind?"

Mind? He sure did! He didn't want her standing a foot closer to Obadiah Grady than necessary.

But the look on her face indicated that she would like to dance with Obadiah. And after encouraging Emily to get out more, he would look like a fool if he raised a complaint.

Swallowing his unsettled feelings, Matt forced a smile. "Go ahead, if that's what you want."

He hoped that she *wouldn't* want, but it seemed she did. Emily reached out and took Obadiah's hand. "Then I'd be happy to accept, Mr. Grady."

Obadiah beamed. Matt stepped aside for them, resisting the fighting urge that swept through him again. He wanted to stand where he was and keep a close eye on them, but that would look odd. Instead he made his way back to Sadie and the kids.

Sadie looked up as he drew near. "How was the dancing?"

"Fine."

"Where did Emily go?"

"She found another partner." Matt stooped to help Grant roll up the cuff of his pants so it wouldn't drag in the dirt—the perfect excuse to keep his face averted. He didn't need her to see just how much Emily's partner bothered him. "Sadie, do you know Obadiah Grady?"

"Sure I know Obadiah. He's one of your closest neighbors."

"He is?" Matt frowned, picturing each of the nearby farms. He knew almost all their neighbors, but he hadn't met Obadiah. "Does he own that place with the big house and barn?"

"That's the place. Obadiah's worked hard to improve his

homestead over the years." Sadie absently picked a piece of grass and twirled it between her fingers. "I'm surprised you haven't met him yet. After Colton died, he was at Emily's place every day for a time. But then I guess he figured that you had things in hand, and he probably had work to catch up on at his place. He goes to the Methodist church, so there's another reason you haven't crossed paths."

"He's married?" Matt tried to keep his tone casual.

"Obadiah? Oh, no. But he's a fine enough man that I don't know why he isn't."

Matt looked away, the knot in his middle tightening. It was even worse than he'd feared. A fine, upright man, who was unmarried and had a beautiful farm that butted nicely with Emily's.

Matt would need to keep an eye on this man.

Matt closed the barn door behind him, took the brimming pail of milk, and started for the soddy. The milk bucket swung at his side as he whistled and paused to wipe his sleeve across his forehead. Even this late in the day, the heat was oppressive. He looked forward to reaching the soddy where it would be a little cooler, provided that Emily had kept her baking to a minimum.

The jingle of harness prompted him to look up. A buggy rattled its way down the lane, occupied by a lone figure—a man, judging by his shape. But Matt didn't recognize the team nor the rig.

Matt moved forward, still lugging the milk bucket, and reached the soddy as the buggy drew to a stop. He started to call out a greeting but froze as the man came closer into view.

Obadiah Grady.

Obadiah climbed down from his buggy and straightened. "Hello, Mr. Keath."

"Hello to you, Mr. Grady." Matt remained rooted to where he stood. Of all the nerve. How could he be so brazen to show his face here?

Of course, when it came down to it, Obadiah had visited Emily before Matt even thought about coming. But he'd just seen Emily the day before at the Fourth of July celebration. He had no reason to visit.

The soddy door opened, and Emily stepped outside. As she stood blinking in the sunlight, Matt was struck by just how beautiful she was. He didn't usually pay much attention to that. The sun glinted off her dark hair, and her eyes caught the light, reflecting it back with even more brilliance. She was good look-ing, all right, and she'd make a prize for whoever married her. *If* she allowed herself to fall in love again.

She broke into a grin at the sight of Obadiah. "Mr. Grady, how good to see you so soon. You're just in time for supper. You haven't eaten yet, have you?"

"No, but I wouldn't want to put you out at all." Obadiah flashed her a charming smile.

Emily waved her hand. "It's no trouble. A friend is always welcome for a meal."

"Well, then, I'd be mighty obliged, Emily."

Matt flinched. He couldn't sit down to dinner with Obadiah Grady. Why, he'd rather share a table with Frank Harvey!

Maybe.

Emily ushered Obadiah inside, and Matt trailed behind. Without a word, he set to work straining the milk, aware of how comfortable Emily and Obadiah acted to be with each other. Their conversation flowed smoothly from the weather to the crops and to the neighbors. By the time Matt returned from delivering milk to the well, they had moved on to talking about the differences in various Indian tribes.

Indian tribes? How had they managed to jump to that?

Matt sat at the table, waiting for Emily to notice him. She sent him a smile that didn't quite match the brilliant one she'd given to Obadiah when he arrived. "Good, you're done with the milk. Would you pray for the food, Matthew?"

At least she'd asked *him* and not Obadiah. Bowing his head, Matt uttered a brief prayer aloud. At the end, he silently added, *And Lord, please help me not to be too unkind to Obadiah tonight.*

Matt didn't attempt to join the conversation, but he listened carefully to every word Obadiah said. He noted each time Obadiah's gaze wandered to Emily and counted how many smiles he offered her.

Emily happened to wear a blue dress today, one that brought out the color of her eyes and that Matt had always thought she looked especially nice in. Now, he almost wished she were in the black dress that she'd worn yesterday. The black wasn't quite as flattering to her figure, and the color did nothing for her eyes.

One thing was obvious—the man was smitten with Emily. He had smiled at her *three times* just while asking for the gravy.

Matt's hands tightened at his side. It wasn't difficult for him to figure out what went through Obadiah's mind. Marrying Emily had probably been the man's intention for some time, but he had been biding his time, waiting for her mourning to end. But after meeting Matt yesterday, he felt threatened and realized that his claim on Emily wasn't as secure as he had thought. So now he was edging in closer, trying to win her favor with all his nice smiles and pretty compliments.

It wasn't going to work if Matt had any say in the matter.

He didn't mind it if Emily remarried. She deserved to be happy, and it would be a relief if she did get remarried. When he returned West, he would never need to suffer another headache worrying about her.

But Obadiah was *not* the man he wanted to see Emily marrying. He talked too smoothly, smiled too much, and . . . Matt just plain didn't like him. Besides, he didn't seem to care much for Joyanna, Grant, or Austin. He gave them no attention until Grant spilled his cup of water onto Obadiah's lap.

There wasn't much water left in the cup, just enough to

dampen Obadiah's pants, but Obadiah fumed, even if he masked it behind a polite expression. Beyond that, he seemed to think that children should be seen, not heard, and they most certainly shouldn't be heard while he was the one speaking.

After the younger children were excused and Emily cleared the dirty dishes away, Obadiah looked at Matt. "Please don't feel that you need to put your work off because of me. If there's work you need to do while it's still daylight, feel free to go ahead."

Clearly Obadiah was trying to get rid of him. And Matt wasn't going to fall for it.

"There's nothing pressing that won't wait for another day," Matt replied, forcing a smile onto his face. "We don't get too many visitors, and I'd hate to miss out on your time with us."

"Very kind of you," Obadiah said through gritted teeth.

If Obadiah thought he could worm his way into Emily's good graces without any resistance—well, he had better rethink his plans. Matt was sure that Emily cared nothing for the man—at least, reasonably sure—so he had no qualms over chasing the man off. He just wasn't sure of how he would go about it yet.

"Where did you live before you came to Osceola?" Matt leaned back in his chair, trying to appear relaxed. In truth, he felt tighter than a wound-up spring.

"Back East. Little town in Maryland," Obadiah replied.

"Near the ocean?"

"Right on the coast."

"Hmm. Bet Nebraska's a heap different than Maryland."

"Different isn't always bad."

The conversation was getting stilted. Obadiah looked toward Emily, his lips curving into another of those sickening smiles.

Matt decided to break all rules of politeness and ask an explosive question. "Why aren't you married?"

Obadiah drew his eyebrows together. "What?"

"Why aren't you married?"

He'd hit a nerve with that one. Red stained Obadiah's face and his nostrils flared. "Didn't your mama ever teach you not to ask such questions?"

"Sorry, my mama passed when I was only five. Didn't mean any harm. Just trying to keep up the conversation."

Obadiah settled down, his jaw clenching when Austin let out a shriek as Joyanna entertained him.

Emily stepped outside to fetch something. As the door snicked shut behind her, Matt said, "So there's a reason you aren't married?"

Obadiah shot him a withering look. "I thought you'd decided to quit prying."

Matt straightened, meeting Obadiah's gaze squarely. "'Fraid not. Not if you're intending to marry my sister-in-law."

Obadiah blew out a rumbling breath. "Stop it, would you? I don't know what you're trying to do—or where you got your crazy ideas—but I can tell you one thing. Colton Keath never would have treated a guest like this, and he wouldn't have liked his brother to, either."

"I know my brother," Matt said coolly. "And I also know that he appreciated honesty above all else."

Obadiah eyed him, obviously trying to figure out just how much of a threat Matt truly was. At last, he eased back, his eyes steely and lips turned up in a thin smile. "Now, no need to fly off the hook, Mr. Keath. I wasn't trying to hide anything, and the only reason I didn't answer your question was because it's deeply personal. But if you insist, then I'll tell you that I was engaged at one time. She jilted me shortly before the wedding, and I haven't had the heart to try again after that. There, does that satisfy you?"

He was trying to make him feel guilty for prying. Matt refused to let his expression betray any shame. "That's too bad.

I'm sorry it happened to you, but what spurred you to try to woo Emily if you are so against marriage after being jilted?"

Obadiah scowled. "Well, aren't you full of questions tonight?"

"That's not an answer."

"I didn't know I was required to answer to you, Mr. Keath."

Matt started to reply, but the door opened. Emily stepped into the room. At least he'd managed to pull one answer to his questions out of Mr. Obadiah Grady.

But somehow, that single answer made Matt even more disturbed. There was nothing evil about Obadiah. He appeared to be a good man. So was it possible that Emily *did* welcome his attention? Was he acting too quickly in trying to drive the man away?

If only Matt felt free to ask her. But no, that would be far too awkward for him, an unmarried man, to press for such answers, even if she was his sister-in-law.

By the time Obadiah took his leave, Matt was sick of the man's presence. Supper had finished hours ago, and Matt had fought back yawns for the past half hour. Despite his feelings, Matt followed Obadiah out the door, determined not to allow him to have an intimate goodbye with Emily. Obadiah glared at him but said nothing.

"Goodbye, Obadiah, and thank you for visiting. You've been nothing but a blessing to our family since we met." Emily's eyes shone in the setting sun.

"Thank you for allowing me to intrude on your evening. It gets awfully lonely sitting alone in my big house."

"Come anytime, and don't feel as if you're intruding. I enjoy your visits. Have a good night, Obadiah."

"You too, Emily."

As Emily disappeared inside, Obadiah leaned close to Matt and whispered, "You asked why I wanted to marry Emily. Well, here's your answer. She's an entirely different woman than

Mary Louisa; she's the kind who will stick with a man through thick or thin. After watching her all these years with Colton, that much is obvious. She's a good woman, but she needs a man. I want a wife, someone to share life with, carry on the Grady name, and we seem to fit together well. She deserves a good man, not a cowboy who would run out on her. And, Lord willing, I intend to be the man who wins her."

It took a moment for Matt to catch the meaning of Obadiah's last sentence. "You're saying that *I* would run out on her if I married her?" The idea sent rage rushing through his blood. How dare Obadiah imply such a thing!

Obadiah straightened, looking Matt in the eyes. "It takes more than a couple months to tame a rowdy, shiftless man. I intend to see that Emily's well taken care of so she doesn't fall into the hands of the likes of you."

Anger quickened Matt's heartbeat, and he didn't trust himself to speak. He might have his faults, but he *did* take his responsibilities seriously. If he didn't, he wouldn't even be there.

"Keep this between you and me, all right?" Obadiah pinned him in place with a hard look. "Emily doesn't need to hear a word of this."

Matt debated with himself but at last gave a tight nod.

"Good." Obadiah clapped him on the shoulder as if they were great friends, then he returned to his buggy.

Matt watched as Obadiah settled himself onto his seat. He gathered up the reins and flicked the team into motion without sparing Matt another glance.

Matt remained standing as Obadiah's team turned out of the lane and onto the road. That was when he sensed someone standing beside him.

"All right, why don't you like Obadiah?" Emily asked, staring after Obadiah's buggy.

Matt tensed, every muscle resisting the use of *his name* on her tongue. "What do you mean?"

"You're friendly when you're talking with Ephraim and Zane and the other men, but you don't act that way with Obadiah. Why? What did he ever do to you?"

Now she was getting defensive about Obadiah. Obadiah, who was in love with her land and the idea of carrying on the Grady name.

"Guess we just don't click is all," he mumbled, not looking at her.

"He's a good man. And he's one of our closest neighbors, so you should try to make friends with him."

Matt folded his arms across his chest. "If you like him, fine, but I'd just as soon the man ate at his own table like he ought to."

"Matthew!" Emily stepped back from him, her eyes flashing sparks. He hadn't gotten that look from her since Colton's birthday, and it only increased Matt's frustration with Obadiah.

"He was practically asking for an invitation to dinner by showing up when he did," Matt said through a tight jaw. "And did he really need to hang around all evening? He wore out his welcome, at least with me."

"That isn't at all hospitable. I will have you know that *all* neighbors are welcome at the Keath table whenever they should choose to stop by. And if they wish to stay and visit longer, then that's a compliment." She whirled and stormed into the soddy, the door banging shut behind her.

A compliment. Emily's words left a bitter taste in Matt's mouth. Did she realize that Obadiah was courting her? And if she did, was she trying to tell him that she considered it a *compliment?*

A hollow feeling formed in the pit of Matt's stomach, and he allowed his gaze to travel around the farm. Obadiah's visit left him feeling strangely insecure. He didn't intend to stay after harvest, and yes, it would be in Emily's best interest for her to remarry. But the thought of being replaced by another man shook him. Would that man, whoever he was, love and understand Emily as he ought to? Would he realize just how special Joyanna, Grant, and Austin were, and would he love them as his own—or would he treat them as a burden, the offspring of another man?

A small body leaned against his leg, and he looked down to see Joyanna. "It's all right, Uncle Matt. I don't like Mr. Grady either," she said, folding her arms across her chest to imitate Matt.

It wasn't right to encourage her to dislike Obadiah Grady, but Matt could see his own expression reflected so clearly on her face that he burst into laughter.

"You know what, Joyanna? You're pretty special," Matt told her, patting her on the head and smoothing down the flyaway wisps of hair that had escaped from her braids.

Joyanna stared back at him, her face solemn. "You're pretty special, too, Uncle Matt."

He laughed again, then he picked her up, threw her to the sky, and settled her over his shoulder. "It's past bedtime for all little girls on this farm, so it's off to bed with you, young miss."

Joyanna squealed. Matt hauled her off to the soddy, temporarily shoving aside the worries that nagged him. Especially Obadiah Grady, who was quickly turning into one big headache.

CHAPTER 23

Things seemed to go downhill for Matt two weeks later when he stepped into church on Sunday. As soon as he finished greeting Pastor Drew, who did he spot but Obadiah Grady, conversing with Josiah and Ephraim just as easily as if he attended the Mission Church every Sunday.

Matt glared at Obadiah, a surge of anger rushing through his veins. Why couldn't the man find another place to be? He'd already visited the farm twice that week. After several disagreements, Matt and Emily had been avoiding all mention of Obadiah, but Emily still delivered him a warning look whenever Obadiah came around in his buggy. It seemed to Matt that he deserved a break from Obadiah for at least one Sunday morning.

"Hey, Matt," Zane said, approaching him. "How are things going out your way?"

Matt looked away from Obadiah and managed to smile at Zane. "Um—we're getting along." *Barely.*

"Good. Been thinking we should talk about this next round of hay. It seems like we're going to have a good stretch of weather, so I was thinking about getting some hay down this week. What do you think?"

Usually, Matt enjoyed talking with Zane about farming. But when every nerve inside him was aware that Obadiah was edging closer to Emily, farming was the last thing on his mind. Forcing himself to keep his gaze on Zane and not Obadiah, Matt said, "Might be a good idea."

"Josiah finished cutting his hay yesterday, so I was thinking I'd start cutting mine tomorrow. Maybe you could wait a couple days and then cut yours. That way we can stagger it so we can get Josiah's hay picked up, then mine, and then yours. We wouldn't have to worry about our fields drying out at once and needing to be picked up on the same day."

Matt nodded, hoping he didn't look too distracted. "Sounds good. We'll go with your plan."

Zane clapped him on the shoulder. "We'll talk more later. Looks like Drew's getting ready to preach."

"Sure," Matt said, and then he walked to Emily and the children.

He slid into what had become his usual place, with Grant on one side and Joyanna on the other. Emily sat on Grant's other side with Austin on her lap. Rustling came from the pews behind him as others took their seats and murmured greetings to each other. He relaxed against the back of the pew. Obadiah hadn't made it around to Emily yet, and if Matt had his way, he wouldn't get close to her after church either.

As if to mock him, a shadow loomed at the end of the pew. "Do you mind if I join you?"

"Of course not." Emily grinned and scooted over to make room for Obadiah.

How was it fair that he could simply stroll in and take a seat so close to Emily, closer than Matt? That man was really starting to get under his skin.

Obadiah's ominous presence at the end of the pew made it nearly impossible for Matt to concentrate on the sermon. His mind warred back and forth. Common sense told him that Emily wouldn't put up with Obadiah if she didn't like him. And yet his irrational side wanted to either send Obadiah sprawling or shake some sense into Emily—he hadn't yet decided which would be more effective.

When they stood to sing the last hymn, Matt couldn't recall a word of Drew's sermon. Tilting his head from one side to the other in an attempt to relieve some of the built-up pressure, Matt heaved a deep sigh. *Lord, forgive me for not focusing as I ought. I shouldn't let Obadiah distract me from worshiping You.* Matt glanced at Obadiah. *But, Father, You know that man is infuriating!*

Pastor Drew's words of dismissal bounced off Matt's mind without sinking in. It wasn't until Joyanna wiggled past him to join her cousins that Matt realized the service had ended. Obadiah was already talking up a storm with Emily. No surprise there. Matt moved closer, silently reminding Obadiah that Emily was *not* his private possession.

"I'm still surprised to see you today, Obadiah," Emily said. "I'm glad you came, but I never expected you to leave the Methodist church."

"Oh, I haven't exactly left the Methodist church. Just decided to change things up a little." Obadiah gave her a charming smile.

Trying to gain points with you, don't you realize, Emily? Matt bit back his observation and gave the floorboards an intent scrutiny instead.

Obadiah and Emily's conversation bounced back and forth, their lightheartedness grating on Matt's nerves. Obadiah seemed reluctant to pull himself away from Emily, and Emily seemed eager to keep visiting with him.

Oh, Lord, please grant me patience. I would welcome even just an ounce. Matt counted to ten, telling himself to listen to his common sense and wait for them to finish. But he wanted to interrupt and drag Emily out the door with him.

Finally, Obadiah said goodbye and turned away. He made his way toward the door, shaking hands with men along the way, and then he stepped outside. Matt let a breath out in a *whoosh*, then quickly straightened so Emily wouldn't see his relief.

"Are you ready to leave?" Emily raised her eyebrows at him, no doubt wondering why Matt was hovering at her shoulder rather than visiting with the other men. In truth, the idea of leaving her side hadn't even crossed his mind.

Before Matt could respond, the decision was made for him. Seemingly from out of nowhere, Mrs. Durmond appeared and bore down on them with the force of a tornado, her black dress only adding to the impression.

Mrs. Durmond stopped in front of them, her gaze pinning them in place with a dozen accusations. Matt squirmed, even though he had nothing weighing on his conscience.

"Emily Keath," she said, "we must talk." She stood stiffly, the pinch of her forehead emphasizing that there was no way out of this conversation.

Emily flinched. "I'm sorry, but I need to gather the children and head home."

"Your dinner can wait. This cannot." Mrs. Durmond edged closer to Emily and hissed, "Emily Keath, do you realize how scandalous your behavior has become? It's a shame to this town. If you don't stop at once, there will be serious consequences for your sin."

"My *sin*? What are you talking about?"

"Obadiah Grady, that's what." Mrs. Durmond's face turned a mottled red. "I heard about what you did, dancing with the man right in front of the eyes of the whole town. Your husband has been in his grave not more than a few months. It's shameful, that's what it is. But even worse, I heard that you're allowing the man to *court* you. No widow should consent to marry a man within a year of her first husband's death, and certainly not when he'd only been gone a few months. No matter how bad her circumstances are."

"Wait . . . I'm allowing Obadiah to court me? What do you mean?" The horror in Emily's eyes told Matt that she hadn't even considered the idea. Despite his growing rage with Mrs. Durmond, some of the tension in his chest dissipated.

"I heard he's regularly visited you since the Fourth. You gave him a little encouragement, and now the two of you are getting thicker than cream, I hear. When others see you cozying up with the young man, it reflects poorly on the community and the church. I'm not going to keep silent a moment longer. Colton would be ashamed if he saw the way you're carrying on with another man so soon after his death." Mrs. Durmond's voice rang with self-righteous conviction. "You best think through your actions and stop chasing after men to solve your problems—"

Emily's stifled gasp was all the fuel Matt needed to drive him forward. *"Enough!"* he exploded, his voice loud enough to make everyone around turn and stare. "You have said enough and more than you ought! Leave Emily alone, and stop picking on a woman more defenseless than yourself. The only shameful thing around here is the way you treat Emily, bringing up such accusations against her."

Without waiting for Mrs. Durmond to say more, Matt hooked his arm around Emily's and propelled her toward the church door. Between Obadiah and Mrs. Durmond, he'd had as much as he could stand for one day. Emily had clearly endured even more.

Not even pestering Mrs. Durmond with his "outlandish" boots was going to help him laugh this attack off.

~

"I cannot bear that woman! How could she suggest such a thing?" The words burst from Emily as she and Matt made their journey home. She had remained silent ever since they left church, but now, as they approached home, she could not hold her anger inside any longer.

For all the years she'd known Mrs. Durmond, she'd never been able to rile Emily as she had the past couple of weeks.

Matt frowned, his fingers tightening around the reins. "That woman is a menace. She had no call to speak to you like that."

Emily shook her head. She hugged Austin against her middle as if he could shield her from the hurt. "I don't know where she gets her ideas. Obadiah Grady, of all people! He's a good neighbor, and he and Colton always got along well, but this is absolutely ridiculous. How could anyone think he's courting me?"

Since Matt didn't answer right away, Emily looked at him. "You don't think my behavior has planted those ideas in other people's minds, do you?"

"Not at all!" Matt said so passionately that her fear on that account disappeared.

"Good. Obadiah certainly isn't thinking along those lines, and I'd hate to think that I've been making others think he has."

Matt fell quiet, his face averted from hers.

Emily's lungs squeezed tight. "Matthew? You don't think he's courting me, do you?"

Matt didn't look up, so again Emily said, "Matthew."

Finally, he lifted his gaze to meet hers.

"I'd like an answer please. Do you think Obadiah is courting?"

He shifted on his seat and gave his head a jerk. "He's courting."

Emily squeezed Austin tighter, her stomach cramping. "How do you know?"

"He makes it pretty obvious."

Matt's answer wasn't at all what she had expected, and it didn't sit well, either. "You can't be right."

Matt shook his head. "He told me in plain words that he was courting."

Emily's breath tangled in her throat. "Obadiah *told* you that he was courting me? I thought you didn't talk to him."

Matt quirked an eyebrow. "I don't any more than necessary."

What else had Obadiah told Matt? Maybe those private visits she'd somehow failed to notice explained why Matt didn't like Obadiah. But it did puzzle her why Obadiah would share such personal information with Matt if they didn't get along well.

Emily sighed and slumped against the seat. "Ever since Colton passed away, everything seems to be going downhill."

"Don't let yourself think that way," Matt said. "I know it's hard without him, but he wouldn't want you to fall into despair."

Emily dipped her head in a nod. "You're right, of course." She nibbled her lip and then sighed again. "Just when I think Mrs. Durmond has said everything she can to rile me, she catches me off guard. I don't know how I'm going to face her again."

"I'm just hoping we don't run into her anytime too soon. If we do, I'm afraid I can't be held responsible for my actions."

Despite the chaos of her emotions, a giggle escaped from Emily. "I'm afraid I might yield to the temptation and come to your assistance as well."

Matt shook his head. His eyes still held remnants of the thunderclouds that had filled them with Mrs. Durmond's accusations, but his lips turned upward. "You're doing good, Emily. Colton would be proud of you."

The strength in his voice made it easy for Emily to believe that Mrs. Durmond was just a sinister weathervane, always being swung about by what she heard. Matt was like a rock. Nothing would budge his opinion, and if he believed the best about her, then she had no reason to listen to Mrs. Durmond.

A mist clouded Emily's vision, and she looked down. "Thank you."

What would she do without him?

CHAPTER 24

Matt swiped his arm across his brow, giving his muscles a break from tossing hay into the wagon. His muscles had hardened after putting up so much of Josiah's and the Hoffmans' hay, but by this point in the day, his arms were certainly feeling weary from all of their hard work.

Matt rubbed the itchy spots on his neck, courtesy of the hay that had embedded itself in his shirt collar. He'd never realized just how much work putting up hay was—or just how satisfying it could feel. There was a sense of security that no matter how nasty the weather this winter, the animals would have feed and there would be fuel to burn. And when it came right down to it, putting up hay wasn't the worst job he'd done in his life, even if it did irritate the skin.

"Giving out on us?" Zane asked from the other side of the wagon, his voice muffled by the mound of hay in the wagon between them.

"Never. Why, I could keep going like this for a whole week if need be," Matt said.

"Then I guess I could go for at least a week and a day, seeing how I'm more used to putting up hay than you are," Zane said, and Matt could hear his grin.

"Not a chance. You're younger than I am. Haven't developed as much muscle yet. You'd give out long before I was ready to call it quits." Matt smiled and pitched another forkful of hay into the wagon. During the whole round of hay, Matt and Zane had been trying to outdo each other in exaggerating just how long they could keep pitching hay. Their arguments grew more far-fetched the longer they worked.

In the wagon bed, Josiah angled his hat to block the sun. "I don't know about you, Sarah, but I'm going to take the lazy choice and call it a day come suppertime. I sure ain't lasting until next week."

Sarah glanced over her shoulder, the reins held lightly in her hands. "I think that's a wise idea, Pa."

"Hear that, Zane? Sarah just called you unwise," Matt called, unable to hide his grin. He'd picked up on the family joke of twisting Sarah's words to use against Zane. In truth, neither Sarah nor Zane had ever let a criticizing word for one another cross their lips. Ephraim always said that Zane could sell off the family silver and Sarah wouldn't say a word against him. That is, if they'd had any family silver.

Now, Matt received the usual reaction as Sarah's face reddened and she shook her head. "You know that's not what I said. Zane is a wise man, and I never implied otherwise, did I, Zane?"

"Not a hint of it," Zane replied.

Matt bit back his laugh. Sarah believed Zane had the last word in everything and that whatever he said was the living, breathing truth. Though it was humorous to watch, the sweetness of Zane and Sarah's relationship made Matt yearn for a marriage just like theirs. A union where, even after however many years passed, their love and devotion to each other would remain as strong as ever. Although they'd been married for three years and had two children, Zane and Sarah still gazed at each other like newlyweds as if they couldn't get enough of each other.

Still pitching hay into the slow-moving wagon, Matt glanced toward the soddy. Emily and Margaret had plenty of work to keep them busy as well—dinner to cook, the garden to weed, and, of course, children to watch. Along with the three Keath children, Byron and Audrey stayed at the house. Sarah seemed happy with the arrangement. Matt suspected she enjoyed being in the fresh air and sunshine, driving the team for her husband, rather than being back at the soddy with Margaret and Emily. Or maybe she liked to do whatever was the most helpful for Zane. It was true that her driving the team made the work go faster; Zane had taught her how to drive well.

Matt's thoughts shifted back to Emily, another woman who was as strong as they came. Obadiah still persisted in visiting, even though Emily's friendliness had somewhat chilled now that she suspected his intentions. Knowing that Emily didn't welcome the man's attention, Matt felt more relaxed around him. In fact, he felt sorry for the man. Almost.

Matt observed the hay stacked in the wagon. "Figure we're close to being ready to bring this load to the barn?"

Josiah nodded. "Yep. Let's just pile her a little higher, and then we'll head back."

Matt paused to wipe the sweat out of his eyes and looked back at the progress they'd made so far. If they worked fast, they could probably have all the hay up by nightfall.

Josiah's yell snapped him out of his reverie. The wagon was no longer beside Matt.

He tracked it up ahead, watching the team gallop away with their heads held high. Sarah had taken hold of the reins in both hands and tugged back on them, trying to slow the horses down while Josiah scrambled over the hay to lend a hand.

"What happened?" Matt asked. Zane had already taken off at a sprint toward the runaway team.

Whatever spooked the horses had sent them into an outright frenzy. Matt jogged after them, though he knew his efforts were pointless. He couldn't outrun the horses. Eventually they would tire out and come to a stop, whether that was still on Keath land or somewhere closer to town.

Unless they hit the drop-off at the edge of the field.

Matt sucked in his breath. They were aiming straight toward it.

"Oh, Lord," Matt whispered, but even as the prayer left his mouth, the team barreled into the barren spot that marked the drop-off. They vanished from view, dragging the wagon after them.

The horses screamed and the wagon bucked. Matt cringed as Josiah pitched out of the wagon—and landed on the ground in a heap.

Matt ran faster than before, screaming to God in his heart with each pounding step he took. Zane was right on his heels, running past Josiah who lay on the ground, sliding down the drop off. Matt's stomach lurched into knots.

Sarah could be anywhere down there.

Josiah pushed himself into a sitting position as Matt reached him. Dragging in a lungful of air, Matt planted his hands on his knees and asked, "You all right?"

"Yeah. I think I'm fine." Josiah moved his arms and his neck, testing them. "Don't think nothing's broken. If you would just help me to my feet . . ."

"Sure." Matt held out both hands to help him as gratefulness welled inside his heart.

Josiah took his hands, and Matt pulled him to his feet. Josiah flinched as he settled his weight on his right leg.

"'Fraid my side took a good beating." He rubbed his hip, then he limped toward the drop off and the tipped wagon.

Matt followed. The horses had regained their feet and were still harnessed together, but had freed themselves from the wagon. A broken piece of wood dragged behind them.

He scanned the area. No sight of Zane or Sarah.

Josiah and Matt slid down the loose dirt of the drop-off and rounded the wagon. A chill slithered up Matt's spine.

Sarah lay crumpled on the ground, unmoving.

Zane bent over her. Matt sprinted the last few steps toward them. Zane's shoulders quivered as he whispered something over and over that sounded like, "Please, Sarah! *Please!*"

Summoning all his courage, Matt touched Zane's shoulder. Zane twisted to look at him, his eyes begging for help.

"Matt, she won't wake up! What do we do?" He grasped Matt's hand in a grip so tight it hurt.

Matt looked over his shoulder to Sarah. Her face was ashen, the skin on her forehead broken and bloodied. One arm lay at an odd angle. Years of working in rough conditions had taught Matt basic first aid, but for one sickening moment, his mind went blank.

But then instinct took over. "We need to keep her as still as possible." He took a deep breath, his confidence returning. "We especially want to keep her neck still in case she has a spinal injury."

Zane nodded, but fear lurked in his eyes.

"How do we get her back to the house?" Josiah asked from behind Matt.

Matt's confidence slipped again. "I—I don't know. I guess the team won't be any help."

"Well, we need to do *something*," Zane said. "And fast!"

Josiah settled his hand on Zane's shoulder. "Calm down. We need to think this through. The last thing we want is to hurt Sarah even more."

Zane bit his lip, chin trembling.

"We need to get her to the house where we can best help

her," Matt said, thinking aloud. He looked at Josiah. "We need to find a way to carry her. Maybe we can find something back at the house to make a travois. Or we could use a board and carry it between us."

Josiah dipped his head toward the wagon. "Should be something there that can help us."

Matt squeezed his eyes shut. What else could they do for Sarah? "We'll want to stabilize her arm before we move her. If we could put it in a sling so it's close to her body and unable to move, that would be best."

Zane leaned away from Sarah and began to unbutton his shirt. "Think this would work?"

"Should be fine." Josiah glanced at Matt. "Somebody better run ahead and warn the womenfolk about what happened. And fetch a doctor."

"I'll do that." Matt settled his hat more firmly on his head. "Can you and Zane get her back to the house by yourselves?"

Josiah nodded and hurried toward the wagon. He tugged at the tailboard until it came free from the wreckage. Matt waited as Zane pulled his arms free from his shirt, then gently slipped it beneath Sarah's broken arm. Using the sleeves, he tied the shirt above her left shoulder.

Satisfied that they'd done all they could for Sarah, Matt scrambled up the drop off and ran across the dry stubble of the hayfield toward the house.

At the edge of the hayfield, Matt paused to suck in a few ragged breaths, then plunged on. His legs burned and his side felt as if a knife were stabbing it. He wasn't used to running like this, and his heavy boots did him no favors.

Finally he reached the farmyard. In a last burst of speed, he ran past the barn and dashed for the soddy, sending a cluster of chickens scattering before him.

Emily must have seen him coming because the door flew open and she hurried toward him. "Matthew, what's wrong?"

He gasped for breath. "There was—an accident. Wagon went over. Sarah's hurt—Zane and Josiah coming with her."

The color drained from Emily's face. "Is it bad?"

With all his heart, Matt wanted to reassure her that all would be well—but he knew she wanted the truth. Not the fluff. "Pretty bad. You'll need to get a bed ready for her, and you might want to give your mother and the kids a warning. I'm going for Doc Stoning." He hesitated, even though everything inside screamed for him to hurry. "You'll be all right?"

Emily nodded and straightened. "Yes. My mind is spinning with a hundred things to do, but I'll be fine."

"Good." Matt reached out and squeezed her shoulder, infusing as much comfort into the gesture as he could. "I'll be back soon."

He turned and ran for Bowie's pen. Even in the midst of his worry, Matt's heart lightened at the thought of being able to ride his horse somewhere. Catching Bowie, he saddled and bridled him, his hands still deft even though he'd been working more with harnesses than saddles lately.

He prepared to mount, but then Emily reappeared, a bucket and dipper in her hand.

"I thought you'd be thirsty after working in the hot sun and then running like that." She thrust the full dipper at him.

Matt suddenly realized he *was* thirsty, and although he chafed at losing even a minute, he reached for the dipper and took a deep drink, draining it dry. Emily refilled the dipper, and he drank again. And again. He took the last dipper and dumped it on his head, the coolness providing just the relief he needed. Grinning a bit sheepishly, he handed the dipper back to Emily.

"Thanks."

"I didn't want you passing out on the way to town." Emily moved back as he mounted Bowie. "Hurry home."

Home. The word touched a chord in Matt's heart. He hadn't attached that word to any specific place for over ten years, but now something inside him yearned to have something solid to tie himself to. To cling to even in life's fiercest storms, like now.

Matt glanced around him, taking in the soddy, the barn, and finally the small woman who stood beside him, the woman who evidently cared enough about him to bring him water.

Warmth filled his heart. He would need to examine that feeling later, but now was not the time to fall into introspection.

"I will," Matt said, tipping his hat to Emily and touching his heels to Bowie's sides. "I'll hurry home."

CHAPTER 25

Matt had never known his body could hold as much tension as it did while sitting in the soddy watching Doc Stoning. The faces of the family gathered in the room with him betrayed their own strain.

"Not only did Sarah break her arm, but she must have also hit her head as the wagon rolled," Doc Stoning said, leaning over Sarah's bed. "I've splinted the arm, so that shouldn't be a problem, but the fact that she is still unconscious concerns me." He surveyed the room, looking at the crowd of family huddled near Sarah. "I bandaged her head, but until she wakes up, it's impossible to determine the extent of her internal injuries. There is nothing I can do right now, so until then, we pray."

Matt hugged Joyanna tightly, and she buried her face deeper in his chest. He glanced across the room to where Emily sat beside her mother, her eyes shimmering with unshed tears. If only it were as simple to comfort her as it was Joyanna. Despite his fierce desire to shield his family from threats, physical or emotional, Matt had no defense against waiting.

Doc Stoning moved away from the bedside, and Zane claimed the spot next to his wife, jaw clenched. He hadn't said much since Matt arrived with Doc Stoning. And though Doc had pushed him aside so he could examine Sarah, Zane never looked away from his wife's still form. *Please, Lord, don't take Sarah from him. She means everything to Zane.* How would Zane even survive if his wife were taken away from him? Those two were truly one flesh, and Matt didn't want to consider how Zane would react to losing his other half.

But Doc Stoning was here to take care of Sarah, and between him and God, they had been known to work miracles before. With the best of care, Sarah ought to make a full recovery, although it might be a long journey.

"You aren't leaving, are you, Doc?" Elkanah Hoffman asked from his seat at the table. Both he and Florence, Zane's parents, had come as soon as they heard about the accident.

"No. I want to be here as soon as she wakes up." Doc Stoning straightened his instruments on the table, peering at everyone over his spectacles. "All of you might feel better with a little rest. Though goodness knows where you can find a place to sleep in this cramped room. No offense, Mrs. Keath."

Emily's lips turned in an attempted smile. "I can't take any offense with truth."

Matt looked around the room. *Cramped* was an understatement. Sarah had Emily's bed. Grant, Austin, and Byron Hoffman were asleep in the second bed. Margaret and Josiah sat at the table with Elkanah and Florence. Emily sat in the rocker with Audrey. And Matt had pulled a chair into the farthest corner of the room and sat with Joyanna, trying to keep his feet out of everyone's way. There was no way any of them, besides the children, could sleep, especially not with all the nervous rustling. The only one in the room who appeared calm was Doc Stoning, probably because he was used to being in such situations.

Joyanna wiggled on his lap, and Matt figured she likely felt as restless as the adults. Standing, he walked across the room to

Emily, tripping over a couple of toys on the floor in the process.

"I'm going to bring Joyanna to my bed in the barn so she can sleep," he told her. "I'll be back."

Emily looked up, her eyes rimmed with red. "Thank you for thinking of that. I can't think past..." She waved her hand toward Sarah without finishing her sentence.

Matt wanted to pull her close, just like he did with Joyanna, but instead he swallowed hard and repeated, "I'll be back."

Matt relaxed as he stepped outside into the cool night, a breeze caressing his face. This waiting was wearing on his nerves. Staying busy was the only relief he could find from the strain. After riding for Doc, he'd tracked down the team and brought them home, slowly since Molasses was limping and both horses were bruised and shaken up. It took him a while to rub them down and treat their injuries, and then it was time for chores. Tomorrow he'd need to mend the harness and check the wagon in the hayfield to examine the damage.

But for tonight, Joyanna and Emily needed him. And he intended to be here for them.

"Do I really get to sleep in the barn like you, Uncle Matt?" Joyanna asked as they walked from the soddy to the barn.

"Sure do," Matt replied.

Even in the dim light from the moon, Matt could see the smile that spread across her face. "I always wanted to stay in the barn with you," she told him, but then she frowned. "I sure do hope Aunt Sarah feels better tomorrow. You think God knows she's sick?"

"I know He does."

"Then I guess we'll just have to pray He makes her get better, right? Byron and Audrey are awfully sad 'cause their ma can't talk to them. I'd be sad, too, if my mama couldn't talk to me."

The idea of Emily being the one injured in the accident sent a chill through Matt's veins. *Thank you, Lord, that she was safe at the house,* he prayed silently, feeling a little guilty. It wasn't that he didn't care about Sarah; he just would have felt worse if Emily were the unconscious one. It was only natural considering he knew Emily better than Sarah.

In the barn, Matt let Joyanna scramble up the ladder ahead of him. He followed her closely to make sure she didn't slip and fall.

"It's pretty dark up here," Joyanna said as they reached the hayloft. "Shouldn't we get a light?"

"Not with all this hay. We don't want to start a fire." Matt picked her up and carried her to where his bedroll was spread out. Laying her down, he said, "There, you'll be just fine."

Joyanna clung to his arm. "Will you stay with me, Uncle Matt? I guess we can't have a light up here, but it's still pretty dark."

Her voice sounded small, and Matt was reminded of just how little she really was. Much as he wanted to hurry back to Emily, he couldn't leave the poor girl alone in a strange bed in the dark. "I'll stay until you fall asleep," he agreed. He stretched out beside her and wrapped an arm around her small shoulders.

Joyanna wiggled closer to his side. Before Matt could count to ten, her breathing had evened out and she was asleep.

Matt fought back a yawn, a wave of weariness threatening to suck him beneath its current. It had been a physically demanding day, and the stress from Sarah's accident only added to his exhaustion. Still, he had to return to the soddy. He wanted to be there for Emily. He'd only lay there long enough to make sure Joyanna was really asleep, and then he would leave.

He yawned again and allowed his eyes to close for just one brief second. He refused to fall asleep.

The next thing he knew, something nudged his shoulder. Matt's eyes flew open, and he tried to sit up, only to find that his right arm was pinned in place. *Oh yeah.* Joyanna was still lying on it. Matt fell back, twisting his head to see what had touched him.

Josiah's face hovered above his in the pale gray light that filtered through the window. "Sorry. Didn't mean to scare you."

"I'm fine." Matt extracted his arm from beneath Joyanna, tingles of pain shooting from his shoulder to his fingertips. He flinched and rubbed his arm, trying to restore circulation. "What time is it?"

"It's morning."

"Morning? Already? I didn't think I fell asleep."

"Guess you needed it."

Perhaps—but no more than Josiah or any of the others at the soddy.

"How's Sarah?" Matt tucked his shirt back into his pants. Silence stretched between them. The look in Josiah's eyes answered him even before he spoke, and Matt's heart missed a beat.

"She's gone." Josiah rubbed a trembling hand over his face. "She passed away an hour ago."

"Gone? You mean . . ." The words were so terrible that Matt couldn't vocalize them.

Josiah nodded, the lines across his features sinking deeper, making him appear older.

Matt's hands fell to his lap. Sarah Hoffman. A wife and mother of two children. Only twenty years old. Just like that, she was gone. It couldn't be true. Her family needed her. The whole community needed her.

"Zane." The single name broke through Matt's confusion. "How is he?"

Josiah swallowed. "I . . . don't know. He said he wanted to be alone, and then he left. I'll check on him later to make sure he's all right."

Emily? Matt didn't say her name aloud, but his concern was enough to drive him to his feet and toward the ladder. "You shouldn't have let me sleep."

"Figured at least one of us should get some decent rest. There was nothing you could do anyway."

Matt knew Josiah was right, but at the moment, all he wanted was to get to Emily.

As soon as Matt's boots hit solid ground, he took off at a sprint. The barn door banged shut behind him, the sound setting Snooty to lowing in the barnyard. Matt flew across the ground between the barn and the soddy, but strangely, when he reached the door of the soddy, Matt skidded to a stop. Or maybe not so strangely. He had no idea what mental state Emily would be in.

"Oh Lord, we need You," Matt whispered into the early morning air. "Please help Emily. Give her strength to accept this loss, especially since it's so soon after losing her husband. Help us all, Lord, to trust You even though nothing makes sense."

Matt reached for the handle and opened the door. Stepping inside, his gaze swept around the room. Grant and Austin slept in the corner, Margaret made up the empty bed where Sarah had been, and Emily stood at the stove with her back to him. Matt couldn't move forward, couldn't get any words past the lump lodged in his throat.

Emily turned and saw him. Her reddened eyes widened, but she seemed to be struck by the same thing that held Matt in place. She said nothing, just stood there holding the spoon suspended in midair.

Emily and Matt faced each other, with Matt's heart full of all kinds of emotions that threatened to overflow. Then Margaret caught sight of him, and dropping the coverlet onto the bed, she hurried toward him.

Tears brimmed in her eyes. "Oh, Matt, dear, I'm so glad to see you. Josiah told you?"

Matt nodded.

"Such a terrible thing." The older woman stopped in front of him, fumbling for a handkerchief. Without even thinking, Matt folded his arms around her. The woman had been motherly toward him ever since he arrived in Osceola, and he ached along with her in the loss of her daughter.

For a long moment, Margaret clung to him, then she stepped back and wiped her eyes. Matt locked gazes with Emily. She set down the spoon and moved forward into his arms.

Matt held her tightly, patting her back. "I'm sorry," he whispered near her ear. "So sorry." The words sounded weak, but he had nothing more to offer. He could only try to will some of his own strength into her.

A crowd of mourners watched in silence as Sarah's body was laid to rest in the Osceola Cemetery. Pastor Drew stood next to her grave, sunlight playing across his face as he delivered the service. "We therefore commit this body to the ground, earth to earth, ashes to ashes, dust to dust, in sure and certain hope of the Resurrection to eternal life."

Matt had heard the words many times before—for his mother, his father, and now for Sarah Hoffman. Somehow, the more often he heard the words, the more they tore at him. Nothing about Sarah's death was right. She was young, and she meant so much to so many. Her death had shaken the whole community. He could see it just by looking at the faces gathered for Sarah's funeral.

Beside him, Emily was rigid, not even flinching when the first shovelful of dirt hit the lid of Sarah's casket. The stony set of her face was so unnerving that Matt wished she'd just burst into tears, even though he had never known how to handle a weeping woman.

Zane also showed no emotion as the dirt slowly claimed his

wife's body. He stood with arms folded across his chest, face expressionless. If Matt hadn't known just how crazy Zane was for his wife, he might have thought he didn't care.

On the inside, Zane was probably just as dead as his wife. The impact of her death had knocked the very life out of him.

The moment Pastor Drew finished the prayer that concluded the graveside service, Matt grabbed Emily's elbow and whispered, "Let's go home." There was no use prolonging the agony by lingering and attempting to visit with neighbors.

Her chin quivered. "In a moment. I need to see Sarah's grave up close."

Matt nodded understanding. The sight of a grave was powerful enough to make the reality of the situation sink in fully.

"Take your time," he said, taking Austin from her. She turned away, hugging herself as she trudged toward her sister's grave.

With all the children in tow, Matt made his way toward the Hoffmans, knowing he ought to give them his condolences. But his feet dragged, and when he crossed paths with Ephraim and Sadie, he was glad to pause and visit with them.

"Well, Matt Keath, aren't you brave to take on all three of those young'uns?" Despite the pain in his eyes, Ephraim smiled, some of the lines easing from his face.

Sadie nudged her husband. "Now, Ephraim, Matt's a good hand with kids, so don't give him a hard time."

Under normal circumstances, Matt would have laughed. That was one he hadn't heard yet. No one had ever said he was *good* with kids; he considered himself to be only tolerable. Why, it wasn't too long ago that Emily was outraged with him for terrorizing her children!

"How are you?" Matt asked, hoping they would see the words as more than just politeness.

Their faces sobered. "We're fine, all things considering,"

Ephraim replied. "Sarah's death is a complete shock. Never would have seen it coming."

"And now her poor children are motherless." Sadie wiped at her eyes. "First Colton and now Sarah. It's been one rough year for our family."

Ephraim reached out and covered her hand in his. "It's been rough, but we'll weather this storm as well. The Lord knows what He's doing, and He can bring good even out of this. Why, just think. Colton's passing was bad, but it brought us Matt."

"True." Sadie patted Matt's shoulder. "And what a blessing he is."

They walked on, and Matt stared after them. When he'd first arrived, Sadie had called him an angel. And now, months later, she still considered him a blessing, even after all the rocky times he'd caused. He felt that all the blessing was on him for having such a wonderful family.

Finally, Matt moved on, pulling Joyanna and Grant after him. He reached Elkanah and Zane and stood to the side, waiting while old Mrs. Ruther clucked over the misfortune and patted Zane's shoulder. Mrs. Ruther was well known for stretching what could be said in a sentence into a whole paragraph, but by this point she seemed to have decided she'd said enough. She hobbled on, her cane tapping in tune to her uneven gait and her neck craning as she searched for someone willing to listen to her prattle.

Matt stepped forward and held a hand toward Zane. He accepted it without making eye contact.

Matt squeezed his hand but didn't try to say anything. Then he turned to Elkanah. "Let me know if you need anything," he said, holding out his hand.

Elkanah gripped his hand with enough strength to make Matt flinch. "I will. Thank you, Matt. It's good to know we have such dependable neighbors."

"Anytime."

Matt glanced at Zane again, but he doubted Zane needed to hear more words of condolence. Mere words couldn't resurrect his wife.

Matt swallowed. Shifting Austin to his other arm, Matt took Grant's hand, and motioning for Joyanna to follow, he led them away from the crowd gathered around Sarah's grave.

Colton's grave wasn't far off, and Matt found himself walking toward it. It had been some time since his last visit, and Matt let himself think of all the changes in his life since then. Last time, he'd been determined to keep Colton's family at a distance. He was at war with Emily, annoyed by Joyanna, and couldn't get the boys to stop screaming at him. Matt smiled. He'd been a mess, all right.

Matt studied the marker in silence. He didn't know how Emily had put up with him during those first couple of months. He'd thought *he* was the one who was going to sweep in and save the day, when really, Matt was the one who was the most bankrupt. It was no wonder they'd had such a hard time getting along together.

"Matthew?"

Emily's voice made him turn. She stood not too far behind, Audrey in one arm and holding Byron's hand.

"I hope you don't mind. I told Florence we'd take Byron and Audrey home with us. Florence tried to get Audrey to take a bottle, but she wasn't having any of it. The poor little thing wants her mama, so I offered to take her—um, home with me. And I thought Byron might as well come, too. It doesn't seem right to separate the two of them during such a time of upheaval."

Matt hadn't even considered that Audrey was still the age where she needed to nurse. He cleared his throat. "That won't cause problems, will it? With Austin, I mean?"

"He's about able to be weaned, anyway. It will be fine."

"Zane doesn't mind if we take his children?"

Emily shrugged. "Florence was grateful. I didn't ask Zane, but he's not in any shape to make decisions right now."

"Then I guess we'll take them home." Matt was struck by how, even in the middle of her own pain, she still thought of the needs of those around her. Not many women would act like that. Or men, for that matter.

"You're pretty special, Emily," he told her without thinking. Instantly he felt embarrassed that he'd spoken his thoughts aloud, but there was no taking his words back now.

Emily blushed, her gaze dropping to the ground. "Thank you," she murmured, then spun away. "Guess we better get home."

Looking around at the children who were now under their wings, Matt figured she was right. He wasn't sure about many things, but he did know that the two young children would add a good deal more work to their lives.

Slowly, Matt followed Emily, aware of a tug in his heart. It felt similar to what he'd felt the day he said goodbye to her, right before he rode off for Doc Stoning. But again, there was no time to think the feeling through, and there probably wouldn't be anytime soon. Not with all these children to look after.

Maybe that was all right though. Because whatever he felt was unsettling, at the very least.

CHAPTER 26

"All right, old girl, here we go again." Every time Matt settled onto his stool to milk Snooty, he recited those same words. At first he'd used them out of dread for the task, but now they were merely habit. He and Snooty had gotten used to each other, and she behaved surprisingly well… most of the time.

Matt scooted the stool closer, grabbed hold of her teats, and squeezed, sending milk pinging into the pail. Truth be told, he'd come to almost enjoy milking. It was a peaceful task that allowed him to think clearly. The quiet of the barn coupled with the rhythm of milk hitting the bucket were like a balm for his mind— particularly now when the house had become noisier than ever.

It had been three weeks since Sarah's funeral and slowly the family was starting to adjust. Matt still shuddered when he remembered those first days following her death. Audrey fussed constantly, setting everyone's nerves on edge and keeping Emily up long into the night. Byron too was not an easy addition, as he couldn't comprehend why his parents were gone. After the initial joy of playing with his cousins wore off, Bryon wanted to go home. Whenever someone opened the door, he tried to bolt outside and run home.

A couple of days of dealing with his screams left both Matt and Emily exhausted and questioning if they'd made the right choice bringing the two children home with them.

But with time, Byron and Audrey were adjusting to life in the Keath house. The tears and screaming had subsided, and no one made attempts to run home. Matt hoped they could finally have peace from the chaos that Sarah's sudden death had brought on them all.

Zane visited a few times. He seemed lost in a fog, and Matt had given up on trying to have a conversation with him. Instead, Matt allowed his presence to remind Zane that he was available if Zane needed him.

Matt worried about him. Zane had lost weight since Sarah's death, and his face looked haggard. Matt couldn't help but wonder if Zane had even gotten a decent night's rest since the funeral. The only time he appeared to be aware of his surroundings was when his children were in his arms; otherwise, he seemed lost in a different world. His grief was natural, but Matt feared that if the fog didn't lift soon, Zane might seriously hurt himself.

Matt sighed, stripping the last of the milk from Snooty's teats. Sometimes life just didn't make sense. He'd rehearsed the accident many times in his mind, trying to figure out what they could have done differently to prevent Sarah's death. Was there something he should have noticed that day? Something about how the team was acting? Would it have made a difference if a man had been driving the team instead of a woman?

The only conclusion he could come to was that the Lord hadn't turned a blind eye to their pain. He knew what they were going through, and all circumstances remained under His control. It might not make sense to Matt—but he wasn't God, so he didn't need to keep going over the situation, trying to find a reason to criticize himself. What had happened was in the past and couldn't be changed.

Snooty shifted, and then her foot swung forward, striking the bucket.

"No!" Matt yelled, but he was too late. The bucket flew, and milk spilled in all directions.

Matt leaped to his feet, sending his stool tumbling backwards. He jabbed an accusing finger at Snooty. "You unmannerly beast! After all this time of getting along, how could you do such a—"

A bad word almost slipped out, and Matt clamped his mouth shut. He hadn't felt such an overwhelming urge to swear in a long time. He also hadn't been this mad in a long time either. *Take a deep breath. She's only a dumb old cow, and what she's done isn't worth dirtying your mouth over.*

Matt sucked in a breath and whirled away, not trusting himself to stand close to Snooty without hitting her. He needed to get his mind onto something else, not on all the choice expletives that he would love to blast.

Matt snatched the pitchfork, stalked to the horses' stall, and set to work scooping muck with a will. Then, at the top of his lungs, he belted out a hearty rendition of "Amazing Grace," his voice reverberating through the walls of the barn.

"*Amazing* grace, how *sweet* the sound that *saved* a *wretch* like *me*, I *once* was *lost,* but *now,* am *found,* was *blind,* but now I *see!*"

The tension in his neck eased, and he swung into the second verse, yelling as loud as he could. He was actually starting to enjoy this.

He drew a deep breath, prepared to launch into the third verse. But in the brief second of silence, he heard a slight cough from behind him. A shape lingered in the entrance, half-shrouded by darkness.

"It's good to hear a man singing while he works." Josiah stepped into the barn, the corner of his lips twitching.

Matt's face burned. "Josiah. Wasn't expecting you this evening."

"No, probably not." Josiah chuckled. "But then I would have missed a most interesting concert.

Thinking of what he'd truly wanted to say to Snooty, Matt felt an immense wave of relief that he hadn't yielded to his old habit of swearing. That would have been a real cause for embarrassment if Josiah had witnessed that.

"What brings you this way tonight?" Matt asked, setting his pitchfork aside.

"I brought something you might want to see." One of Josiah's eyebrows quirked. "It's out in my wagon. You have time to come take a look?"

"I figure so." Matt shot a glare at Snooty. "The cow can wait a couple more minutes."

Falling in step behind Josiah, Matt walked outside into the sunlight.

"I was in town today, and I happened to come across this . . . *thing*," Josiah said, striding toward the wagon. "He seemed to think you wouldn't mind seeing him."

Matt looked toward the wagon, shielding his eyes against the sun. A man sat on the bench, staring out at the field as if he'd never seen such an interesting sight. As Matt drew closer, the man turned, a grin igniting across his face.

"Well, if it ain't Matt Keath! When'd you take up singing hymns acapella?"

Shock nearly knocked the breath out of Matt. "*Flick?* Are my eyes giving out on me?"

It made no sense. The man looked like Flick and spoke like him, but Matt couldn't reconcile the idea of Flick, an all-out cowboy, appearing in the heart of a farming community.

And yet, no amount of blinking would make Flick disappear.

A tumult of emotions washed over Matt, not all of them making sense. Pleasure at seeing his old friend. Uncertainty over how to react to Flick after all the changes in his life. And —uneasiness?

Flick gave Matt a skeptical look. "You really meant it when you said you wanted to play farmer, didn't you?" he asked, tacking on a pair of questionable words.

Matt stiffened. "I usually follow through with my words."

"So you do know him." Josiah glanced from Matt to Flick. "He told me so, but I wasn't sure if I should believe him. That being the case, I'll be heading home now." He motioned to the horse tied behind the wagon. "You got a place for this feller's horse, Matt?"

"I guess," Matt said slowly.

Flick scrambled down from the wagon seat, and within a few minutes, Flick's few belongings were stacked on the ground beside the wagon and his horse had been put in the same pen as Bowie. Evidently Flick had carried along all his earthly possessions.

Now Matt just needed to figure out why he was visiting.

Matt focused his attention on Josiah. "You want to stay for supper, Josiah? Emily and the kids would be happy to have you visit a little longer."

Josiah shook his head. "Thank you, but no. Margaret would wonder what was taking me so long in town."

"Suit yourself," Matt replied. "Just make sure to stop by sometime soon."

"I will. Nice meeting you, Flick." Josiah tipped his hat to them. Climbing up into his wagon, he clucked, and his team plodded forward.

"Well." Flick turned to Matt. "I didn't believe you'd last this long."

Matt folded his arms across his chest. "You made that abundantly clear back in Scottsbluff."

"Oh, don't go getting all riled up about what was and wasn't said in the past. You're supposed to fall over with joy at seeing a familiar face from your *real* occupation." Flick arched a brow, eyeing Matt's clothing. "You haven't decided to quit cowboying, have you?"

"Not on your life," Matt said. "Farming's not so bad, but I'd choose riding horses to following behind them any day."

"Good. Seeing you in such a getup made me fear you were losing it."

Ignoring the jab at his outfit, Matt asked, "So what brings you to these parts?"

Flick waved a finger at him. "Not so fast, Mr. Keath. You shouldn't ask me to get into a long explanation like that on an empty stomach. Something smells mighty fine, and I'm so starved that my stomach's becoming friends with my backbone. Besides, don't you want me to meet the family?"

Meet the family. No, Matt realized, he *didn't* want to take Flick anywhere near Emily and the kids. Flick had been a good friend back in cattle country, but standing there in the barnyard, Matt was struck by his rough nature. Flick wasn't much on manners or controlling his tongue. Even Matt used to grow weary of all the expletives that salted Flick's language. With Flick, it wasn't a question of *if* he would use unsavory words; it was a question of *how many* he would use.

But Matt suspected that Flick hadn't traveled all the way from Scottsbluff just to say hello. Something must have brought him there, and until he revealed that purpose, Matt had to humor him.

"Fine." Matt gave a sigh. "Emily should have dinner about ready. But Flick?"

"Yeah?"

"Remember this isn't the Bar K. You're about to talk to a lady and children, not to cowhands."

Flick swore and held up one hand. "Relax, Mr. Family Man. I'll be on my best behavior. No need to get yourself worked into a sweat."

That did nothing to ease Matt's worry. After all, he knew what Flick's best behavior usually entailed.

CHAPTER 27

Matt closed the door behind him with a heavy thud and blew out his breath. His fears had been confirmed as soon as they walked in and Flick burst into a string of profanity. "You told me your brother had a couple kids, not that he was trying to repopulate a whole county!"

The look of horror on Emily's face made Matt wish the floor could swallow him alive.

"You got a place I can spread my bedroll for the night?" Flick asked, his spurs jangling as he shifted from one foot to the other.

Matt shot him a quick glance. "You planning on staying some time?" He had hoped that Flick would decide to move out soon. Maybe that night, given Emily's reaction to him.

"Depends. I'll need to bunk down for the night at least."

Matt let out a breath of relief. So he didn't plan to stay long. "You can sleep with me in the hayloft. Plenty of room there for both of us."

"If it's good enough for you then I guess I can handle it."

Matt pushed away from the door and marched down the path leading to the barn, motioning for Flick to follow. He intended to get some answers out of Flick, and whatever Flick had to say was sure to contain multiple bad words. Matt didn't wish Emily and the children to overhear.

He'd walked this path so many times over the summer that he could probably walk it in his sleep. He kept his gaze fixed on the ground, determined not to look at Flick and give him an opportunity to start talking. Not until they were settled down for a long talk.

But then a pair of boots came into view, and Matt jumped back just in time to avoid colliding with Zane.

Zane jerked as well. "Sorry. Didn't see you there."

"I'm the one who's sorry. I wasn't watching where I was going." A movement behind Zane caught Matt's attention, and his heart plummeted. *Obadiah Grady*. Again. Did the man never spend his evenings at home anymore?

"Mr. Keath." Obadiah tipped his hat to him, but his gaze strayed to Flick. "I see you have company."

Matt nodded. "This is Flick . . ." He suddenly realized that he didn't know Flick's last name. Was Flick even his real name? A person's name wasn't too important out West. Whatever a man took as his handle was accepted without question—but etiquette was different here in Osceola.

"I see." Obadiah surveyed Flick. "A cowboy, I take it?"

"That's right." Flick swore, but he was grinning.

Obadiah stepped backward, his face reflecting his disgust. "So this is the kind of company you keep, Mr. Keath? *These* are the kind of people you invite into your home, and expose Emily and the kids to?"

"Oh, come on," Flick said before Matt could respond. "Matt ain't choosy about who he rubs elbows with, unlike *some* gents." He narrowed his eyes at Obadiah.

Obadiah glared right back. "Matt should remember that he has more than just himself to think about when he's here on

Emily's farm. If he wants to associate with filthy, uncouth, swearing—"

"Obadiah, leave them alone. I'm sure Matt knows what he's doing." Zane stepped forward, appearing more alert than he'd been since Sarah's death. "Let's not be too judgmental."

Obadiah wheeled to face him. "Think, Zane! It's bad enough that Emily has to put up with the likes of Matt, but for him to invite his rough and tumble friends over is the last straw!"

"The last straw?" Zane frowned. "I didn't realize we were counting straws. Matt's been good help to Emily."

"But he's rowdy and shiftless. Nothing like the kind of man Emily deserves."

Matt clamped down on his tongue, reminding himself to choose his words carefully. But then Flick let out a whoop, and Matt realized that holding his own tongue was the least of his concerns.

"I think this here no-good busybody needs to be brought down a notch. What do you say, Matt?" Flick looked at Obadiah, his eyes glinting with a dangerous spark that Matt was all too familiar with.

Matt inserted himself between Flick and Obadiah. "No, Flick. You will *not* so much as touch him."

Obadiah stumbled a step back, his eyes round. He had gone too far, and now he was nervous. He ought to be.

"I haven't heard Emily complaining about Matt's help, so come on, Obadiah," Zane said, interrupting the stare down. He tugged on Obadiah's arm. "Let's get moving."

With a final glare at Flick, Obadiah hurried to follow him. But when he reached the door, he paused to call back, "This isn't over, Matt. Before tonight ends, you won't be feeling quite so cocky."

He disappeared inside.

Flick stepped forward, and Matt grabbed his arm. "Just let him go."

"No, *you* let me go, and I'll teach him a thing or two about how he talks to us. I'll bet no one's ever given him a black eye in his life, and I'd like to teach him how it feels."

"Settle down, Flick, or you're going to get me in trouble. This isn't the West, and if you go around delivering punches, people aren't going to take very kindly to it. Obadiah's not a bad man. He says what he truly believes, and he's just trying to look out for Emily."

"Why should he care? She's your sister-in-law."

"But he wishes to make her his wife."

"Well, if she accepts his court, she's crazy, that's what. Crazier than a mustang on locoweed." Flick shook his fist one last time at the soddy, then turned to face Matt. "Say, is it really true that there's no saloon in town?"

Matt blinked, surprised by the sudden change of subject. Not that he should've been. Flick was always ready to jump into a good fight, but he quickly forgot why he was fighting, the only reason Matt had ever been able to drag him out of a fight before he killed his fool self.

"There's no saloon. Osceola is a dry town."

Flick swore. "Leave it to church folks to put a damper on everything fun. How can you stand it this long without a good drink?"

Matt looked at him evenly. "I don't drink, in case you forgot."

"Oh, yeah. You always have been a tee-totaler." Flick muttered another expletive. "That's just because you never gave drinking a good try."

Matt remained silent. He'd already tried arguing with Flick countless times in the past, tried to explain how he'd watched countless men ruin their lives and destroy their families because of liquor. But finally he'd given up. Flick knew where he stood, so there was no reason to get into yet another fight over it.

Flick shrugged. "Fine. Live your life like a straight-laced puritan if that's what you want. I don't care."

Matt kept quiet, waiting until they reached their horses' pen. Then he faced Flick. "Care to explain what brings you here?"

"Impatient as ever, ain't you?" Flick leaned back on the fence and folded his arms across his chest.

Oh, yes. This was Flick he was talking with. The man who had always dragged out every piece of news as long as possible. Matt resisted the urge to roll his eyes and instead leaned back against the fence like Flick. He might as well settle in for a long wait.

Flick uncrossed his arms and spread them along the fence rail, releasing a sigh. He reminded Matt of a cat stretching out in the sun, lazy and content. Even his voice almost sounded like a purr. "Keller sure was smug about firing you."

Matt studied him out of the corner of his eye. "What do you mean by *firing* me? I quit."

"Not by Keller's version of the story. He says he fired you. And let me tell you—he's made up at least a dozen stories for why he did. Told them all over the saloon. Your reputation as one of the best cow punchers in the north is sadly smudged."

Matt sucked in his breath. That was *not* the news he'd expected Flick to deliver. "Why? Why would he do a thing like that?"

"Why do you think?" Flick asked. "You were the one who turned your notice in to Keller. Was he mad then?"

Matt slumped back against the fence, the wood biting into his back. "Oh, he was mad, all right. Wanted me to ride as foreman for him."

"He did? Then for pity's sake, man, why didn't you? You've dreamt of that job!"

"You know why. I was needed here more than I ever was at Keller's."

"Well, I hope you thought through what you were tossing out. Your job here is only temporary, while your job as a cowboy's gotta last you a while. You would have been in real good shape if you'd taken that job Keller offered you."

Matt scanned the farm, a piece of land that had come to mean more to him than Keller's spread or any other ranch ever had. This summer couldn't last, but the memories of his time here would always be close to his heart—and far more precious than any memories he carried from working for Keller. "Doesn't matter. I don't regret coming here, and I didn't want to work for Keller anyway. He's too pushy."

Flick raised an eyebrow. "Think beyond your position at Keller's, Matt. In turning down Keller's offer, you also made an enemy out of the man, and he's made sure that you won't find a position anywhere near the Bar K. No one around Scottsbluff is going to be too eager to hire you if you head back there."

Matt chewed on his lip. So, the promising career he'd been intending to fall back on was gone. He'd worked hard to get himself to the point he was at when he left. Now, when he returned, he had no choice but to start from scratch—but even worse since his reputation had been ruined.

He glanced at Flick. "All very interesting, but what does this have to do with my question? What brings you here?"

Flick's eyes lit. "I'm going to Texas."

"But—why?"

"Why not? Things were getting too boring around Scottsbluff, so I figured I'd set off on a new adventure. Meet some new people, see some new sights. There's cattle in Texas, and since cattle's my trade, I figured I'd sashay down that way."

"Oh." Matt frowned. "And you decided to travel miles out of your way to visit an old friend who's made decisions that you think are dumb?"

"Exactly."

And that made no sense to Matt. "But why did you decide to come visit *me*, of all people?"

"*Now* we're starting to get to the point." Flick leaned closer, jabbing a finger at Matt's chest. "I've got a proposition for you."

"You don't say."

"I want you to come to Texas with me."

Matt looked down at Flick's finger still poking at his ribs, then took a step back, distancing himself from the man. "I told you back on the Bar K that I wasn't going to Texas—and I haven't changed my mind."

Flick heaved a sigh. "I thought I'd explained this. You're a cattleman. Your reputation back in Scottsbluff is in bad shape. You should be jumping on this opportunity to make a fresh start."

Matt shook his head. "No. You know I intend to stay until harvest, and that's still a couple months off. There's no way I'm leaving yet."

Flick frowned. "If you're worried about the bet we made, forget about it. I'm willing to call it off if it means you'll go to Texas with me."

"What bet? In case you forgot, I declined your bet. And you better be glad, or you'd be handing me a nice chunk of cash. *You* were the one who said I wouldn't last longer than a day on the farm."

"I never said that! I clearly remember saying that I didn't think you would be back any *sooner* than a few days on the farm."

Matt resisted the urge to roll his eyes. Flick never appreciated being put in his place. "That's beside the point. I'm not going, and that's the end of the matter."

"Not quite. You haven't heard the details yet." Flick turned and sauntered into the barn.

Matt looked after him. Had Flick just dismissed himself and left him with a couple dozen more questions? It wouldn't surprise him. Flick always liked to make his exits with as much drama as possible.

But after a moment, Flick appeared in the doorway again and marched back to Matt, a newspaper tucked beneath an arm. He stopped in front of Matt and unrolled the paper. "I didn't want to scare you—but since you refuse to listen to any other reasoning, read this."

Matt hesitantly took the paper, his pulse quickening. He didn't bother to look at the advertisements like he had before when receiving a newspaper from Flick; instead, he immediately flipped to the front page.

He scanned the headline, his stomach pitting. "What!"

"Told you it would spook you." Flick leaned against the fence, his words playfully taunting.

Matt lowered the paper and looked at Flick, his heart thundering in his ears. "Ryker? He killed *Ryker*, of all people? Why? Ryker was only the jailer."

"I'm telling you, Frank Harvey's got a grudge a mile wide."

"As I recall, you laughed at me for being worried about Frank Harvey after he killed Telmond."

"Did not!" Flick jerked upright, his hand fisted at his side. "Anyhow, killing Telmond was one thing; killing the jailer is another. You bet your boots, Matt, you're a marked man."

The tightness in Matt's gut had already confirmed that for him. He raked a hand through his hair, trying to sort through his jumbled thoughts. One stood out from the rest and finally made it to the forefront of Matt's mind. "Frank doesn't know I'm here, so I'm safe. Just as long as he can't find me."

"Wrong again. Old Frank is bound to have figured out you're here by now. News that you gave up being a puncher to help your family on their farm in Osceola spread through the area like wildfire. It's no secret where you disappeared to."

Matt rubbed harder at his scalp. It seemed like the gossip of others was causing him a heap of trouble.

"But relax, old boy. That's why you're going to Texas with me. No one will know where you've disappeared to. You don't even need to tell your family. Then, when Frank Harvey comes snooping around for you, he won't have a clue where to even begin searching. See? It's perfect."

"Perfect—except that I'm not going to Texas. I have work to finish here, and I'm not going to let Frank Harvey dictate how I'll live my life."

"You crazy man!" Flick let loose a string of expletives. "You won't have much life to live your way with Frank Harvey out for the kill."

Matt stared back, refusing to flinch. Not even if Flick's words did hold some truth. "I don't intend to die. I've got a crop to harvest, and Emily needs me here to bring it in. Running from Frank Harvey won't take care of that."

"Find someone else to help her. You won't be of any use to your family if you die."

"It's not that simple." Matt rubbed his jaw, stubble abrading his palm. "Hiring help costs money, and a hired hand isn't going to be as concerned about seeing things done right. I promised I would stay, and I'm not breaking my word."

"You fool!" Flick aimed a couple more expletives at Matt and tilted his hat back, scraping his fingers through his hair. Then his face brightened. "I've got it. Get Emily married off."

"What?" Matt recoiled, Flick's words scalding him.

"Marry her off. If she has a husband to take care of her then your worries are over. He won't cost her a cent, and he'll be pleased as pie to have a field ripe for harvest when he didn't have to sweat a drop over it. It works well for everyone."

"Never." A sick feeling swirled through Matt—far more powerful than Flick's words warranted. He swallowed hard, but the nausea refused to completely go away. "Emily's not an old shoe that needs to be disposed of. I have no intentions of marrying her off to someone just to make life easier for me. She wouldn't stand for it in the first place."

"I think she would. You have a lot of sway over her."

"Me?" Matt's next breath choked him. "How would you know? You just met her."

Flick smirked. "I know how to read women. It was written all over her face."

Unsure of how to fight against Flick's words, especially since he *didn't* read women at all, Matt shifted his stance. His mind buzzed with words that he wanted to say, but it was impossible to string together a coherent sentence.

Flick took advantage of his silence. "Find someone who would be willing to marry her, and then get them together. You said Obadiah is courting her. Push her toward him. Half your work is already done."

"Marry her off to *Obadiah*? Not on your life!" The idea sent a blaze of heat through Matt's veins, hot enough to burn.

Flick shrugged. "He *is* a big pain, so I don't blame you for not wanting to tie him into the family. How about the other man who was with him? Is he married?"

"Zane?" The heat in Matt's blood only increased. "He was married, but his wife passed on. Byron and Audrey are his kids."

Flick snapped his fingers and grinned. "See? We've got it. He didn't seem like a bad fellow, and Emily's certainly got some charm to pull him in. She needs someone to help her run the farm, and he needs someone to watch his kids. It's perfect. They could both help each other."

Matt shook his head. "Impossible. Zane's wife passed away only a few weeks ago. He's hardly able to think straight, let alone agree to marry another woman."

Flick scowled. "Don't be so pessimistic. A man's got to live and eat even if he's lost his wife, right? He'd have some clouded thinking if he couldn't see the merits of a union with Emily."

"You underestimate Zane. He wouldn't marry just to get a cook and housemaid. He loved his wife like you've probably never loved anyone in your life."

Flick's features darkened. "Don't go lashing out at me when I was only trying to help. You act so defensive of Emily. You got a little sweet spot for her yourself?" He began his usual pattern of mocking, pretending to fall back against the fence and clasp his hands over his heart with a look of love-struck desperation. "Oh, Emily, my dearest. I have a man right on my tail who seeks to kill me, but since I could never fathom seeing you married off to another man, I offer you the rest of my days and promise that I shall stay with you until the day he ends my life with a bullet."

"Cut it out, Flick." Matt scowled, trying to cover the erratic thud of his heart. He wasn't smitten with Emily, not by a long shot. But he *did* feel unsettled by the idea of her and Zane making a match.

There was a little truth to Flick's words. Getting married would take care of many of Emily's and Zane's problems. The only real trouble was that Zane was still in love with Sarah, so how was he supposed to give Emily the love she deserved as his wife?

That was it. That was the real reason he didn't want to see the two of them married. Now, if the right man came along with the ability to provide for Emily and the children and love them unconditionally, then Matt wouldn't hesitate to congratulate them. The only reason he couldn't shake the discomfort he felt whenever he considered her remarrying was because none of the suggested candidates were right for her.

"Well, at least I tried." Flick threw his hands into the air. "Land sakes, I tried, but arguing with a rock only wastes a fella's breath. You sleep on this tonight, and tomorrow we'll talk more about heading to Texas, all right?"

Matt frowned. "You sure are stubborn."

"Same to you. But this time *I'm* in the right, so you'd be wise to listen to me. Frank Harvey means business. And if you think you can stay here and escape him, you're a simpleton. Telmond and Ryker were both smart men. They saw enough of the hard side of life to know better than to leave their backs exposed. I'm warning you—if you run into Frank Harvey, you can say goodbye to this life forever."

"We'll see," was all Matt would commit to saying. "We'll just wait and see."

CHAPTER 28

Emily risked a peek at Obadiah over her mending. He flashed her a smile, and she ducked her head, fixing her attention on the patch on Grant's overalls. Obadiah was a puzzle tonight—a puzzle she couldn't figure out.

When he marched through the door an hour ago, his mouth had been pressed into a hard line, his face red. Emily couldn't think of why he would be upset, but after a brief greeting, she focused on Zane, giving Obadiah time to calm down. And he had. Ever since then, he'd been charmingly polite.

Or maybe she was wrong and he *hadn't* been mad at all. Maybe he'd just been out in the sun for too long.

Matt had opened her eyes to the suspicion that Obadiah was courting her, and since then, she'd been trying not to give him reason to think she had stronger feelings for him than she did. He was a good man, and she didn't want to hurt him. But there was no way she could marry him. She still loved Colton too much—and when it came down to it, she supposed that she would *always* love him too much to remarry. There wasn't a man on earth who could take his place.

But Obadiah didn't seem to understand her hints—and he

proved it now by leaning forward with another of those too-charming smiles. "Emily, would you like to take a walk with me?"

Emily missed her next stitch and jabbed the needle into her finger. She yelped and dropped her mending to rub the tip of her finger.

How would she find a polite excuse for turning down a walk with Obadiah? A walk away from the soddy *did* sound nice, but Obadiah would take it the wrong way.

Then she gave Obadiah a smile of her own. "I'd love to go for a walk with you, Obadiah, and I'm sure the children would too. Kind of you to offer."

Joyanna cheered, and even though the younger children didn't understand, they followed her example, creating a racket that made Obadiah flinch.

"I meant just the two of us, Emily. Alone," Obadiah said. "Every adult needs a little time away from the house—*without* the kids."

"Sorry. I can't leave the children alone, so I guess a walk isn't happening." Emily picked up her mending and the children stopped whooping and went back to their play.

"I'm sure Zane can watch them for the few minutes we'll be gone," Obadiah spoke through gritted teeth. "Right, Zane?"

Zane looked up from the rocker where he sat with Audrey, his gaze lingering on Emily rather than Obadiah. "If that's what Emily wants."

Did he, too, realize that Obadiah was attempting to court her? Emily certainly hoped not. The fewer people who guessed Obadiah's intention, the better.

"I think we both want to walk." Obadiah rose from his seat and stopped in front of her. Plucking the mending from her lap, he took her hand and pulled her to her feet. "Coming?"

Emily snatched her hand out of his, tempted to put him in his place and give him a firm *no*. But on second thought, maybe a walk with him was a good idea. If they could be away from the children's listening ears then maybe they could clear the air of all misunderstandings and Emily could break the news that he stood no chance of winning her heart.

Bother. Why hadn't the man taken a wife years ago?

Giving in, Emily nodded and led the way out the door. Obadiah followed, his footsteps determined, and the door closed behind them.

"Where shall we go?" Obadiah asked, holding out his arm for her.

Emily pretended not to notice his offered arm. "Let's walk toward the road," she said, setting off before he could say more.

He hurried to fall in step beside her. They walked in silence toward the road, the dirt path muffling their footsteps. Emily glanced toward the fence where Matt talked with Flick, but they were involved in an animated discussion, and neither of them noticed her. Perhaps that was just as well. Matt would be sure to give her an I-told-you-so look if he saw her with Obadiah.

"Why are you looking at him?" Obadiah asked, his tone sharp.

Warmth flooded Emily's cheeks. "I like to keep track of my family. That's all."

"Matt Keath doesn't need anyone to look after him. He's got enough self-confidence for a troop of men." Obadiah narrowed his eyes at Matt.

Wisdom told Emily that it might be best to hold her tongue, but she couldn't keep silent. "I don't understand why you don't like my brother-in-law. What's he ever done to you?"

Obadiah came to an abrupt stop. If only Emily *had* listened to wisdom. Now she'd made him mad.

But his expression softened. "Don't you understand, Emily? It's only for *your* sake that Matt Keath gets on my nerves."

"Me?" Emily widened her eyes, her pulse freezing. "What does this have to do with me?"

"Everything. You have a prime piece of land in your possession, and you're a beautiful woman. Any man would be attracted to you." Obadiah scanned her face. "Don't you see? It's your hand Matt's been after this whole time, no matter what he states publicly."

"Never. You don't know Matt. He doesn't care about land—at least not farmland. And as far as his feelings for me, we've spent most of our time together getting mad at each other and making up. Not very romantic. I wasn't convinced that he even liked me at first."

"That means nothing. The truth is that Matt Keath is smitten with you, and he's going to try to marry you."

Emily's head spun. Matt had told her that Obadiah was trying to wed her, and now Obadiah told her that *Matt* was the one attempting to marry her. What did they have to gain by making her believe the other was pursuing her?

"Emily." Obadiah inched closer. "I can't bear to see you stuck with a man like Matt for the rest of your life. I care too much about you to see that happen."

Emily couldn't grasp his words, especially not when he was hovering so close. "A man like Matt? What do you mean?"

"He's not your type." Obadiah's face hardened. "He's a loose man, never tamed and never will be. He might stay for a few months, but eventually he'd leave you and the kids in pursuit of the adventure he craves. You'll be left broken-hearted, wishing you had never met him. Men like Matt have hard cores. They may change outwardly but not deep-down. And I refuse to let you be subjected to such a life."

Emily stared at him, her breathing hitching. "Matt is *not* that type of man."

"I've read the signs, and they all point to that conclusion. I, of all people, should know." He clenched his jaw. "My pa was that kind of man. He drank and abused us. Dragged us all over the place until we couldn't take it, and finally he abandoned us with my grandparents in Maryland. My sister died a month later. Ma didn't last much longer. And after my grandparents passed on a few years later, I was entirely alone. Pa never returned."

Emily's heart ached for him. "I'm sorry you had to go through that. But Matt—"

"Emily, you aren't seeing him in the right light. He might look like Colton, but he doesn't act like his brother. I'm only trying to look out for you. I couldn't bear to see you become like my mother, a woman who was broken and worn out. I care about you too much for that." His eyes met hers. "I love you, Emily. Is it too soon to ask you to be my wife?"

Emily's breath caught in her throat and panic grabbed at her chest. No, she was *not* ready for this. She wasn't ready to respond to love. And apparently she wasn't even prepared to hear it proclaimed. She wanted to speak out and stop him, but she couldn't seem to pry her mouth open enough to get the words out.

Obadiah closed the distance between them, his expression gentle. "Please, Emily, I can take care of you and the kids. You need someone to help you, and I'm willing to be that help. I think we'd make a good team. Marry me. Please."

Emily took a small step back. "No, Obadiah. I can't. It's—it's too soon since Colton . . ." She couldn't finish.

Obadiah studied her. "Do you mean you don't wish to marry *any* man? Or you don't wish to marry me?"

"Any man. It wouldn't matter who it was."

"Even Matt?"

Irritation broke through Emily's panic. "Yes, even Matt. He's included in the category of *any man*."

"I see. So you're telling me no."

"Right."

"It was too much to hope for." Obadiah heaved a sigh that raised his shoulders. Then a hard glint flashed through his eyes.

"Well, at least you won't be marrying Matt. That's the one thing that eases the disappointment."

Irritation jarred Emily again. "You're quite preoccupied with Matt."

"I might have some reason for that." Obadiah jerked back toward the farm. "I guess there's no use in lingering when we've said all that needed to be said."

Emily murmured her agreement, her heart heavy. It was too bad that Obadiah had gone and decided to make more of their friendship than was there.

Things would never be the same between them again.

CHAPTER 29

"Everyone ready for church?" Matt asked as he stepped into the soddy. Joyanna and the boys cheered, and Matt resisted the urge to cover his ears. They were deafening.

The noise didn't bother him as much as it did when he first arrived, but there were still times when he longed for peace. As loud as the soddy usually was, it was no wonder that Flick had been avoiding the soddy as much as possible, choosing instead to stick to Matt's side or hide in the barn.

"Perfect timing." Emily picked Audrey up and motioned Joyanna, Grant, Austin, and Byron toward the door. As she passed Matt in the doorway, her black skirts swishing around her ankles, she asked, "Where's your friend?"

"Flick's not much for church," Matt said, keeping his response an understatement. Truth was, Flick had given him so much grief about going to church that it was embarrassing. So far, Flick's visit had resulted in Matt's reputation plummeting in his eyes—and he'd made sure Matt knew what he thought quite clearly. The only thing that puzzled Matt was why he didn't just head to Texas and leave him behind.

Emily's eyebrows arched. "So what's he going to do while we're gone?"

"He'll find something." And Matt knew just what that *something* was, though he didn't say it. Flick must have brought some whiskey with him. The last time Matt checked on him, he was out cold. He'd be spending the rest of the day sleeping off his hangover, just like he did on his days off back at the Bar K.

"He better not complain if he gets bored," Emily said, walking to the wagon that Matt had pulled around to the door.

Matt couldn't help but shake his head. She was naïve—but he liked her that way.

Before closing the door, Matt grabbed his rifle. He'd checked it over the night before to make sure it was in good shape. Of course, that had caused Emily to give him an odd look, but thankfully she hadn't asked any questions. She probably thought he was planning to go hunting.

Now he watched her forehead furrow as he tucked the rifle safely behind the wagon seat.

"Why are you bringing that along?"

"Never know what you'll find," Matt said, keeping his tone light.

He climbed up onto the wagon bench beside her, gathered up the reins, and freed the wagon brake. The team plodded toward the road, and Matt exhaled when Emily turned her attention to the children in the back of the wagon without asking more questions.

Matt had been doing heavy thinking since Flick told him about Frank Harvey closing in on him. Since he wasn't going to run, the best thing he could do was to never be caught off guard. He intended to talk to Sheriff Becker at church this morning and tell him to keep an eye out for Frank. If Frank did travel this far to get him, he would surely stop in town to find out where Matt lived.

Hopefully warning the law would be enough, but Matt

wasn't staking his life on that hope. From then on, whenever he was away from the farmyard, he intended to bring a firearm with him. He didn't want to be unarmed even on his way to church. Letting down their vigilance was what got Telmond and Ryker killed—and if he did run into Frank Harvey, Matt didn't want to go down without a fight. There was no harm in taking a few precautions, but being caught off guard was sure death.

"Do you happen to know why Flick has been making hints about me marrying Zane?" Emily asked, interrupting his thoughts.

Matt twisted to look at her, his arm bumping against Austin who was squeezed onto the seat between them. "He hasn't."

"Yes, he has, and multiple times." Emily arched a brow. "Would you like to explain why he cares?"

Matt mentally groaned. Would there be no end to the trouble that Flick had caused him? "Don't mind Flick. He's just pouting because he has some silly idea about me going to Texas with him."

"Texas?" Emily frowned. "What does that have to do with me marrying Zane?"

Matt nibbled on his lip, hating this awkward conversation that Flick had forced on him. Keeping his gaze straight ahead, he said, "I told Flick that I wouldn't leave until harvest. But he's stubborn, so he started making up plans about marrying you off—"

Emily gasped. "Marrying me off!"

"He suggested Obadiah, but he doesn't like Obadiah much, so he switched to Zane, merely because Zane is the only other man he knows around here. I told him he was crazy and to mind his own business, but Flick always has to stick his nose where he shouldn't, and that about sums it up."

Matt didn't look at her, but the silence beside him was deafening. At last, Emily said, "I'm not sure about Flick."

"Then I guess we're agreed on that."

Emily fell quiet again. When Matt finally risked looking at her, she met his gaze and asked, "Do you *want* to go to Texas?"

Matt shook his head. "Not at all. That's Flick's idea."

"You're sure?" Some of the lines in her forehead smoothed.

"Very sure." Matt smiled. "Remember? I need to see how that harvest turns out."

Emily smiled in response.

"Now, may I ask you a question?" Matt asked.

"Of course."

"Why were you walking with Obadiah a few nights back? And why hasn't he visited since?"

Emily's cheeks reddened. "You saw us walking together? I thought you were busy talking with Flick."

"I was, but that doesn't mean my vision became impaired. Care to explain what you were doing?"

Emily's lips pursed together. Then the words came tumbling out. "You were right. Obadiah insisted we go for a walk, and he proposed to me, but I turned him down."

"Mmhmm." Matt resisted the urge to remind her that his predictions had been right. But he did send one glance her way.

Emily's face reddened even more, and she gave his shoulder a solid whack. "Matthew Keath! You will not say that you told me so."

Matt held up a hand to defend himself. "I didn't, so don't go flying off the handle with me."

"You didn't say it, but it was written all over your face."

"I'm sorry," he said, but the laugh that escaped made it sound unconvincing.

Emily shoved him again. "You aren't helping your cause by lying. You aren't sorry."

Matt gave up and yielded to the laughter building up inside him.

Emily eased back on the seat, staring at him like she'd never seen a man laugh before. "I don't see what's so funny."

Matt tried to control his laughter. There was nothing funny about the situation. Nothing besides the memory of Obadiah yelling after him that Matt wouldn't be feeling so cocky come evening—and the sight of small Emily Keath so furious with him. He really shouldn't tease her, but it was fun getting a reaction out of her.

The laughter did make him feel better. For the past couple of days, his worries over Frank Harvey had been stringing his nerves tight, and the laughter eased some of the built-up pressure.

Matt reached out and took Emily's hand, giving it a quick squeeze before releasing it. "Thank you."

Emily's face reflected her puzzlement. She wouldn't understand, of course—but if it hadn't been for her, he probably would have spent the whole trip musing about Frank Harvey's whereabouts. And now they were pulling into town, and he felt better than when they first left home. A few months ago, he never would have believed it, but he found that spark of temper in her the most refreshing.

Sheriff Becker was not at church.

"I'm sorry. He had to take a trip to Columbus and won't be home today," his wife Jeanne told Matt, swaying back and forth to keep the baby in her arms asleep. She gave Matt a sideways glance. "If you need to talk to a lawman, Deputy Wilson is at the jail today."

Matt shook his head. He'd met Deputy Wilson before, an older man who was dedicated to his job but unbelievably forgetful. Matt had never seen a more disorganized man, and he figured it would be best to talk directly to Sheriff Becker about his concerns.

"When will Ethan be back?"

"He should be in town by tomorrow at noon."

Noon. That wasn't too long for Matt to wait.

He nodded. "Thank you. I'll talk to him then."

"Do you want to leave a message for me to pass along to him?" Jeanne asked,

"No, that's all right. It can wait." It would take a while to write the details on paper, and he didn't want to hold up Jeanne. Besides, if he told Ethan himself, the sheriff could ask any questions he might have and verify anything that didn't make sense.

He would just need to find an excuse to head into town tomorrow, an excuse that wouldn't arouse Emily's suspicions. There was no use in worrying her for no reason.

"Tomorrow will be quite soon enough," Matt said, and tipping his hat to Jeanne, he left to round up his family to head home.

CHAPTER 30

"I'm going to make a trip into town today if anyone wants to join," Matt announced at breakfast the next morning. "I plan to leave right after lunch. You need anything, Emily?"

Her eyes brightened. "I'll do some looking and make a list. Since you're going to town, I might as well come along and get my shopping done. It's not often that I get offered a ride into town." Then she frowned. "What do you need from town?"

Matt had expected the question and was prepared. "Before I leave, I want you to have a good roof over your head. I'm going to pick up some lumber in town and shingle the roof some nice day." It wasn't a new idea. He'd decided to put a new roof on the house long ago, back when he first got hit by a glob of mud from the ceiling. There was no way he could leave Emily and the children with a roof that slowly crumbled around their heads with each rainfall. And now that he needed an excuse to go to town, the timing seemed perfect for the project.

Emily froze with her fork halfway to her mouth. "You're going to *what?*"

"Redo the roof. Shouldn't be too hard of a job as long as we get a nice stretch of weather for it."

Emily gave a slow shake of her head. "I don't have the money for that."

Matt blinked. She thought he would come up with the idea and expect her to pay for it without even discussing finances? "You don't need to. I'll pay for it."

Emily stared at him, then lowered her fork to her plate. "You can't. Do you realize how much lumber costs out here?"

"I've looked into it already and I have the money."

"That's not it." Emily bit her lip. "I can't let you make such a large purchase on our behalf. The roof is fine. We've gotten along this far with it, and I guess it will hold out for a few more years."

"I've already made up my mind, and a roof is what I want to invest in." Matt leaned forward in his seat. "Please. Let me do this. I came to take care of you this summer, and I won't feel right leaving if I know that the next heavy rainstorm could bring a load of dirt down on your heads. You wouldn't want me to have a guilty conscience, now, would you?"

Emily hesitated. When she finally looked up at him, her eyes glistened. "Thank you, Matthew."

He eased back in his seat, trying not to smile too broadly. He felt as though he'd just been granted permission to own the world.

"So, we can go to town today?" Joyanna asked, looking from Matt to Emily.

Emily nodded, and Joyanna's face broke into a grin. As she drew in a deep breath to let out a cheer, Matt placed a finger over her lips.

"Shh. You can't be too loud or else you'll scare Mr. Flick. You see, Mr. Flick spooks real easy, so we gotta talk quietly, or he'll act just like one of those little prairie dogs running for cover in its hole, all right?"

Joyanna's face turned sober, and she darted Flick a quick glance. Leaning close to Matt, she whispered, "Okay. I wouldn't want to scare him." Even her whisper was loud enough to be heard beyond the soddy.

Flick scowled at Matt. Taking a heaping bite of eggs that were wrapped in pancake, he hunkered lower in his seat.

"What do you say, Flick? You want to stay here or come with?" Matt asked, fighting to hide his smile.

Matt expected him to say that there was no way he would sit crammed in a wagon with a bunch of yakking kids. But without even looking up from his breakfast, Flick said, "Reckon I'll go along."

Matt couldn't keep from staring at him.

Flick glanced up, a smirk tugging at one corner of his mouth. "What? It's boring as a prairie dog hole here, and even a trip to your stuffy old town would be welcome. I'm sticking with you wherever you go. Unless, of course, it's to church." His smile turned a touch mocking. "Seems to me there's a Bible story about some fella who said he'd follow some other fella wherever he went."

"I believe you're thinking of the story of Ruth."

"Ruth. Yeah, that's it." Flick settled his elbow on the table and took another bite of his pancake-egg sandwich. "From now on, just call me Ruth."

The first thing Matt did when he arrived in town was drop Emily and the children off at Ephraim and Sadie's mercantile. Flick turned down Matt's suggestion that he do some window shopping and he chose to stick with Matt instead.

"Seriously, Matt. I don't know what's gotten into you lately," Flick said as Matt guided the team toward the lumber yard. "Milking cows, letting all those little kids hang on you, buying lumber. I think you've been out of touch with real living for too long."

"Actually, I've never felt more alive," Matt replied. And that was true. He'd never felt so alive or as if he had more purpose than he did since arriving.

It didn't take Matt long to pick up the lumber. In no time, he and Flick were heading toward the center of town again. Next stop was the sheriff's office.

Matt hitched the team at the rail across from the sheriff's office, and Flick raised his eyebrows at him. "What're you doing?"

"Just wanted to have a quick talk with Sheriff Becker," Matt said, coming around the side of the wagon.

Flick remained slouched on the seat. "Why? He won't do you any good. Frank Harvey doesn't exactly go around introducing himself to lawmen."

"But if Frank does come looking for me, Ethan might be the first person to sense that something is off. It never hurts to put him on his guard."

"Oh, come on, Matt. He'll just tell you to hang up your gun and leave the hunt to him. Lawmen always have an inflated opinion of what they can do."

Matt knew Flick had a low opinion of the law, and his comments irked him. He turned to face him, but then his gaze caught on a man farther down the street. He was far enough away that Matt couldn't make out his features, but the Stetson on his head immediately caught his attention. Not too many men in Osceola wore those.

Running his gaze down the man's frame, he took in the broad shoulders and stocky frame. The swaggering gait. His blood went cold.

"Matt?" Flick leaned closer, blocking Matt's view of the man. "What you looking at?"

Matt moved sideways so he could get another look at the man, but already he was convinced of who it was. He glanced toward the sheriff's office, then back at the man. He had disappeared—right into Mayfield Mercantile.

That decided it. Matt took off toward the mercantile, his heart hammering. He prayed he had mistaken the man's identity, because if he was right, then Frank Harvey had just walked into the same store as his family.

"Matt!" Flick called after him, but Matt ignored him. Hopefully Flick would have the sense to hang low and keep quiet.

Matt couldn't think twice about his next move. He ran around the side of the store and opened the door leading to the Mayfields' living quarters. No one was around and all was quiet. Ignoring his uneasiness at barging into Ephraim and Sadie's home, he made his way toward the door leading to the store.

If Frank Harvey laid so much as a finger on his family, he would feel the full weight of Matt's wrath.

CHAPTER 31

Unsure of how quickly Matthew would want to leave town after he returned with the lumber, Emily directed Joyanna to entertain the younger children and hurried with her shopping, refusing to let herself linger over the crisp new bolts of fabric. That could come later, provided that Matt wasn't in a rush.

"Well, sister of mine, I'm glad you could come patronize my store today," Ephraim said when she piled her goods on his counter.

"Of course you are. You thrive on my money, don't you?" Emily added a spool of thread to her pile, trying not to smile. In truth, she didn't think her older brother had a greedy bone in his body. There had been many times over the past year when he had waved her money aside, telling her to count her purchase as a gift.

"Are you and Matt getting along fine on the farm?" Ephraim asked, totaling up her purchases.

Emily nodded. "Matthew's buying lumber to replace the roof today."

"That's awfully kind of him." Ephraim didn't look up from his notepad, but Emily didn't miss his tiny smile.

"What? I don't see anything funny about it."

Ephraim's lips straightened. "No, nothing at all. Matt's very kind."

The door opened, and Emily turned. A man stepped into the room—a man wearing a hat she recognized well. She opened her mouth to call Matthew over, but stopped short as the man lifted his head.

Not Matthew.

The stranger scanned the room, one hand adjusting his hat. Emily's gaze slid to his belt where a pistol dangled from his holster. Few men in Osceola toted a pistol, especially not in the mercantile.

"Hello!" Ephraim called out. "How can I help you today, sir?"

The man gave him a brief wave. "Finish with the lady first."

"I guess that means I better keep moving." Emily retrieved her reticule and paid for her goods, then gathered them into her arms. "Hopefully Matthew will come quickly." She glanced back at the dark-haired stranger, her pulse quickening at the way his gaze settled on her.

She hoped Matthew came *really* quickly. His presence always made her feel safe.

Moving to the counter, the stranger fixed his eyes on Ephraim. "I wondered if you could maybe help me?"

"Depends on what you mean by *help*," Ephraim replied. His tone lost none of its friendliness, but the lines around his eyes tightened just a bit. Maybe he had picked up on something about the man as well.

"Do you happen to know a man named Flick?" the stranger asked. "I'm looking for him."

"Sure. He's staying at Emily's place right now." Ephraim nodded her way.

The back of Emily's neck tingled. Flick was just passing

through the area, yet this stranger looked at her with a glint in his eyes, almost as if he had *expected* Ephraim's words.

He had better not expect her to invite him to stay in her barn too.

She swallowed. "Flick is in town today and I'm sure he'll be here shortly. He was helping with a load of lumber."

The man's mouth curved. "Perfect."

Without another word, he turned on his heel and left the store. Emily gave her shoulders a shake, trying to ward off the chill the man had given her.

No sooner had the bell over the door stopped jingling than the door leading to Ephraim and Sadie's private apartment creaked open. Emily turned, expecting to see Sadie. Instead, Matt stood in the doorway as he scanned the room.

"What—?" Emily began, but Matt cut her off.

"Did you see a man in here with dark eyes, black hair, and a hat kind of like mine?"

Ephraim blinked. "Actually, yes. He just passed through the store, but he already left—"

Matt took off toward the door, muttering something under his breath. Emily stared after him, awed by the power that emanated from him. This was a side of him she'd never seen before. As the door closed behind him, he called over his shoul- der, "I'll be back soon. Whatever you do, stay here, Emily!"

"Well," Ephraim said, shaking his head as the bell bounced off the door. "That was odd."

Emily frowned, a knot gathering in her middle. Matt didn't usually act like that. He had to know something about the dark stranger that he wasn't letting on.

She only hoped he wasn't getting himself into hot water.

"Matt Keath, would you mind telling me what in tarnation you're up to now?"

Matt stepped away from Mayfield Mercantile and speared Flick with a look. "Not so loud! He'll hear you yelling my name from clear across Osceola."

"Who?" Flick ambled over to him, his voice lower but still too loud.

"Frank Harvey, that's who. Looks like you were right about him coming after me." Matt glanced first in one direction, then another, but Frank was nowhere in sight. Motioning to Flick, Matt stepped into the street. "Come on."

Flick fell in step behind him. "Where are we going?"

"The sheriff's office, of course. Emily and the kids are safe for now, but I'm not going to let that man run loose even one more hour. He's already caused too much damage." Matt quickened his step and cast a glance over his shoulder. Seeing Frank in person had been bad enough, but losing track of him was even worse.

"I still don't think the lawman's gonna be much help."

Matt said nothing and kept walking. He didn't care to get into an argument with Flick now, of all times.

Reaching the sheriff's office, Matt scanned the area behind him once more, then turned the handle and pushed the door open. "Hello?"

Sheriff Ethan Becker and Deputy Wilson huddled together over some papers on the desk, but they both looked up as he entered.

"Matt, pleasure to see you," Ethan said, rising from his seat. "What brings you here today?"

"I've got a problem." Matt moved to the side as Flick joined him in the room. "I think I've got a man out to kill me. And I just saw him here in town."

Ethan's eyebrows drew together, and he motioned Matt to an empty chair. "Explain."

Matt took a seat and briefly outlined his past with Frank Harvey and how he'd seen him there in Osceola. Ethan's expression didn't change as he nodded and jotted down a couple of notes, but Deputy Wilson frowned.

"Sounds like you didn't get a real good look at this man," he said when Matt finished telling them all he knew. "How do you know this *is* Frank Harvey? I mean, given the distance, you could've been mistaken."

"And he's been awfully spooked lately," Flick spoke up, keeping space between himself and the sheriff. "He's been seeing Frank Harvey under every rock since I showed him that newspaper."

Matt opened his mouth to argue—preparing to tell them that he was sure of it. But Ethan was already putting on his hat. "We'll hope for all our sakes that the man wasn't Frank Harvey, but this definitely bears some looking into. I'll go to the telegraph office now and send a message to Arcade and Stromsburg and some other nearby towns so they know to keep an eye out for this man. Then I intend to search this town from top to bottom and circle outward from here."

Deputy Wilson nodded. "Good idea."

"I can help look for him, too." Matt offered.

Ethan hesitated. "I don't think so. If he's out to kill you then you should stay out of this."

"He doesn't know that I saw him. He doesn't even know I'm in town."

"But if he sees you and drags you into a bad situation—"

Matt gritted his teeth. "I know what he looks like. You only have my description to go off. I'd really like to get this taken care of as soon as possible."

"I understand, Matt. But—" Ethan rubbed at the furrows between his eyes, then he finally looked up from the floor. "On the other hand, having you along would be helpful. I'd like to get this taken care of quickly too. It's not my policy to allow criminals to run free through my town any longer than I can help it."

"I'll be careful," Matt said quickly, deciding to take Ethan's comment as permission.

"I'll guard his back." Flick gave a long sigh. "Would've been a heap better if you'd just gone to Texas with me, Matt."

Ethan glanced between the two of them, his eyebrows working, but at last he nodded. "I guess I can't keep you from searching for the man, but please be careful. I don't want either of you winding up in a bad spot."

"I'll be careful," Matt said again, then he headed for the door without allowing himself to think of what he would do if he actually *did* find Frank Harvey.

CHAPTER 32

With Ephraim occupied with a customer and all now quiet in the store, Emily wanted to go home. The fun of the trip to town was gone, replaced by thoughts of all the chores awaiting her return. She looked out the display window, scanning the street for Matt. No sign of him.

But the team and wagon were hitched just across the block. She glanced at the children still playing peacefully, then made her way to the counter where her packages still sat. She might as well bring her goods to the wagon so they'd have only the children to manage when Matt returned. That should help speed their trip home.

Emily gathered her merchandise into her arms, then fumbled to open the door and slipped outside. She crossed the street, looking around as she walked. The town was quiet—unusually so. At least none of those noisy locomotives were barreling into town.

At the wagon, she arranged her items in the bed. Then she slowly made her way back to the store, looking for Matt. What *was* he doing?

She crossed the street again and made her way toward

Mayfield Mercantile. As she passed the gap between Mary Couther's seamstress shop and the mercantile, a man suddenly materialized in the alley. Before she could even let out a scream, his hand covered her mouth. Gripping her arm, he yanked her into the shadows of the alley.

"All right, just cooperate with me and you won't get hurt," he said, his breath hot against her ear.

Her heart pounding, Emily did the first thing that came to mind. She bit his hand. He hissed, his grip loosening. Writhing, Emily kicked at where she thought his legs must be.

The man swore and his fist connected with her chin, sending pain radiating through her jaw. The world dimmed and humming filled her ears. By the time her vision cleared, he had her crushed against himself, his arms an iron band around her middle.

"There now," he said, breathing hard. "No need to get all feisty. I just need you to answer one little question for me. You can do that, can't you?"

Tears pressed against her eyes, but she said nothing. There had to be some mistake. She couldn't know anything he would care about, but what would he do to her when he realized that?

"Your husband," he growled. "Where is he?"

"M-my husband?" Emily gave her head a shake, but the movement hurt. "My husband is dead."

His grip tightened until it was hard for her to catch her breath. "You're lying. I know better than that. If he were dead then I would have heard so before now from—a source of mine. You have one more chance to answer me." He paused, then asked, "Where is Matt Keath?"

"*Matthew?*" Emily inhaled sharply.

"Yes, Matthew. He must not have told you that he was expecting a visit from me."

Emily wasn't sure what to think, but she did know that this man would use everything she told him as leverage against

Matthew. "I—I don't know where he is," she said. It was partly true. She didn't know exactly where he had disappeared.

The man said nothing. Before Emily could determine her next move, he shoved a foul-tasting rag into her mouth. She tried to scream, but the rag muffled the sound and threatened to choke her.

"I see you aren't going to do this the easy way." He dropped to one knee. Dragging her with him, he held her against his leg and pulled out a rope. "That's all right. I have time, and I'm sure that by the time we finish our little visit, you will be more than happy to tell me where your husband is."

The rope bit into her wrists, and tears flooded her eyes. Things like this weren't supposed to happen in Osceola. Maybe in other towns but not here.

The man paused and lifted his head, and Emily stilled. Voices rumbled nearby, drawing closer to the alley. She could make out Flick's overly loud voice, and a wave of nausea washed over her. If Flick was approaching, then Matt must be as well.

The man shoved her to the ground. In one smooth motion, he leapt to his feet, gun drawn. He almost seemed to be expecting Matt.

Emily shifted just a bit, not enough to catch the man's attention but enough to get into a better position. Staying focused on the alleyway, she winged a cry for help heavenward.

This wasn't going to end without a fight.

Since Sheriff Becker was on his way to the telegraph office to send his messages and Deputy Wilson prowled the depot, Matt decided to tackle the storefront across the courthouse. He walked quickly but still maintained his caution and remained aware of his surroundings, taking care to scope out each alleyway before emerging into view.

He took a right at the end of the street, strolling past several buildings and Louger House. Still no luck. Not a single trace of Frank.

He moved eastward, taking Central Street and then making a right onto Main Street at the school junction. For him and Frank, this pursuit was like an intense game of hide-and-seek—one where being "tagged" meant much more than simply losing a game. Their lives were the forfeit.

Flick lagged behind, keeping up a steady stream of complaints to let Matt know that he wasn't happy about traipsing all around town.

"We've walked four blocks so far," he told Matt as they turned onto Main Street.

"Five," he said as they crossed the corner at the Mission Church.

"Six—and my shoes pinch," he added at the next corner.

Matt gestured to the sheriff's office that they had arrived at and to the wagon parked across from it.

Flick shook his head. "Not unless that's where you're going."

Matt crossed the street, walking toward the mercantile. Flick grumbled and fell into step behind him.

At the gap between Mary Couther's seamstress shop and Mayfield Mercantile, Matt paused and peeked around the corner down the alleyway. But this time something was different. There was someone in the alley.

Matt jerked his head back, his mind reeling from the impact of what he had just seen. Frank Harvey—but not just him. Although he couldn't be sure from the momentary glance, he thought he had also seen Emily on the ground.

A shudder wracked his frame. *Emily.* He never would have guessed that Frank would go after her. He couldn't step into the alley with his gun blazing—not without risking Emily's life. And yet, if he tried to fetch help, he had no doubt that Frank would hurt Emily. Or worse.

"Harvey?" Flick's voice was too loud. Matt nodded.

Think! He had to think. There was always a way out of situations like this. He leaned against the brick of the sewing shop, frantically running through his options. Which were pitifully few.

He heard Flick's breathing behind him, closer than he cared for Flick to be. Before he could speak, Flick whispered, "Sorry, buddy."

Abruptly, Flick's shoulder slammed into Matt from behind, shoving him away from the shelter of the wall and straight into the mouth of the alley. Shock coursed through Matt. Without even understanding what had happened, Matt reached for his revolver—only to find that it wasn't there. He'd been unarmed without even realizing it.

Flick.

He'd been betrayed.

Matt swung to face Frank. Sunlight glinted off a metallic object in Frank's hand, and, even as he aimed the gun, Matt dodged.

The gun cracked, and fire stung his arm. His heart thundered in his ears. Emily kicked Frank in the leg, trying to destabilize him, but Frank already had his revolver cocked, ready to fire again.

Frank's arms lifted, and Matt lunged at him. Grabbing the revolver's barrel, he shoved it sideways with one hand and hit Frank's wrist with his other. He twisted and jerked the revolver out of Frank's hands just as the gun discharged with a roar.

The bullet kicked up dirt in the ground behind Matt, but pain seared through the hand that clenched around the smoking gun barrel. His grip loosened, and he dropped the gun.

He dove for the revolver and nearly butted heads with Frank as he grabbed for it at the same time. Frank caught a fistful of the front of Matt's shirt and shoved him with enough force that Matt almost went down. Breathing hard, Matt grabbed the wall to regain his balance, then he aimed a well-placed kick at the revolver to keep it out of Frank's reach. No way would he let Frank get ahold of that.

"Matt Keath." Frank's face filled Matt's vision, his grip on the front of Matt's shirt turning into a choke. He swung his fist at Matt's face.

Matt threw his arm up to block it, turning away from Frank's hold on him. He was a fraction too slow.

The blow grazed his arm and connected with his eye, sending a shockwave of pain through him. Tears blurred his vision, and Matt blinked fast, trying to get rid of them. He needed his eyes if he was going to win this fight.

His right eye cleared enough for him to see Frank's fist coming at him again. Matt ducked sideways. Frank's fist hit the brick of Mayfield Mercantile and he let out a roar followed by a string of expletives.

His breathing hitched, Matt aimed an upward punch at Frank's jaw. Frank's head snapped back, his hand slipping from Matt's shirt. Matt spun toward the revolver on the ground and dodged for it, scanning the area around him as he did. Emily had edged back from the fight and was struggling against her bonds. Flick was gone.

Good.

Matt's hands closed around the revolver, and sweet relief flooded through him. Time to end this once and for all.

Emily cried out. Before he could straighten, Frank's boot slammed into his side. Pain, white hot, flashed through his side. Then it grabbed his chest, refusing to allow him his next breath.

Matt crumpled, agony slicing through him. The gun slid a couple of inches from his hands before his fingers curved and tightened around the grip. He couldn't lose the gun. Had to keep his focus.

Frank landed on top of him, expelling the last of the air from Matt's lungs. Another jolt of agony shot through him. Frank grabbed for the gun, and with all his strength, Matt writhed, curving to shield the pistol with his body. His efforts earned him only an elbow to the middle.

Air. He couldn't grab enough air. Darkness edged his vision, threatening to take control of him.

He couldn't give up. He was dead if he did.

Frank shifted, and Matt dragged in a shallow breath. He could do this. Matt forced his arm away from where it wanted to curve against his burning side, then struck at Frank's jaw. A weak blow, at best.

Frank grunted, but his gaze remained fixed on the revolver. His knee crushed Matt's arm against the ground. In one quick twist of his good hand, he jerked the gun away from Matt.

The cock of the gun echoed in Matt's ears. He knew he wouldn't make it this time.

CHAPTER 33

Matt fully expected to be blown to glory, but even as Frank swiveled the revolver's barrel toward him, something else flashed above him. There was a solid crack, a garbled sound from Frank, and then Frank's limp weight crashed down on top of Matt.

Matt stared at Frank first, and then he looked up. Emily held part of a broken crate in her hands, breathing hard.

"You—you knocked him out," Matt stammered. He wouldn't have believed that Emily was capable of it.

"It was either him or you." Emily lowered the board, the fire in her eyes quenched beneath a rush of tears. "I was afraid I wouldn't untie myself in time. Are you all right?"

"I will be once Frank is off of me." Matt didn't trust Frank, even when he was unconscious. It was only a matter of time before he came to again.

Matt shifted, hissing at the pain that shot through his side. Maybe it was a bit ambitious to say that he would be *entirely* all right once Frank was off him.

Footsteps pounded on the boardwalk, and he snatched the revolver, motioning for Emily to move behind him so that he had a clear line of fire. If Flick dared show his face again, he'd be ready for him.

Emily crouched behind him just as the footsteps skidded to a stop beside the alley. Matt blinked hard, trying to clear his vision. Everything had gone blurry.

"Hello?" a familiar voice called.

Matt's breathing slowed. *Ethan Becker.* Just the man he needed.

He lowered the revolver and let his head fall back against the dirt beneath him. The impact, light as it was, made him wince. Now that the fight was over, pain crowded its way into his focus, sending a burn through his whole body. He couldn't decide what hurt worst, his head, his ribs, or his arm.

He pulled his focus together, narrowing in on his injuries. Actually, his head and his ribs were winning the pain war. His arm hurt, but no more than if it had been scratched.

"Looks like you found him, all right," Ethan said.

Matt grimaced. "Looks that way."

Metal clanked, followed by the familiar snap of closing handcuffs. Matt cracked his eyes open to find Ethan dragging Frank off of him.

"I heard the gunshots on my way back from the telegram office," Ethan said. "I met your friend Flick, too, running the opposite way. Seemed odd, especially since he didn't seem happy to see me. So I left Deputy Wilson questioning him while I made my way here. Looks like you had it all under control though."

Frank groaned. As his eyelids fluttered, Matt said, "Well, I'd say your timing was none too late."

Emily moved closer, and Matt heard her suck in a breath.

"What?" he asked.

"You look terrible."

"Thanks."

"And," she lifted her voice, "I'd like to know if there are any other reprobates I should keep an eye out for. I can't believe you never mentioned that man to me, Matthew Keath. What were you thinking?"

Matt was aware that she had been badly frightened. Still, he was grateful that she was angry with him instead of being in tears. He couldn't handle a woman in tears.

"Apart from Frank, the only reprobate I can think of is Flick." Matt glanced at Ethan. "I hope Deputy Wilson saw fit to bring him into custody, because he's about as guilty as Frank."

Anger gnawed at him at the mere thought of Flick's betrayal. But he pushed his feelings aside. For now, getting to his feet was going to take all his focus and energy. Matt tried to sit up, but pain stabbed his side, snatching his breath and knocking him onto his back.

Emily turned all sympathy. "You need to see Doc Stoning right away. You must have broken something, and you certainly don't want to further injure yourself."

"I never see the doctor."

"Then I guess it's time you changed that." Emily planted her hands on her hips, and Matt noticed the raw marks on her wrists. He winced.

"Are *you* all right?" Matt asked. "Did he hurt you?"

She lowered her hands and hid them in the folds of her skirt. "I'm fine. He hit me once, but that's all."

Even once was too much as far as Matt was concerned. He shook his head. "I'm sorry. This was all my fault. I dragged you into this—"

Emily held out a finger, silencing him. "Enough, Matthew," she said, her voice gentle. "I'm just thankful you're all right. It could have ended much worse. If anything had happened to you —" Her voice cracked.

Tears shimmered in her eyes, revealing just how deeply she felt.

He swallowed hard. She was right. It could have ended way worse, but it hadn't.

She was fine, and that was all that mattered.

~

After leaving Doc Stoning's office, Matt made his way to the jailhouse. Ethan met him on the lawn outside and cut straight to business.

"The two of them are half-brothers," Ethan told Matt. "That's the connection."

Matt closed his eyes, processing the new revelation. *Half-brothers.* After all his years of knowing Flick, it was only now that he knew the truth. Flick must have been aware of Matt's connection to Frank from the very beginning. There was no telling how long he had been in cahoots with him.

Matt opened his eyes again—or rather, his right eye since his left one was swollen shut. "I guess that explains why Flick was helping him."

He exhaled, his side aching from even that simple motion. He would probably be in pain for a good while. Doc Stoning said he had two broken ribs and had wrapped his chest tight, which somehow only made the pain worse. It would be three to six weeks before they healed, Doc said. In the meantime, he needed to take it easy, something Matt doubted would be much fun.

Especially since Emily said she'd keep an eye on him to make sure he didn't overdo it. She was bound to take her guard job too seriously.

Matt shook his thoughts aside and asked Ethan, "Could I see Flick please?"

Ethan didn't act surprised. Instead, he stepped aside and motioned for Matt to enter the jailhouse.

The walls of the jailhouse seemed to close in around Matt as he stepped inside. The imprisonment would be a hard form of punishment for Flick. The man was like him in that way, and he never liked to be confined by four walls.

Heat still raced through Matt's veins when he thought of Flick's betrayal. All those days spent together working at the Bar K, the times when Matt had dragged Flick out of fights that could have ended worse for him than just a knot on the back of his head—Matt had been loyal to him even in the tough times. And *this* was how Flick had rewarded him?

Matt hadn't even wanted to see Flick at first. But he had time to think as he'd sat in Doc Stoning's office and gotten patched up. Flick had gotten himself into deep water this time. Despite his betrayal, Matt still felt duty bound by their friendship—or at least what *he* had considered a friendship—and knew he couldn't leave town without at least trying to see him.

Matt stopped in front of Flick's cell, and Flick looked up from where he slouched on his cot, his eyes narrowed. "Well, would ya look at who's showed up to gloat. Bet you're real happy to see me getting my desserts, huh?"

Matt leveled his gaze at him. "That's not true. It doesn't give me pleasure to see a man behind bars."

Flick gave a harsh laugh. "Sure it does. You ought to be dead right now, you know? No amount of religiousness is going to make you feel anything but pleasure at seeing me here."

"I won't deny that you hurt me. You also hurt my family, and that was even worse."

"I know. And what if I told you this, Matt Keath?" Flick leaned closer. "I'd do it all over again. Only difference is that I would make sure you got effectively silenced, and I would make a clean escape. No sitting in chains and waiting for a court trial. If you came here expecting an apology, forget it."

"I didn't come for an apology." Matt inched closer and rested his forehead against the cold bars of the cell. "I can't say I understand your reasoning behind lashing out at me like this, even if Frank is your brother. I've always considered you to be my friend—"

"You can forget that too," Flick said. "This has been in the works for a long time, Matt. Longer than you'd want to know. Everything would have been perfect if you'd stayed on at the Bar K. Frank was almost ready to move in, but then you up and left. But that was all right. Everything still would've worked out if you'd just gone to Texas with me. Frank would've waylaid you on the way, and it would have been over just like that." Flick snapped his fingers. "Done."

Matt could only stare at him, stunned by how duped he'd been. "Maybe that is how things always were, Flick. For you, at least. For me, I considered you a friend who always had my best interests in mind, even if we didn't agree on what that was. But now that I see how things really are, I guess there's only one thing left to say. I forgive you."

Flick snorted. "Don't need your forgiveness. I planned your downfall. I don't even care if you hate me."

"Well, I don't," Matt said, and he felt a sense of freedom as he realized that he meant it. "To plan such misery for me, you must feel pretty miserable yourself. So I feel sorry for you. I'm sorry you've missed out on some of the very best things in life, things I'd been missing too until I came to Osceola. Things like family. Love. God." Matt paused. "I forgive you, Flick, even though you haven't asked. But here's something more for you to think about. God is offering you forgiveness as well, despite the nasty things you've done. No matter what happens, it's never too late for you to turn your story around."

"I'm accused of attempted murder. If I don't swing, then I'm aiming for years in the state penitentiary. And you think *I* have the power to change *my* life?" Flick barked a laugh. "Grow up, Matt. It's over for me."

"Your future isn't the victim of your past choices. You have the power to change your eternity." Matt eased back from the bars. "It's up to you. Do you want heaven or hell? God's forgiveness or your own reasoning for why your sin isn't all that bad?"

Flick refused to comment. Instead, he remained on his bed, slouched against the wall and arms crossed.

Matt turned his back to the cell and walked away. He glanced at the desk where Ethan sat and dipped his head. Ethan nodded back.

Matt stepped outside, the sun's rays washing over him and scrubbing away the image of Flick's brick and iron cell. His heart ached over Flick's decisions, but seeing him once more truly had been the final step in closing a chapter of his past. He couldn't hate the man. Not when he could still see the bitterness etched on Flick's face.

Matt walked to the wagon where Emily and the children waited for him, drawing the first deep breath he had since Flick's arrival.

Thank God he had chosen this precious family instead of Texas.

CHAPTER 34

Matt was awakened by the rooster's crow, prompting him to pull the pillow over his head in an attempt to muffle the sound. Fool bird. How could anyone think roosters only crowed at sunrise? Spending the summer living in a barn with the chickens made Matt more aware than ever that roosters vocalized whenever they felt like it, regardless of day or night.

Feeling wide awake now, Matt started to stretch but then caught himself, remembering his broken ribs. He groaned as he pulled the pillow away from his face, still annoyed that his body had betrayed him. Even stretching was off-limits now, so he scowled at the ceiling instead.

Emily had been true to her promise to keep him from overdoing himself. She'd taken the doctor's word too seriously. She hardly let him do anything, including the milking. Even worse, she seemed to have a sixth sense that told her when he was considering doing something that he shouldn't. She always popped up to ruin his plans before he could get any work done.

But she wasn't alone in warning him not to overdo it. During the first week, there had been a steady stream of visitors

—men offering to help with whatever he needed and women who brought meals to help ease Emily's burden. Of course, they were eager to hear the whole story of how Matt was injured, but their offers to help were genuine. Josiah had assured him that he would get a couple of men to help redo the roof of the soddy; after all, he had the lumber, and it was a shame to let it sit around and gather dust, especially when it could be put to good use. Everyone was making too much fuss over Matt, but he still appreciated the help.

Zane had been his greatest source of help. He didn't ask Matt if he needed help; he simply showed up every morning in time for chores and told him to put him to use. "You've helped me so much with Byron and Audrey that it's only fair," he said.

After a couple of days of witnessing Zane travel back and forth, Matt had the idea to ask if he wanted to move into the barn with him for a while. Zane agreed so fast that Matt wondered if he was looking for an excuse to flee from his empty house. Matt couldn't blame him. It had to be hard trying to overcome his grief when, every day, he was surrounded by memories of Sarah. Since Zane's house was situated on the same farm as his parents', not more than a stone's throw away from theirs, his pa and brothers could take care of the livestock without him. In fact, Elkanah had gone out of his way to thank Matt for giving Zane a reason to leave the farm.

"He works hard. Too hard. He's not the same as he was before Sarah's death. He needs a change, or else he's going to collapse," Elkanah had told him, his expression evidence of the concern he held for his son.

Matt knew that he spoke the truth. Ever since Sarah's death, Zane didn't look like he'd been eating or sleeping properly. He couldn't continue in that state for long and still remain healthy.

Matt looked across the loft to where he could just barely make out Zane's sleeping form in the dark. Moving in with Matt had seemed to be just the change Zane needed. The dark smudges beneath his eyes had disappeared, and he seemed more clearheaded than he'd been since the funeral. And best of all, he was able to spend more time with his children.

Matt only wished that he would've invited Zane to move in with him long ago. He'd grown closer to him in the past several days, and now he felt almost as if he had become the younger brother that Matt never had. It made him even more determined to help the young man overcome his devastating loss.

The rooster crowed again, and Matt gave up on attempting to fall back to sleep. Matt rolled out of bed and winced at the pain in his side. It wasn't as bad as it had been at first, but he didn't appreciate the reminder of his injury.

Matt pulled on a new pair of pants and stuck his feet into his boots, then pulled on his shirt and buttoned it up. He tried to keep his movements quiet, but Zane stirred.

"Morning already?" Zane asked, stretching in a way that Matt couldn't.

"Little early yet, but the rooster woke me up, so I figured I'd get something done. You can keep sleeping."

Zane rolled out of his pile of blankets. "Nah. I'm already awake, so I might as well get started too. Besides, I'm scared of what you'd attempt to do if left unsupervised."

Matt snorted. "You and Emily both act like I can't do anything. It's not like I'm an invalid."

"Would be easier to keep an eye on you if you were."

Matt gathered his dirty clothes and started for the ladder. "I'd be sitting with my feet up all day if you and Em had your way. Got to keep pushing my limits, or else I'll never be allowed to do anything again."

"Em?" Zane's voice held mild curiosity. "Since when did you start calling her Em?"

Matt paused. "I guess I don't know." But he rather liked the nickname. *Em.* Short and sweet, just like the woman.

Matt shrugged and moved to the ladder, discarding his

clothes so he had both hands free. Since his mishap, he'd gotten into the habit of making sure he could use two hands when grabbing the ladder rungs, lest he slip and exacerbate his injury.

"What are you doing now?" Zane asked, his tone warning that Matt better not be testing his limits.

"I'm just going to get the milk buckets for you. Then I might fetch the cows."

"Right. And start milking if I'm not there immediately." Even in the dim light Matt could see Zane shake his head. "Behave yourself, Matt."

"Of course I will," Matt replied, making Zane snort.

When he reached the bottom of the ladder, Matt picked up his laundry and started for the house, his heart lighter than it had been in a while. No, he didn't like being hurt, but he had to admit that the fussing wasn't all bad. Especially since he knew that they fussed because they cared about him. The only trouble was that sometimes they overdid it.

Matt opened the door to the soddy. A light shone from the inside, and Emily looked up from where she sat at the table, her Bible opened before her.

"Morning, Matthew. Aren't you up a little early?"

"Couldn't sleep any longer." Matt raised his eyebrows. "And aren't you up a little early, too?"

"I couldn't sleep either." Emily studied him, her forehead knitting in a frown. "How are you feeling? Does your side hurt?"

"It gets better every day."

"It seemed like it wasn't doing well yesterday after you mucked out the barn."

Matt waved his hand. "A little pain is expected."

Emily wagged her head. "And that's why you need someone to look out for you. You push yourself too hard."

"You're one to talk. You keep too busy yourself."

That was true. Even now, in the lamp light, the lines of her face were more defined than they should be, and the shadows beneath her eyes were more pronounced.

"Didn't Sadie mention on Sunday that there's going to be a sewing group meeting at the church today?" Matt asked.

Emily gave him a guarded look. "Why do you ask?"

"You should go. Take some time to relax."

Emily shook her head. "That's ridiculous. I haven't been to a sewing group in months."

"All the more reason to go."

Emily cocked an eyebrow at him. "Someone needs to keep an eye on the children and cook supper for them. The chores won't care for themselves."

"I can take care of things here. You need to go and enjoy yourself." Matt nodded firmly to indicate that the matter was closed.

Emily stared at him, mouth ajar. "You aren't supposed to be overexerting yourself."

"For pity's sake, I'm not an invalid," Matt snapped. "I'm perfectly capable of watching the kids. They won't give me a bit of trouble, I'll bet you."

Emily looked doubtful. "And I'll bet you that you've cut more work out for yourself than you realize."

"Hardly. The kids will be of no trouble, and I'll keep supper simple. Bacon and flapjacks."

Emily looked even more incredulous, and Matt added, "I do know how to do a little cooking. I've made bacon and flapjacks countless times and I haven't killed anyone yet."

Emily still didn't look convinced.

"Trust me," Matt said, picking up the milk bucket. "We'll be just fine. Zane will be here too. A few kids and a simple supper is nothing to fret over. What time will you need to leave?"

Emily sighed, still shaking her head. "You've really made up your mind, haven't you?"

"Yep, and I'm not changing it."

"I'm not changing mine either. So what do you plan to do about that?"

Matt tilted his head. "I'll pull the wagon around, then I'll come after you and carry you out to it if that's what it takes. Then I'll injure myself even more, and you'll feel terrible because your stubborn resistance sent me into such an agony of pain."

Emily stared at him, then snatched a dish towel from the table and threw it at him. "You incorrigible man! Get out of here, now!"

Convinced he would get his way, Matt ducked out the door with a laugh.

~

"You're sure you'll be all right?" Emily asked for what seemed like the tenth time as she gathered up the reins.

Matt looked up and gave her his most confident smile. "Of course. Just enjoy yourself and don't worry about us."

"I still think you're crazy, Matthew Keath," Emily replied with a smile.

"And I still think you're overly worried about this." Matt stepped back as the team started forward. "We'll be fine. You'll see for yourself."

"Goodbye, Mama," Joyanna called out, waving enthusiastically. The boys' goodbyes sounded a little more uncertain, and Austin kept his thumb tucked securely in his mouth as the wagon rolled farther away.

Matt waved a final time, then he turned to the four children in front of him. What did Emily think could go wrong? He could handle one girl and three boys. Emily had even taken Audrey with her, the only child Matt hadn't been so sure that he could oversee. So without the baby, the rest of the afternoon ought to be fair skies.

The four children stared back at him as if waiting for him to tell them what to do. Matt cleared his throat. "How about all of you find something to play outside? I've got some harness to oil, so I'll be outside the barn."

"I gotta use the outhouse," Grant piped up.

Matt's smile faded. "Oh. Then I guess that's what we'll do first."

All of the children insisted on tagging along. Once Grant finished, each of them had to take their turn at using the privy. Matt released a breath of relief when he finally closed the door behind them.

"Now, time for you to find something to do," he said, ushering the children toward the barn.

None of them seemed too sure of what they wanted to play, but Joyanna eventually took the lead. "Let's play hide-and-seek. Grant can be 'it' first."

Grant covered his eyes. Even though Joyanna dashed away, Byron and Austin took their sweet time in finding easy hiding places.

Matt fetched his harness from the barn and sat outside the door, positioned so that he could keep an eye on the children while he worked. He studied the leather in front of him, twisting it around in his hands. Just as he was about to settle down to work, Joyanna popped up at his side.

"Uncle Matt, Grant isn't playing fair. He peeked when he was counting to ten."

Matt sighed, tamping down his impatience. "He's young, and he probably doesn't understand what it means to not peek. Why don't you send him here to count? I'll make sure that he keeps his eyes covered."

Joyanna bobbed her head in agreement and sprinted away.

Every so often, Matt was interrupted and had to hold his hands over a little boy's eyes to make sure he wasn't peeking. As each moment passed, he questioned why he'd even taken the harness out in the first place. He was barely making any progress.

Finally, Joyanna had to take her turn at being "it." That freed Matt's hands so he could return to his work. As Joyanna chanted the numbers to ten from behind him, Matt again picked up his rag and set to work on the harness. Squeals and giggles filled the air around him, but he blocked out the noise and instead thought through his priorities for the next month.

One of the tasks he needed to do was put up a final round of hay. Josiah had already said he would help.

As for Zane, he remained silent about haying. Maybe the memories of Sarah's accident and their last day working together were still etched on his mind. Matt wouldn't blame him if he chose to busy himself with other things instead of assisting in putting up hay, but losing Zane's help would be a severe cut in their efficiency.

And of course, harvest was just around the corner. The corn husks filled out nicely. Matt watched the sky daily, praying the weather would continue to cooperate. They were so close to being able to bring it safely in—

A sudden scream pierced the air. Matt dropped the harness and leapt to his feet, searching for its source.

"Uncle Matt, come quick!" Joyanna yelled. "Austin fell in the cattle tank!"

Matt took off sprinting toward the cattle tank before she could even finish her sentence. A child in the stock tank was no joke, and he willed himself to move as fast as possible, ignoring the ache that began in his side.

Matt reached the tank where the other children were gathered. He vaulted over the fence and landed on his feet next to the cattle tank. It was only half full, but Austin couldn't seem to get his feet under him. Matt plunged his hands in and grabbed the boy beneath the armpits, hoisting him up out of the tank.

"You all right, Austin?" Matt asked as the boy coughed up water.

Austin began to cry, and then he gagged up more water and cried even harder.

Matt rubbed Austin's back, struggling to control his own breathing. His side felt like a knife was stabbing through it, especially after all the running, twisting, and leaping. But he refused to relax his grip on Austin. That had been a close call, too close for comfort. Many children had died by falling into animal troughs, and Matt hated to think of what might have happened if Joyanna hadn't noticed.

"'Ook, Unca Matt. 'Ook at me," Byron spoke up from behind him. Matt turned to see Byron holding out two hands that were filled with a sticky yellow substance. It oozed down his arms and stained the front of his shirt. The enthusiasm in Byron's brown eyes showed that he thought Matt would appreciate his offering after what had happened.

"Byron!" Matt fought to keep his voice from escalating into a yell. "You're not supposed to be taking the eggs—and definitely not crushing them!"

Byron's expression fell. He gazed at his hands, clenching and unclenching them, letting pieces of egg shell and scrambled eggs slip down his forearms.

Matt exhaled a long breath, grabbing on to his patience with both hands. "It looks like we've got two boys who need some cleaning up. Guess we better get on with it."

This time around, hopping over the fence was a real challenge. His ribs screamed as he tried to clamber up, and there was no adrenaline in him to urge him on. After fetching buckets of water from the well to clean their clothes, Matt felt even more exhausted than after being in a rodeo. Still, he couldn't afford stopping for a moment; it was already late in the afternoon, and he wanted the meal ready before dusk. He'd need to hurry if he wasn't going to miss that goal.

He entered the soddy, and Joyanna, Grant, Byron, and Austin insisted on trailing him around as he studied the equipment he needed to work with. After rustling around for several minutes, he found a spoon and a bowl to use for the flapjacks mixture. He wiped the back of his hand across his forehead. Why, exactly, had he suggested this in the first place? He should have listened to Emily when she told him that his idea was ridiculous.

She'd been right.

Joyanna came to his aid and helped him find the flour. Then she insisted on helping him dump in each ingredient, spilling a little on the table during the process.

While she stirred the flapjack batter, Matt turned his attention to the bacon and lined the frying pan with the thin strips, then placed the pan on the stove. He held his hand above the stove to test the temperature. It wasn't warm like it should have been.

Matt groaned. How could he have forgotten to add fuel to the fire this afternoon?

The boys lost interest in Matt's cooking and began to play by themselves—some kind of game that involved wrestling. Joyanna sang, still stirring the flapjack batter. The noise pressed in on him, smothering him in his inability to escape it. A dull throb started at the base of his neck which quickly progressed into a full-blown headache. By the time he had managed to start the fire in the stove again, the pain was in full force and fighting for attention with his sore rib cage.

Now, things could be worse, so don't start complaining, he told himself.

As he adjusted the pan of bacon, the door opened. Matt swung around, expecting to see Emily coming to save him from this mess.

But it wasn't Emily. Instead, Zane lingered in the doorway,

holding a milk bucket and frowning. "What are you doing?" he asked.

"What's it look like?" Disappointment snapped into his voice, and he made no effort to filter it out. "I'm trying to make supper."

Zane sent a skeptical look toward the pan on the stove. "What are you making?"

"Flapjacks and bacon."

"Really?"

Matt massaged his aching side and scowled at Zane. "Yes, really. I *do* know how to cook. Done it dozens of times before."

"On a stovetop?" Zane asked, still eyeing the pan.

He had Matt cornered with that one. "Well, not exactly. I'm more experienced with cooking over a campfire. But I figure there can't be much of a difference."

Zane shook his head. "I don't know a thing about cooking, but something gives me the notion that there are differences between cooking over a campfire and cooking over a stove."

"I know at least something about cooking, and I say that there is no difference. They both have fire. They both cook food. Same thing." Matt massaged the back of his head. "And for your information, I've never killed anyone with my cooking, so there you have it."

"There's a first time for everything," Zane muttered. Then he whipped his attention over to Joyanna and shouted, "Watch her! She's going to drop the bowl!"

His warning came too late. The bowl slid off the table and landed on a chair. It somehow remained upright, but some of the batter splattered over the edge, spilling onto the chair and the floor.

Zane groaned. Matt squeezed his eyes shut, forcing himself to keep his temper under control. It was only an accident, only a mess that could be cleaned up.

"You know, I just remembered that there was something I

wanted to talk with Pa about," Zane said, intentionally not looking at Matt. "I think I'll head that way after I finish chores. Don't count on me for supper."

Before Matt could respond, a popping sound from the stove jerked his attention back to the bacon. He lunged toward the stove and started to reach for the pan—but then he remembered that it was hot. He snatched a wadded up towel and used it to push the pan back from the full heat of the stove. The bacon no longer looked like bacon. It resembled charred sticks instead.

Zane took the milk he'd strained and edged toward the door. "Glad you found a way to stay out of trouble, Matt," he said as he left.

Matt stared at the door. That was all he could say? *Glad you found a way to stay out of trouble?* The man must be crazy, and he had no grasp of how chaotic Matt's afternoon had been. Watching children and cooking supper was *not* an easy job. In fact, it was just as physically demanding as milking the cow or carrying feed to the pig—maybe harder. This afternoon had left him feeling worse than he had since Frank Harvey pummeled him.

"Uncle Matt?" Joyanna called. "You gonna get the pancakes cooking?" She watched as Austin sampled the batter that had spilled on the floor.

"Yes—no, Austin! Yucky." Matt scooped the boy up from the floor in one swift motion. He wasn't picky about his food, but the idea of eating pancake batter that had mingled with the dirt floor was enough to disgust even him.

Austin howled, wriggling to get down and return to his treat, but Matt held him firmly. He'd take care of the mess in a minute; for now, he needed to cook those pancakes.

But something didn't seem right with the stove. The first couple of pancakes Matt cooked remained doughy. Then they started to burn, and try as he might, Matt couldn't flip them fast enough. The worst thing about it was that the outsides were black while the insides were still undercooked. Mustering patience, Matt tried again and then another time. He adjusted the pan from one spot on the stove to another. None of them turned out right.

Matt flung the flipper aside and turned his back on the pancakes. It was time to focus on making coffee instead. Supper might be a disaster, but at least he could have coffee ready by the time that Emily returned. That was one thing he'd never failed at yet.

While waiting for the coffee to boil, Matt turned around and surveyed the room. It was a mess. Piles of flour and salt stood among the dirty dishes that littered the table. Pancake batter dripped from the chair onto the floor. The mere sight of it worsened Matt's headache. This had to be a nightmare.

"I'm hungry," Grant announced, looking at Matt as if he actually expected him to have a solution.

Joyanna and Byron chimed in their agreement. The pressure made Matt feel like the air was slowly being squeezed out of him.

Austin returned to tasting the pancake batter on the floor. At least that was one thing Matt could take care of.

Matt picked him up and growled, "Austin! I said no."

Austin's high-pitched wail caused Matt's ears to ring. Gritting his teeth, Matt secured his hold on the boy as Austin tried to push away with his arms and legs flailing. Then Austin struck a blow at Matt's injured ribs, and fire erupted in Matt's side.

"Austin!" Matt nearly dropped the boy and stumbled back a step to regain his balance. He tripped over Byron, and Byron fell on his bottom and started to wail.

Matt teetered on the verge of what must surely be insanity. The crying, the mess, the failed attempt at supper. It was all too much. Way too much. He'd tried to remain patient throughout the entire afternoon, but he was only human. He had limits. And those were limits that he was nearly about to reach. He couldn't handle even one more thing.

But then he heard what he knew would become the last straw . . .

He turned around and—yep. The coffee had boiled over.

Matt ran to the stove. Without even pausing to think, he snatched the pot and pulled it away from the heat. Pain seared through his fingers at the touch, and Matt jerked his hand back.

Fool! his mind screamed. *You know better than to touch a hot pot with your bare hand.*

His hand throbbed, the pain burning deeper with each pulse of his heart. He darted a look around the room in desperation. There—a bucket of water sat near the stove. He quickly submerged his hand, the coolness engulfing his skin and quenching the fire in his hand.

Somehow, even through the cloud of pain and the crying from the children, Matt could make out the click of the door opening. He lifted his head and glimpsed what he was sure must have been an angel. Emily stood with the door half opened, her eyes wide as she took in the chaos before her. She stood there, unmoving, for barely more than three seconds before she glided into the room and took over.

Matt watched in amazement as she restored the room's peace. She placed a sleeping Audrey on the bed, then crossed to the stove and removed the coffee from the heat. After seeing the scorched flapjacks and bits of bacon, she discarded them for the animals. She ordered Joyanna to clean the batter on the chair, and then she picked up Austin from Matt's arms, calming him and Byron down. It was nothing short of a miracle.

"We'll keep supper simple tonight and have eggs and bread," she said, stopping in front of Matt. "Let me see your hand."

Matt grimaced as he let her take a look at it.

She held his hand, studying it. "Doesn't look too serious, but

I'm sure it's painful. I'll get some salve and bandage it up for you."

Matt endured her fussing as she returned with the salve and a strip of cloth. Why had he never noticed how much work she did in the house? Oh, he'd always known she kept busy—but now he realized that without her all of them would be lost.

In a gentle motion, Emily smeared the salve across the red streak on his palm, then she picked up the bandage. Winding the fabric around his hand, Emily looked at him with an eyebrow raised and a suspicious twinkle in her eyes. "You had no trouble this afternoon, did you?"

Matt intended to say that he didn't know how she survived even a single day. Or that the next time he conjured such a crazy idea, she had his permission to lock him up until his sanity returned. But the words that spilled out instead were, "I love you, Em."

Emily stared at him, her smile frozen in place. "I'm sorry. What did you say?"

How had he been so blind to the truth before? All those times when he'd flinched at the idea of Emily remarrying, the times when he teased her just to see her smile. When he went out of his way in an attempt ease her burdens. None of the nice reasons he'd given, attempting to justify his actions, were the real reason behind why he did them.

It was because he loved her. That was all there was to it. He couldn't evade the truth any longer. The idea of returning to Scottsbluff didn't even remotely appeal to him anymore, not when everything he could ever dream of was right there in front of him—a farm and a perfect, ready-made family this side of heaven.

And Emily. The sweetest, fieriest, most loveable woman he had ever encountered.

"I love you, Em," he repeated, unable to look away. "I love you with all that I am. Will you marry me?"

"Matthew Keath!" Emily held the end of the bandage suspended midair, her mouth dropping open. "Has this afternoon done something to your head?"

"Yes. It made me realize just how much I need you. *Need* you, Emily. I'm lost without you." Matt wanted to say more, to make her realize just how powerful his current of emotions was. But he wasn't good with words in the best of times, and he certainly wasn't at his best right now. Not with the ache in his side, the throbbing in his head, and the fire in his hand. And although he didn't know much about proposals, he figured this wasn't exactly a conventional one. Not when Emily bandaged his burned hand with a roomful of children as their audience. But he meant every word of what he'd said. His love for her ran deep, all the way to the core of who he was.

Emily studied him, her eyes widening as she realized just how serious he was. Her mouth became a thin line and she turned her gaze to his hand, skillfully wrapping the bandage around it without saying a word.

Matt waited. When she didn't speak, he finally said, "Well?"

She tied the end of his bandage, then lifted her eyes to his. Matt was unprepared for the fire that flashed back at him—along with the tears.

"Never, and I mean *never*, let me hear you say such a thing again," she snapped. Without another word, she spun away from him.

Her words sliced through him, overwhelming him with a pain more intense than anything physical. She didn't love him.

Heat burned through his face. Why could he never hold his tongue when he ought to? If he had taken a moment to think logically and consider her reaction, he would have known exactly what she would say. He'd heard her declare multiple times that she had zero interest in remarrying. Of course her response to him would be no different.

But really, she should know that there were benefits to

marrying him. Did she think he was going to stick around forever and work on the farm for nothing? She was putting her family's future in jeopardy by refusing him. She ought to at least marry him for the sake of convenience!

Matt worked up a slow burn thinking through all the reasons she should have heard him out. Too agitated to sit still any longer, he rose from his chair and stomped out of the soddy.

"Matthew, where are you going?" Emily called after him. "Supper's almost ready."

"I'm not hungry!" Matt yelled, and he let the door swing shut hard behind him.

Matt fled to the barn and stormed up and down the aisle several times. With each circuit, his pace slowed until at last, he stood in the center of the barn, unmoving. He wanted to cling to his fury, use it as a shield to protect himself from the pain of her rejection. But try as he might, the anger disappeared.

Deep down, he knew that his argument for why Emily should become his wife wasn't strong. Neither of them wanted to tie the knot just for practical reasons. He knew that.

Besides, her heart still belonged to Colton. She wasn't ready to move beyond the pain of losing him just yet.

Matt sighed, raking his fingers through his hair. How could he ever get out of this mess? He'd made *yet another* stupid move, one he would pay for over the next month. He had promised to stay until harvest—and he would—but his relationship with Emily wouldn't be the same after this. His thoughtless words had made *that* impossible.

He wanted to look on the bright side and hope that maybe, within a few weeks, Emily would change her mind. But thinking like that would only delay the pain. In his heart, he knew Emily would never agree to marry him—not for love or for the security he could offer. He might as well accept it now.

So, his plans needed to remain unchanged. After harvest, he

would go to Scottsbluff, regardless of how much it tore his heart. He couldn't stay—but he was going to miss his newfound family. Joyanna, Grant, Austin, and . . . Emily.

Each one of them had gained a special place in his heart.

Another stab of pain knifed its way through Matt's heart. If she had only said yes, everything would have been perfect.

He sucked in a deep breath and lifted his head to look at the cobwebbed ceiling.

"Lord, I don't know what Your plans are behind all this," he whispered. "But You must have a purpose. You never let Your children suffer in vain." His shoulders slumped. "Couldn't You make this one easier? Couldn't You just make her love me?"

The dead silence that followed was his only answer. It enveloped Matt like a thick fog, making him feel lonelier than he had ever felt before.

CHAPTER 35

Matt somehow kept going even though his heart was heavy. He had the roof secured on the soddy, the hog butchered, and the fields harvested, bringing in greater yields than he had dared imagine. When he brought the grain to the new elevator in town, he got a good price. Yet inside, Matt knew that each finished task brought him one step closer to leaving.

Time was running out on him.

Even after the harvest was safely put up, he delayed his departure to weatherproof the farm. He also cut enough wood to keep Emily's stove burning until spring—or, as Josiah said when he saw the pile, enough to heat all of *Osceola* this winter.

But at last, Matt had to face the truth. *Who am I trying to kid?* he asked himself as he drove the team down the road one chilly afternoon in mid-October. He no longer had a reason to stay. Emily didn't love him and she never would.

Matt's fingers tightened around the reins—as if squeezing the life out of the leather could solve anything. He didn't want to leave, but his desires couldn't change facts. His time in Osceola had ended.

He'd attempted to express his love for Emily, although he hadn't said the actual words. Not since that one impulsive exclamation. He'd hoped that she could see it in his behavior and in the way he looked at her and spoke to her, but he was ultimately unsuccessful. He'd lost the battle.

"All right. Fine," he said aloud. "If she doesn't want me here, then I'll leave. Tomorrow morning."

Putting his leaving into clear words, with a set time to depart, made it unavoidable. He could no longer postpone it. Short of Emily altering her feelings for him, he had no more than twenty-four hours left with his precious family.

"Tomorrow," he said again, and his shoulders slumped. He knew she wouldn't change her mind.

Matt snapped out of his thoughts and realized he had almost passed the turn for Edvin Nordstrum's lane. He reined in the horses, backed them up, and made the turn slowly, glancing around to make sure no one at the house had been watching him.

Matt always found the trip to Edvin Nordstrum's blacksmith shop strangely peaceful. In fact, Edvin's entire farm seemed to radiate peace. Everything was in order, from the wooden farmhouse to the shop and the straight lane leading up to the farm. Whenever Matt visited, there would always be somebody from the family with a friendly face and something nice to say. The only problem was that it seemed like Matt always had some kind of broken machinery when he stopped by.

But somehow, even when he was feeling his most harried, a trip to the Nordstrums' improved his state of mind—even if Edvin didn't have a favorable report on his broken equipment. That was just the attitude that the Nordstrums infused into those around them.

And if there was anything Matt needed now, it was peace.

Matt drew the team to a stop in front of the barn, far enough from the blacksmith shop that the noise and flying sparks wouldn't spook the horses. He hopped down from the wagon, grateful that his side no longer felt even a twinge of pain from the motion, and tied the team to a post. He started toward the shop, but Edvin was already coming his way, wiping his soot-covered hands on a rag dangling from one of his pockets.

"Matt, *god dag* to you! How goes it with you and your family?" Edvin asked, the words heavily tinted by his Swedish accent.

"Fine," Matt replied, even though he hardly felt *fine*. But he wasn't about to heap his miseries onto poor Edvin.

"Good, good." Edvin's gentle smile remained in place. "You've come for your plowshares, *ja*?"

"If you have them ready." Matt felt a dull twinge of pain. He wouldn't need the plowshares come spring, but whoever was farming Emily's land would. And Matt intended to leave all of Emily' equipment in pristine condition when he left.

Edvin nodded. "Oh, *ja,* we have them done. If you'll give me a moment, I'll fetch it from the shop, and you can be on your way. Good?"

"Very good."

Edvin nodded again then hurried back to his shop, whistling to himself.

At least *someone* was happy today. If only Matt could close his mind off to all thoughts, including the regrets that lashed at him. Unless Emily changed her mind, this would be the last time he'd see Edvin. The last time he would bring farm equipment to a blacksmith shop, period.

Matt tilted his head back and glared at the sun. How could it have the audacity to shine today? The sunrays should have had enough decency not to come near him, let alone caress him with their light. He would have preferred the weather to be storming hard enough that he had to push his way against the wind. At least then he would have something he could fight.

The barn door opened, and one of Edvin's children stepped

outside. It was the youngest child—Katrina, if Matt remembered correctly.

"Hello, sir," she said, her accent lighter than her father's. "Lovely day, isn't it?"

Before Matt could answer, a puppy tumbled out the door after her, its pudgy legs scrabbling to regain its balance. Two more bounced out after it, and the three of them fell in a pile, nipping at each other and pretending to growl.

Katrina chuckled and reached into the pile to scoop one into her arms. "Silly little thing. Give you a bit of fresh air and sunshine and you're happy, aren't you?"

However stormy Matt had felt before, he couldn't keep from smiling now. "How old are they?"

"Eight weeks." Katrina tilted her head. "Perhaps you'd be interested in buying one? Every farm needs a good dog, you know, and these puppies' mama is a good hunter. Always bringing dead rats and rabbits up to the house for us."

Matt moved closer and rubbed the puppy's head. "I wasn't really in the market for a dog, but—" He gently tugged on the puppy's ears. "On second thought, maybe I am. How much are you asking?"

"Two dollars."

Matt bit his lip. "Sorry, I'm afraid that's too much."

A smile arched her lips. "Then ask me to lower my price. You aren't giving up that easily, are you?"

She was little more than a kid—Matt guessed no older than sixteen. But she was obviously used to bargaining. "Fine. Katrina Nordstrum, would you be willing to come down on your price?"

Her blue eyes sparkled. "I just might be able to. How about a dollar fifty?"

Matt considered that and nodded. "Very well, young lady. You've got yourself a deal."

"Good. I have one buyer who wants one, but he didn't specify which he was taking. That being the case, you may take your pick of the whole lot. But if I were you, I'd consider that one." She pointed to the door where a fourth puppy stood, its eyes scanning the barnyard and tail whisking back and forth in short, jerky motions. "Go ahead. Pick it up."

Matt took her offer and bent to scoop it up. It quivered slightly, but when Matt brought it to his chest, it snuggled right down as if it had found home.

"She's a little smaller than the others, as you'll notice," Katrina told him. "And she has a bit of a limp. It's not a very noticeable one, but it's there nonetheless. My brother Ivar's horse stepped on her a few weeks ago. I treated her as best I could, and she's been healing nicely. With time, she should come out of the bit of limp."

"That's my Katrina." Edvin came around the corner of the barn, Matt's plowshares in hand. "Always fixing whatever's broken." His face creased into his usual smile. "Trying to sell you a puppy, *ja?*"

"She already sold me on one." Matt stroked the puppy in his arms, teasing her floppy ears. "I think you're right. I'll take this one."

Katrina beamed. "*Ja,* that's a good choice. She has a good temperament, and she should get along well with all those little ones at your house. And just look. She's already claimed you, I believe."

Matt smiled as the puppy stuck out its pink tongue to lick his finger, but his heart felt heavy. The puppy wasn't his. He couldn't expect a mere dog to take his place when he left, but maybe it would provide a bit of distraction for the children. That way, they wouldn't notice his absence so much. When he left tomorrow, the puppy would remain.

After paying for both the puppy and the work that Edvin

had accomplished on the plowshares, Matt climbed into the wagon, the puppy tucked between his shirt and his coat.

Edvin stepped away from the team and ran his fingers through his silver-blond hair. "You take care, Matt, and enjoy the puppy. Be sure to stop by sometime, and you could bring that sweet family of yours as well."

Despite Matt's intentions to keep his personal problems to himself, he found himself shaking his head. "I'm afraid this will be the last time I'll see you. I leave tomorrow."

"You're leaving?" Edvin frowned. "To go where?"

"Back west." The words emerged more harshly than Matt intended.

Both Edvin and Katrina studied him without blinking. "And you are not excited?" Edvin asked.

"I don't have much choice." Matt forced himself to inhale deeply. "I'm sorry, but I need to get home."

"Of course." Edvin's gaze traced his face, the lines around his eyes gentle. "I don't want to hold you up."

Matt nodded and picked up the reins. He had to escape before the dam that held his emotions in check broke and he said things he'd later regret.

"Matt?" Edvin stepped forward. "Listen. I don't know what your circumstances are, but God does. I will pray for you."

"All of our family will," Katrina added. "He can give you the answer you desire—and also the answer that you need the most."

Matt looked from one to the other, the back of his eyes beginning to burn. "Thank you," he murmured. He didn't know the Nordstrums very well since they attended the church in Swede Home rather than the Mission Church in Osceola. But he wished he'd taken the time to get to know them better. They must be special people if they were willing to pray for someone they hardly even knew.

Edvin stepped away from the team and waved goodbye. "*Ha*

det bra, Matt—have a nice day. Remember that only One can grant you peace."

~

After taking care of the team, Matt brought the plowshares to the barn, the sleeping puppy still tucked in his coat. He stepped into the building and found Zane seated at the work table.

Zane barely glanced up from the pieces of wood scattered before him. "Edvin get them sharpened?"

Before Matt could answer, the puppy squirmed awake and let out a whimper that turned into a yowl.

Zane spun around and stared at him. "What on earth—what do you have there, Matt?"

Fighting back a grin, Matt unbuttoned his coat to pull out the puppy. "How do you think the kids will like this?"

"A puppy?" Zane's mouth curved upwards, the first hint of a smile that Matt had seen from him in a while. He stood, holding out his hands, and Matt deposited the puppy into his arms. "How old?"

"Eight weeks." Matt let the puppy lick his fingers, then rumpled her ears. "I couldn't pass her by. Thought the kids might like a dog."

"Of course they will. She's a cute one."

For several minutes, the only noises in the room were the little sounds the puppy made. The quiet only made Matt's shoulder's tense, his throat ache with the words he knew he needed to say.

Matt inhaled, then blew his breath out. "I'm leaving tomorrow."

Even though he had his eyes fixed on the puppy in front of him, Matt could sense the quick lift of Zane's head. "Why so soon?"

"It's past time I was gone. Should've left long ago."

"Seems like you've been getting plenty done around here."

Matt sighed. "This is a farm. There's always something to be done. I need to leave now while things are quiet."

Several heartbeats passed before Zane spoke. "I don't think you're making a good choice."

"Choice?" The single word drove Matt a step backward. "What choice? I have no other option!"

Zane looked up at him, his features unreadable. "Oh, there's always a choice. Maybe you just haven't looked hard enough."

"Zane, you have *no* idea how hard I've thought this through."

"Emily turned you down, didn't she?"

The argument on Matt's lips died, and he stared back at Zane. "What?"

"You asked her to marry you, and she turned you down."

Matt grabbed the back of his neck, scrubbing his hand over the skin. The action did nothing to ease the pressure inside him. "So how'd you figure that out?"

"I've known for a long time that you care about her. It was pretty easy to see. Take Obadiah, for instance. You fairly bristled whenever he was around."

Matt blinked. "Surely it wasn't that obvious."

Zane nodded. "That obvious. And when you and Emily started acting all funny around each other, it didn't take a brilliant mind to figure out what had happened. Besides . . ." He lowered his gaze. "I was in love once. I should recognize the signs."

Matt took a few steps away from Zane, picking up one of the pieces of wood from the work table. He turned the wood over in his hands, not truly seeing it, then dropped it and spun to face Zane again. "I can't stay. It would be too uncomfortable to hang around, and besides, winter's almost breathing down our backs. We can't live here in the barn much longer."

Zane studied him, his features unreadable apart from a slight pinch at the corners of his eyes. "If that's the way you feel."

Matt started toward the barn door, then swung around and stopped in front of Zane. "All right, so you don't think I'm making the right choice. What, then, do you suggest I do?"

"It's not my place to tell you what you should do."

"I'm willing to listen to any advice, so tell me what's on your mind."

Zane met Matt's gaze. "If you were thinking clearly, you would have come to the same conclusions I have. I don't think you're ready to listen."

"Of course I am. Come on, Zane. I could use a little help right now."

Zane shook his head. "There's only one thing I'll tell you. Emily needs you, but she won't admit it to a soul, not even herself. And she loves you. I see that clearly, but she's deluded herself."

Matt couldn't restrain a bitter laugh. "Impossible. I have eyes in my head, Zane, and that's not what I see. She's better off without me. Have you noticed the way she's acted around me lately? She can't draw a decent breath when I'm nearby. She's even more prickly than when I first arrived."

"Exactly my point. She's trying to protect herself in the best way she knows how. And what is it that she's trying to protect herself from?" Zane waited as if Matt should know the answer. When Matt said nothing, he answered his own question. "The truth that something inside her is responding to your love."

Matt started shaking his head before the words had fully escaped from Zane's mouth. "Thanks for trying to encourage me, but that's just wishful thinking. She doesn't want me around. And even if she did, she would tell me so before I left. So, if she doesn't say anything, then I'll know for certain that she doesn't care."

Zane frowned but kept quiet.

Matt folded his arms across his chest. "What's *that* look about? I can tell you don't agree with me."

Zane's frown remained in place. "You're both so stubborn that I could knock your heads together. Seems like you're determined to ruin your lives."

Matt pressed his lips together. "She *will* tell me if she wants me to stay. And if she can't get the words out, then too bad."

Zane sighed. Matt braced himself for another argument, but Zane only said, "You're right about winter being almost here. I should probably head back to my own house." He grimaced.

Matt exhaled, allowing the fight to drain out of him. "Is it any easier?"

Zane shrugged. "In some ways, yes. But in others—I don't think I'll ever get over her."

Zane never referred to Sarah by name anymore. In fact, he usually didn't refer to her at all.

Although part of him warned that he should be careful where he tread, Matt couldn't hold his tongue. "You, of all people, should understand that Emily hasn't recovered from her loss of Colton. Do you think you'd be ready to remarry in just a few more months?"

"No. But that's different." Zane frowned at the puppy he still cradled in his hands. "Different people, different circumstances. Emily needs to remarry. Those kids need a pa, and she needs someone who can care for her farm. You've already stepped into that role whether you realize it or not. Emily's healed more than it might appear from the outside. You've already made her do things that I never would have imagined she'd do so soon after Colton's death. Maybe she isn't ready to accept the truth, but she is ready to remarry."

"And *you* don't need to remarry? Your kids don't need a ma? Your house doesn't need someone to look after it?"

A shadow fell across Zane's features. "For me, there was only one woman. She isn't replaceable."

"No spouse ever is. The question is whether the spouse left

behind will choose to be satisfied with their life without them or if they'll move on beyond it. Neither choice is wrong." Matt turned away. "If Emily's ready to move on, then she knows how I feel. But if she isn't, then I might as well leave. Waiting won't change a thing."

309

CHAPTER 36

E mily was always thankful when supper had ended.

As soon as she politely excused herself, Emily pushed back from the table and set to work on the dishes, glad to turn her back to Matt and those eloquent blue eyes of his. Maybe he didn't mean to allow his eyes to reflect his thoughts, but Emily could plainly read what went through his mind. It unnerved her. She had never anticipated that he would care for her so much. She hated hurting him, but she couldn't give him what he wanted.

There appeared to be no end in sight to the uneasy truce they had struck.

The door clicked shut, and she glanced behind her. Matt was gone. Her shoulders lowered, some of the inner tension draining away.

Then the door opened again and Matt stepped back into the room. Turning her back to him, Emily fixed her gaze on the dirty dishes in front of her, listening as Matt walked over to the chair he usually occupied.

"Joyanna, boys, come here. I've got something for you."

Emily made herself stay at the dish basin, but she had a hard time resisting the temptation to turn around and look as the children gathered around him.

A strange sound carried across the room, a squeaky *yip* that almost sounded like an animal.

The children squealed.

"Oh, look!" Joyanna said. "Is it yours, Uncle Matt?"

"No, it's yours. All of yours," Matt replied.

Joyanna squealed again, and Emily couldn't resist peeking over her shoulder to see what was causing all the excitement. For a moment, she couldn't see beyond Joyanna's body as she flung her arms around Matt's neck, smothering him with a big hug. When she dropped to her knees again, Emily caught a glimpse of an animal's black nose and curly brown fur. A puppy.

Emily's view became blocked again by several small heads leaning toward the puppy.

Matt's gaze met hers. "Nordstrums had some puppies for sale. Every farm needs a dog." Though his words were innocent, his eyes searched hers with depth of emotion that Emily didn't wish to read into.

Unable to hold his gaze, Emily ducked her head in a nod and returned to the dishes. Of course he would get the kids a dog if he thought they needed one. That was just like Matt, always doing more than he needed to for them.

Emily sniffed back the moisture gathering behind her eyes. Why must he always do things like this, giving without expecting anything in return? It made her feel guilty.

Emily felt a presence beside her. She glanced up to find Matt hovering over her, far too close for comfort. She panicked and quickly averted her gaze back to the soapy water she was washing dishes in, scrubbing the plate in her hands with too much intensity. *Ignore him and he'll go away.* She struggled to keep her breathing even, despite the way her heart hammered in her chest.

He didn't move, but he seemed to be waiting for her to look

at him again. That was not something that Emily had any intentions of doing. The plate in her hands slipped and fell back into the water with a *splash* that sent water droplets flying. He made her so nervous that she couldn't even think straight.

"Are you trying to ignore me?" Matt's voice was so low that Emily wouldn't have heard it if he hadn't been standing so close.

She couldn't lie. "Yes."

"Well, if I talk, will you listen?"

"Maybe." She absently foraged through the soapy water for another dish, but there was none left. A trickle of perspiration ran down her neck as she sighed in frustration.

Why couldn't he just leave her be?

As if to answer her thoughts, Matt said, "I'm leaving."

Emily nodded. But when he didn't move, she looked at him. The seriousness in his eyes struck her with the full impact of his words.

Emily felt the blood drain from her face. "Leaving?"

"Tomorrow. At dawn." He paused, as if waiting for her to respond.

But Emily didn't know how to. She couldn't. The news she'd dreaded more than anything else had arrived. She wanted to cling to Matt and beg for him to stay, even if only for a little while longer, but she held herself in place. He'd been more than kind in setting aside his own time and plans to help her this summer. It would be selfish of her to ask for more. Especially when she could give him nothing in return. Not even her heart.

Silence stretched between them, broken only by the children's squeals and Zane warning the children to be careful with the puppy. Even in her discomfort, Emily noticed that Zane had his back to them, affording them a little privacy.

She took a deep breath and looked back at Matt. "You'll write?"

A shadow crossed his face, but he nodded. "I'll keep in touch."

She started to turn back to her dishes, but his voice stopped her. "Em."

Emily raised her gaze again. Her heart fluttered at the range of emotions that emanated from his eyes.

Love. Pain. Longing.

For a moment, the look in his eyes drew her into a whirlpool of emotions she hadn't felt in ages. She couldn't seem to move or even catch her breath.

Finally, Emily gathered the strength to step back and suck in a deep breath. The spell had been broken, and the look on Matt's expression had vanished.

"You'll write if you need anything?" he asked, words stiff.

She swallowed. "I will. Be sure to stop by if you're ever in the area."

He nodded in response.

"Well, I guess that's it." Matt took a step back. His gaze darted to Joyanna and the boys, and a flicker of pain crossed his face. "I better tell them goodbye. I don't intend to stop by the soddy tomorrow. I want to get an early start."

It was all happening far too quickly. Again, Emily fought back the urge to cling to him and instead forced what she hoped looked like a smile. "Goodbye, Matthew. I hope all goes well for you."

"Thank you," he replied, voice flat. "I hope things go well for you too."

Then he walked away before Emily had a chance to express her gratitude for all the work he'd done over the summer.

She looked away as he knelt at Joyanna's side, unwilling to hear what she knew he was going to say. Tears threatened to spill over her eyes, and she desperately tried to keep them in check. *I can't let him go. I can't.*

But she gave her head a firm shake. It would be better for him to leave. He had probably missed his cowboy work and was likely eager to return to it. Before long, he'd forget about them and find a wife who could love him the way he deserved. She refused to be selfish and try to keep him from leaving.

From the corner of her eyes, she saw Joyanna launch herself into Matt's arms, the puppy entirely forgotten as she buried her face in her uncle's shoulder. Emily's resolve nearly broke.

Please, Lord, help me to bear this. Give me the strength I need to stand and watch him leave. Don't let me hold him back, she prayed. Because if she were truly honest with herself, she was frightened by just how deeply she would miss him.

Emily's first thought upon waking was of Matt. She rolled out of bed and crossed to the window, peering outside. It was too dark to see a thing.

Going through the motions, she got dressed and started the stove. As she set the frying pan on to warm, she heard the door open and she spun around, her heart skipping a beat. Had Matt changed his mind? Or was he only coming to tell her he was leaving?

But it wasn't Matt. Instead, Zane stepped into the soddy, closing the door softly behind him. Emily's heart sank.

"Did Matt leave?" she asked, hardly recognizing her own voice.

"Yes."

With the single word, all of Emily's lingering hope was destroyed. Her shoulders slumped, and she struggled to restrain her tears. "I see."

Zane picked up the milk bucket. "If you'd asked him to stay, he would have."

Emily inhaled deeply and lifted her chin. "Maybe, but I wouldn't ask him to do that."

Zane muttered something beneath his breath about "knot-headed fools," but Emily chose not to listen.

As he walked toward the door, Zane said, "I'm thinking about moving back to my place today. It's getting too cold in the barn, and now that Matt's gone, we might as well make our adjustments at once. But don't worry. I'll still be back to take care of the chores. It's the least I can do after all you've done for me and the kids."

Emily nodded, but his words barely penetrated. Matt was gone.

The door closed behind Zane, and Emily squeezed her eyes shut. She would not cry. This hurt, but it was probably for the best. She was starting to depend on Matt too much. He had no commitments to tie him to their family, and if he didn't move on now, he would at another time instead. She needed to stand on her own two feet and stop pretending he was going to be around forever.

And yet, she couldn't deny that her heart felt as if it were being torn in pieces by longings she didn't understand.

Sinking into a chair at the table, Emily buried her face in her hands. *Oh, Colton, love, I'm so confused. There's so much I don't understand since you left. There's no man on earth who can take your place—and yet, why do I feel so devastated over the one who just walked out of my life?*

CHAPTER 37

Cold wind bit at Matt's very bones as he slid down from Bowie's back and scanned the land around him. The horizon looked no different than it had an hour ago, or the hour before that. Bleak. Dead. Just how he felt.

One and a half days since he left, and already he was almost sick with longing for Emily and the kids. *Goodbye.* That was all he'd left them with.

I did my best. I did my duty to Colton, so there's no reason to feel guilty, he tried to tell himself, but the words did nothing to ease the numbness of his heart. If it were merely a matter of duty to his brother's family, then Matt could have left long ago, satisfied that he'd done all that Colton would have expected of him and more. But duty had long ago been tangled with love, so the two couldn't be separated. Duty without love was cold, but love without duty was pointless.

"I just miss them so badly," Matt whispered aloud, the wind snatching the words away even as he spoke.

Not many months ago, he'd been happy with this kind of lonely life, no one depending on him or needing an account from him. But now it felt hollow. He needed to think about his future, plan his next step for how he intended to regain his reputation in Scottsbluff as one of the best cowboys around, but his mind kept wandering back to a little farm outside of Osceola.

He couldn't stop worrying about them. Winter was almost there. Zane had promised to take care of the animal chores. But what if a terrible blizzard hit the area and he couldn't make it? How would Emily manage then? And what about this summer? Who would take care of the fields and the other farm work that pressed to be done? There was too much for a grown man to get done, let alone a woman who had children to look after.

He tried to shake his worries aside. It wasn't his concern anymore. Emily could have asked him to stay. It wasn't his fault that she didn't want him around.

But it still hurt.

Matt sighed, the sound drowned out by the wind. He never should have come. He couldn't seem to settle down to his "real" work now.

And yet, if he hadn't come, then he would still be the same arrogant cowboy he'd been all along, blind to some of the most meaningful things in life—family and God.

He knelt on the frozen ground, pulling back the dead grass to clear a spot for a fire. Then he rocked back on his heels and simply stared at the bare dirt.

Emily would be fine. Just like she'd told him long ago, she didn't need *him.* She had neighbors and God.

He hadn't asked her what her plans were now that he was leaving, but strong woman that she was, Emily had probably started rearranging her life by now. A life without him.

How long before Joyanna stopped missing him? How long before his name fell out of use around the family table and the boys forgot that "Uncle Matt" had ever come to visit? How long before he could think of something other than the family he'd left behind?

"Lord, I don't know what to do," Matt whispered aloud, an odd prayer since he had already made up his mind. He was going to return to life as a cowboy.

But the words resonated somewhere deep inside. Raising his voice, Matt yelled, "I don't know what to do!"

The words echoed off the empty plains and faded away without bringing him an answer.

He was out of choices; he knew that. Since staying on the farm would be too uncomfortable, the only thing he could do now was to move on.

Staying would be uncomfortable, would it? a little voice whispered. *For Emily—or for you?*

Emily, of course. He was thinking of how she felt. She practically arched away from him every time he came too close.

And he couldn't be expected to work Emily's fields for free the rest of his life. He needed an income, for pity's sake! Besides, Emily had pride. She wouldn't let him keep helping for no charge forever.

But had he really been thinking of Emily's feelings or of how uncomfortable *he* felt? He didn't like facing the truth every day that he'd been turned down, that Emily wasn't flattered enough by his proposal to accept him. His pride had suffered because of Emily's rejection. And, in reflection, he had felt a little mad about it.

Well, to be honest, there were moments when he'd been downright furious.

He had to face it. They *could* have gotten along just fine. Maybe not as easily as before, but they would have managed. And the way they felt didn't change how things would be for Joyanna and the boys now that he was gone. Not only had they lost their pa and their uncle, but now Emily would be busier than ever trying to keep up with everything.

There's always a choice. Zane's words returned in a whisper, but they hit Matt right in his stomach. He'd made a choice in leaving. No one was forcing him to leave; he'd arrived at the conclusion to leave on his own.

There's always a choice. Maybe you just haven't been looking hard enough.

He hadn't been looking for another choice, period. He had *wanted* to leave. Leaving was easier than staying and facing the pain. Sometimes, love could hurt.

He hadn't figured love into his decision to leave. Perhaps there *had* been other options rather than leaving, but Matt had chosen to take the easy way out. He'd wanted his way or no way, and he hadn't been willing to consider other alternatives. Nor had he been willing to allow room to love that precious family of his.

"True love is a choice we make, even though it doesn't always come easily," Josiah had told him long ago.

And true love put others first, not self. The way that he felt made no difference. If he was needed, then what kind of a man was he to just walk away, trying to ignore the hurts of those he'd left behind? The ones he loved?

There had to be another way out. If the barn was too cold to sleep in, why not ask if he could move in with Zane? His farm wasn't too far from Emily's; if Zane could make the trip every day to take care of Emily's chores, why couldn't he? And if Emily didn't want him to work her fields for free, why couldn't he rent the land from her?

Here, alone with Bowie, Matt knew that his heart was too tied up in his family to leave. He would never forget them, nor did he want to. It was time to lay aside his pride and make some new choices.

"Lord, forgive me for not seeing before," Matt whispered aloud. He had thought that God wasn't listening to him, but the truth was that Matt had been too intent on pushing for his own way to hear Him.

So you love Emily and Joyanna, Grant, and Austin, do you? Then what are you waiting for? Go back there and show them.

This time, Matt was more than willing to listen to that little voice. He stuck his foot in the stirrup and swung himself up onto Bowie's back, letting out a whoop. "C'mon, boy. We're going home."

Bowie started off at a lope, tossing his head as if saying, *Thank goodness the daft man finally came to his senses.*

CHAPTER 38

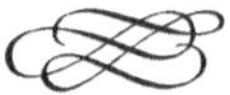

With each passing hour that Matt was away, Emily's heartache only intensified. She couldn't believe how much she missed him. While the house was full of children, it still felt lonely without him.

All went well during the first day of his absence. Life continued as normal, even though his empty chair at the table taunted her.

And then came the blowup at suppertime.

It started off simply enough. Glancing to where her daughter set the table, Emily said, "Joyanna, you can put one of those plates back."

Joyanna paused. "Uncle Zane's not eating with us?"

"Oh, he is. He'll be in from chores soon."

Silently, Joyanna counted plates then shook her head. "We do too need all of them."

"Oh, honey." Emily suddenly realized the error. "We don't need a plate for Uncle Matt."

"Oh." Joyanna set the plate away, but her forehead furrowed. "When will Uncle Matt be back?"

"What do you mean? I thought Uncle Matt told you that he was leaving."

"He didn't say when he'd be back." Joyanna folded her arms across her chest. "When will he be home?"

Emily shook her head. "Joyanna, he isn't coming back. He's gone."

"*Gone?*" For a long moment, Joyanna stared back at her. Then she started screaming like Emily had never heard her scream before. Throwing herself across the bed, Joyanna slammed her fists into the mattress and kicked, the covers doing little to muffle her shrieks.

Emily stared at her. How could her sweet little girl throw such a temper tantrum? *Oh, Heavenly Father, grant me grace, because I don't know how to deal with her,* she prayed. As frayed as her own emotions were, a tantrum was the last thing she needed.

When Joyanna's arms and legs stopped flailing, Emily cautiously approached. Sitting on the edge of the bed, she reached out to rub Joyanna's shaking shoulders, relieved that her touch didn't set off yet another round of screams.

Joyanna's muffled voice came from beneath the covers, and Emily leaned closer to hear.

"I want—Uncle Matt," Joyanna said with a hiccup. "I don't—want him deaded."

Emily sucked in a breath. "*Deaded?* Oh, sweetheart." Emily drew Joyanna into her arms and rocked her back and forth, tears stinging her eyes. "Uncle Matt's not dead. He's just as alive as you and me."

Joyanna pushed back and glared at her. "You said he was gone and that he wasn't coming back."

"I didn't mean that he was dead. He's going to live somewhere else." Emily rubbed Joyanna's back again.

Some of the defiance faded from Joyanna's face. "Why can't he stay with us?"

How could she explain the complicated circumstances to a little girl who only wanted her uncle back? There was no way she could understand the tangled way a grown-up's heart acted sometimes. Emily didn't understand it herself. "He works with cows, remember? He only came to help us for a little while, and now it's time for him to go back."

"He likes cows?"

Emily nodded. "Yes, he likes them."

"More than he likes us?" Tears filled her eyes.

"No, I'm sure not…" Emily began, but Joyanna started to cry.

"I want him to come home." She leaned close to Emily, her small body shaking with sobs. "He's ours. Why can't he stay with us?"

The boys stared at Joyanna. Then, one by one, they joined in her tears. Emily gathered them close, unable to explain why Matt was gone. Not when the question her own heart asked was *Why?* Why had she ever let him go?

By the time Zane stepped through the door, the crying had hit its peak and Emily felt like she might just join in with the wailing. She didn't blame Zane for his swift glance toward the door as if he wished he could make a run for it.

Things only worsened the next day. It began to rain at night and continued through the day, keeping the children locked inside. All of them were in a bad mood, and before long, Emily felt as if their bickering and crying were going to drive her mad.

The rain, arguing, and crying continued on into the next day. By noon, Emily was desperate to escape the house.

"Is there any way you could watch the kids for a couple hours this afternoon?" she asked Zane when he came for lunch.

He nodded. "I suppose. Just as long as I don't have to make supper. I learned my lesson from Matt."

"Poor Matthew." Emily tried to laugh, but it sounded more like a sob.

Emily rushed to wash the dishes and put them on the shelves

where they belonged, then she dressed in her best black dress and pulled her hair back into a bun. She knew exactly where she needed to go—Sadie's.

If there was anyone who could bring sunshine back into her world, it was Sadie. She had always been close with her, but now that Sarah was gone, Sadie was more of a sister to her than ever before. She was the sister of her heart.

As muddy as the roads were, Emily didn't dare push the team too hard on her way into town. But she was tempted. The rain held off until she was nearly to the mercantile, then it came in a wave that made her rush to tie the team to the hitching rail and run inside.

Bells jangled as she pushed the door open and stepped into the store, out of breath. Sadie bustled in from the family's living quarters at the back of the store, her face brightening when she saw Emily.

"What a good surprise! Wasn't expecting you to stop by today. Most people are staying home because of the weather. How can I help?"

"Truthfully, I don't need anything. I only came to visit. The kids were just getting to be too much." Emily unfastened her cloak, aware that she was making a puddle on the floor.

Sadie beamed. "I'm glad you came to me. I've been dying for someone to visit." She motioned toward the door leading to the living quarters. "Come with me and I'll get you something hot to drink."

"I'll make tracks on your floor," Emily protested, but Sadie waved her hand.

"This is a store. I have men stomping through here with muddy boots all day. The little bit of mud on your shoes won't make any difference."

With a shrug, Emily let Sadie lead her past the counter and into the kitchen where a kettle was already steaming on the stove.

"Ephraim can keep an eye on the store for now. He just stepped outside to get some more wood from the shed. Throw your cloak over the back of one of those chairs so the fire can dry it out before you go home," Sadie told her. She took two china cups down from the cupboard. "Margie's at school, and the youngest three are down for a nap, so we'll have a little time to ourselves. Just take a seat and get yourself warmed up."

As much as she loved her brother and nieces and nephews, Emily was relieved that she and Sadie could talk without interruption. She waited until Sadie handed her a cup of tea and a cookie, then spoke. "How are things going for you?"

"I thought you'd never ask." Sadie grinned. "I probably shouldn't tell you so soon, but I'm expecting again. Ephraim can hardly keep from telling the whole world because he's so excited. But I told him he better keep it to himself for a while since the baby's not due until May, as close as I can figure."

Sadie radiated with joy. Emily was always excited about a new baby in the family, but today, tears burned against her eyes. "That's—good. Very good."

Sadie sobered. "What's wrong, Emily? Are you all right?"

"I'm fine, I'm fine," Emily replied, but a tear slid down her cheek. "I'm sorry. I'm excited for you, but—I just haven't felt right all day. I'm—I'm so sorry."

Sadie set her cup aside. "Come now, Emily, surely you aren't going to hold out on me. Tell me what's wrong."

Silence stretched between them. Then Emily drew a shaky breath. "Everything's been wrong since Matthew proposed to me."

"He proposed to you?" Sadie sat upright in her chair. "Why, Emily, that's good news! The very best. Are you going to tell him yes? Of course you are. You'd be crazy to turn him down."

Emily lifted her chin. "Then call me crazy, because I did turn him down."

"You *what?*" Sadie half rose from her chair. "Why on earth did you do that?"

"I thought you, of all people, would support me." Emily blinked back tears. "Don't you see? Colton hasn't been gone for even a year. It's too soon to think of remarrying."

"So when *will* it be time to think about remarrying? You have a farm to run and little ones who need a pa. It seems to me that there's no time like the present. Matt's a good man, and I know he'll take good care of you and the kids."

Emily crossed her arms. "Yes, there would be plenty of bene-fits in marrying Matthew, but I'm not looking for a *convenience* marriage. Matthew deserves better. He deserves someone who will love him."

"And you don't?" Sadie asked.

"No."

Sadie's eyebrows arched. "Are you sure?"

"Yes."

"Really?"

"Sadie! Of course I'm sure. I loved Colton, and I know what love feels like. What I feel for Matthew is not like that."

Sadie seemed to think for a moment. "Do you love me?"

Emily sent her a look. Sadie knew the answer to that. "Yes."

"Do you love Ephraim?"

"Of course."

"But you don't love us in the same way, do you? For one thing, much as you love Ephraim, you would never have this conversation with him, right?"

The idea of telling all this to Ephraim was horrifying. It was embarrassing enough talking to Sadie.

"No," Emily admitted. "But if you're trying to say that no love feels the same way as another, then don't waste your breath. I know that love feels different for different people, but I also know that I don't have the kind of love I need to marry Matt."

"You mean you don't feel you can commit to being with him forever? You don't want to be there for him in sickness or health, whether he's rich or poor?"

Emily frowned at her. "That's the easy part. I'm not afraid of commitment."

"So if it isn't the commitment part holding you back, then it must be the love. You're afraid to love, aren't you?"

"That's not it! I'm not afraid to love."

Sadie fingered the handle of her teacup, but her gaze remained fixed on Emily. "I think you are. You're afraid to move past the old, the familiar, and step into something new. You might claim you're letting him go because your heart still belongs to Colton, but the truth is you're afraid to let yourself love another man. You don't want to lose him and endure the heartache you felt when Colton passed on."

Emily's protest died on her lips. Was that how she felt? Surely not. She had loved Colton like she could never love anyone else. She wasn't ready to move on. What they shared was too precious to be set aside mere months after his death. It wasn't that she was afraid to love someone as deeply as she had loved Colton. She just didn't *want* to.

"On second thought, it's probably a good thing you turned Matt down," Sadie said, drumming her fingers on the tabletop. "You can do better than him. He's changed a lot in the last few months, but he's still got a lot of growing to do. Besides, he hardly knows anything about farming. Only cattle. I'm sure you can find yourself a man who knows much more about what it takes to run a farm, and one who's more settled too. Matt's so used to moving around all the time that you probably shouldn't trust him too much."

Emily's mouth dropped open. "What are you talking about? I thought you liked Matthew. You liked him even before I did!"

Sadie stared into her cup. "Yes, but liking him as Colton's

brother is different than liking him as your husband. I want better for you, Emily."

"Better?" Emily's anger kindled, sending a rush of heat through her veins. "What do you mean? Matthew would make the perfect husband. He has some growing to do, just like all of us. Pastor Drew talked about how only dead people don't grow in one direction or another. Matthew's been incredibly kind and helpful. He's reliable, trustworthy, and willing to learn. He may not be like Colton, but he shares many of his same qualities, and I wouldn't be afraid to spend the rest of my life with him."

Sadie looked up from her tea, eyes twinkling. "Why are you defending him? I thought you said you didn't care about him."

"I don't—" Emily began, but then she stopped short. She'd been baited.

Her cheeks flamed. It was unfair for Sadie to talk her into a corner like this, but she had meant everything she'd said, hadn't she? She was willing to admit that she cared about Matt. She respected him, admired him, and felt safe when he was nearby. But as deep as her feelings ran for him, she hesitated to go so far as to declare that she loved him. She didn't feel that deeply for him, did she?

"Emily, do you mind if I tell you something?" Sadie leaned forward and took her hand. "Over the summer, Ephraim and I have been watching you, and we've made a few observations. You needed Matt. You were wearing yourself to the point of exhaustion, trying to keep up with the farm before he came. But he also needed you and those sweet children of yours. He's softened since he came here. Just think—at first he wouldn't so much as touch the children, and now he swings them up onto his shoulders as if it's the most natural thing in the world. You both keep each other on your toes. And what's more, the two of you seem to complement each other.

"Do you want to know what else?" Sadie asked, giving her

hand a gentle squeeze. "When Colton passed, your family became incomplete. And then Matt arrived. After you all stopped fighting each other, you became a family, whether you were conscious of it or not. Emily, trying to get rid of him now would be like cutting off a part of yourself. God brought Matt into your life for a purpose beyond what either of you could have dreamed.

Emily absorbed Sadie's words in silence. Was it true? Maybe she *was* afraid to love. For the first time, Emily dared to examine her heart. She had to admit that Matt did seem to belong to them. She hadn't asked for his help, but he'd taken it upon himself to see to it that they were protected and provided for, that they didn't lack anything. And, with time, his presence had touched their emotional needs as well.

Just thinking about the wonderful man who had stepped into their lives not long ago made Emily's heart ache. She missed him. And now, when it was too late, she admitted the truth to herself. She loved him. Without even realizing it, he had stolen a place in her heart long ago, sneaking past the barriers she'd formed. She loved him, and she'd let a future with him slip right through her fingers.

The dam that had been holding back her tears burst, and Emily let herself give way to the sobs. "Oh, Sadie, how could I have been so blind? I love him, but it's too late!"

"Fiddlesticks. It's never too late." Sadie banged her hand on the table for emphasis. "Just go home and tell him how you feel—"

"I can't. He's gone." The truth brought a fresh rush of tears into Emily's eyes.

"Gone?" Sadie's voice reflected her shock. "Where?"

"Back West."

"Foolish man!" Sadie slammed her fist again. "There's got to be a way out of this. Write to him. Tell him how you feel. And if that doesn't work, then—then I'll sic Ephraim on him. I'll go after him myself. I'll grab him by the ear, drag him back, and lock him up until he comes to his senses."

"It's my fault, not Matthew's." Emily blew her nose on her handkerchief. "He waited for me as long as any man could be expected to, but he couldn't put his future on hold forever."

"The man runs off on you, and you're still defending him." Sadie made a sound that was almost a growl. "Something needs to be done about this. As sure as my name is Sadie Mayfield, I won't rest until the two of you are good and married and can't escape each other."

Despite her heartache, Emily couldn't help but smile at her sister-in-law's determination. Then another rush of tears came. "Thanks for your help, Sadie, but I'm afraid it's too late. He's gone, and I couldn't ask him to come back now. He has his own life. And I'm sure that before long, he'll forget about us entirely."

CHAPTER 39

Emily managed to control herself and stop the tears, only because she knew that she would soon be home and would face Zane and the children. She let the team pick their own pace, in no hurry to get home despite the falling rain.

Matthew had seen that they belonged together. Why hadn't she listened more closely to him and realized the truth? In her effort to hold love at arm's length, she had lost something precious, something she feared that she could never recover no matter how hard she tried.

Lord, do You see us right now? Do You see this mess that we've gotten ourselves tangled in? Was it Your plan for Matthew to stay or to leave? Either way, I need You more than ever. Matthew's gone . . . Tears stung her eyes once again. *Oh, Lord, I really do love that man. I just don't know how to let him go.*

The rain came down harder and turned to sleet by the time the team pulled into the yard. Climbing stiffly from the wagon, Emily rubbed her hands together, trying to restore feeling to her fingers. Her mittens dripped, and the wind cut through the thin material. Maybe her hands would have been warmer without the soaking wet mittens.

Her teeth chattering, Emily made her way to the horses' heads. "All right, girls, let's put you away so I can warm up."

As cold and wet as it was, she probably shouldn't have made the trip into town today. But she couldn't feel sorry, not after all the truths Sadie had helped her see. Even if she had seen them too late.

Her fingers fumbled as she tried to undo the harness. Cold seeped right through her cloak and skirts until not a single part of her was warm. She scowled at the harness, trying to get her clumsy fingers to work properly.

"Let me do that, Em," a familiar voice spoke beside her, and a pair of strong hands brushed hers away from the harness.

Shock jolted through her, stealing the breath from her lungs. She jerked her head around to look up into the very pair of blue eyes that she longed to see. *Matthew.* She must be so cold that she was hallucinating. He was gone and had no intention of returning.

Matt's lips curved into his familiar teasing smile. "By the way, can you tell me if Emily Keath lives here?"

Her heart had nearly stopped when she first saw him, but with his words, it took off with a leap, pounding so fast that she half feared it would fly away. He was real, all right, and just as roguish as ever. And handsome. Devastatingly so.

There were so many things she wanted to say, so many things she wanted to ask him. And most importantly, she wanted to confess her love for him. But instead, she heard herself say, "Matthew Keath, must you really scare a body like that?"

His grin widened. "Yep, I guess Emily Keath does live here."

It was almost impossible for her to think straight when he smiled at her like that. Emily stumbled back, fully aware of how drenched she must look after her trip through the rain and mud. She brushed her skirts and cleared her throat, trying to compose herself. "When did you get back?"

"Maybe half an hour ago. I already saw Zane and the kids. Joyanna gave me a good scolding for leaving." His grin faded into a gentle shadow of a smile, and his eyes searched hers. "I've been doing lots of thinking. We need to talk."

Emily nodded. "I know. There's something I need to tell you, Matthew—"

He held up a hand to stop her. "Don't tell me anything until you get out of those wet clothes. You're going to catch pneumonia standing outside in this cold. The weather's too crazy for you to be out and about. Don't know what was so all-fired important that you had to be out in this."

"It was very important." Emily wanted to shout right then and there about how deeply she cared for him, but he was right. She'd rather tell him when her teeth weren't chattering and she didn't look like something the river had washed up.

Matt shooed her toward the house. "Go on, now. I'll be in for supper soon, but first I've got chores to take care of and a little business with Snooty."

"Snooty?" Emily frowned.

"You know. The milk cow."

"You mean Candy?"

Matt arched one eyebrow. "A cow with a temperament like that one has no business being called Candy. After the very first time I milked her, I renamed her Snooty. Just a little revenge for the trouble she gave me."

Emily choked back a laugh. "I'm sorry. You really have had a hard time with that cow, haven't you? Maybe Zane would be willing to milk her before he goes home."

"Not on your life. No one's laying a hand on that cow except me tonight. I've been pining to milk that cow since the day I left, and no one's going to take away my opportunity. Why, bless that cow. She could even kick the bucket tonight and I wouldn't mind."

Emily smirked at him. "I thought you hated milking and

everything that had to do with farming."

"*Hate* it? What are you talking about? I love farming."

"But you're a cowboy—"

"I found that I've sort of lost my love for that kind of life." Matt shrugged. "Farming's not so bad, not when you're surrounded by the right kind of people."

Emily's heartbeat quickened. "I'm glad you're home, Matthew," was all she allowed herself to say, but she infused the words with as much feeling as possible.

"Me too." Something flickered in his eyes, a look that made Emily feel soft and warm inside. But then he stiffened and pulled his gaze away from her, focusing instead on the harness. "Anyhow, you shouldn't be out here. I told you to hurry inside before you catch your death of cold."

His mood seemed to have taken a sudden swing from teasing and gentle to all business, and Emily decided it would be best to listen to him. Besides, her feet were numb, and she was still shivering.

She turned and hurried toward the soddy. "Thank you, Matthew," she called over her shoulder.

His response was so quiet that she almost missed it. "Anytime, Em. Anytime."

She smiled and pushed the door open, stepping into the warmth of the soddy. She had no doubt that Matthew Keath would be there for her anytime. He was a rare man to turn around and come back for them. She looked forward to their talk with all her heart. Whatever he'd been thinking, she was very interested in hearing it.

Unless . . .

Her steps faltered. Unless he'd changed his mind.

She bit her lip. What could have swayed him enough to bring him back? Surely he hadn't decided that he didn't actually love her. No, she refused to entertain the notion. There had to be a different reason. At least, she prayed there was.

"Mama, guess what? Uncle Matt came home!" Joyanna leapt from the floor and danced around Emily. "You said he wasn't never coming back, but he told me that he wasn't gonna leave again for a *long* time."

"That's good news." Emily watched as Zane stood and placed the sleeping Audrey on the bed. The boys gave her a brief wave before returning to their activity with the wooden figures Colton had sculpted so long ago.

"All seems quiet here," she said. "How did you get things under control?"

Zane shrugged. "We read a few books—a *lot* of books, actually. Then everyone took a little nap and woke up happier."

Emily shook her head. He was such a good father. She once again felt thankful that her little sister had found such a wonderful man to marry. If only those shadows would leave his eyes.

Zane walked to the door and tugged his coat on. "I'm headed home. Matt said he'd take care of the chores, so no need to worry about those."

"Thank you, Zane. I needed this afternoon." Emily took off her own dripping cloak. "I still can't believe Matt's home."

Zane pulled his coat lapels together and turned toward the door. "I can. I knew he'd be back. Just wasn't sure how long it'd take for him to straighten things out in his head."

Before Emily could ask him to further explain, the door shut behind him. Emily frowned, then shrugged her questions aside. Kneeling in front of the wooden trunk at the end of her bed, she flipped the lid open and rummaged through the items inside. She hadn't dared to do that since Colton's death.

She set aside the extra quilts and pillowcases that, with her mother's help, she had sewn as a young girl, back when she dreamt of the day she'd marry and have a chance to use them.

She pushed aside some books and a couple of crude gifts she'd received from students that she taught so many years ago.

Then, moving aside her wedding dress, she found what she was looking for at the very bottom of the trunk—a couple of dresses she had thrust into its depths Colton had died.

As she pulled out each dress, tears came to her eyes as she recalled why they were put away. They both had been Colton's favorite; he used to say the blue calico brought out the hue of her eyes and the lavender made her look like spring. It was too heartbreaking for her to wear either of them after his death, remembering that Colton would never be there to admire her dresses again.

Emily sighed as she surveyed the dresses hanging from pegs on her wall. Those everyday dresses were faded, and the black dress she'd never liked still hung there. She picked up the lavender dress before returning it to the trunk, but she kept the wrinkled blue calico in her hands. She breathed it in. It smelled good, like the rose petal sachets she stored in the trunk as well.

Emily started to close the lid of the chest, but a small picture frame caught her attention. She paused. There it was; her and Colton's wedding picture that she had tucked away with the dresses. She picked it up and stared at the man she had married that day. The pain still twinged in her heart from all the memories they had shared, yet it was not as sharp as it used to be—not paralyzing like when he first passed away.

Sadie's right. I have *healed,* she thought, amazed that she could face such a traumatic blow as her husband's death and still find her own heart beating. She felt more than alive. She had grown since that terrible day when all the light seemed to drain out of her life.

She ran her thumb along Colton's face pictured in the photo. "I'll always miss you, Colton," she whispered. "I know you would understand what I'm about to do."

Emily delicately set the picture back in the trunk and closed the lid, latching it shut.

There were many things that would have made this moment easier. The number one thing, though, was if Emily had worn her black mourning dress rather than that frilly, beribboned dress that made it difficult for Matt to stick to his resolve of avoiding any conversation about love or marriage.

Matt sneaked a look at Emily from across the table, even though he knew he shouldn't. He'd known she was stunning but hadn't realized the extent of her beauty until they were face-to-face tonight. He could have been knocked over when he stepped through the door earlier and saw her standing by the stove, her hair swept into a fancy hairdo. That pretty dress he'd never seen before brightened her features, especially her mesmerizing eyes. And the smile she'd given him—*that* was what kept him from saying a single coherent word. She should've known better than to look at him like that. It made a man start hoping for things that he had no right to imagine.

It had been far easier to keep his resolve when she was wet and muddy from her trip to town. That was the Emily he knew how to deal with. But now, it was all he could do to keep his wits together enough to ask her to pass the salt.

Thank goodness for the children. At least Joyanna kept up a steady stream of chatter throughout supper and kept him from needing to say anything. Chances were, if he dared to open his mouth, the only words that would come out would be a plea—"I love you. Please reconsider, won't you, Em?"

But when Emily excused Joyanna and the boys from the table, Matt knew he had to gather his thoughts and carry through with his decision.

"We need to talk. Can the dishes wait?" he asked more abruptly than he intended.

Emily nodded. "They can wait. We do need to talk."

"Good." He became momentarily sidetracked as he admired the deep shade of blue in her eyes. But then he jerked his thoughts back to hard business facts. "I've been thinking, and I figured out a way we can make this work."

Her eyes encouraged him to continue.

"I decided that I can't just leave. You need someone here to help run the farm, and I want to be that person." Matt pulled his gaze away from her face. "I care a lot about you and the kids. I'm going to worry myself sick about you if I'm anywhere but here. So, to save my own sanity, I figured out a plan. Please consider because I really think this could work."

Emily folded her hands on the table. "Then let's hear it."

"First things first—I'm going to move in with Zane. I already talked with him earlier, and he said that he has more room than he knows what to do with and would love for me to stay with him. So that takes care of the problem of the barn being too cold. Next, I'd like to rent the farm grounds from you. The money from the rent will cover your expenses, and the harvest will cover mine and keep me in business. Plus, I'll be close enough to help if you need anything." Matt paused and risked a glance to look at her. "So, what do you think?"

Emily's smile faded into a frown. "I don't think that's what either of us want."

Irritation flared to life inside Matt. Maybe this wasn't *exactly* what he wanted, but it was the closest he could get to his dreams. He was determined to make her see that she needed him, even if she didn't want to admit it. There was no way he could make himself return to Scottsbluff now.

"You better give it some more thought," he argued. "It's not a bad idea. I've been working on the details for a couple days now. It's a win for both of us. We'll both have an income and the extra help. What more could you ask for?"

"Do you love me?"

Her question caught Matt off guard. Was this a trick question? He'd kept his promise and had said nothing about love. How did she pull love out of his *strictly business* talk?

He examined her as she remained seated across the table looking more attractive than necessary.

"Yes, of course I do," he said. "I wouldn't joke around with something as serious as that."

"So I suppose you've decided that you wouldn't marry me for anything?"

Matt's heart thumped. "You know that's not true."

"Then ask me."

Surely he'd heard her wrong. "What?"

"Ask me if I'll marry you."

Now Matt *knew* it was a trick. But he couldn't think straight with her blue eyes fixed on him. Even though he knew he shouldn't, he said, "Emily Keath, will you marry me?"

"Yes."

Matt frowned. "Yes what?"

"Yes, I'll marry you."

Matt's pulse raced and his breathing shallowed. He *couldn't* have heard her right. "Could you say that again?"

Now Emily laughed. "Matthew Keath, I love you, and I will gladly become your wife."

Her words finally registered. Matt sprang from his chair,

tipping it behind him as he grabbed her by the elbows and spun in a circle, shouting, "Hallelujah!"

Matt did a quick sidestep to dodge a toy on the ground, but then he collided with the bed. Both of them crashed into the table, and as it was about to topple over, he released Emily to catch it. "We ought to consider constructing a bigger house," he said.

"We're certainly outgrowing this one," Emily said, glancing around.

"But for now . . ." Matt squeezed her hand. "What changed your mind?"

"I didn't change my mind. Sadie just helped me to understand what my real thoughts were. It's time that I stopped trying to fight my love for you."

Matt shook his head. "I still can't believe this. And to think I was determined not to come back." He shuddered. "How soon can we set a wedding date?"

Emily tipped her head to the side. "That depends. If I were to ask Mrs. Durmond, she would say no sooner than spring. A full year after Colton's death."

"Spring? Seriously?" Matt could hardly fathom the idea of waiting so many months. In his mind, he was already cozying in for winter with his new family. He wouldn't even mind if they were snowbound until April as long as he had them.

"My, my. Just a few minutes ago, you didn't think I would *ever* marry you, and now you're complaining about a few months of waiting?"

She had a point. Matt lowered his voice and leaned closer, brushing a loose strand of hair back from her face. "If you want to wait a few months, then that's your choice. I'll wait as long as you want me to." Though it would be a *long* winter.

"Maybe it *would* be proper to wait a full year. But since when did we ever listen to Mrs. Durmond, anyway?" Emily's eyes twinkled. "I'll marry you on Sunday."

Matt's heart skipped a beat. "*This* Sunday?"

"Yes. It's only practical to get married soon; I'd hate to see you going back and forth from Zane's to here. But there is one condition."

"What?"

Emily grinned. "You'll have to deal with Mrs. Durmond."

Matt exhaled in relief. "Emily, if you'll marry me on Sunday, then I'll face any number of lions you ask me to. I'm not a very patient man."

A giggle escaped from Emily. "I've noticed."

"Hey, now—" Matt began, but he stopped when he felt a tug on his leg.

"Are you really going to marry us?" Joyanna asked, looking up at him intently.

Matt smiled at her use of the word "us."

"I'm going to marry your mama," he said, "and I'll be your pa if you want."

Joyanna threw her arms around his legs. "Grant, Austin, did you hear that? Uncle Matt's gonna be our pa!"

Matt was rooted to the spot with all the tiny hands that clung to his legs, something that would have sent him into a fit of terror when he first arrived on Colton's farm. But there was plenty that he did now that he never would've done back then.

He hugged as many of the kids as he could. *Praise the Lord.* It had been a crazy ride to reach this point—why, he doubted he could have even survived if it hadn't been for prayers from people like Ephraim and Sadie, Josiah and Margaret, Zane, Pastor Drew, and the Nordstrums. They all seemed to grasp what was going on even before he and Emily had.

Matt flashed a smile at his bride-to-be. "Sunday it is, then. And don't you dare try to back out on me, Emily."

Emily quirked an eyebrow at him. "I assure you, I have no desire to escape from you, Matthew Keath."

And Matt laughed with pure joy.

Beginning this new series has been a joy for me. Osceola has always held a special place in my heart, and to be able to use it as the setting for my story is both a delight and a privilege.

I spent the first fourteen years of my life on a farm just a couple of miles outside of Osceola. My siblings and I were the fifth generation to live on the land, and we spent our childhood climbing trees my great-great grandma planted years before and chasing kittens in the barn where my great-great grandpa used to bring his draft horses in after a long day in the fields. Hearing stories and seeing pictures of just how much work my grandparents poured into the land gave me a deep appreciation for where we were and the legacy that had been handed down to us.

For *A Choice of Love,* I found it delightful to take a look at Osceola through the eyes of a man out of his element. And there was some very fun research that went into this book.

Cowboys and farmers are not synonyms, as some may think. Cowboys worked primarily with livestock while farmers worked mainly with the land. During the early days of western settlement, the two groups kept strictly to themselves, but as more farmers emigrated from back East, conflicts broke out as ranches and farms warred for the same pieces of land. This created a lot of tension, as mentioned by Matt early in the story.

Sod houses were another aspect of the story that I had a fun time researching. I spent far more time diving into old books than the story warranted and learned everything from how to build one to tips for how to best live in one.

To my surprise, many of the people reminiscing about their growing up in a soddy actually spoke fondly of the buildings. It could have been because of the passing of time and a rose-colored view of the olden days. However, as Emily pointed out to Matt, there were benefits to sod houses that made them more desirable than frame houses for many years. The insulation the dirt provided made the sod house more fuel-efficient than many of our modern day houses.

And according to one man, the difference between a comfortable sod house and a miserable one had to do with the finishing of the walls. If the inside walls were well plastered, no bugs or vermin could sneak inside to join the family. But the houses that *weren't* plastered gave rise to horror stories of snakes dangling from the rafters and frightening the housewives.

Researching for this series has only deepened that appreciation and made me fall in love with Osceola all over again. The people who first settled this town had a faith, strength, and grit that saw them through circumstances even more unbelievable than fiction.

I'm honored to be able to claim such people as my ancestors, and it's my prayer that our generation will think more like them, considering what is lasting and what kind of legacy we wish to leave behind for our children to inherit.

I hope that you'll join me for the next installment in the Home to Osceola series! *A Time of Proving* will release in 2025, so be sure to sign up for my newsletter at www.alenamentink.com for updates.

ABOUT THE AUTHOR

Alena Mentink is a Nebraska author who enjoys mixing history with fictional characters to create a story for God's glory. The Midwest claims the number one spot as her favorite setting for her stories where her characters manage to find plenty of trouble to keep them occupied. When she isn't busy writing, Alena can usually be found somewhere around her family's farm where she lives with her parents and eight siblings.

LOVED THE BOOK?

Leave a review! Whether you read this book because you bought a copy, were gifted one, or checked it out from your local library, you have the power to leave a review. Simply visit the retailer or a review site like Goodreads, give it a (hopefully) five-star rating, and jot down your thoughts. Even just one sentence about why you liked the book would be greatly appreciated. Thank you for helping other readers find *A Choice of Love*!